THE DEADENING WAKE

"Get the drive," I repeated.

"Yeah," he said.

"Call the number." That was next.

"Exactly."

"And even the score," I finished, staring at the mercenary with eyes I knew looked dead inside. Because eyes were the window to the soul, and that part of me was empty.

I had tried to do the right thing.

And I had failed.

"If that's your choice," Merc said. "The way I look at this, we're even now."

He smiled then, something quick and light. As if he had a happy thought.

"The next time we meet though, that one will settle things."

BOOKS BY CHRIS J. CRANFORD

THE DEADENING WAKE

CHRIS J. CRANFORD

FORGED IRON PRESS

This is a work of fiction. Names, characters, businesses, places, events, locales, and incidents are either the products of the author's imagination or used in a fictitious manner. Any resemblance to actual persons, living or dead, or actual events is purely coincidental.

Copyright © 2022 by Christopher J. Cranford

All rights reserved. No part of this book may be reproduced or used in any manner without written permission of the copyright owner except for the use of quotations in a book review. For more information, address:

contact@chrisjcranford.com

First Paperback Edition Dec 2022

Cover Design by Sadia Shahid

Published by Forged Iron Press
www.forgedironpress.com

www.chrisjcranford.com

Acknowledgments

I went to college in Augusta to get a degree in Creative Writing. At the time, I wanted to see if writing was something I was good at, if it was something I *could* do, and going to college was the only way I could make that measure, of myself.

As I navigated classes, read various literature, wrote reports and spoke with professors, I stumbled upon a personal truth. Especially while reading *The Faerie Queene*, studying Spenser, Shakespeare, Milton and Joyce.

It struck me that hundreds of years ago people told stories, *fiction* stories, because I believed they were working out our reason for existence in their writings. How we can become better. How we might be able to advance humanity, and what that might really mean.

A powerful lesson for me. That fiction, that a good story, can impart as important a life lesson as any self-help book.

I wanted to thank Professor Kisting with *The Deadening Wake*. Talking with him in class, after class, in the Caffeinated Brain, helped me to understand what I needed to write, and more importantly *why* I needed to write.

Thank you sir, for opening my eyes a little more, to a little wider horizon, and a much greater—and always growing—understanding.

CHAPTER
ONE

I started this particular Wednesday eating breakfast in my apartment. One of those single-bedroom flats in Boston people rent while they were looking for other, larger apartments. A transitionary kind of place for most, but I'd been calling it home for over a year.

Most people would describe my place as small. Or modest. Possibly with a roll of their eyes. It was definitely homey, a long room being both the living and dining room, a small table on one end carefully aligned to the kitchen. There, a sink was lodged in a tan Formica counter, electric metal burners topped an old oven, and an ancient microwave sat with some of its numbers worn to a pale transparency.

There wasn't a lot of color. A white fridge tucked against the wall. An old black phone hanging by the hallway next to the fridge, the kind of phone a curly black cord hung from. There was yellow backsplash against the wall, but it could have just been white backsplash colored with age.

The living room was much the same. A couch, a coffee table, a television. A picture next to one coaster in the middle of the table. The sports channel on the television, flickering highlights of the games from the night before.

There was one chair at the table. I sat at it, looking around the apartment, the bare walls, and my breakfast in front of me. It was a routine I had developed over the past few years. Not the looking. The breakfast. Two eggs—over easy—with a couple pieces of rye toast, a side of sliced grapefruit, and a glass of orange juice.

It was the same as the day before, and the day before that. And the week before that. Nothing had changed in my life for quite some time, and I suspected nothing would for quite a while longer. I seemed to be going through the motions, and not for the first time I contemplated why.

I picked up my fork and used the side of it to cut into my egg, did the same with the toast, then stabbed them both and ate them together. The toast was dry. I swallowed a little orange juice to get it down. The combination was scratchy in my throat and bitter on my tongue.

Eating was a rinse and repeat thing. Eggs warm, the yolks a little runny. The thick, earthy rye bread soaking up the yolk so that each bite was a little sweet, with a hint of caraway. Occasionally there were tinks and clinks as the silverware struck the stoneware plate.

I dragged pieces of the rye bread through the eggs. There was never enough yolk, and the toast always got dry, going down. I swallowed a couple of times, forcing the mix down with a gulping sound, sipping the orange juice. Took my fork and cut into the egg again.

Rinse and repeat.

The television sound was on, low, in an attempt to mask the clicks and clinks of eating. They sounded a little like the cleaning of a gun, the sounds of breaking components down and assembling them again. My life didn't need that kind of reminder.

The old phone hadn't rang since I had installed it. Though I could sense its presence there, a dull pressure between my shoulder blades.

Like a dull knife held tight to my spine, waiting for word to go in. I waited. It waited. My whole life now seemed to be a wait.

Once, it had been very different.

I ate some more. I turned to the window in front of me. There was nothing outside but the bare branches of fall awaiting the first grasp of winter, the gray-blue sky of morning, bare of clouds. The branches waved slightly in the wind, from a tree that had long since given in to the season's chill.

Somewhere there came a *tap-tap-tapping* of a bird. A shadow fluttered along the windowsill. Some sports show was on the television now, and I could hear a couple of anchors wonder about some team's chances this season.

I wondered very much the same about mine.

Every day I forced myself to at least go out and do something. Today was Wednesday, and Wednesday had its routine in my life like any other day. Sometimes I thought of my life as a mile marker on the highway, the numbers slowly counting away to my end destination.

At some point the road would end. The numbers would stop. But today the mile markers were still counting, so after breakfast I cleaned up and left, heading towards the gym.

The gym, like breakfast, was a staple of each day. Rehab has a way of drilling that into you. For a tool to be used properly, it has to be ready. Both the body and mind need to be sharp. So though I tried to vary my day in little ways, I always started them all at the gym.

The gym was large, with tall three-story walls. Plenty of air and light. Lots of new, fancy equipment, white and shiny. Black dumbbells, black plates, dark red benches and seats. Squat racks and bags in one corner. Men and women everywhere.

I put in some loud music and put on a punishing routine. I liked to completely exhaust my body, I worked each rep until the last one, making sure to reach that shaky feel of pushing up the bar for the last time. To hear the *clink-clink* of the bar settling back into the rack, to take the big breath after pushing myself to the limit. It was a feeling of accomplishment I lacked in life, but I nourished it here.

Rinse and repeat.

Each day I worked my full body, contrary to what many trainers and magazines and experts would tell you, because I believed each day could be my last. If it was, I wanted to go out without anything left. With burning as much as I could out of myself.

And, if I was being honest, that kind of exhaustion helped me to sleep. One of the few things that did. Like my routine, exhaustion had become something I needed. Almost craved.

I finished up with a little rehab on my right leg, the big tibia aching under the weight of memories, the reminder of a bad fracture from years ago. A rod still lay in there, thick titanium hammered through the bone. Two years ago it had been the only thing holding my leg together, bits of bone stacked on it like a jigsaw puzzle, and thick scars remained where screws held my ankle together. The latest X-rays had shown everything had knitted back more or less like it should, like the doctors said it would, but in the picture little dark lines still ran across the tibia, so the puzzle of bone still wasn't quite a complete picture, yet.

I took a shower at the gym. The water was hotter, and ran longer than at home. I ignored the guys who looked at my scars. There were plenty. All part of me. Except for the long zig-zagged scar along my right leg. The edges of the skin, where it had been stitched together, were still marked with where the thread had held the wound together. The scar tissue always turned a deep, angry color after my workouts, leaving little dark crimson crosses strung up along my leg.

The juice bar was next. I stopped by for a shake and a little small talk with the girl making them. I didn't talk a lot, but this was part of this routine. Being a little social, with a familiar face. Something I forced myself to do.

"You going to watch the new Impossible Force movie?" she asked, putting my shake in front of me.

"You mean Mission Impossible?"

Posters of it were everywhere. Commercials with all kinds of crazy stunts, motorcycle chases, and explosions. Movies about a secret government agency saving the world.

"That's the one," she said.

"I doubt it." I wasn't into those types of movies. Maybe they hit too close to home.

"You look like the guy in it," she said. "Just taller."

I picked up the shake, the glass was frigid in my hand. Lots of ice blended in it. The shake was a little brown from all the almond butter. I was uncomfortable with this kind of talk. These kinds of reminders.

She tilted her head. "More angry, too," she said, smiling a little, as if she was joking.

I shrugged. There was a little more talk from her than me, until another few customers stopped by. Then she was happy to move on. Most people were, people sensed something about me. A gut instinct, telling them to stay away.

That hadn't been the case a few years ago. But I was happy to have that aura now. I didn't want to meet too many new people. New people broke up my routine with new conversations and questions, sometimes leading to new thoughts, often leading to old ones. Like impossible missions.

I wanted none of that.

I sat a while longer and sipped my shake. It tasted like bananas and almond butter. It was thick and tasty and just icy enough to cool me down. My body cooled down, a bit of energy coursed through me as carbs and electrolytes sped through my arteries and reached all the muscles I had worked, the torn fibers accepting the proteins and enzymes and building itself up a little stronger, each day.

I looked over the gym as I drank, like I always did. There were bodybuilders jacked up and pumping out rep after rep, powerlifters grunting and screaming out each of their lifts, a few women on the cardio machines running with earplugs in, ignoring both the bodybuilders and the powerlifters. Some bags and mats in a back corner where everyday different people practiced kicks and punches, as if that could prepare someone for who they might meet in a dark alley.

Trust me, no one is ever really prepared for that. When it happens, you're either the type of person that gets out of it, or you're not. That's all there is to it.

As always, there were the mixed crowds of people. Groups hanging around a machine, talking about last night's show, or work, how to approach a lift. Form. Technique. Weather. Scores of games. Sometimes a few guys talking about how tight that girl's shorts were on the glute machine. The same people, day after day, talking about whatever.

I felt like they missed the purpose here. This place was to make sure your body was strong enough to handle anything. Those people, the talkers and laughers, I didn't understand.

A man came up and sat on the stool next to me. He was fresh from the shower and wore a dark blue suit he had already started sweating through. One hand adjusted a striped tie, gray and blue and black. The other sat a briefcase down and waved his face, beaded up with sweat.

He flagged down the girl and tossed out an order with what sounded like thirty or forty different additions to it. I guessed he was the typical executive, rushing in from the desk to get a quick workout in, so later he could sit back in a large chair and give people orders and feel like he was the alpha male in the room.

The man grinned at me. "Just finish?"

"Yeah." My voice was a little low and rough. Unused.

"I could tell," he said. "You got the look." The girl brought his shake. "Me, I got a ways to go but a couple more shakes a day ought to help. Protein, you know." He said it like he was letting me in on a secret.

"Sure." I looked at the girl and she rang me out. I slid her some cash for my drink, with a little extra. I didn't use cards, and she was used to the drill.

"I drink one before and after my workout," the man kept talking to me. He leaned a little closer. "And a couple more times a day. Trying to pack it on, you know. Gets harder as you get older."

I nodded, looking past him. My eyes surfing the crowd, not picking anything or anyone out. I sipped the last of my shake, and wished I had ordered something orange-flavored instead. The fake peanut butter and banana flavor was a little gritty.

"Let me ask you something," the man asked. Friendly enough, just a guy talking to another after a workout. "How do you get like that?"

"Let me stop you there." I turned away from the crowd and caught his eyes. He had thin brown hair, a spray tan, and his teeth had been whitened a shade too bright. His smile revealed one crooked front tooth. I was surprised he hadn't had that fixed. "I'm not interested."

"Hey," the guy said, instantly affronted. Pulling back. "I'm not selling you anything. I'm just talking."

"You misunderstand me." I stood up, setting my glass on the counter with a tiny thunk. I looked around at the powerlifters and bodybuilders, the counter girl and the customers and the groups. All the small talk. The questions. The answers. The corner of my lips lifted, barely. "I'm just not interested."

He didn't know what to say, but he wanted to say something. You could argue I was being an ass, and I wouldn't disagree. It was just that, when you lived what I lived, survived what I survived, it was all I had left in me. The rough spots.

I walked out of the gym. An older lady there was trying to fit a walker through the double doors. The aluminum legs of the walker kept snagging on the lip of the doorway, and then the lady would *click* the walker back to the sidewalk angrily and try again.

One of the lady's legs was wrapped in one of those blue casts, the ones that look like a soft, thick piece of dark blue cotton, but it was really just a cover to protect a thicker shell underneath. Her face was lined with wrinkles, her hair had a good amount of gray, eyes were scrunched, teeth gritted with an internal fury I recognized.

I took a moment and held the doors, making sure she got through both sets and into the lobby.

I might be an ass, but I'm not a monster.

THREE

It was Wednesday. Wednesday was mall day. Or, more specifically, the bookstore at the mall day. Part of my routine was to include myself in society. To keep things other than my body sharp.

I drove over in my car, a red sedan, one of the four-cylinder foreign cars that lasted forever. I used to be an American guy, but now I just wanted something that ran. I had bought it new, with cash, just a stock vehicle with no options. The dash just held a radio, no fancy screen with a camera showing the rear of the car, or even a compact disc player.

The car still smelled like vanilla. That was the air freshener in it when I bought it. Not the usual new car smell. I always just replaced it with the same scent when the little tube ran out.

The sedan fired up quietly. I drove towards the mall, working my way through traffic and stoplights with the steady patience of a turtle. The license and registration in my glove compartment wasn't in my name and didn't have anything to do with my history or age or race, but I drove carefully all the same. There was just no real need to rush.

I still had to stop, again and again. Even though I stayed in the right hand lane, and kept the car at the speed limit. Other people, in sports cars, SUVs, trucks, and little square hybrid things, they all would speed past me and cut in front at the last second, in the least possible room, slamming on their brakes as if shouting out to everyone, *Hah, I made it!*

One guy, in one of the newer Chargers, the newer version of the muscle car, couldn't make it in front of me. I didn't slow down for him, but I didn't speed up to block him, either. He hit his brakes and slowed his black Charger down, the engine revving, and rolled down a tinted window.

I looked over at him, like I had looked over the crowd at the gym. A surfing glance, flicking over to him and back, catching everything and nothing. The driver of the Charger was a younger man, in a tank top and a crew cut. Muscled arms and shoulders. A tiny guitar dangled from his rearview mirror.

He got ready to shout something. Then he took a look at me and something changed in his face. A second later the Charger slowed down, drifting back through traffic, until I lost him.

Like I said, people could sense something in me.

The bookstore was busy. I had to park out to the side, out into the parking lot. The sun was out, the sky was cloudless, so the air was a mix of a cool chillness combined with the warm rays of the sun. It felt good, breathing in the fresh air and feeling the sun on my skin.

The mall was large, with three levels. Plenty of large chain stores inside, like Macy's and Dillard's and JCPenney's. The doors closest to me were on the second level, someone had driven through them years ago. The driver had been drunk, as he kept blaming his wife when the cops put him on the ground and arrested him. Apparently she had spent a lot of money there.

One end of the mall ended up in a weird semicircle, where an outdoor stretch of stores sat in a large arc, like a strip mall. A sidewalk in front of the stores, so people could walk along and shop. If I formed a large C with my hand, the mall would be the back of my hand and the strip mall would run along my forefinger. My thumb would be the bookstore, and the gap between the thumb and fingers the parking lot.

A water fountain sat at the entrance to the mall, close to the bookstore and the row of shopping stores. Its jets pushed the water hard enough I heard the splashing almost from where I had parked. A few people sat on the stone rim, sunglasses on, laughing and talking together. Some with their phones in hand, texting furiously.

The bookstore was part of a huge chain. It had a coffee shop inside. The front of the store was all framed glass windows, one after the next, giving people inside the ability to sit and look out over the lot, the stores across the circle, the water fountain. A large Chinese restaurant sat in the open parking lot, at a triangle to both the strip mall and the bookstore, with a pair of large stone horses in front of it.

I liked my time at the store. If I liked a day enough to be a favorite, it would be Wednesday. Normally it was quiet, peaceful. I could sit by the front windows and watch people come and go, from shop to shop. I watched the outside like others watched television, observing people living their lives, and not being interrupted by too-loud commercials pushing different drug after different drug. Years ago I maybe would have gone to the airport and done the same thing, but then someone had flown a few planes into the World Trade Center and the Pentagram, so being in the terminal required a ticket nowadays.

So the bookstore now, instead. As far as life, it wasn't much, but it was my Wednesday, and I liked it. I had been doing it for a year or so now, and I would probably do it for plenty more. Maybe it was the one time I allowed myself to think of other lives, other plans. I could imagine them, these people walking around, what they were doing, what they were going to do, what they were thinking and saying and planning. Parties over the weekend, dinner plans, maybe a weekend at the beach.

Of course, I would deny it, if asked. I had lived the life that had gotten me here. My future was this, such as it was. The routine. Today. Tomorrow. And that was it.

CHAPTER
FOUR

Today the bookstore was packed, mostly with younger kids on laptops. It felt like it was around that time where finals started in the local college. The strong aroma of coffee greeted me, from the coffee shop in the back of the store, followed by the faint smell of newly printed paper. The smell of paper was something I liked, the smell felt warm to me, a scent that relaxed me. Maybe it was the memories of my mother taking me to the library, as a kid. Anyway, I breathed it all in and walked in.

Bookshelves funneled everyone down the same lines. Fiction books, non-fiction. Mystery and thriller. Cookbooks, life stories. Spines of all types of books colored the shelves, of all kinds and types and sizes. A small round table lay in the middle of the entryway. It was positioned right in front of the doors, where the biggest name authors had their newest hardback books stacked, facing outward in symmetrical little rows.

I wandered to the back of the store and stood in line at the coffee stand, watching a single barista take the orders, make the drinks, and serve everyone in a fluid motion that looked monotonous and repetitive.

There was the order, the money, the pour, the foam, the syrup, and sometimes the whip.

Like the guy back at the gym, some of the orders went a little overboard, with different kinds of milk and different temperatures requested. Additions and subtractions to their drink, until each person got exactly what they felt they needed. One customer even ordered a small soy latte, extra-hot, a pump of sugarless vanilla, with regular whip, and had it all placed in the largest cup.

All that was crazy to me. So when the barista got to me, I just ordered a large black coffee.

"Really?" She looked at the assortment of flavors, foams, and spices scattered around the counter. Maybe not sure how to handle a coffee she didn't have to mix and modify into something else. "Is that how you like it?"

"No," I said. Though I didn't not like it that way, either. "But I'm a fan of simplicity."

She smiled, a little tiredly, thinking I was making a joke. Then she took my money, got my coffee, and quickly handed over a hot cardboard cup, green with little snowflakes across it, and a white plastic top. I took them, left a tip, someone else taking my place with their particular order.

I took the coffee and maneuvered around tables packed with students, all of them tapping laptops or cell phones. The cup was warm in my hand, the coffee hot and bitter, almost burning my tongue as I sipped at it. I passed a group of kids talking animatedly among themselves, with some kind of game on all of their laptops. Quite a few others with headphones tucked in their ears. All of it louder than a bookstore should be.

As I moved along I passed a few bookstands. The last one held a bunch of classics, modernish authors like Dickens, Austin, and Twain. Older works such as Chaucer, Milton, Dante. I grabbed one of the bigger books from that stand and plopped down in my favorite spot, a table in the corner, where one of the big windows met a set of book-shelves.

The front of the store faced southeast a little, during this part of the day the sun lit up the area, warming the surface of the table. The worst part about it was the sunlight, on a bright day, would flash directly into someone's eyes who was sitting there, which was the reason I thought the table was usually open.

I sat the book on the table with a heavy thump, unlooked at and unopened. It was part of the routine I usually picked a book and sat it on the table, allowing it to take up more space than just me by myself. People didn't usually sit with me, but on a crowded day I liked to take a precaution.

Most days I was satisfied to just sit and watch people. I angled my chair a bit, taking little sips of my coffee. The taste hadn't changed, it was still black and bitter and hot. Constant burning reminders of my life.

I placed my feet up against the windowsill ledge, making sure to cross the right leg over the left. I tended to cross them the reverse when I wasn't thinking about it, and after a while the right leg ached under that weight.

Constant reminders.

In front of me stretched the long window of plate glass, slightly tinted. It was just enough that I felt like I looked through it and onto another world. Like watching a movie through a transparent screen.

There was the half-circle across from me, the stores stretching side by side along the strip, cars parked in front of them. To my right was the restaurant, both horses facing me, the door to the place between them. Between the restaurant and the stores was more of the parking lot, with rows of cars following along the strip until it met the main lot.

The restaurant was fairly new. I had watched them build it over the past year, Wednesday after Wednesday. From the beginning it had been flooded, one of those fancy Chinese fusion places, a chain people flocked to. Especially now. It was close to lunch, and businessmen and women headed in to eat, make small deals, take and give interviews. Most of them wore the regular business attire, gray suits, blouses, dark pants.

I sat, sipping bitter coffee, lost in the universe of interactions and movements happening outside. My heartbeat slowed, my breath became long draws in, followed by soft, lengthy exhales. Sitting there, I imagined this was how I now took part of the world around me. Just kind of existing. Not quite a bystander, not quite a participant.

A toy store sat in the middle of the strip mall. Tiny kids occasionally bounced out of it, parents struggling to slow them down. Their small hands usually held some kind of electronic handheld game, or one of the square DVD boxes of a video game, sometimes a doll. There was one everyone wanted this year, a small green baby-like figure with pointy ears.

My parents had been farmers. We had never had much, but we went to the library weekly, and on special occasions, they would take us to one of the large toy stores, with rows and rows of playthings for all ages. I had walked out with Legos, more often than not. Occasionally gaming books, monster manuals, guides. Things I could build or imagine or dream, back when the world had been open to me, and I could do anything.

My coffee cooled down. I wasn't drinking it fast enough, I guess. I went and got a refill, returning to my spot with another hot cup. This time the line was short, and the barista asked me if I wanted something else, but I had her just give me a second cup of the black. A bitter drink suited me today.

I snorted, quietly, to myself at that thought, and settled back in. No one had taken my spot, or my book. The lunch rush was in full swing. Women strutted out of some of the nicer stores, in nice blouses, matching coats, and slim, form-fitting pants. Most of them had a bag hung from their elbows, which were positioned *just so*. Sunglasses hid their eyes, and their hips sank with every step. I knew their heels clicked against the sidewalk at a steady pace.

The crowd thickened with managers, bosses, and other executives. All of them parking and rushing around, trying to fit what they could in the hour they had off. The movement of everyone outside increased, slowly, something only the most careful observer would be able to tell.

I could see it, feel it, when it happened. There was a pace everyone moved at, and that pace increased, poked and prodded by the people in a rush. Crowds moved as one, yet every action of one person affecting another, so that chain reactions would string from individual to individual; people who were, for the most part, unaware of how together they really were.

A bright white sports bike idled along the first row of parking spaces, the bike in perfect balance, with a young woman leaning against the bike's gas tank. Her form stood out prominently on top of the bike, a long sinuous curve arched delicately above a thrumming motor, a ponytail of dark hair hung out from her helmet and lay down the middle of her back. I watched her for a bit, the bike rolled past the fountain, then a crowd of people crossed between us and I lost her from view.

The crowd had to stop midway through the lot. A car sped down the row, not paying attention to people walking, braking hard in front of the restaurant. It was a silver BMW with nice rims, and had heavily tinted windows. A head motioned in the car, almost a vague bobble looking left and right, maybe for a parking space. The head stopped moving, and the BMW pulled into the single parking space left open for pickup orders.

I rolled my eyes. The guy hadn't been looking for a parking space, he had just been looking for witnesses.

I sipped my coffee again. Still hot, still bitter, but mellowing now on my tongue as the liquid began to cool. The BMW guy got out of his car, a young man in a suit who shut his door quickly and rushed inside the restaurant, checking his phone the entire time. The taillights of the BMW beeped twice, as the restaurant doors closed behind him.

I checked my watch. Fifteen minutes passed. That was the limit on the sign in the pickup order parking space. The young man stayed in the restaurant.

I was curious about the kind of person that would take a parking spot—reserved to help everyone—for their own personal use. That type of person likely existed at the center of their universe. Everything that happened in their world, happened only in relation to themselves.

There was no room in that universe for thinking about others, taking the time to make life easier for someone else. Small things, small acts that meant nothing to that person, in the center of their world, but might help someone else tremendously. That kind of selfishness was an animalistic, primal urge to do what's best for your own person, no matter the consequences of your actions to others.

The lid of my coffee cup popped off and fluttered to the floor. I took a breath and relaxed my hand, letting my thoughts go. Then I fished the white lid off the floor and sat it next to me on the table. The top made a light, plastic scratching sound on the polished wood surface.

"Hey," a voice said, as a backpack was tossed on my table.

The action startled me. I twisted a bit, seeing the biker I had watched earlier. She stood at the corner of the table, holding the strap of her backpack in one hand, a helmet in the other. It was a modular helmet, one you could lift up by the chin and pull the face shield up. The helmet was white, with an intricate design painted alongside either side, golden and silver curls that spread out like wings.

Her hair was loose from the ponytail, as if she only tied it up on the bike. Dark strands shimmered over her shoulders, long and black with tints of dark red. Tints of gemmed studs in each earlobe. Nothing fancy, and something that said this was *her*.

She had a slight grin, as if apologizing for interrupting me. Her eyes caught me, they were a bright emerald green, and almond-shaped.

I nodded a hello.

"Mind if I sit here?" she asked. "Place is packed."

Her voice was smooth, but carried a timbre underneath the tone, like someone who maybe performed on stage. It held a hidden power I could feel. She had a tiny hoop in one nostril, and this late in the fall her skin was still a healthy, dark tan. I couldn't have guessed her ethnicity, maybe Italian or some kind of Latin DNA. Certainly something that began in Europe, before making its way across the ocean.

I nodded again, sliding my placeholder book to my side of the table. Then I shifted my chair so that my legs pointed along the window, which gave me more of a view of the fountain and the strip stores, less of the parking lot and the restaurant.

The biker sat down deftly, tucking her helmet in the chair across from me and quickly sliding a laptop out of her bag. I thought of her in her mid-twenties, five to ten years younger than me. Young enough to still be a college girl, old enough to be looking for a career instead of just a job. Maybe going to school for the second time.

Her eyes flicked up and caught me staring. Her lips curved a bit, like being stared at was something she was used to. I imagined it was. I nodded for a third time at her smile, acknowledging the moment, and she went back to her laptop.

I turned back and kept watching people circle around outside, but nothing jumped out at me. I had lost the movement of the crowd, the intricate way people walked in and out from around each other. Or maybe I had lost interest. Beside me a steady *tap-tap-tapping* of a person who knew their way around a keyboard started up.

The coffee was cool again. The BMW still sat in the carryout parking space. Thirty-five minutes now. Every now and then a car would pull up and wait there, until the owner finally drove away and parked somewhere else. Each time that happened, a few minutes later a harried person would hurry into the restaurant, then a few minutes later hurry back out, holding several large bags.

The biker girl said something. I didn't realize she had said it to me. I felt a silence between us, like she was waiting. One of those things I realized at a subconscious level.

I glanced over. Her laptop was closed, as if she had finished what she wanted to do, and I got the impression she had been watching me watching others for a little bit, a small square white thumb drive twirling in her fingers. Her lips curved again, her smile held a little devil in it. Impish.

"What was that?" I asked.

She didn't answer immediately. Instead, her eyes met mine, and her smile brought out glints of gold in her green irises. It caused them to shimmer a bit.

I held her gaze and waited. Not moving. The rest of the store became background noise, the kids gaming, the orders of coffee, the random shouts of kids. Neither of us broke the stare, and she finally repeated what she had said before.

"Now, sir knight, show what you be," she said again, her voice relaxed but carrying a power, a timbre that resonated in me. As if she was on stage, speaking out to a crowd. "Add faith onto your force, and be not faint."

I'm sure my face looked as confused as I felt. "Umm, excuse me?"

One eyebrow lifted, in an elegant arch. "Spenser," she explained, as if she had just quoted him.

That didn't make it any clearer. "I don't know who that is."

Her gaze flicked down to the book I had picked up. *The Faerie Queene*, the cover of the book black, a white shield on its face, a solid red cross painted across the shield. With Edmund Spenser below the title.

My face grew warm, my cheeks flushed a bit. It wasn't often I was caught off-guard. Even in the tiny details.

"It's a favorite line," she said, still with that half-smile. "It looked like it fit you."

I shrugged. "It's just a book I grabbed."

"Just a book, huh?"

"Yeah," I repeated, holding my coffee on the table, both hands circling the cup.

"You don't seem like the kind of guy who does something without a reason," she teased in a friendly way, maybe sensing my discomfort. "I've seen you in here before, haven't I?"

"Maybe." I shrugged again. "I'm here on Wednesdays."

"Just Wednesdays?"

"Just Wednesdays," I said.

"Why *just* Wednesdays?" she said in a way that mimicked me, not in a mean way, just so I could hear her echoing me. Light teasing, maybe.

I looked out the window again. I was uncomfortable explaining my routine. It was what I did, and that was all. "It's just what I do," I ended up answering.

"Huh," she said, again.

I glanced back, and she caught my glance and laughed. It wasn't loud, but it was from the belly. A laugh at the moment.

Something real.

"Certainly, that's not all you do," she said, putting the laptop into her pack, dropping a few things in with it. Leaving a thin spiral notebook out, something small with a tiny pen nestled among the spirals. One of the telescoping pens, meant for a quick jotting of notes.

"I'm not sure I know what you mean," I said.

"Hmm," she said. It seemed like her mind worked that way, sharp quick answers mixed with thoughtful, slow reposes. Her mind worked through something, as if calculating days or times or schedules. "What do you do tomorrow?"

"Thursday?" I said. "Thursday is park day."

"Park day?"

"The park down by the marina," I said. I liked the boats down there, they had large yachts, schooners, a lot of smaller craft. It was another way for me to get through a day, watching waves crest out from the powerboats, the ripples roll across the water.

"What do you do down–" She stopped herself and looked at me, then the window. Putting things together, quickly. "Do you just watch things, there, too?"

I shrugged again. The way she asked it made me feel like I was missing something. But the opposite was true. I had experienced way too much in my life. Watching people, in my mind, evened things out.

She shook her head a little, puzzled. "What kind of work just lets you have that kind of time?"

I hadn't been asked that in a long time. My job had defined who I was, for quite some time. I wasn't out of work, now, but I wasn't at work, either. The people I worked for, they were waiting. I thought I was, too.

Did they think I was too broken to keep going? I didn't know the answer to that question. All I could do was keep the tool sharp.

Could I trust them, like I had before? That was an answer I did know. Unequivocally.

No.

So I wasn't defined by my job, not anymore. Not right now, at least. Now I was defined by my routines. My breakfast, in the morning. The same sports show. The same executives at the gym telling me how they work out. I had Wednesdays and Thursdays and Fridays, all the days of the week, over and over again until they made up what I was.

She waited for my answer. I got the feeling she was fascinated. It didn't look like she was losing any interest.

I wasn't sure I wanted her to. That feeling was new, and like all new things scared me. It threatened the routine.

"Right now, I guess I'm kind of between things," I finally said.

"Huh," she tilted her head. In that way that meant she was processing my answer thoroughly. "But you used to do something, right? You have that look."

"That look?"

"Yeah," she said. "You have that *look*."

I looked away. I wasn't sure what look I had anymore. The way she had said the words, it sounded like she knew all about my past. Those memories and feelings had been buried, for me, deep in my mind, behind a thick concrete wall that would never come down. And yet I could feel them, even now, stirring and rumbling behind that barrier.

I was scared of this conversation. Of this girl. Of things large and mountainous shifting ever so slightly between my past and I.

She figured out I wasn't going to answer. One hand reached out to my book, and a long, elegant finger tapped its cover. She smiled, as if easing the conversation back to more friendly areas. "In all that time you have, you might want to give this a chance. I get the feeling you might relate."

"Yeah," I said. *Not* thinking about my past. "Sure."

"Seriously," she said, her eyes intent on me, knowing the effect she had on others. On *me*. "Not many people recognize their own truth."

I swallowed. Played with my coffee cup, mostly empty now. The coffee cold now, and losing its hot bitterness. For some reason, I thought next Wednesday would no longer be bookstore day.

"Hey," she said, waiting for me to look at her. Her smile was back. The impish one. I wasn't sure if she was teasing me still, but the color and curve of her lips were intriguing. "You got anyone you spend all that time with?" she asked.

It took a second for me to realize she was asking me out.

I looked at her, really looked at her. She was pretty, but there was something underneath that made her spectacular. Something in what she knew, or what she was made of, that wasn't in other people. Something that kept your attention. She knew she had it, she knew I was affected by it, and she knew I knew all of those things.

There was something in her eyes, as well. The emerald green irises were bright with her smile, but there was a shadow behind them. A past she had overcome, maybe. A pain she had felt, and so could see it in me.

I was afraid of her. Not her, but what she meant to my life. My routine.

Her stare, even now, unsettled me. I knew, I *knew* that if I spent any time with her, she would learn every secret about me. She would understand what had happened, and might be able to help me get over my past. She carried the possibility of healing things I thought might never heal, and goosebumps rippled along my forearms as that realization hit me.

I bit down, hard. Pressing my teeth together until it felt like they might crack.

The pain I carried was all that kept me going.

I *needed* it.

I didn't want to move on to other things. I *never* wanted to get better. I wanted all the anger and rage and pain because it was something I was *owed*, dammit.

My routine was all that kept it at bay. People may have talked with me and come away thinking I was depressed, clinically so. That I lived out my days in a bare minimum kind of way, because that was all I felt like I had.

Those people would have been wrong.

Inside I carried a rage. It burned deep inside me, blisteringly hot, a fiery ball consuming anything I allowed it to touch. The only thing that kept it at bay was the routine. Focusing on the next thing I needed to do, the next day. Thinking too far into the future, or too close to the past, would cause it to erupt.

The routine allowed me to hold the anger in check. It kept it cool, cold. The fire, the fury, the anger and rage were all caught behind the icy walls of my routine.

What was the saying? Revenge is a dish best served cold? If so, I had a five-star meal waiting on ice. Waiting for the day I needed to serve it. There would be a day a reckoning would come, where the icy walls I had built would melt and collapse, where towers would tumble. Where mountains fell. Where aircraft carriers sank.

It was a fine balance, working my routine, keeping my thoughts from my immediate past. Rehabbing my leg without thinking about how it had broken. Glancing at the scars of bullets tattooed across my chest without thinking of how I had gotten them. Or the woman that had put them there.

Even now thinking about it raised the temperature in my body. My heartbeat sped up. My fingers tightened and dug into my palms. I pushed the thoughts and memories away, building up the mountain of ice that was all that could hold my anger at bay, until it was a floating iceberg, miles and miles of ice hidden deep underneath the ocean of my routine, until all that was left was a cold frost of fury, in search of its Titanic.

This girl threatened it all. It was all too soon. I couldn't afford to be around a person like her, because of what I was due...

What I was due, it was something I was owed. *Owed.*

The girl watched me, fascinated. I understood, at that moment, that she had a feeling for everything going on inside of me. Some intuitive instinct inside of her. She didn't say a word, because she understood it would tip me one way or the other. As if I was a wild animal, hurt, trapped, and any movement or sound would cause me to flee, or die in the attempt.

Her eyes stayed on me. Deep. Intense. Understanding. Like she had been where I had been. Like she had a past that in some way could relate to mine.

That wasn't possible.

And yet a connection had formed between her and I. Maybe even before we had met, when I had seen her on her bike, felt something in her that called to me on some universal, yet personal level. Something we had both felt the instant she had sat down.

This woman had something to her, something that already had started working on my mind, had me thinking of changing my routine, almost changing without thought, of letting go of the anger I held...

I wanted those thoughts, of letting go of the anger and the hate, that part of me *gone*. The anger was all I had left, and I would not give it up. Not for anyone.

Just then a loud beeping noise came from her jacket, a miniature car alarm kind of sound. It startled both of us, she jumped just as much as I had. She quickly pulled out her phone and glanced at it.

Her body language instantly changed. Her tan skin whitened. She moved quickly, her motions fast yet rigid. Her chest swelled in and out, over and over, as if she couldn't get enough air.

"I've got to go," she said, not waiting for me to say anything. She jammed her laptop into her bag, a book and a notepad falling out. It was a spiral notebook, the kind with the college's name on the front. I picked them up, handed them over, and she stuffed them back into her bag as she ran out of the store.

I watched her go. She slammed through the front doors of the bookstore, and out into the crowd. Her strides were choppy at first, then opened up as she got to the fountain. Fleeing to her bike.

Whatever her emergency was, I was relieved to see her go. She had represented too much change in my world. It wasn't something I was ready for. It might be something I would never be ready for, again.

A large truck sped through the semicircle. A big black Escalade, with windows tinted far past the legal levels. Something you might see in a motorcade. The truck hit its brakes sharply, seeing the biker, and the truck slid to a stop with a long squeal of tires locked on asphalt.

The driver's door stayed shut, but three guys got out of the truck.

Dressed in jeans and hooded sweatshirts. I knew I was getting every detail. All the jeans were blue. All the shoes the same brand, the same blue and white color with the same symbol on the side. All the sweatshirts gray, with hoods tightly pulled over their heads, hiding their faces. Each of the men had a good build, like they worked out.

I found myself on my feet. The girl had stumbled when avoiding the Escalade, and was backing up now. Holding her hands out, with her bag in front of her, as if trying to protect herself.

The guy on her side caught her quickly. She struggled and screamed. The other two guys jumped in and all three of them wrestled her into the backseat of the truck. The truck took off even as the three men got in, the doors swinging shut as the Escalade spun down the row.

I moved. Running. I burst through the doors of the store, pushing through a surprised family there, and into the parking lot. Not as nimble as I used to be, my leg ached sharply at every pounding step, but fast enough. Faster than most.

The back of the Escalade was already swinging around the Chinese place. I started sprinting, and got to the side of the restaurant just as the truck reached the far end of the strip mall, where the stores met the fields of parking lots that stood around every mall. It didn't brake, but swung left and headed for the main entrance.

I kept running, but the Escalade increased the distance between us easily. Steady pulsing aches burst from my right leg, but I pushed through. Faster, sneakers slapping pavement. Not admitting to myself the race was already over.

The vehicle spun around a large set of bushes and fled up the ramp, to the main road. My last sight of the truck was as it ran the stoplight at the top of the entrance, turning left onto the highway and heading towards the interstate. Brakes squealed from above me, from other cars up and down the street as they swerved to avoid the Escalade.

For a long moment I didn't do anything. I stood there, not breathing hard, not moving, just watching. Feeling my heartbeat echo in my right leg, a painful throbbing that echoed through me. Wondering what had just happened. Wondering what I was doing.

There was quiet all around me, broken by a few calls and shouts from behind me. Back by the bookstore. Over all of that there was the rumbling of the Escalade, getting louder and louder, then the transmission downshifting as it hit the interstate ramp, and rolled away.

Over one hundred Wednesdays had passed, each of them the same as the last. I had made sure of that.

Today had been different.

My fists clenched with that realization. I had been waiting, a tool without a purpose. Waiting to be picked up again. But something else, someone else, had picked me up.

I didn't know if I was the right tool for this job. I had been sharpening myself for something else. What I had left in my life was a single purpose, a biblical type of revenge. Justice. I didn't know if I was the person I needed to be, now. Not for this.

The fury inside didn't seem to care. It was always that way with anger, madness didn't care what pipes it broke, when the pressure got too high. The raw emotion just grew and swelled and pushed and pushed to be released, against whatever container tried to hold it.

I didn't know who the girl was, but I could find that out. I didn't know who the guys were who took her, but I could find that out as well. They wouldn't be thrilled to see me.

I walked back towards the bookstore. A little stilted, my right leg dragging a bit after each step. There was a small crowd surrounding the door, pointing my way. The silver BMW was still parked in the fifteen minute parking space.

I limped past the car. My reflection cast back at me, by the tinted windows there.

You have that look, she had said.

What look was that? A man with burning eyes. Short black hair, too curly for its short length. A five-o'clock shadow. Protruding cheekbones and a sharp jawline, one that came from clenching teeth tightly together.

What look did I have? What kind of man was I now?

Not the man I used to be, that was for certain.

I left the BMW with several footprint-sized dents along its side, its lights flashing, its car alarm blaring to be rescued from the man kicking it.

Some people never learn, but I'd give them the opportunity.

The first thing I did was find the girl's bike. It wasn't a Ducati, but it was a nice sports bike, well taken care of, bright white with blue and red stripes down its sides. The bike was parked in the center of its parking spot and kicked on its stand, allowing plenty of room for the cars next to the bike to open their doors.

I quickly searched the bike, not finding anything and not really expecting to find anything. A bike wasn't like a car, where you kept your registration and insurance in a glove-box, but I was hoping there might be something somewhere. I've known some people to stick a laminated emergency number card under their seat sometimes, or on the back of the license plate.

Speaking of which, I looked at the plate number of the bike and memorized it. Then I felt like it was time to get moving, before the authorities showed up. Not that I had anything to worry about there, but I didn't want to be slowed down.

Some of the people from the bookstore walked my way. That reminded me that the girl had left her helmet back in the store. I headed back to our table, found the helmet still in the chair where she had left it, tucked under the tabletop.

I grabbed the helmet, it was bright white with a tinted face shield. The intricate design looked like a custom paint job, a pair of wings spread out over the sides of it, starting at the front and painted in a way that the tips of the wings met at the back.

The wings blurred a bit over the ears, as if invisible streams of air flew over them. I could imagine the wind rushing by the helmet as the bike accelerated, the design appeared to be slowly blown away in tiny streamers of gold and silver.

A signature rested at the bottom of the back of the helmet. It was tiny, and hard to make out. Not legible, but maybe someone would recognize it.

I took the helmet and headed out. Then I stopped and went back to the table. I picked up *The Faerie Queene* and ran by the front register to purchase it.

Then I headed to my car. The parking lot was full of people, standing around and talking to each other. Pointing in the direction of the black truck, one or two pointing at me.

I ignored them, focused on my next step. I decided to try my luck with the Department of Motor Vehicles for the license number. If that didn't pan out, I'd track down who had painted the helmet.

The car started up quickly, in the way small cars do. I put the book in my gym bag and sat that in the backseat. The helmet sat in the co-pilot chair.

It was a twenty-minute trip to the DMV. I drove a little more urgently than I had to the mall, and the people cutting me off didn't sit as well with me this time. I wrestled the sedan into tight spaces, ran through yellow lights, creeped up on the bumper of an old pickup truck going way too slow for the posted speed limit.

When I pulled into the parking lot, I grabbed the helmet and got out. Inside the DMV I had to take a number, and then sit around some people who looked like they had been sitting there for a few days now. Listless. A tiny sign flashed the next number in red, blinking every few moments like you had won something on The Price Is Right. The chair was hard, metal, with a very flat pad on the top of the seat.

Everyone has been to the DMV. Most of us would understand that they weren't going to give me anything useful. Maybe I wasn't thinking clearly. Or maybe I hoped I would get that one person who just didn't give a shit anymore. There's a number of those in government work.

I waited until my number flashed on the sign, and then walked up to the open spot on the counter. A lady sat there, typing into her computer, not even really looking at me. She had rimmed glasses and gray hair, and was much, much heavier than a person should be. Whatever tall chair she sat on, it had to be reinforced.

"New plates?" she asked, in a monotone voice. Hopefully the tone of an employee just getting through the day. Her nametag said her name was Madge. She definitely looked like a Madge.

"No," I tried a smile at her. I got nowhere with it. It was something I hadn't had a lot of practice with, lately. On the plus side, Madge hadn't run away screaming. I took a breath and pushed forward. "I've got kind of a weird situation, and I was wondering if you might help me."

"That depends," she said. "Do you need a new license? Or a renewal?" she added the last bit on with a bit of hope. As if that was the extent of what she could do.

"Not either, really." I held up the helmet. "A girl left this."

"And you're here because?"

"I was hoping you would be able to put me in touch with the person." I showed Madge the artwork, and tried another smile. I was hoping she would feel like she was helping me help another person. "I used to bike, and this is a custom paint job, I'm sure it cost a small fortune. I have the bike's license plate, I was hoping you could help me find out who it belongs to."

Madge looked at me funny, and I realized how odd I had phrased it. Like I said, I was a little out of practice with these things.

"That's not something we do," she finally said. Her slightly hopeful face had given into something much more weary.

I tried a different tack, something a little less stalkery. "I'm not asking for their address or anything. Just call them from here and let them know their helmet is here. It was the only thing I could think of."

I sat the helmet on the counter, sliding it closer to Madge, like I was handing it over. Carefully, I faced the reflective shield towards the monitor. Reading things backwards was something anyone could do, and it was something I had practiced, once upon a time. If I could just get her to bring up the information, I would have the address.

"I don't know," Madge said. She tried a smile. It looked more like a frown. Maybe it was something she didn't do often, either.

"Look." I went for a good Samaritan look. It was a look my face wasn't built for. "I'm just trying to help someone out. It's not like people put ads in papers anymore for lost and found."

"Well..." Madge thought about it for a second, then another. Finally, a thought struck her. "Maybe if I saw your license?"

"Sure." At least she was making sure I was on the up and up. I handed it over. It wasn't my real name on it, and if she ran it through the system I knew it would come back clean.

Madge took my license without a word and keyed in some information from it. She looked satisfied with what she saw, and got up, very slowly, making sure her bulk was centered under her feet. "I'm going to make a copy of your license real quick."

I nodded like I understood, and watched her wander to the back of the room, towards a big heavy printer that looked like it had been built in the seventies. In the helmet, I saw that she had my information on the screen, my address, etc.... The screen was black, the letters were that computer-green, glowing against the dark background.

I waited, hoping that she would come back and check the biker's plate out for me. I knew they would find out nothing more about me than what was on the screen. That was certain.

Madge came back after a minute with a piece of paper, my license, and an older guy. This man was black, stick-thin with glasses, and had on a gray suit, with dark blue slacks, a white shirt and a blue tie.

She handed me my license, and grinned at me triumphantly, like she had won a race I had no idea I was running.

"Sir," the old man began, with the tone older people reserved for unruly children. "If you wouldn't mind following me, we can wait in my office while we get your information."

"It's not my information," I said. The old lady had called in her superior, which I should have realized was what was going to happen, if I tried this.

Smiles weren't the only thing I was out of practice on.

Still, I went on. Knowing that the older man had already called his superior, and maybe the police. Madge had pulled one over on me, and I was an idiot for even trying this. Who actually gets help at the DMV? I picked up the helmet, as if showing it to the older man. "I'm just trying to return this."

"Sure sir, sure," the old man said, waving me around the counter. "Just come on into my office and we'll get it all taken care of."

"I appreciate it," I said, looking at the old lady and rolling my eyes a bit. Point to you, Madge. It was a hard world when you couldn't trust little old ladies anymore. "But I've got something to do."

A few seconds later I was in my car and rolling out of the parking lot. The helmet in my seat. The old man had followed me out, and I watched him getting my plate number as I left.

That would limit the time I had to find the girl.

Strike one.

I didn't have a smartphone, or a laptop. I wasn't really interested in being available anywhere I went with just a slide of my thumb across the phone. Same with surfing the internet, it just didn't interest me to look through thousands of ads or click hundreds of links to find something I needed. Either one of those would have helped me now, but I would have to do things the hard way.

I stopped by the first bike store I saw, a little old place with Harley-Davidson Motorcycles all over the lot, thick Fat Boys and bigger Road Kings mixed with smaller Softails and Sportsters. On the far side were a few Yamahas and other brands of bikes. Nothing Japanese or sporty, just street bikes. Maybe they had been traded in for a Harley.

I operated on the belief that the paint job on the helmet was local. It wasn't going to help me if the graphic was something ordered from an artist in California.

The guy in the first store didn't know much about the helmet or the paint job. He just had a black skullcap of a helmet, and never had bothered with anything but that for his own use. He was an older man with a long beard and a black headband, and he looked like he had ridden

Harleys all his life. He was helpful enough to point me in the direction of a nearby place that sold sports bikes, though.

It went that way for a bit. I made my way east, towards the ocean, stopping at dealerships along the way. The sun got brighter above me in the cloudless blue sky, as the traffic of early afternoon thinned out as people returned to work. It was just a matter of keeping up the search, no matter how many dealerships I went to.

So the next place didn't help me, or the place following that. The third or fourth, either. Not even the eighth. Still, I kept moving on to the next, coming closer to the ocean, and at the tenth place I hit the jackpot.

The dealership was all foreign motorcycles, sports bikes that screamed along the roads at faster than a hundred miles an hour, painted in bright yellows and reds that appealed to a younger generation. The building was large, covering the corner of the block and all the bikes were inside.

I walked, smelling that new tire smell of brand new rubber, present in the air of every dealership. I glanced at everything, taking quick stock of the place. Rows of bikes spread across the store, all facing the front of the shop, with two walkways crossing through the rows in the middle of the place, so that all of the motorcycles were in one of four quadrants. A few back walls held helmets, vests, jackets, all the gear with all the logos.

There were a few young men walking around, browsing the wall of gear. A group of younger women at the center of the store, where the aisles crossed each other. They all were dressed in a way that made them high schoolers in my eyes, tight pants, tied off shirts revealing tight, flat stomachs. Everything this group of girls wore, they wore in a way to pull attention to them, screaming *look at me*.

Something the biker in the bookstore hadn't needed. She had a presence. An elegant kind of call. Something I knew that would always draw attention, no matter what she wore.

A group of three guys stood in front of the girls, one of the guys in the front doing most of the talking. He had one hand on a bright red Ducati, and kept motioning to it as he spoke. Maybe trying to sell the girls the bike or, more likely, sell them a ride on the bike with him.

I walked down the aisle. My tennis shoes were quiet against the hard tile floor. The pair of guys with the salesman looked up at me, in a way that made me think they were taking my measure. Which made me smile, a slight curve of the side of my mouth. These kids were too young for that kind of thing.

The salesman himself was too involved with one of the girls. A young lady with thick golden hair that fell over her face, tight black yoga pants and even tighter sports bra. Likely a size too small. I thought it might be too cold for wearing that, but I couldn't argue... the *look at me* was strong with this one.

The young man was talking about handling, and curves, and how the bike felt in just the right hands. All the innuendos a young guy would hint at. The young lady was listening to the guy hard, her eyes focused on his, and occasionally letting the tip of her tongue brush her top lip. He wore Ducati gear, bright blue pants and a tight white and blue shirt with the name of the company down his legs, across his back and chest.

Golden-hair had a group of girls with her, three of them, all various blondes with dark streaks dyed in their hair. Or maybe it was the other way around. All of them watched the guy and the girl, as if this was going to be their entire afternoon.

I stood by the guy for a moment and waited, not sure who was trying to hook up with who. The three blonde friends all looked me over once, almost at the same time, then turned back to the conversation. I waited patiently a moment, holding the helmet in one hand.

The young man wasn't going to acknowledge me, though. I knew he knew I was there. And he knew that I knew he knew. But he was invested in Golden-hair, and he wasn't going to let a thing like a customer stop a good thing.

And here I was, waiting on this guy hitting on girls too young for him, when a woman had been kidnapped. When she needed help.

I was a patient guy, when it was just me. But when what I was doing affected someone else, the patience seemed to evaporate.

"Hey," I interrupted. "Have a sec?"

The young man flicked his eyes to me, obviously disappointed. He had a cocky grin on, and turned back to the girl, holding his hand out to me, palm up. Making a show of it. "I'm with a customer, bro. Come back in a bit."

The girl looked at me too, sizing me up. One of those glances looking to see if I had money, how did I look, how did I match up next to the guy she was talking to, was I interesting enough to interrupt their day, those kinds of things.

She must have come to a positive decision, because the blonde licked her lip again, briefly, and smiled at me. "It's okay, Trick."

Trick. I rolled my eyes. What kids were calling themselves today.

Trick wasn't happy about the girl smiling at me.

"I won't take much of your time," I told him, as nice as I could. It had been a while since I had needed certain conversation skills. "It's a little urgent."

Trick's frown deepened. He still had his hand up. This wasn't going according to his plan. He glanced at my sneakers, and came to a conclusion. That I wasn't here to buy anything.

"We're a bike shop. Finding the right bike takes time," he explained, letting me know where I stood. "When I'm done with the lady, and she finds what she likes, I'll help you out."

He wasn't wrong. I wasn't going to buy anything. But we both knew the golden-haired girl wasn't either. So I tried again, maybe not as nice as I could have been.

"Trick, I'm just asking for a second of your time. Then you can go back to Goldilocks and the three blondes."

Goldilocks' eyes widened. Her friends looked like they couldn't figure out whether to be offended or interested. I think they all settled for something in between, striking various poses.

"Bro," Trick said. Still with the hand.

Maybe he felt like he had to defend the girls. More like he wanted to recover his reputation. Either way, Trick didn't look like he wanted to help me.

I grabbed his shoulder, right where the clavicle meets the neck, and squeezed. I had moved fast, but in a way like I was pulling an old friend closer to me. I squeezed my fingers with enough pressure to make it uncomfortable on the young man, and pressed down hard enough to keep him standing there, unless he wanted to look like a fool and try to jerk away in front of the girls.

Trick tried to jerk away, anyway. So I gripped tighter, until he winced and stopped. One hand grabbed at my hand, and then he caught my eyes.

"Hey," he said. Then again, "Hey." It looked like he didn't know what to say next. Maybe, in suburban America, he didn't realize things like this could happen to him.

The faces of the girls all lit up. The two young men by him looked like they wanted to do something. They were just unsure of what, and settled on swelling their chests out and facing me. The guy on my left took out his phone—*when did that become the first thing someone did in a fight?*—and held it out, facing me.

I held Trick tight, not letting him move. I looked at both of his friends. I knew what my face looked like. I knew what they would see, looking at me. I knew what they would find, if they understood the cold fury waiting in the backs of my eyes.

The two guys stepped back. I stared at the one with a camera until he held up both hands, phone loose in one, thumb barely on the back.

"Show me," I said.

He turned the phone around. The camera app hadn't been brought up, yet.

"Photos," I said, knowing there was a folder or album somewhere.

"Sure man, sure," the guy said. His hair was too long for his head, and it got in his face as he nodded. He turned the phone, did something with his finger, and then turned it back.

The first picture was of the group of girls, coming in. Then one of them wandering the store. He looked at them, looked at me, and swallowed. I nodded. He swiped again, showing a picture of the girls from behind, close and tight on their asses.

A few of the girls let out a gasp. I shook my head.

He swiped a couple more times. Pictures of him and the two guys standing next to him, by a group of bikes at a track somewhere. Pictures of a sunrise. Something with maybe his mother, an older lady, in what looked like a kitchen.

"Good," I finally said. No pictures of me. "Put it away."

I nodded, and he slid the phone back in his pocket.

"Hey," Trick said again, bending his legs as if trying to drop out of my grip. I pulled him up, and closer.

"I just asked for a second, Trick," I told him. "That was your chance to do the right thing. Now we're going to do it my way."

I put my face real close to Trick's. I brought up the girl's helmet, turned around so he could see the graphic, and the signed name. He turned his head, not looking at me, so all he could see was the helmet.

"You see this kind of artwork before?" I asked. Increasing the pressure in my grip on his shoulder.

"Hey." Trick had become really short on his vocabulary. "I don't know man, I don't know. I just sell the bikes."

"So you don't know dick about bikes, then?" I asked.

"No, no." He looked at the girls. Some part of him hoping he could salvage this. "I ride 'em bro, I just ride 'em. A few races. We don't paint anything here. No custom work."

"I'm not asking if you paint them," I said. "You would know this, if you took the time a few minutes ago. I'm asking if you know who does."

"I don't know," Trick said again. He grimaced under my hand. Goldilocks looked disappointed.

"That looks like Charley's work," one of his friends volunteered, then. Not the kid with the phone, the other guy. He had red hair, and pale skin. Black ink in the shape of some kind of lettering or tribal tattoo appeared from under his shirt, and scrawled along the side of his neck. "I'd try them."

"Charley's?" I asked.

"Yeah, like where Dorchester hits Fourth," the friend said. "Graphics shop, does a lot of tattoos and custom ink. Can't miss it."

"Any other places you know, does this kind of stuff?" I asked Red Hair.

"Not really, man," he said. "Been to Charley's. It looks like something they'd do. A lot of custom work is done on the side, though. If they didn't do it, they might know who did."

Looking at the helmet, the first big loop of the signature almost looked like a C, and maybe a lowercase H after. I couldn't be sure, because it looked more like a scribble than anything.

Still, it was the most information I'd gotten.

"Thanks," I told Red. "I appreciate the help."

I let go of Trick. He straightened his shirt out, moved his neck around, and looked at me. "Man, you can't be doing that to people. I'm going to call the cops."

"It's a free country," I said, looking right at Trick. "Though we just had that lesson about choices and consequences."

His eyes met mine, then looked away. His face followed suit. I stayed there, relaxed, on the balls of my feet. It wasn't like I was going to fight any of these kids, but adrenaline was adrenaline, and my body was squarely on the fight side of the fight-or-flight response. Always had been. So I stayed there, aware of everything, and ready for anything. Waiting.

Trick swallowed. His friends stood by, quietly. Goldilocks stared at me in wide-eyed attention, with Goldilocks still biting her lower lip. It must be her thing. Her friends had forgotten their poses, just looking at me with open eyes. I had suddenly ratcheted up their interested list.

"Tell me," I said to Trick. "One way or the other."

"I'm not," he finally said. "I won't."

"Won't what?"

"I won't call the cops," he said.

I nodded. Both of his friends looked at me, shaking their heads as well. Hands out and open. There would be no videos or pictures or calls to the police. From any of them.

"Appreciate your time," I said, and walked out of the store.

CHAPTER
SEVEN

Dorchester wasn't hard to find. It was closer to the ocean than the dealership I just left, all I had to do was keep driving east, going through an older part of town, closer to the wharfs. Cobblestone and brick buildings that had been around for a hundred years or even longer, most of them rebuilt and reconstructed to provide an old-time feel for new-time prices. Dark shingled roofs with chimneys poking out on top, windows and doors slightly smaller than the doors and windows of today.

The roads were older, more damaged, with the humidity coming in off the ocean mixing with the hot summers and late, freezing winters. Roads covered by ice throughout the day, salted and plowed, until the pavement gave in and cracked, until even the newer highways quickly became acne-pitted scars dotting the face of new concrete. As I headed closer to the ocean the road got older and older, there were more and more cracks in the pavement, more potholes, some holes new and gaping, others closed, filled with a dark asphalt that never seemed tamped down enough to be flush with the road.

The car hummed quietly underneath me, bouncing over the mounds and jouncing across the pits. I made good time. Traffic had lightened up some, being in that period of time after lunch, and before the end of the workday. Later, during rush hour, these streets would be packed tight like sardines, cars funneled through each stoplight, horns blaring as the light flicked from red to green to yellow back to red.

I knew I had the right place as soon as I turned onto Fourth. Charley's was a graphic design and tattoo shop, its name actually was Charley's Angels, just spelled differently from the television show. A large painted sign with the name stood above the shop, Charley's Angels in a gothic font, with an angel on the left of the name, and a devil to the right.

More angels spanned the glass windows of the store, with demons sprinkled in here and there. One angel had a set of wings that looked almost exactly like the pair on the helmet. On this angel, the streams flying by the wings made it look as if he was flying high into the stratosphere.

I pulled up the helmet and looked on the back. More and more the scribble looked like the name Charley's Angels, signed with short, loopy lines and a pair of long lines, a horizontal one underneath the name split with a vertical line between the two words, like a cross.

I walked through the door. A little digital bell dinged me in. The outside motif of heaven and hell continued inside the store, all kinds of different angels and demons of different sizes and colors printed on hundreds of pieces of paper, square, posted in rows across every wall. Occasionally I would see some of the tribal stuff, armbands and such, as well as goth tattoos. Different sizes and shapes of skulls, reapers, tombstones. Serpents, scythes, all of that and more.

The back of the store held a couple of tattoo chairs. A person was lying on one of the chairs with their shirt off, their back towards me. A guy stood over the person, weaving a tattoo gun in hand, a tiny wisp of smoke drifting up from the gun. He had a dark blue tank top on, and a skull bandana tied tightly around his head. A fan blew across the chairs so that the smell of hot ink and burned skin drifted through the store.

A girl waited by the front counter, leaning against it, one arm bracing herself on the top. A laptop on the counter in front of her, open, the back of it facing me. She had long braids of black hair, each of the ends bleached white. The braids on the side of her head were shorter than the braids on her back, so that the bleached ends looked a little like a staircase, curving around to the back of her head, each step lower and lower. She had on a tight black cotton shirt, so tight it flattened her breasts.

She looked at me, oddly. She might have been thirty, or thereabouts. She had too much makeup on to really tell. Her gaze found the helmet in my hand, and her eyes opened in recognition.

"You," she said, drawing the word out, "aren't here for some ink."

It was nice to get right to it. I held up the helmet. "You know who painted this?"

She didn't even need to peer at the signature. "Sure," she said.

I waited for a second. And she waited for a second. I waited a bit longer. The girl seemed happy to leave the conversation there.

I finally asked her, "Would you mind telling me who, then?"

She smiled, not a real smile, but small. The kind you indulge children with, when you are explaining something. "Depends," she said.

Then she waited a bit longer. She seemed to be good at that. After a moment her gaze went to the back, watching the one guy tattoo the other.

I sighed. "Depends on who's asking, right?"

Her smile got real. "You're damn right," she said. "And what they're asking for."

"Well, I'm the one asking," I said, and gave her my spiel about the girl forgetting her helmet in the store.

The girl shook her head when I finished. "You don't want to return it."

"I don't?" I asked.

"Nah," she said. "I don't know how you got the helmet, but you're not looking to return it. You want to find the girl who owns it."

"I do?" I said. Giving her my indulging smile. Or something like it.

Her voice was calm and low, her eyes watching me. "I'm guessing you met her."

"What if I did?"

"If you met her, you'd know," she said.

"This is kind of circling around a bit," I said, letting out a huge exhale. But I continued. "Know what?"

She leaned a little more over the counter. Like we were conspirators. She lowered her voice. "I'm not in the habit of giving stalkers information on the girls they're stalking."

I was feeling like I was going to go oh for two. I used to be a lot better at these kinds of things, but first Madge had gotten the runaround on me, and now this girl. There was a time when people would have wanted to help me. But I guess that had been a different me.

Still, the girl needed some help. And I was the guy who could give it. Even with my routine.

I realized I had made the decision to help her without even thinking about it. Somewhere back in the parking lot, while I had been chasing the Escalade. Maybe my body had been on autopilot, doing things I had done before. But even after that, I had gone to her bike. I had grabbed her helmet. I had gone to the DMV.

I had tossed my routine aside. And that frightened me. Because the person I had been before, I wasn't that guy anymore. Without my schedule, the focus on the next moment, and not the future, I didn't know what would happen.

Not to the girl. I was going to save her, or die trying. Knew it, without a doubt. But what would that cost me? Where was this road steering me? What would happen to what I was *owed*?

I guessed I would find out.

"Kind of a stretch, isn't it?" I said, rolling my eyes. "Me, here, with her helmet. Trying to find a girl, just to what?" I waved my arms. "Watch her through a window?"

"There's worse than watching a window out there," the girl said. "You seem to be the type of guy that would fall into that category."

The tattoo guy had come up, while we were talking. He had a tightly trimmed goatee and long sideburns to go with his black skull bandana. He wore a tank top to show off his muscles. He looked like he went to a gym. And he felt like he was tough.

The guy handed the girl some cash. The guy getting the tattoo walked out of the door, the electronic bell dinging him out. I had that effect on people.

Then it was quiet in the store. The pregnant kind of silence, with just the box fan blowing in the back. The smell of hot ink. Burned skin.

And us.

"This guy bothering you, Charley," the guy asked. He carried himself loosely, on the balls of his feet. He looked at me with a grin, just a twist of his lips. As if he had taken out trash before, and would again.

"Charley," I said, looking at the helmet again. "This is your work."

"Yep," she said, then talking back to the tattoo guy without missing a beat. "I'm good, Dave."

"You got it," he said, and turned away without looking at me again. He headed back to his chair, as if he and Charley had worked with tough customers before, and trusted her decision.

I realized then that Charley's other hand was below the counter. Arm angled in such a way that her hand was pointed at me. It wasn't hard to imagine what she might be holding in that hand.

So I took a deep breath and tried to relax. Maybe it had been Madge, maybe Trick, or maybe the break in the routine, but I knew how I looked to Charley. I understood how the rage had me stand, tense, every muscle tight and ready to spring into action. So I loosened them up. I knew the sharp line of my jaw protruded too much, because I knew how tight I was grinding my teeth. I took a deep breath and tried to relax.

And I knew my eyes held something behind them, pain and anger and a dark fury, and people could feel it all, when they caught my glance. So I...

Well, two out of three wasn't bad.

"Okay," I said, holding my hands at my sides, a little up, the helmet loose in my grip. "I think we got off on the wrong foot."

"Maybe," Charley said. "Not sure there's a right foot to be had."

"You got Wi-Fi here?" I said. Hoping I was right in my next guess. It had been hours since the kidnapping, and Charley was the only link I had to rescue the girl.

"It's twenty-twenty," she said. Talking about the year. "Wifi is everywhere."

"Okay," I said, keeping my hands up. "Do me a favor and get on your computer. Do a quick search for me. See what you see."

She looked at me for a long second. Keeping her one hand below the counter. Keeping her eyes on me. Then she pulled back a bit, off the counter, and her arm there slid a laptop over. That hand opened the case, and both of us waited until the startup tones finished beeping.

Charley kept focused on me the whole time. Her laptop squared to me. So I took a step back, trying to give her space. Making her feel more comfortable. Her free hand worked the mousepad, clicked on something, and I gave her the name of the mall.

"Search for that," I said. "And kidnapping."

Her eyes had been watching herself type the name of the mall in. When I said kidnapping though, they flicked back up to me, and the arm under the counter tensed.

I took another step back. Holding my hands higher. From the back Dave started singing, a low voice, more kind of humming the tune and breaking out with a few words, here and there. Maybe what he knew. I glanced over, he was cleaning up his station, a spray bottle in one hand and a white cloth in the other. Paying no attention to Charley, or me.

I looked back to Charley. "Please."

She pursed her lips and thought for a moment. Then she finished typing something in, with just the one hand, tiny ticks of each hunt and peck of letters as she entered them. Then Charley hit the return key with a final, hard click.

Something must have come up, because her eyes opened. She moved her hand and I heard another click, and then her eyes travelled from side to side. Her mouth moved, as if she was reading the words aloud.

Then she clicked something else. I heard the braking of the Escalade, as it swerved out of the parking lot. The sound was tinny, coming out of the tiny speakers of the laptop, but I still heard the rumble of the engine as it started to pull away.

Then she hit a button. The sound stopped. She looked at the screen, then me. Then back at the screen.

"She's been kidnapped," she said, finally.

I nodded, and kept my hands up.

"You were there," she said. "That's you, chasing the truck."

I let out a breath. News was out, and someone had captured me. Likely a cell phone somewhere.

"It was," I said.

"You could be with them," Charley said, looking like she was trying to understand the video.

I rolled my eyes, looked at her a little more seriously. "Really?"

She was a little shocked. Her eyes kept looking back to the screen, as if Charley was having a hard time believing what she saw there. After a quick moment or two, she shook her head, slightly. "No."

"I'm just a guy who happened to be there," I said. Then I looked at Charley, knowing what I looked like. "But the wrong type of guy, for those people."

Charley looked at me, then slowly nodded. "You look like you would be."

"So I'm looking for anything to do with her," I said. "Someone kidnapped her for a reason. I've got to figure that part out. Work forward from there. And I have to do it fast, because whoever took her needs something from her."

"You met her, didn't you?" Charley said. "Angie?"

So, her name was Angie. I didn't like it. Angie was how you called someone you were hanging with, someone you met at the beach for a game of volleyball, or maybe for a group of girls grabbing drinks after work. It was likely short for Angela. I liked that name better, it seemed to fit the woman I had met. Someone confident. Composed. A touch of elegance, a hint of a painful past, someone who had built who she wanted to be.

I nodded, more to myself than answering Charley's question, though the motion served to do both.

"That's why you're doing this," Charley said.

"Doing what?" I said. Then motioned my arms around. "This?"

Charley nodded again. "If you met her, you'd understand."

I did meet Angela. And I thought I did understand. I walked by hundreds of people a day. Stared at thousands. Just trying to make it to the next day. But some people, they stand out among the thousands. They have a quality that pulls you in. That breaks routines. That makes you feel something.

"I understand," I said. "Can you tell me more about her? Maybe where she lives? Works? Something to help me figure out how to find her?"

She would have something somewhere. People don't get kidnapped without a reason. And the phone call she had received, just before, that had been something else. Something that had scared Angela. If I dug enough, I would find something. Or someone. Either one would bring me closer to finding her, and if I knew one thing, it was how to take one tiny step at a time, each step taking you just a bit closer to your goal.

Until you got there.

Charley came to a decision. "I still don't know much about you."

For a brief second I thought about taking the information. Rushing

Charley, despite the gun she might be holding. Taking on singing Dave. Knocking them both out. Searching her computer for something I could use.

That was the anger in me. The fury behind the wall. Wanting to be realized, be unchecked. And these people seemed like good people. Whatever I needed, it wasn't something that I could take by force. However much I wanted to.

I took a deep breath, and let it out. A long inhale and exhale. Besides, there could be a hundred Angela's in Charley's laptop. Or there could be none. I softly rubbed my forehead with the palm of my hand, in little circles. I slowly let go of the side of me that would have done anything to find out information about the girl.

"Fair enough," I said. "But just so you know, I'm still going to find her. All you're doing is delaying the inevitable."

"Maybe that's a good thing," Charley said.

"Maybe," I told her. "Or maybe your friend will be dead by then, and you'll regret the chance you had to help her."

"Why not just call the cops?" she asked.

"They aren't going to want help," I said, shaking my head. "Especially not the help I'd give them. Besides, they already are ahead of the game, now. They know more. Her bike's in the lot. Her picture's on the video. What more do they need from me? What's the helmet going to help them with?"

Charley just looked at me. I could see the scales weighing in her mind.

"I'll tell you something else," I said. "The police aren't me. They've got a million cases to handle every day. All I have, is this." I took a step forward, knowing Charley could sense, feel what I was telling her in the back of her mind.

I didn't know where this was headed. I just knew it was a place I had to go. A path I needed to follow. Someone was in trouble, and once I had been a person who had answered that call. It wasn't that long ago, and some small part of me still wanted to be that guy.

Anger surfaced in me. Different from before, from the fury I used my routine to keep in check. It confused me, and then I realized it wasn't the anger of betrayal. It was more of a righteous wrath. Maybe I was blending emotions, mixing old scars with a new wound, that of feeling impotent when someone needed me, but I knew Charley could sense what I was feeling. Enough to convince her I was the right guy for this job.

"You'll have to trust what I say here. This is something I'm good at," I said, my voice low, not quite hoarse. My hand in a fist. "These people, these kidnappers, aren't going to be happy to meet me. I'm telling you, I can find her, and when I do, they're going to regret kidnapping her."

She smiled a little, a real smile. Acknowledging the truth of my words, maybe. "I can believe that."

"Then give me a chance to help her," I said. Not quite pleading.

Charley took a last measure of me. Something clicked in her eyes, some decision. She inclined her head once, and started typing something into her computer again. Pulling her other hand from below the counter.

"Tell you what," she said. "I'm not going to tell you where she lives. I still don't really know you. But I'll help you."

"Help me how?" I asked.

She hit return and looked at her screen closely. "I'll take you to where she lives."

CHARLEY DID SOMETHING ON HER LAPTOP AND CLOSED IT.
Then she talked to the tattoo artist in the back for a few minutes, then
grabbed a purse from under the counter and followed me out to my car.
Outside, traffic was picking up a bit, cars crowding the street, an occasional roar from a muffler as a car accelerated quickly from a stop.

The both of us were quiet. It was my natural state, but I thought
Charley was probably wondering why she was helping me. I was
surprised she had agreed to take me to Angela's house. She probably
was too.

We got into my car. The doors thunked shut, and I started it up
with the quick muscleless rev of a four-cylinder engine. Charley took a
big breath in through her nose, and looked over at me, with one
eyebrow raised.

"What?" I asked.

"I didn't figure you for a vanilla guy," she said.

The air freshener. "I'm not. It was just what was in the car, when I
bought it."

"Huh," Charley said, and grinned at me. "You sure it's not because
they don't make brimstone-scented air fresheners?"

I rolled my eyes. "Funny."

"Maybe broken bone is more your style," she said. Cracking herself up. "Or ash."

We pulled out into traffic and headed west on the boulevard. I flipped my visor down to block the descending sun. It was still midafternoon, but starting to edge towards evening, and the air was chilly enough that I could feel the warm rays of the sun through the windshield on my face and arms.

I usually drove without the heater or air conditioning on. Charley looked at the controls, and fingered the radio dial a bit before not turning it on. The road noise was a steady humming inside the cab of the car, with the whooshing sound of us passing other cars.

For a while we just drove along, her telling me to turn here or go straight there, until we hit a long stretch of stoplights and slow cars. We idled at each light, then took off, only to have to stop at the next. My hands tightened on the steering wheel, and I had to force them to relax.

I used to be so calm. Collected. Ready for action. Knowing what I did helped others.

"I can tell why she likes you," Charley said, while we were stopped.

"Who?" I asked.

"Angie," Charley said.

You got anyone you spend all that time with? Angela had asked.

My heart raced with the memory. Excited.

My hands were tight again on the steering wheel.

"Why would she like me?" I finally asked.

"You got to know her story," Charley said. "Something in your eyes. Dangerous. But some pain there, as well. She wouldn't be able to resist it."

"I don't understand what you mean," I said, hitting the gas before hitting the brakes again, a moment later.

"I'm guessing here," Charley said, "but you seem like a quiet guy. At ultimate rest."

"Still not getting it," I told her.

"You were sitting there at the bookstore, right? Just watching things, not moving."

I shrugged. "It's my routine."

"So you were there. Relaxed. Then you probably looked at her, like you did when you walked into my shop," Charley said. "You caught her eye, and she saw something powerful and dangerous and empty and dead in you, and that would intrigue her."

I grunted. "You've got a large imagination."

"I'm an artist," Charley said. "I notice things. And I bet I'm right about you. I can see it in the way you carry yourself. Unnoticed, maybe even trying to fade into the background, but sort of looming with violence."

I shifted in the seat a bit. A lot of what she was said was close to the truth. Uncomfortably so. "You an artist," I said. "Or a psychologist?"

"I'm just saying, I pick up those kinds of vibes," she said.

"Yeah, well, it's not about her liking me," I said. "Or me even liking her. It's about doing what's right."

"Is it?" Charley said. "She's not some princess you're trying to save? Some damsel in distress?"

Again, close to the truth. Again, not something I wanted to talk about. We made the next light, stopped at the next, and I looked over.

"Whatever she is doesn't matter," I said, feeling the lie as I spoke it. "Not to me."

"It's not?" Charley said.

"No," I said again.

"Then why are you trying to find her?"

I gritted my jaw a bit. I couldn't tell Charley the answer to that, because I didn't fully understand why I was trying to find Angie either. "I can't explain it," I said. "Why do you care?"

Charley smiled. "You noticed the shop, right? Charley's Angels?"

I didn't answer.

Her smile disappeared.

"I believe in all kinds of things," she said. "Angels. Demons. I've been a part of a little Heaven, a little Hell. I've fallen down. I've gotten back up. I've seen redemption."

Charley paused. "And I've seen enough to know retribution, when it's right in front of me," she said. "And the one thing about retribution, the person who is taking the eye for an eye, they only do it because they care."

She wasn't wrong. I was the guy who took an eye for an eye. Maybe I was even the guy who took *eyes* for an eye. But she also wasn't right.

I didn't know Angela well enough to care for her. I didn't know her enough to understand why I was interested in her. And I couldn't afford to feel anything for her. Hell, I barely knew her. All I had was a five minute conversation, and now I felt like some kid back in high school.

I knew what happened, when you got involved with someone else. When you cared about someone enough that you placed their wellbeing, their happiness, above yours. That kind of trust existed only so it could be betrayed.

I wasn't going through that again. So I packed it all up. Put it behind the wall, with everything else. Pressed the gas pedal when the light turned green, and headed to the next stoplight. Took a breath and released it.

"Turn up here," Charley nodded left. "We're getting close."

CHAPTER
NINE

Angela lived in a part of town that worked hard to try to reclaim itself from the slums. I turned down a street with buildings painted in graffiti, liquor stores, and cardboard homes for the homeless. After a few blocks, fresh coats of paint began to cover the graffiti. Smaller mom and pop places took over the corners of streets instead of liquor stores. Iron bars on the windows disappeared, leaving panes of glass. There were real people here, struggling to stake a claim to some kind of life, take a stand, and keep what they owned from falling into the ocean of welfare, drugs, and paid-for cell phones around them.

We passed a large poster, almost like a billboard, across the face of a building. One of those political campaign posters, with the picture of a confident man, dark hair with a touch of gray, firm chin. The words Bigger and Better underneath.

Charley motioned for me to stop as we came to a tiny block of brick apartments. I pulled off on the opposite side of Angie's building, by an open parking meter in front of another apartment building. A small coffee shop was open beside us, with just a few people out front, this late in the day.

I wrestled some loose change out of the console and got us thirty minutes at the meter. The two of us crossed the street to Angie's building, avoiding some of the traffic. Tiny trees had been planted there, in a row down the sidewalk, which was clean except for a few cigarette butts by one of the trees. Which just showed there was an asshole in every crowd.

A bunch of tall teenage kids stood down the street, hanging around, one of them holding a basketball. Laughing and joking. The ball bouncing occasionally on the pavement.

Three steps led to the front door of the complex. It was old, maybe from the fifties or sixties, and six stories tall. The brick face had been washed recently, none of the windows had bars, and the windowsills held a variety of potted plants. A few windows were even up, letting in the cool air, and sounds of a television came out of one.

The ringer on the outside of the entryway was clean, a slight circle of polished brass, but I didn't have to ring anyone to go in. The door was unlocked. I opened the door and went in, Charley following me into the entry hall.

The tile floor lay before us, old black and white squares. It had been recently mopped, with the faint smell of lemons and bleach lingering in the air. A staircase led up to the next floor on our left, with an old black-iron banister, the stairs doubling back on itself to the third floor, all the way to the top. There wasn't an elevator.

"Fourth floor," Charley said. She started to go up the stairs, but I held her back. I would be first.

The banister didn't move, it felt tight as I grabbed it. My leg protested a bit going up, but I made sure every step was silent as I placed each sneaker on the hard tile of the stairs. Charley had a pair of low, thick-heeled pumps on that clicked against the steps, until I looked at her with my eyebrows raised, motioning for a little more quiet.

I didn't know why I felt like I had to be quiet, it was just a sense I had. Intuition. Something old, that I had trusted once, coming back to me.

At the second floor Charley whispered, "Apartment 404."

I winced. Whispers carried a bit, something in the way it was pitched. When I heard a whisper I almost always knew someone was up to no good. It immediately gave a person a bad feeling. A low, soft voice was the better way to go. Low voices talking were almost background noise.

We made our way up. On the third floor I saw my first drop of blood. Dark and teardrop shaped, the end pointing up the stairs. A few more were scattered on the tile, as I made my way around. Even more up the third set of stairs, as if someone had been bleeding and running and trying to bandage up at the same time.

My intuition was usually right about things. I didn't rush up the stairs, but stayed quiet. Let the calmness overtake me, so that I'd be ready.

At the fourth floor I held out a hand to Charley, motioning for her to stop. Six apartment doors circled the stairs, one every twenty feet or so. The one at the top was labeled Apartment 401. Two more doors circled the stairs, 402 and 403. Apartment 404 was at the other end of the hallway, where the steps led up to the fifth floor, and across from 405.

I saw all that at the same time I saw the drops of blood leading from 404, and the door to Angie's apartment open, slightly pushed in. There was a single long splinter in the gap there, kicked back from the door jamb, where the deadbolt would have been.

"Wait here," I told Charley, in a very low voice.

"Why?" Charley went to push past me. Voice louder than it needed to be.

I grabbed her shoulders, holding her and looking Charley in the eyes. She went to say something and I shook my head. Thankfully, she stayed quiet, and when she stopped struggling, I told her, very softly, to wait again.

Charley saw the door then. Her eyes opened. I held out my open hand. "Let me check it out."

"What if Angie's in there?" she said.

I rolled my eyes. Every sound was important. I mouthed the next words. "Wait. Here."

Charley took a big breath. She had been good at the waiting game back in her store, but here was a part of life I ruled, and I knew I would win that game here. Still, one of her hands snaked into her purse.

I leaned closer. Charley pulled back, and I pulled her closer, placing my lips near her ear. "Come in after. Count to thirty, then follow."

Her frown told me what she thought about that.

"I don't need Wild Bill Hickok," I told her, glancing at her purse.

She didn't say or do anything. I didn't think she was going in immediately, but I didn't think she was going to wait, either. My jaw clenched a bit. I kept hold of her shoulders.

"I need you to acknowledge what I've told you," I said.

Charley shook her head and waited for a long moment. Then she finally answered, again in that whisper, "Fine."

I nodded and let go of her shoulders. "Start counting after I enter."

I flowed down the hall and towards the door, not making a sound. Old habits never go away, though my right leg twitched a little, like a numb limb coming back to awareness. An ache, but also an itch, needing to be scratched.

I got to the door and hunched a bit, pressing my ear to the crack. I listened for a long three-count, hearing the soft scrabbling of someone walking around, the clicks and clacks of items being thrown around. Enough noise for at least a person or two, and loud enough that I held out hope they hadn't heard Charley.

I could smell something light in the air. A faint, sweet smell. Copper-like. Almost metallic. The scent brought back memories of people. All of them dead.

My heart picked up a bit, beating to an urgent drummer. I forced it to slow down and slowly pushed the door open. My fingertips light against the door. It opened without a sound to a short hallway, painted in a light color, a few pictures on the wall.

Down the hall was a small living room. Pillows on the couch, a blanket across one arm, and more pictures across the walls there, giving the place a sense of life my apartment never had. A door beyond the living room which led to a bedroom, or a bathroom. That door was shut.

A tall counter was to my left. Beyond it was an open kitchen. In the back, a wooden table had been pushed against a white refrigerator door.

And there was a guy standing in the middle of the room.

The entire kitchen was a mess, a phonebook had been tossed to one side, notepads and dishes all over. Drawers were open, next to a sink, with stuff pulled out of them. The guy faced away from me, staring at something in the middle of the kitchen floor. Something the counter prevented me from seeing.

He was wearing a white T-shirt and jeans. Dots of blood had dried on his shirt, and there were thin lines of it across his front and back. His hair was cut short on the sides, and just a little longer on the top, the high and tight most military men preferred. His complexion was dark enough that it told me he spent a lot of time outdoors.

He turned his head just then. I knew he saw me at that moment.

I had learned winning a fight most often boiled down to two things.

The first thing was knowing when a fight was about to happen. It never mattered what the fight was about, or what weapons people brought to it, whether it was guns or knives or fists. None of that mattered. It only mattered if you knew, without a doubt, the moment the fight was about to begin.

After that, it was just a question of timing.

If you had a sense of the exact moment a fight was going down, then all you had to do was get your strike in first. If you struck with overwhelming force or intense quickness, or both, the fight was going to end. Right then. Ninety-nine times out of a hundred.

I had always been good at feeling that moment. Over the years, I had honed my intuition to a place few had. Knowing *when* was a sixth sense for me. I always knew. I always got in the first blow. So when I felt the moment, I struck. Always as quick as I could, and with as much force as I could bring to bear.

Like now.

The guy was still turning his head when I moved. One of his hands wrapped around to the back of his jeans, at the same time I slid around the kitchen counter. There was a gun tucked in his waistband, something black and square with slide-action. His hand wrapped around the handle and pulled it out. His body turning to me even as I got to him.

I pushed his gun hand out to the side, my hand on his wrist, my fingers digging into the place between the gun and his thumb. Yanking his thumb out, breaking it with a loud pop.

At the same time, I gut-punched him with my other hand. Three times in rapid succession. Aiming right at the corner of the solar plexus, and digging each fist deep into his stomach. Feeling something, likely a rib, crack under the last blow.

The gun clattered to the floor. And then the guy was kneeling on the floor and dry-heaving, both hands holding his ribs.

Fight sensed.

Fight won.

I quickly grabbed the man's gun, a Beretta 9mm. It had been awhile since I had held one, but the memory of it fit my hand well. The man was still retching, so I held him by the hair on top of his head. It was short enough that it made it difficult to keep a grip on him. So I dug into his scalp until I felt some of his hair pull out.

The guy was still dry-heaving a bit from the punch. Trying to get in a breath. Close-up I could see the patterns of blood across his chest, dark lines crisscrossing his shirt. This man had been in a fight recently.

Here. One of his hands pawed at the hand holding his hair. Until I placed the barrel of his gun against his forehead.

The guy stopped. Making gulping sounds while he held down whatever stomach bile might be trying to come up. I made sure he held as still as he could, because all of a sudden I was highly interested in what the guy had been standing in the middle of.

It was a mess.

More thin lines of blood crossed over the kitchen. As if the fight had been right there. They ran both left to right and right to left. Maybe someone's arm had been cut, and while that person had been swinging, blood had been slung around. The blood was not quite fresh, it had begun to dry in places, mainly because it was thin.

Somewhere in my head, the timer hit thirty. I yanked on the guy's head, pulling his face up to me. He was still trying to catch his breath, holding back his heaves with one arm still pressed tight to his belly. I turned to see Charley in the doorway to the apartment, gun out and pointed in my direction.

Her hand wavered, and her eyes were so wide open there was no way she could blink.

"Get in here," I said. "And shut that door."

When Charley did nothing, I told her it again.

"What happened?" she asked. "Who is that guy? Where is Angie?"

"Shut the door first," I said. "Cover your hand with your shirt when you close it. Questions later."

She stood there, like she was under a time-delay. Hearing what I told her way long after I had spoken the words.

The guy struggled again in my grip. I pulled him back and swung him around by his hair, placing his back against one of the floor cabinets. There were lines of blood on the floor, just like the walls and cabinets, and sliding the man smeared the liquid a bit over the tiles. He bit back a scream and stopped struggling. When I checked, Charley had shut the door.

"Over here," I said.

Charley came around the counter, her gaze taking in the mess. Then her eyes seeing the blood. I didn't think they could open any wider, but they did.

I let go of the guy and pulled Charley to the middle of the kitchen floor. Little drops of blood were on the tile, but stepping in those couldn't be helped. I placed her where the table had been shoved against the refrigerator. I held her arm so she pointed her gun at the guy.

Charley did all those things listlessly, like she was in shock.

"Keep the gun pointed at this guy," I told her. "If he moves, pull the trigger."

She didn't say anything.

"Charley," I said.

She didn't respond.

I slapped her. Lightly on the cheek. Just a pat, really. She shook herself and glared at me.

"Keep your gun on this guy," I said. "If he moves, shoot him."

"I can't shoot him," she said.

"You were going to shoot me, in your store, weren't you?" I asked.

"That's different," she said. She didn't sound confident though. "You kind of came across like an ass."

"Well, this is different too," I said. "If this guy moves, and gets to you, he might kill you."

Charley swallowed.

I looked at the guy. He had gotten control of his breathing, and had laid back against the counter, one hand holding his broken thumb. His eyes were narrowed, and his jaw was set.

"Won't you?" I asked.

The guy said nothing. He knew the type of guy I was, soldiers always recognized each other. But he also knew Charley was nothing of the sort, and he had a sense that she was going to hold me back.

I patted him down. He had a knife in his back pocket, the gun I held now, and that was it. So he was somewhat competent. Nothing to iden-tify him, no phone either. Part of a competent group.

I opened the knife. It was something you could open with a thumb, pushing a little nob so the blade would come out of the handle. Some-thing people could carry easily. The blade had been wiped, but some blood still hung where the blade sat in its cradle.

"Do nothing," I told the man, "and you'll live."

He sneered a bit. It was cocky. Like he had been in more dangerous situations and made it out okay. Maybe he thought he was good enough. He had just beaten someone, and testosterone could make people feel invincible.

I knew all about feeling invincible. And what it took to break someone.

"Do anything else," I said, simply. Using a voice I rarely used. "And you won't."

His sneer slipped a little. Maybe he believed me. We'd probably end up seeing.

"Charley?" I asked again. "Can you or can't you?"

"What?" she asked. Her hands were trembling, holding the gun. It was a big .45, with a cylinder. An older Smith & Wesson. Like some-thing from the old west, long and heavy.

"Can you shoot him?" I said.

She shook her head a little, her eyes still open.

I let out a breath. Charley couldn't hold the guy there, and I couldn't look through the apartment without someone keeping an eye on this guy. So I'd have to tie him up.

Some towels hung out of one of the open drawers. Little yellow things, long and a little fluffy. The kind you use to dry dishes. I yanked a few out and used the man's knife to cut strips out of them. Then I used those strips to bind him. At his ankles. Then his knees. And then his wrists. Until he was as tied up as I could make him.

"Jesus Christ, that smell," Charley said, ducking her head and muffling her face with one arm. She still had the gun in both hands, loose in her grip now. "Is that blood?"

Maybe there was more here than I thought. It had smelled faint to me.

"Yeah," I said.

"Angie's?"

"I doubt it."

Looking at the drying liquid, it was hard to tell. I thought the fight had just happened, in the past hour, but I wasn't a blood spatter analyst.

"You want to tell me?" I asked the guy.

He kept his sneer going.

So it could have been an hour. Likely not longer, but I didn't really know. Fucking Madge. Fucking Trick. Maybe if one of them would have actually helped me, I could have stopped whatever had happened here.

If this had come from Angela... the quiet anger inside me got a little louder. The crossed lines on the man's T-shirt appeared to grow darker before me. Thicker. Pulsing.

I took a deep breath to push the emotion back down. It made no sense for her kidnappers to bring her here, just to kill her. They would have waited to take her when she got home. This was something else. Something unknown.

"Who is that guy?" Now that Charley could talk, she was full of questions. Like most people coming out of shock, she was trying to find her bearings. Trying to put it together.

"I don't know," I answered. "Let's find out."

I turned back to the guy. I had placed him so his back lay against the dishwasher. He was young, maybe mid-twenties, and looking at him he had the confidence of youth. The feeling of invincibility. He was clean shaven, and his eyes watched Charley and me, remembering everything we said. Memorizing how we looked.

"Who are you?" I asked.

The sneer really never left that guy. Maybe it had frozen on his face as a kid, and he had been stuck with it since. The man shrugged.

"I get it," I said. "I've been there. You recognize it." I tried giving him a chance. "Let's not make this more difficult."

His eyes flicked to Charley, then the door, then back to me. The man made a little motion with his head, as if asking me if I was willing to wait forever. That someone, sooner or later, would be walking in. Or walk by.

Maybe he had a partner. Maybe that guy was following the other person who had been hurt. I didn't know, but I had a sense I didn't have a ton of time, either.

I took a breath and stood. "Watch him," I told Charley, pushing her gun so that it pointed to the ground. "Just watch him. Give me a shout if he moves."

"Where are you going?" she asked.

"Just watch him," I told her again. This wasn't twenty questions. "Touch nothing."

I waited until she nodded. I found a pair of latex cleaning gloves under the kitchen sink, which I put on. I wasn't worried about my prints, but it made sense to have less of them around than I needed to. It had been a long time since I had done something like this, and I felt less prepared than I had ever been.

Both Charley and I had stepped in the blood. A lot of it had dried, but it still left little prints on the floor. Solid shapes from her pumps, part of a sneaker pattern here and there. Not much, but I wiped them up, and put the towel I had used down so Charley could stand on it.

I searched the apartment. The kitchen I covered quickly, assuming this guy had looked through it pretty thoroughly. Everything had been pulled out of the drawers and tossed on the kitchen counter, on top of the blood there. It was still wet, so everything was stained with pink smears. I shoved aside batteries, measuring cups, tacks and butterfly clips, all the stuff that ends up in the junk drawer in the kitchen.

A few letters caught my eye. I slid the envelopes to the side, laying them blood-side up. The address from a local college. Bills. I caught her name on one of them. A phone bill. Angela Martinez. Something in me noted I had guessed her name correctly.

Charley stood there watching me, shoulders slumped, gun held loose in one hand. I could almost read what was going through her mind. She had thought she was going to check on a friend, and make sure I was on the up and up. Instead she was in her friend's apartment, with her friend nowhere in sight, with blood on the wall and a guy with a gun.

The way some mornings go, right?

I worked quickly through the apartment. The pictures on her wall were mostly of her and a much younger version of her. Maybe six or seven years younger. I guessed a sister, or a cousin. The photos on the wall showed them at a variety of places, enjoying a variety of things. Boating, motorcycle rallies, groups of friends going out. A race track, with expensive cars lining the wall in the picture where Angela stood. Pictures of friends, people I didn't know, couldn't know, all tipping back big-bowled glasses of margaritas. Some of her and her sister in Boston's harbor, the tall masts of sailboats behind them, the boats tied loosely to the docks, drifting on dark watery waves.

There were some of Angela on a stage, a large beautifully dark plat-form with grand props of buildings behind her. In some she was dressed in old Shakespearian clothes, and stood among other actors doing the same, always in the middle of some action. Her eyes caught me, as if she was staring into the crowd, directly at the person taking the shot.

In one picture she was alone on the stage. She wore a white dress, something tight to her body, shimmering along her curves, and the snow-like pureness of the dress looked great against her naturally tan skin. The picture was again from the crowd, catching row after row of dark shadowed heads in front of Angela, hidden from the spotlight that shone down directly on her. She appeared as if she were singing—eyes partly closed, head tilted up, mouth open and slightly curved, chest expanded in the way singers do when they are holding a long, long note.

I imagined that note. The crowd. The breathless anticipation of a climaxing moment.

All signs of a life that would never be the same, after today.

The whole place had been tossed, vents pulled out of the walls, closets broken in. Clothes thrown everywhere. Her bedroom had a small bed, maybe a full. It was one of those pedestal frames with plenty of room between the box spring and the floor. Both the mattress and the box spring had been cut up and torn through. No monsters hiding there.

Whoever had broken in before me had done a number and had been messy, but they had been thorough. Everywhere I looked though, I saw tiny drops of blood. On the backs of pillows. Dotting the white fluffy stuffing of the mattress. One smear against the couch, as if the guy had leaned over it.

No monsters hiding. Just one in full sight. There was nothing else to help me, all I had left was the guy.

So that's where I'd have to start.

I came back to the kitchen. The guy there looked at me like he had been waiting. Charley looked at me as if she had a hundred questions.

"What's happened here?" she said.

"Nothing good," I said. "The place is tossed. These people kidnapped your friend for something. They're looking for it."

"What the hell could Angela have?" Charley said.

I shrugged. It didn't matter what she had. All that mattered was finding her.

"Who does this?" Charley asked, her eyes still wide open. Unbelieving.

"Bad people," I said. Then looked at the guy. "You ready to talk?"

He rolled his eyes. He had decided I wasn't going to do anything, which may have been a fair assumption a few years ago. I was a different person now. Less forgiving.

I glanced back over at the wall. A picture there had grabbed my attention. It was Angela, maybe a few years ago. Much younger, maybe a teenager. She held her younger sister in front of her, the sister might have been ten or so, Angela's arms wrapped around her sister's chest.

Angela's face was nestled to the side of her sister's face and their smiles together could warm the coldest of souls. But it was her eyes that had caught me. In the picture they were open, sparkling, without the hint of pain I had seen in the bookstore.

Sometime between then and now, something had happened to her. Had robbed her of the innocent happiness in that picture, with who I thought was her sister. And maybe even, in some way, was tied to the kidnapping now.

That last could have been my imagination. But the picture affected me in a way I had thought long gone. Or maybe it was all the drops of blood, scattered through the apartment, dark reminders of a recent violence.

Happiness was a fleeting thing in life, though I used to believe it was a natural state. Something we always returned to. Now I only knew the emotion as a way for people to measure how horribly their lives had gone wrong, by remembering how long in the past they had experienced joy, before the memory of the feeling faded away.

Someone had cost Angela something. And then that person had involved me. Whoever that was, whoever was responsible for the kidnapping, they were going to soon know that same level of unhappiness.

I let out a breath. Charley had been staring at me. So had the guy.

I wasn't going to change his mind, so I had to change his perspective. There had been some brown packing tape on the floor of one of the closets. I grabbed it and came back to the guy, ripping a section of tape off and taping his mouth shut with it. After that, his nose whistled a bit, like it had been broken a few times, even though it hadn't looked it.

The guy had good medical. I hoped he still did. He was going to need it.

Next I went to the bathroom. Grabbed a few towels there, big fluffy blue things. Then I cut the shower curtain off its rings. It had some kind of art on it, patterned yellows and blues woven together. I grabbed the curtain and the liner and the towels and came back to the kitchen.

The guy looked at me a little differently, now. His nose whistled a little faster.

"Hey," Charley said, clearly uncomfortable. "What're you doing?"

I stayed quiet. I knew how I looked. The guy recognized it as well, and understood he may have made a critical error. He started to struggle, but this wasn't my first rodeo. Strips of dishcloth or not, I had tied him tight.

He kicked at me with both legs. I grabbed the bindings at his feet and held him up in the air, so that his body swayed underneath me, and his head was cocked on the floor, stuck in the corner of it by the dishwasher.

I put a foot by his head, my leg underneath his back, and kept pressure against him, so that his head stayed pinched and his neck cocked a little oddly. He stopped struggling.

"Hey," Charley asked, her voice pitched a little higher. "What're you doing?"

I laid the shower curtain on the floor. The liner on top of it. Then one of the towels. I did all of that with one hand, keeping the guy against the dishwasher with my leg.

Then I stepped back, put his legs in the middle of the curtain-liner-towel arrangement.

He kicked at me again, so I kicked him back, in the stomach. He let out a big whooshing sound and bent over.

That let me get a knee across the bottom of his legs. I tucked the second towel in front of me, like a loose apron. Then I grabbed his throat with my other hand, forcing him up and pressing him tight against the dishwasher. The plastic tape fluttered in and out, over his mouth, as if he was trying to gasp for air. It made odd crackling sounds. Then his nose whistle started and stopped again, in an odd rhythm. Fast then slow.

"Going to throw up?" I asked, softly.

He looked at me. His eyes were wide open. He was afraid and trying hard not to show it. The guy finally shook his head.

"How about now?" I asked, bringing his knife up in my free hand. Thumbing it open.

"Jesus," Charley almost screamed it. "What are you doing man?"

"Getting answers," I said. Then looked at the guy. "Talking or not talking?"

His nose whistled, high and long. Then he shook his head.

"Your call," I told him. Then stabbed the knife into the meat of his right thigh.

The guy arched off the floor, biting back a scream. His throat made a moaning sound, instead. I still held his neck against the dishwasher, and my knees sat on the bottom of his legs, so all the guy could do was thrust his hips up. My right leg ached a bit, trying to hold him pinned down. I left the knife in his thigh, letting it waggle back and forth, and kept up my stare into the guy's face.

Nothing was more scary than an implacable stare. A gaze without any feeling or emotion. Just the understanding that nothing could stop what was happening to the person having the damage done to them.

I understood that, better than most.

"Jesus, Jesus, Jesus," Charley kept saying, behind me.

The guy took a long breath through his nose, then started coughing. The plastic of the tape fluttered in and out, harder and harder.

"Air?" I said.

He nodded.

"Going to tell me anything?" I asked.

He stopped his nod.

"Your choice," I said, pulling the knife out. Blood immediately welled from the cut, and soaked a circle into his jeans before trickling into the towel underneath.

Then I stabbed the knife back in, an inch or so above the first cut.

He screamed again and then started coughing. Little spurts of blood spat from the first cut, all over the curtain and both towels. I kept my hand over the wound, pressing down on it.

I hadn't hit anything major. Yet. Both the guy and I understood this part of the game. Which was unfortunate. I could cause him pain, but he still didn't think I was going to kill him. Not with Charley there.

There was a time when I knew I wouldn't have, either. And I didn't know that I was that guy now. But the rage in me said differently. The dark wrath screamed to get out, in any way it could. I think Charley saw that all in my face.

"Guy," she said to me. "You can't do that."

"*You* can't do that," I corrected her, feeling the muscles of my face all tighten up, my eyes narrow, my eyebrows lower. "*I* can."

I glanced back at the guy. "Ready to talk?"

The brown packing tape popped in and out of his mouth. His eyes were open, his chest heaved with trying to force air through his whistling nose. I took the knife out of his leg and wiped the edges of the blade quickly on a clean part of a towel, and then reached out to cut an opening in the tape with a flick of the wrist.

The guy jerked his head back. I held him by the hair and cut the tape. Then he gasped in air, a long, deep, noisy inhale, the whole in the tape flittering with the sound. He gulped another piece of air down, then spat a curse at me.

"Look," I said. "I can keep this up until I hit an artery. Or I can take this knife and dig into your kneecap until you walk with a limp the rest of your life. I'm giving you a chance here to tell me what you know, before any of that has to happen."

I looked him right in the eyes. Thinking of the picture of Angela and her sister. The one before she had encountered pain in her life. Years before now. The Escalade, peeling out of the parking lot. Angela telling me I had *that look*.

My hand tightened around the hilt of the knife. "And if you don't talk, that's happening. Believe it," I said.

He took a last deep breath. His eyes flicked to Charley, then back to me. Then he set his jaw and looked away.

I admire tough. I thought I had been that way once. But if I could be broken, anyone could. This guy just didn't know it yet.

"Fair enough," I said, flipping the knife around in my hand so the blade pointed down, placing it on the inside of his kneecap. Trying to keep the emotion out of my voice, the dark anger inside.

But a switch had flipped. Maybe it was memories of my own leg, maybe I could blame what I was doing on that. Or finding the girl, the pictures of Angela, happy in a life that had suddenly been disturbed.

Whatever it was, this guy was going to pay that price.

I pushed the knife into the side of his leg. Right under the edge of the kneecap. There was a thin line there, between bone on bone, and I felt that hard bone catch the blade. So I leaned into it more, working the knife slowly under the cap. A bit at a time. Blood dribbling out and soaking his pants, the towel.

At some point, my face had changed.

I stopped. Took one last look at the guy. His eyes scrunched up, and tears of pain welled up in their corners. I grinned, from a dark and nasty place. A grin someone had once shown me, when they had been working on my leg. It was a smile I'd never forget.

A wet spot spread out from his groin, and the smell of ammonia drifted up from his jeans. The smell of real fear. The man all of a sudden didn't know where this was going to end. He had misjudged me. Maybe misjudged Charley being there.

I had broken through.

"Stop," Charley said.

Something in her voice made me pause.

I looked at the spreading urine stain on the man. The tip of the knife, angled up and into the side of his leg. The veins on my forearm there, popping out of the skin with the effort.

I felt my face, contorted into a creature's face. Twisted. The skin there stretched into someone I might not recognize.

Or maybe I would.

I took a deep breath. Then another. Relaxed my hand around the knife. Let the blade go. Watched the handle waggle slowly, bob up and down. Once. Then once more.

The man's eyes were pinched shut now. His face turned aside. Not looking at me. At what I had become.

I swallowed something hard down. Then turned to Charley.

She had her wild west gun back in both of her hands, and she had pointed the thing at my head.

I knew what she was doing. I understood what she had seen, in what I was doing. In who I had become. But the words came out anyway. "What are you doing, Charley?"

"You can't do this," she said again.

"You're wrong," I said. "I can do this. *He* can do this. He *has* done this before. He's even done it recently. *Look* at him."

I didn't need the bloody lines on the T-shirt to tell me this guy was a killer. I could always tell. It was in their reactions. How they stood. A certain confidence that someone had, when they had killed to survive, or maybe for other reasons. It was a power few people understood, and fewer people could actually carry.

The man had been a soldier. Like I had been. He was young, and if I had to guess, this guy had a dishonorable discharge in his recent past. He was likely a mercenary now. Most guys who were good at killing stayed in the service, at least for a bit. Even if they wanted out, they still stayed in. Hard to find a better way to legally get better at killing people.

So the man had gotten out, and had found the one thing that would allow him to still keep doing what he liked doing. If not legal, at least it paid well. A mercenary's pay usually did, and if you were good, you might even live to enjoy it.

Merc was afraid of me. He sensed the same thing in me as I did him, we both had the same feel of being *in the service*. He knew I had killed before, just like I knew that about him. He'd have sensed it.

We were different though, even if we both were killers. He would take money and do a job, regardless of what the job was. He'd do it for the pay. Or because he enjoyed the thrill. I had given the merc a choice. It wasn't my fault he had picked the consequence.

Even if I had gone a little too far, just now. Even if I had been lost in something I couldn't define. A past that had marked me.

Once I had been considered a good person. I had done things to help others. What I had just become, what I had just done, proved that person was long gone.

We all make choices. These choices take us to whatever point in time we are at in our lives. We walk a path, each path is a step, each step a choice. Step rightly most of the time, and you live a pretty good life. Step wrongly most of the time, and you wander into a deep, dark abyss. Some call it sleeping in the bed you've made.

I couldn't avoid my bed any more than Merc could avoid his. I never slept well, anymore. I had to deal with that. Consequences were something we all faced, sooner or later. I could guess the mercenary's life. His choices. If he hadn't thought about where those choices would lead him, if he couldn't have predicted where his path would end, he should have known he would have ended up with someone like me.

Maybe even someone worse.

"I don't care," Charley said. Her voice shaky, but loud. As if volume could harden the decision. "I'm not allowing this."

"Not?" I wasn't sure how my voice sounded, but Charley immediately stepped back, bumping into the table beside her. Her hand jerked and I thought the gun almost went off, and when she pointed it back at me her grip was so tight her knuckles were white.

I froze. I released the guy's neck and held out both hands. Knife lightly held in my left. My knee loose on the bottom of his legs. Then I took a deep breath and let it out.

I had been close to losing it. To giving in to the hate and the rage, to losing the *me* I had carefully reconstructed over the past couple of years.

The routine had built that me. It was what kept the anger and rage at bay. I was due a reckoning, for the leg, for the betrayal, but that time wasn't now. This wasn't the place. What I was owed wasn't here, with this merc. Wasn't with Angela, and what was going on.

It was hard for me to believe I was here. That was the old me. Not this one, broken and rebuilt. Maybe the old me was here, now. Maybe the old me had let go of the knife, and left it waggling in this guy's kneecap. Trying to recover a small part of who I had been.

Charley had helped with that. She had given me a moment to feel the rage inside trying to control me. The pit of fury overwhelming me. I hadn't even really felt it, as it happened. I could only recognize it by looking back. It had been a cold rage. Some implacable, undeniable force. Something without pity or compassion, just the need to see this act through.

If I let that anger out fully, that small part of me would cease to exist. I would become someone else. A person unrecognizable to those who had known me. The people who had raised me as a kid. My family. My sister. The few of my friends I had gathered, through the years. I would become a monster, and the old me would be...

Gone.

In a way the routine was all that kept that from happening. And I was far off the routine now. After working so hard to hold on to that small part of myself, the old me. Through the year of rehab. Trying to get my leg to work again. Through the years of nightmares, waking up in a sweat, night after night.

The routine was the last thing tying me to the person I had been. And right here, right now, I had almost lost it all, and become the monster. I closed my eyes and silently gave thanks that Charley had seen it, and had the courage to stop me.

"Okay," I told her. "Okay."

Charley's hands shook. The Smith & Wesson shook. I wasn't sure she trusted me. Actually, I knew she didn't. So I stood up, both hands out, stepping back from her.

The whistle of a long exhale left the merc's broken nose.

"We're leaving," Charley said. "And then I'm calling the police."

"Fair enough," I said. I held out my forefinger with one hand, in a *one-second* type of gesture.

The guy looked at me. Whatever had gone through my face, when Charley had held her gun on me, had scared him more than anything I had done before. His skin was pale, and his chest rose and fell quickly.

"Tell me one thing," I said. Hoping the answer would be what I needed it to be. To stay the person the routine had made. "Do you know where the girl is, right now?"

The guy stared into my eyes. Then he gave a shake of his head.

That made sense to me. And I should have put it together before. But violence had led me here. I had wanted to hurt someone, it didn't matter why or who or how. That, I knew, was how the anger would change me.

I nodded, almost to myself. This guy wouldn't be here tossing the place if he had the girl. Or if whoever he worked for had her. He was here for something else. Something Angela maybe had. I should have known that, intuitively.

"Let's go," Charley told me. I could tell she was out of patience, but she wasn't going to shoot me, now. Which I felt was a good sign.

I did a few more things before I left. I taped up the guy's leg, keeping a towel with pressure on it. I wiped his gun and knife down, and left them on the counter. Cleaned the floor again where we had stood. Charley hadn't touched anything, so I thought we were safe enough with her. Anything I left behind, I wasn't worried about, as far as prints.

I looked at the counter again. Took the few pieces of mail there. The bills and the letter from the college.

Angela had something that someone else wanted, that people would kill for. Likely *had* killed for. I would have to dig into her past, quickly, and figure out what that something could be.

Her eyes had pain in them, hidden pain. The kind of pain that came from a tortuous past. There was something there, in her life, an event or person who had hurt her. Something she had overcome to become who she was now.

I knew that kind of pain. She had recognized it in me. And it was likely that whatever had hurt Angela back then, that person would be behind what had happened to her today. Things like that didn't let you go.

That, I knew firsthand.

CHAPTER
ELEVEN

THE CAR RIDE FELT MUCH DIFFERENT GOING BACK TO Charley's than before. I had been hopeful then. Now, I didn't know where I was at, and the car echoed my thoughts, riding quietly along the unknown, silently, the tires rolling across the road without sound. The traffic was thick, we stopped at every light with a tap of the brakes, and each time all that could be heard was the whirring of the vent fans pushing out reconditioned air. Everything outside the car was muffled, like we were in our own world.

Before, Charley had been a little outgoing. Interested in who I was. How her friend might have been interested in me. Joking about how my car smelled like vanilla.

Now, she wanted nothing to do with me. She had seen a side of me not many saw. That I was, if I was honest, unaware I had. When we got into the car she just asked me to take her back to her shop, in a small voice.

Her purse stayed on her lap though. Her hand in it. The purse angled towards me. She was shaken. A lot had happened in a short period of time, things had gotten a little out of control.

As if thinking about it, she glanced back, as if she could see the apartment. Then she reached her other hand into her purse and pulled out a cell phone.

"You do that, and the police will know you were there," I told her.

"Does that matter?" she said, in almost a whisper.

"Maybe not to you," I said. "Whatever you think of me, of what happened back there, you still should know I'm the best chance your friend has."

"She doesn't need you," she said. "She doesn't need *that*."

"Did you see the blood?" I asked, quietly. Understanding what she had seen, in me. "Whoever took your friend, they aren't playing nice."

She was quiet, for long moments. We stopped at a stoplight. A couple walked across the street in front of us, holding hands. The guy laughing at something the girl had said.

The light changed to green. My eyes were still following the couple. A horn behind me told me I needed to get moving. I let off the brake and pushed the gas.

Charley did something with the phone. Searching something on the screen. Then she typed in some numbers and waited.

"Yes," she asked. "Is this the Twelfth Precinct? It is? Thanks. Look, I saw the news. My friend was the person taken by the Escalade. I tried calling her home but her sister is not answering. I have her name and address, if you want them."

After a moment she rattled off the information. Then said, "Thank you. My name is Charley Taylor. You have my number. I'd be happy to help out in any way I can."

Charley gave them her shop's address, next. Then she hung up the phone, not looking at me still, her hand in the purse.

We went that way for a long time. I thought about what I knew about Angela. She had a decent place. In a recovering neighborhood, so not as expensive as a place could be, but still some money. She owned a nice bike. Her furniture—before it had been cut open—had been tasteful.

So she had money going out. Which means she should have a job. She was taking classes, so that was a place I needed to visit. Something in her background would tell me what had happened to her, would point me in a direction.

The blood on the walls bothered me. The fight spoke of something urgent. It spoke of something, or someone uncontrolled. I recognized it, because I had just experienced it. A quiet, hidden rage.

That was different from what had happened at the bookstore. That had been executed well. It had been planned in advance.

I didn't think the same people had come to her apartment. So there were at least two groups of people searching for Angela. The blood escalated everything. And escalation meant there was an urgency to the situation. And maybe even a time limit.

I let out a breath. We headed east, along the boulevard again. Dark gray clouds darkened the horizon in front of me, presaging the coming night. Promising rain, and who knew what else.

Nightmares, for me. Always the nightmares.

Charley shook in her seat. Her skin was pale, and I could see bits of moisture at her temple. Coming down off the adrenaline. I turned on the car's heater, warm hair blew across us both from the dashboard, smelling a little like the air from a hairdryer.

What she had done, it had been brave. I knew what I looked like. I knew how I was acting. And I knew what I had been gripped by.

"Thank you," I said, quietly.

Charley looked over, eyebrows raised.

"Look," I said. "I wasn't always like this."

"Like what?" she asked. "A monster?"

The word hurt, but accurate enough. In the quiet of the night I could pretend to be proud of who I was. Who I had recovered enough to be. But in the light of day, when push came to shove, I hadn't come as far as I wanted to. I shrugged. "Maybe just an ass."

"Well, *ass*," she said. "Don't thank me. If the police come and talk to me, I'll be telling them about you."

"Fair enough," I said. Choices had consequences. I understood that, better than most.

Her arm lay on her purse. It still shook. I worried about the gun going off. "You're not going to shoot me, right?"

Charley snorted, took a second sniff and then wiped her nose with the back of her hand. I was surprised to see a tear roll down her cheek. Then another.

"That's the thing," she said. "It's not even loaded."

I was surprised enough that I almost stopped the car. I know I looked at her longer than I needed to. It told me a lot about her, but it also told me a lot about how I had been, back in Angela's apartment. About what it had really looked like I was going to do.

Charley had been really brave then. Facing something like me, a situation like that, with an unloaded gun.

"It was my grandpa's," she explained. "I don't even know why I carry it."

I understood, maybe a little. Things like a gun make people feel safe. Easy enough to carry it around. And if it brought back memories of a friend, of family. Of maybe going out with a grandfather and shooting in a field, well, those memories made you feel good as well.

"It was a brave thing," I told her. "I wish I could tell you it hadn't been needed."

She sniffed, then wiped her nose again. Wiped her eyes as well. Her face was wet, and I wanted to find some tissue or a towel for her, but my car was bare of most things people had in them.

"Who are you?" she asked.

"Someone different from who I used to be," I said. "But I promise you, if I can help Angela, I'm going to do that."

"Don't promise me anything," she said. "I don't want to be a part of it."

"Understood," I said. "I just wanted you to know."

"You're not doing it for me, anyway," she said, her voice thick, low. "Or even for her. You're doing it for you."

The boulevard was closing in on the beach, and traffic had thickened up again. People, heading for an evening by the water. I had to slow down some, but the turn for Charley's place wasn't too far ahead.

Charley might be right. I still didn't know why I was helping Angela. Especially when it came close to threatening the life I had created for myself. Such as that was. But what had happened back in the apartment, that scared me. Not being in control threatened the revenge I had built my life around.

Something had happened to me, when Angela had sat down at that table in the bookstore. Something that had clicked a switch inside, or turned some knobs, and had me running after the Escalade. Part of it might have been because of the person I used to be. Maybe one of the knobs had swung that way. Part of it was maybe Angela herself, the way she had made me feel, even briefly. Interested and excited and somewhat afraid of both.

Was I helping her just to feel that again? Feel *something*? Anything, but the past?

"I don't know," I said. I didn't used to be that selfish. I wanted to believe I was doing it, because in my mind I had once been a knight, with shining armor. Shield, lance, and sword. I had believed I had been born for great things. To slay dragons.

"Maybe," I finally admitted. "Maybe."

I turned, and we pulled in front of Charley's Angels. Charley unclicked her seat belt, but I lightly lay a hand on her arm before she got out.

She looked at me. Angry.

"Load the gun," I said. "Things are happening here, and who knows what happens next."

"I don't need it," Charley said. Then shook her head. "I *didn't* need it. I've got Dave."

"Dave won't stop a bullet," I said. "At least, not in a way you'd want."

We stayed like that for a minute. The warm air blowing across us both. The swishing sound of cars driving by us. Then one horn, from a car behind me, loud and obnoxious.

Her arm remained tense under my hand. Hard and unyielding. I sighed and pulled my hand off. Charley got out and slammed the door shut. Then marched across to her store and walked in, not looking back.

It was the effect I had on people, now. Like the guy in the gym, something I had cultivated. A very small part of me wished I was different, but the larger portion swallowed it up. It was what worked for me. No reason to change it.

The horn blared again behind me. My hand closed, as if it had spasmed shut at the sound. I forced it open, grabbed hold of the steering wheel, and took off. It was a near thing, but I resisted the urge to flip the finger at the car behind me. That could lead to me getting out of the car. And the person behind me wouldn't want that.

CHAPTER
TWELVE

The skies opened up on the way home. I was headed west, getting on the interstate, but the darkness caught up to me and then the rain came. Big heavy drops spattered on the windshield, making loud popping sounds. One of the rains that came in off the ocean, the air warm enough to pull in all that moisture, before heading inland. Meeting enough cold for the clouds to let go, all at once.

The rain got so thick the wipers couldn't keep up. Even at their fastest speed all they did was *rubbb-rubbb-ruubbb* across the glass, flicking just enough water off the windshield for me to keep driving. I slowed down, passing cars with their hazard lights on, blinking out their watch-for-me signals. Some of those had pulled to the side of the road, others were driving at ten or twenty miles an hour.

Normally I got dinner out, at a place nearby. The rain was just another break in my routine. I went straight home, to my apartment. Found a parking space in front. It was raining too hard to dig around in the trunk, so I left the helmet there and dashed in. The rain drops were cold and heavy and hit me like icy metal pellets. As quick as I tried to be, I still got soaked.

The apartment was dark. It smelled a little wet. The rain kept thundering against the windows. I checked them all shut, tightening all the locks. The apartment was old, and water got in somehow when it rained.

I emptied my gym clothes into my hamper. Found *The Faerie Queene* and set the book on the coffee table. Changed into some dry clothes, jeans and a dark T-shirt, and sat on the couch a bit in the darkness, listening to the rain. The occasional rumbling of thunder. The bright flickers of lightning, illuminating the window in brief little flashes, before leaving the dark night in its place.

It was too early for sleep, not that I slept much. Only as much as the nightmare let me. And I wasn't ready for that yet. Normally at this time I'd be in line at a restaurant, getting my regular order. Today it would have been a sandwich place. They had a nice peanut butter and jelly, something fancy on thick bread, with a caramelized banana sliced and cut inside, the bread toasted and warm. That would be nice now. I would have gotten one of those and came back home. Turned on the sports station, and waited until it was time to go to bed.

Tonight though I sat on the couch and watched the storm outside. Felt very much the same, inside. After a bit I noticed the book again on the coffee table. *The Faerie Queene.* It was next to the photo on the table, the only photo I had. A five-by-seven thing in a cheap black frame. The pointed end of a gondola in the center of the picture, behind it shimmering dark water, lit by a bright sunny day. In the background lay one of the many arched stone bridges of Venice, the rock tan, the people walking through a mix of bright sun and dark shadows.

The handle of an oar spanned the bottom of the picture. The handle was dark and smooth, the wood worn by a hundred thousand uses over the years. Two hands held the oar, a small one and a big one, as if two people were pushing away from the side of the canal and, at the same time, one of them had snapped the picture.

I had snapped that picture. I still remembered the feel of Samantha leaning back against my chest. Pushing hard on the oar and shaking with laughter, trying to tumble me out of the boat, even as we were attempting to steal the gondola and push it away before the gondolier came back.

We hadn't been together long. Sam had just gotten to our team, a few months before. The two of us were still in the newness of the relationship. The need to be physically close to someone. To touch smooth skin, feel the shuddering laugh, the press of her warm lips against my chin.

The gondolier had chased us, running down the canal. The two of us had abandoned the boat, gotten wet getting out. We had found a place to stay, a tiny hole in the wall, cheap plaster on old stone, a tiny bed that was too soft, but we didn't care, we had yanked our clothes off each other and...

My right leg suddenly twinged, a sharp pain. Deep in the bone there.

My heart beat too fast in my chest.

I clenched my fist. Tipped the picture over, face down. The frame clicked against the table. Then I looked at the book. Angela had mentioned a truth to be found. I wondered what that truth would be, for me. What it might hold. I was a little afraid of discovering it.

"Be not faint," I said quietly, almost to myself. Remembering the words Angela had quoted to me. "Show what you be."

The words sounded silly when I said them. I picked it up. It was a heavy, thick paperback, though the cover itself was thin and curled back as I opened it. I went past all the notes in the beginning, about the history of the story and the author, Spenser. Some preface, by some historian or professor somewhere. I got to the first chapter and read.

It was written in old English. All the words seemed to have an extra *e* or two. It took me a bit to get the rhythm of the stanzas down. I kept having to stop and figure out what each stanza was trying to tell me. The pages were thin, almost transparent, the concentrated black ink on the back of the page showing through to the front every time I flipped a page.

The experience gave me a feeling of puzzling something out. A mystery in the making. Words I had to dig through, to discover real meaning. Each page had footnotes, explaining what the footnote marked, or substituting a different, more modern word for an older one. Sometimes I preferred the older. I read, and puzzled, and figured, and all of it took a while. A lot of going back and forth. A lot of looking at the same line, over and over.

But I began to gather an understanding about the story. Initial thoughts. Feelings. Intuitions I would put together later, maybe.

The tale started with a knight. Someone clad in a hard outer shell, shiny newly-built armor. He stood over the scene of a battle. He carried deep wounds inside. Pain he kept to himself, but shielded others from, letting the world see the bright red cross he bore. The burden was so heavy he carried the cross twice. Once on the shield that protected him, and once on his chest. Perhaps a wound he could not hide, as if the cuts were so deep they kept bleeding, and would never heal. Until all that was left was wrath.

I took a break, and leaned back on the couch. It still rained outside, but it was night now, dark outside. I couldn't see the storm anymore, but the drops still splattered against the window with tiny thumps on the glass. A heavy sprinkling now, as if the storm could come back again, harder, more violent. Or move on.

The dark glass of the window itself looked back at me. Showing the couch, the coffee table, the light on the end table beside me. The book with the large red cross on the front of it in my hand. The lamp itself sat a little behind me, and held a low-wattage bulb, yellow. The straw-colored light that made it past the lampshade was just enough to read by. Timid illumination, just over my shoulder. Where I sat in the window was just a shadow. Formless.

I went back to reading.

The knight was with a lady. Fair. Pure, or held a kind of purity to her. Something inside the lady radiated it, though it was hidden a bit, as if by a veil. She seemed to be his guide, in some way. Or, when bigger moments happened, she was the voice that advised the knight. Or directed him.

The lady carried a sadness deep within her. She was pale, dressed in white, on the outside the very symbol of purity. Or maybe truth. But on the inside she held some inner care, hidden from the rest of the world. Something she mourned. Maybe something she had lost.

The pair of them were on a journey. I didn't know if they were in the middle of it, or at the beginning. It all started with the field, where an assault had taken place. The knight and the lady left there and promptly became lost. Old paths they walked disappeared behind them. New paths began and wound through the forest around them.

The two of them tread along, taking path after path. Doubting their direction, but carrying a resolve to press onward. Until they came upon an obstacle, preventing them from continuing another step forward. A hollow cave, with something dark and monstrous waiting inside. Some evil beast called Error.

An odd name for a monster. To me it was as if a wall, or a mountain, rose up in front of the knight. Something too huge to climb, with but one path to follow. The path leading to the creature.

The two of them conversed. The lady issued caution. The knight understood she had endured evil in her life, and that event haunted her. The event had shaped her, and whatever that event had been, the knight rashly rushed into the cave.

The knight couldn't stop himself. He was full of wrath and fire and fury. And so inside the cave he faced Error, and battled the monster. It wasn't long before the foulness of the creature overwhelmed the knight, wrapped itself around his armor, until he was trapped. The knight in a cocoon of the beast, of Error.

Here was the part Angela had quoted me.

"Now, sir knight, show what you be," she had said, her voice relaxed but carrying a power, a timbre that resonated in me. "Add faith onto your force, and be not faint."

The knight found a way to strangle Error into submission. Then he chopped off its head. Ridding the world of the monster. I thought then that the story was over. It's how most tales did end. Heroes victorious. Maiden saved. Evil killed.

Check. Check. Check.

But the story was just beginning. Killing Error hadn't been the end. I was still at the start of the tale.

Error was dead, but the spawn of the creature appeared. The knight froze in place as the spawn of the creature appeared. Thousands, millions of tiny monstrous babes crawled into the light, offspring of Error. Error was dead, yet it still lived on in the creatures it had birthed, parasites suckling at the dead corpse of their mother, growing larger and larger and larger...

I closed the book, and put it down on the coffee table.

The storm had quieted down, dissipated. It had moved on. The tiny light on the end table in the living room threw a small globe of yellow around me. I could feel the darkness in the room, outside the light, pushing in on me. The window was black with it.

It was late.

I got up and moved around, making sure things were in their place. The book, carefully placed to the edge of the coffee table. The photo, picked back up and placed to one side. The windows all shut. The door locked. The counters wiped down.

The lights off.

The bedroom was cold. It always felt cold. I got undressed and slid underneath chilly sheets and waited for my body heat to warm the bed up. My bed was a bed in name only. It was a mattress on the floor, though a well-made mattress.

It wasn't because I didn't want a real bed. I just couldn't sleep in one anymore. I had found that monsters lurked in the darkness there, between the shadowy gap of frame and floor, evil things that lay in wait beneath you and waited to strike until you were at your weakest. I felt them all, all the laughing and the hunger and the evil delicious pleasure of the creatures, all of them staring at me through the mattress, murmuring and giggling among themselves while I waited for the cold pinprick of hard truth to stab me, over and over.

So I had no bed frame. It allowed me what little sleep I could get. It was what I could do.

On the floor above me someone walked heavily, stomping around and getting ready for bed. The thumping beat oddly, as if the person wandered around their bedroom, not knowing what they were doing next. Heavy thumps mixed with lighter thumps, fast thumps and slow ones. Like some kind of ballroom dancing CrossFit class.

I focused on taking deep, even breaths. The day whirled in my mind. I had no doubt I would get up tomorrow and go back to finding Angela. I was on that path, I had walked it without knowing it, and even if I didn't understand where it was taking me, I was going to finish that journey. No matter what was in front of me.

You have that look...

What look was that? The look of a broken man, who had duct-taped himself back together, thinking it would shield him. Or maybe protect others from him.

Show what you be...

What the fuck was I showing? A guy living each day basically the same. Varying small things, to keep himself interested. Afraid of varying anything larger, because if I did, it could upset the one thing I couldn't afford to remember.

Be not faint...

I hadn't been faint. I had let the anger slip, and almost killed someone today. Someone who may or may not have deserved it. But not then. Not by my hand. The wrath had jumped out of me and I hadn't been able to control it. Years of putting myself together, and I had cracked open just like that, without thought. I hadn't used to be that way. I hadn't. I said the words like a mantra, over and over, until all I could feel was the dark around me, the pounding of the guy above me, and the cold sheets that couldn't seem to get warm wrapping around me.

You can't do this...

No kidding Charley. No kidding.

I kept my eyes closed and kept trying to ignore everything. Just waited for sleep, and the nightmare to come.

I didn't have to wait long. And when it came, it was the same. But also, oh so different.

———

THE NIGHTMARE ALWAYS STARTED WITH AN ICY CHILL OF realization. Like my spine had turned into a block of ice. Like a winter tempest coursed down the middle of my back. The kind of chill a person got when they answered a phone, when they answered a call out of the blue, with a thin, *tinny* voice on the other side telling them that little Johnny had been playing in the street and a car had sped by and hadn't seen him and *Oh my god I'm so sorry...*

Cold. Icy. Realization. When it hits you, you always know. And you never forget.

In the dream I stood in the same room as always. A small security office, where the realization had hit me. Two doors in front of me, a bathroom and a breakroom. The smell of dark Turkish coffee was always strong in the dream. Black and bitter.

A body lay face down on the floor to my right, wearing the same gear I was wearing, dark black tactical gear, a gun in one outstretched hand, seemingly a soldier just like myself. The 9mm—a Glock—had been cold back then, but in the dream smoke always drifted out of the end of the warm barrel.

"Sam?" I said. My voice tiny, in the room. So small there was no echo in the small security office. A square card table with folding legs in the center of the room. A light shining bright on the center of the table. A case sitting on the card table, in the middle of the spotlight, facing me.

The vials in the case were shattered this time, a dark thick yellow liquid, so dark it bordered on brown, soaking into the gray foam inside the case. Two syringes missing. The virus they contained released, or worse.

Long black curly hair hid the guy's face, though I knew it was Aaron. He was the only other person there. Sam was missing. She was always gone, in the dream, and there was nothing but the sound of gunfire behind me. Cracks of bullets against the walls. Ricochets pinging around me with high-pitched whines. The shots getting louder. Closer. Always, like all nightmares, getting louder and louder, closer and closer, until you knew, if you turned around, it would all be *right there*.

The dream sometimes confused things. The vials were shattered in this one, whole in others. The liquid was usually a different color, though the burned yellow was dominant. Aaron was never in the same position, but he was always face down. Sometimes his gun was a Glock, sometimes a Beretta. Once it had been a knife, but even that smoked. The gun always smoked.

Once, Aaron wore a suit. Sometimes I wore my old army camos, and when I did those varied from the old desert green and blacks, to the winter white and blacks, to the desert tan and browns.

Often in the nightmare there was an alarm ringing, blaring like a fire alarm. Sometimes the alarm was a bell, tolling ominously, echoing throughout the dream each time its metal tongue clapped against its side. Sometimes the alarm was just the shouting of a town crier, calling out what was happening like he was narrating the dream, telling me I had tripped the alarm, or telling me it was Aaron.

But the nightmare was consistent about a couple of things. I always was frozen, feet locked down as if they were made of concrete. I couldn't move. Could never move. Couldn't turn back and see the guards coming up from behind. Couldn't step forward and see if Aaron was alive. I was always frozen until the guards came up from behind me and a final bullet cracked through my chest.

Maybe not moving was just something common to all nightmares, but I had always believed this dream wanted me to see that open case. The missing virus. Sam. The betrayal. My mind always wanted me to remember what trust could be turned into. How it could be used.

One other thing was always the same. The icy cold realization, such a chill down the spine that I always shivered. My skin, always clammy. Other things stayed consistent. Aaron was always face down. Smoking gun. Case open. Syringes gone. Samantha missing, as if she had never been there. It was like my mind was trying to watch the same movie, over and over, trying to show me something I refused to see. To believe.

I had lived this nightmare so many times the betrayal felt like a part of me. It wiggled inside me like a worm, a dark anger that grew each night. That wrapped around my belly, eating what I ate, swelling in hate and fury.

I could never turn from the open case. It was the empty openness of betrayal. From *Sam*. And I stood there, enduring this nightmare like every other, and it was a long time before I realized this one, this one was different.

The room was no longer the security office, with the smell of coffee. Now it was a cave, dark and shadowy, and the air carried a moist, thick metallic scent. Torches flickered around me, throwing shadows on the walls, across the floor, the darkness obscuring Aaron.

Then a last torch flickered, and it was just me, the table, and the open case. On the rock wall ahead of me was one word. Spelled in bright red blood. Fresh and dripping down the stone.

Error

Little rivers of blood streamed down from the word, each rivulet forming a new letter, the blood curling around on its own until I saw the trails were spelling out the same word, over and over. Little cursive trails of *errors* until the walls around me were covered with it, until the ceiling above me was written with it, until the blood reached the dark floor and started its dark inscription there.

Errors circled around me, the creeping of the bloody words crawling closer and closer, each word smaller than the one previous to it, but being spelled out faster and faster across the floor. So much blood it couldn't have been from one person, but thousands. Maybe millions. On the walls the spelling began anew, writing the same words in the same way, over and over and over.

With my feet frozen in place. Locked. Until the first red letter touched my foot. The blood was shockingly hot, almost burningly so. Like I had stepped into the blaze of a firepit.

Then I jerked awake.

It was now that I was happy to have my back flat on the mattress. The mattress flat on the floor. All kinds of monsters could hide in the dark of the room. Anything could have been hiding underneath the bed. Monsters, *errors*, I could never see, but always waited until my back was turned to rise up and swallow me whole.

The sheets around me were damp with sweat. My skin hot. The air under the sheets warm, though the air in the room was still at the chill temperature I had fallen asleep to. I lay there and took deep breaths, trying to slow my heart. Feeling the heat leak out around me. Trying to not remember the shot that took me, high and right in my back. The soldiers that had grabbed me.

And the torture that had followed.

It was funny to me, in the kind of way these things are, that I never had nightmares about the torture. About the guy coming in with a five ounce claw hammer and breaking my leg, little by little. Like he was chiseling a block of stone, chipping away pieces of it, trying to reveal the truth it held inside.

No, I never dreamed about that. It was always the room.

The subconscious mind works in mysterious ways. Mine seemed to be stuck in reverse. Fixated on what I had missed. The betrayal. Some piece of information I had missed, something the room wanted to show me, over and over and over. Night after night after night.

An error of another life, perhaps.

This life was what I had now.

So I got up, like I always did. Changed out the sheets. Threw the damp ones in the washer. Started it and listened to the water rush in and fill the tub, before the machine thump-thump-thumped through its cycle.

The clock read 4:23 AM. More sleep than I usually got. I wanted to get going early, Angela was out there, so I started breakfast. The same as yesterday, although today the bread was pumpernickel. A little like rye bread, earthy, sweet, but no caraway seeds. The orange juice, the other half of grapefruit, the eggs, all the same.

Just like the nightmares. Always the same. Though this one had been different, maybe because of what I had read. Maybe not. Still, I had awoken the same. Jerking awake, burning out, heart racing. Sweating that cold sweat. Feeling a little wild. Uncontrolled. A cold knot in the middle of my back, from the knife of ice planted in it.

It was why I had started the routine. Something to focus on, immediately afterwards. A pattern. Something to do *next*. Something to put my mind to, to occupy it with. Something to dull all the pain and anger and betrayal to a quiet whisper, a murmuring in the background that was my new life. Something that allowed me to function, at some level.

Each day ended the same. So I tried to begin it the same. Tick the clock to the next moment. Because for me, the routine was all. I couldn't trust what would happen, what I would do, who I would become, if it wasn't.

I CLEANED UP AFTER BREAKFAST. I NEVER USED ENOUGH dishes for the dishwasher, so I had cleaned them in the lukewarm water and the apple blossom scented dish soap. Then I dried them and put them back up, hearing the tiny clink-clink of a cheap plate slipping on top of another cheap plate. After that I sprayed some cleaner across the counters and the table, wiped them down, and tossed the towel into the hamper.

The routine this morning felt like it was holding me back. That feeling worried me. The routine was all, but there was a part of me tense with inaction, that *needed* to move. Another part of me held that part back, but it felt like the grip of that one was slipping.

The gym was usually next. Instead of the gym I did a quick workout in my apartment. The gym would take too long, today. So instead I worked out at home. Wall pushups, upside down crunches, and pull-ups in a cycle, over and over. Another punishing routine. Trying to burn away some of the energy pooling inside of me.

When I was done the muscles in my chest felt tight. My arms burned with exhaustion. But I felt good. Better than I had in a while. The shower was cool and clean and refreshing, the water felt just right on my skin, somehow. Cool enough to refresh, warm enough to have me linger a bit underneath the spray. The soap lather hinted at cucumber and honeydew melon.

I got ready. I didn't have many clothes, most of my stuff was work-out-related, or jeans and polo shirts. I did have a pair of chinos, not sure why I had them. Tan. I matched that with a white button-up shirt and a brownish sports coat and hoped I looked more professional than I thought.

Throughout the morning the window lightened. Outside, the dark night became the early gray of morning. The sky thick with clouds, like a sky usually appeared after a heavy rain. The sun was up, but reluctantly so, giving off a pale heat that barely pushed through the clouds. A Boston storm kind of morning.

My first stop today was going to be the college Angela was enrolled in, but I figured the earliest the admissions office would be open was eight. I had a little time before then. And while I was in a rush to find her, I started to believe more and more that I had a little time.

In my mind I was pretty sure, whatever had happened, there were two groups at play. The group that had kidnapped Angela, and the group that had been to her apartment. Those groups were opposite in their actions, and to me spoke of a difference in intent. One had been carefully coordinated. The other brutal in its execution.

These two forces each now had a chip in the game. One had Angela, the other likely had her sister. Despite the blood, I thought each side would do their best to keep both alive, at least until whatever game was being played was finished.

Or at least, that's what I told myself. I could always be wrong. Angela could be dead in a ditch somewhere. Maybe it was even her blood, in her apartment. But I couldn't operate that way. I went on what my gut was telling me, not because I trusted it, but because it was all I had to go on.

I grabbed the pieces of mail I had taken from Angela's and stuck them inside my jacket. Then I headed to the door. Before I got there someone knocked on it. A type of knock I recognized. That anyone from any kind of service would recognize.

Three quick knocks, hard raps against the wood. Formal.

I froze, right in front of the door.

A lady's voice called out.

"Mr. Hamilton?" Her voice was clear, commanding. Using the name from my driver's license. "Boston P.D. We have a few questions, if you can open up. It'll just take a moment."

A moment could be anywhere from a second to weeks. A slight deception, meant to underscore a hidden truth. That the police would keep me however long they wanted. Cops, right? I rolled my eyes and wondered if I was about to be arrested.

I glanced out my peephole. Two police officers stood there, both in plainclothes. Detectives. The woman cop stood a little closer to the door, she had dark hair lined with a little gray. No coloring of the hair, and just little touches of makeup. No vanity. She was maybe in her early forties, and pretty in the classic way—a sharp nose, nice cheekbones, oval eyes, and a firm chin. The nose had a bump in it, likely broken at some point.

Her partner was an older black guy, tall with a massive set of shoulders on him. Big, the way lumberjacks are big. His face was a little weathered. His nose had been broken. He had crinkles near his eyes, from either squinting or smiling, along with some scar tissue there. His hair was cut short on the sides of his head and was all gray, matching a nicely trimmed gray mustache. Where the woman wore a dark jacket over a white blouse and darker slacks, the big man had an old trench coat hanging off his shoulders and tied around at the waist, underscoring the fact that this was a very large, well-built man.

The woman had one hand resting against the door, the other holding open a wallet with her badge, back against her where I could see it clearly through the peephole. Nice. Her name was Brooklyn Baber.

Heck of a name for a detective. Her partner had his wallet open too, but I couldn't read his name. Maybe it was Black Giant.

Angela was out there, waiting. Even before Charley had called, the cops and I were going to meet at some point. Might as well see where all this was at now. I opened the door. "Something I can help with?"

"Detective Baber," the woman said, moving her foot inside the door. It was a small move, subtle, but noticed. "My partner, Frank."

Black Giant just nodded.

"Have time for some questions?" Detective Baber asked.

"I was just getting ready to go, actually," I said.

"Well, let's talk about that," she said, raising her eyebrows. "And see if you're going anywhere."

I looked at her and her partner. Taking in everything and nothing. Getting a feel for what was about to happen. If Baber had already been to Angela's apartment, then she had talked to Charley. If that had happened, she wouldn't be here, not even with Frank the Black Giant. They would be here with cuffs, and more cops, likely. In tactical gear.

I got the feeling that there was more here that I didn't know. I had never liked not knowing things. Not in the past. And even more so, now.

I thought through all of that quickly. Baber knew what I was doing. Both she and Frank watched me carefully. Her foot still in the door, her hand now pressed against it. One of Frank's giant hands tucked in his coat. They both had been in those kinds of situations, where things escalated quickly, and knew how to judge them.

"It's about the incident in the parking lot yesterday," she continued. "And the DMV."

Nothing about Angela's apartment.

"Ah," I said. As if I had been wondering why they were even there.

"Can we come in?" Baber asked again, a little sharply. A little tiredly. "We're asking now. Don't make me go through the rigmarole of getting a warrant, will you?"

"Rigmarole," I said. "That's not a word you hear often."

Frank snorted, and Detective Baber looked briefly up at the ceiling.

"I can't help but feel like if you could get a warrant, you would have," I added, and watching them, I knew that was the case.

They looked tired. Frustrated. Like they had been up a long time and were running down the last lead they had.

"Mr. Hamilton, you could save our department some time," she said. "We've been up late. A girl's been kidnapped. We'd like to find her. And time is wasting."

I wasn't worried about them coming in. Just getting in my way.

"Step on in," I said, opening the door and stepping back.

Baber walked past me, took a quick look around the apartment. The way cops do. Searching out things to identify who lived there, get a feel for them, by the stuff they owned. Pictures on the walls, crayon drawings on a fridge, the type of throw pillows on the couch, maybe the ones saying things like *Be Still and Know*.

I had none of that. Detectives would want to see some of those things, to get a read on the person living there. Get a feel for who they were dealing with. Baber stepped in and cocked her head, taking a glance around. As if reassessing a thought.

"Don't have a lot here, Hamilton," she finally said.

"I don't," I agreed.

"Just move in?" She glanced at the dining room table. There was one chair there. There was only reason for one. I got the feeling she wanted to sit down, so we could be just a couple of people talking comfortably among themselves, but the single chair ruined that.

"No," I said. I leaned back against the kitchen counter, leaving the chair if she wanted it.

"So, what, you just don't own stuff?" she asked. Her voice was sharp, experienced. Commanding. Her eyes narrowed as she looked around the place.

I knew what she saw. I saw it every day. The small, flat television.

Remote underneath. The empty kitchen counters, no containers of ladles, pans hanging, no cutting boards or jars of sugar and flour. Not even salt and pepper shakers.

Frank slid past me, his coat slowly brushing me, quiet for a man his size. It felt like the Titanic had just slipped by, cruising deep waters, pulling me briefly in his wake. The big man stood in the living room and looked around, frowning back once at Baber. Likely at the lack of information.

They both could dig, but there was nothing there to find.

"I own what I need," I finally said.

Baber arched an eyebrow. "You a minimalist?"

"I just own what I need," I said. "The rest is just…" I made a little motion with my hand. "Extra."

For years I had moved quickly. Packed light. I hadn't had a place of my own, but back then, when I had dreamed of one, I had not dreamed of this. I had thought about a little cottage in the woods, made of stone. An open kitchen overlooking a stone hearth. A few shelves of books. Snow outside. And Sam.

I set my jaw. Stopped myself from looking at the phone.

Funny how life never shows you the true end of the path you walk. It's always a guess. Choices lead to consequences, and sometimes never of your own choosing.

Baber's head tilted a little again. It looked like something she did while she was thinking. "That might be the definition of the word," she murmured.

I couldn't tell if she thought that was funny or if she was just being sarcastic. Hard to tell with cops sometimes.

"Why define things?" I said. Pushing thoughts of the stone cottage away. One break in my routine, one difference after almost ninety weeks of building up a wall, and already the memories were creeping up over it. "They are what they are."

"Hmm," Baber said. She ended up leaning her back against the wall in front of me. Folding her arms across her chest, loosely. Making herself comfortable. "I think we agree there. Things do always end up that way."

"Sure," I said. Not sure if I was happy that she agreed with me. "Whatever."

"If you don't have much," Baber said. "Maybe you won't mind if we take a look around."

"I don't know," I said. "Am I under arrest?"

"If you were under arrest," Baber said. "We'd be reading you your rights now."

"Maybe," I said. Likely they would be chasing me somewhere. And I'd be on the run from the police, and trying to find Angela. Which would worsen my odds. I wondered where Baber was going. "I thought this was about a kidnapped girl."

"That's what I said," Baber agreed, looking around the place again. Trying to nail down the feel of me from it, and failing. Blank walls. Empty cabinets. It exasperated her, some. "How long have you been here?"

"Couple of years," I said.

Baber looked like she didn't believe that.

Frank picked up *The Faerie Queene* from the coffee table. He shrugged and held it out to Baber. Raising an eyebrow and setting the book down on the table. Then he picked up the photo, the five-by-seven frame looking very small in his large hands. His thumb moved over the two hands in the picture, and he looked back to me, briefly.

"Venice?" he asked.

"What's it matter?" I said.

"Wife and I always wanted to go," he said. He set the picture back down on the coffee table, next to the book.

"Go to Paris instead," I told him. Better memories, there.

Baber held still, watching me, her head slightly tilted. They could look. They wouldn't find anything. Angela's mail was inside my jacket pocket. There was nothing else here. Nothing from my past life. Nothing that would tell them anything about me.

"Look around, whatever," I said.

Baber nodded at Frank. The giant shifted and moved from the living room to the kitchen., crossing behind me. I felt his movement too much, much like you might feel a mountain of rock hanging in the air above you. The electric tingling in the back of your skull, the quickening fear of a potential landslide. A large and ominous and powerful force, ready to be unleashed at the first drop of a stone.

Held back, but ready.

Frank and Baber were dangerous people. I recognized that, now. Listening to Frank open doors and cabinets in the kitchen. His hands careful, for a man so big.

Baber pulled a pad out, and a pen. Today, cops had all kinds of electronic tools to record notes on. Digital records and all. Maybe she was old school.

"Can you tell me where you were around noon yesterday?" she asked.

I smiled, keeping my back against the counter. Not liking the feeling of Frank moving around the kitchen behind me. The landslide, waiting. I figured he knew the effect he had on people, that Baber knew it too, and that the two of them were used to interrogating people this way. They were comfortable in it.

"I suspect you know where I was," I told her.

At noon I had been at the Department of Motor Vehicles. Dealing with the unhelpful Madge. Baber had likely gotten my license from there, with my fake Hamilton name, but my real address. So she knew where I had been.

Baber sighed. "For the record, please?"

I got a feel for her in that sigh. She was tired, likely up all night. A cop didn't do that unless they cared about what they did.

"Are you arresting me?" I asked again.

Frank opened and closed the dishwasher again. Hard. The counter shuddered a bit, behind me.

"My bad," Frank said. His voice a low rumble. If I looked, I'd bet he'd have a large smile on his face.

I didn't look. I stayed facing Baber.

"At this point," she said. "No."

Which meant on this point, they had nothing on me. They hadn't talked to Charley. Or, if they had, Charley had decided not to tell them about what had happened.

I gave Baber a slight grin. "Then, at this point, I suspect you know where I was yesterday."

She grinned back. She liked the game. I got the feeling she was good at her job, she and Frank were good together, and they were here for a specific reason.

"What are you looking for here, Baber?" I asked.

She tilted her head. Looked at me with a degree of measuring. Some internal scale she weighed me on. "I told you why we're here."

"The kidnapped girl," I said. Then motioned at my apartment and rolled my eyes. "Explains why you want to look at an empty apartment so much."

"A thing like this, I have to dig at every lead, right?" Baber said. Still grinning.

That was something I did understand. I was doing the same thing. Turning over every rock, hoping that I would find something under one, something that told me who had Angela, and why.

I was a rock, for Baber. Something she needed to flip over.

The cop leaned a little closer, like she wanted to tell me a secret. Still grinning. "Let's say I do know where you were at yesterday. And let's say you know I know. And let's say I also know you went to the Department of Motor Vehicles and asked someone there to illegally get you the name or address of a license plate of a person who had just been kidnapped."

"Okay." I nodded back. Two friends, sharing a secret. "Let's say we both know something like that happened. There might be a few details there someone might argue with. Such as, there was never an asking for an address."

Baber's grin widened into a smile.

"As long as we're speculating," I added, then.

"Sure," she said. She reached up and rubbed an eye. Still with the smile, like she had gotten something from me. "We'll say that."

Frank moved along the hallway to my bedroom. I heard the washer and dryer doors open and close with loud metal squeals. The hard thunk of the dryer door snapping shut. The spring on the door was too tight.

I turned back. Frank was standing in the hallway and looking at the phone. He picked it up, curious. Listened to it, the dial tone loud in the apartment. His big fingers punched a few numbers, each press of the key beeping out of the handset, and then he hung it up.

He realized I had been watching him. "Takes me back," he said.

I realized my hands had both tightened up, under the counter, hidden from his view. I carefully relaxed them, taking deep, slow breaths. Pushing the anger back down.

Frank cocked his head at me, then started poking around on the shelf in the tiny laundry room.

I turned back. Baber was watching me with intense eyes. I got the feeling she had seen everything, and was adding it to the need to look closer tab.

"What do you do, Mr. Hamilton?" she asked.

It wasn't the question I expected.

"Let me rephrase this," Baber said. "What *did* you do?"

Baber was good.

"This about the girl," I asked back. "Or me?"

Baber shrugged. "I'm turning over rocks, Hamilton. Maybe both. Why don't you tell me why you wanted to know where the girl lived?"

"I didn't want to know that," I repeated, again. "I wanted someone at the DMV to call her and tell her I had her helmet."

"Oh," Baber said, as if she had forgotten that detail. "Right."

Then she gave me the *silly rabbit, tricks are for kids* face. She flipped some pages on her notebook, then read something off of it. "I have here that you said '*You don't have to give me their name or address or anything, you could just call them from here. Just let them know I have their helmet*'."

"See," I told her. "I never asked for her address."

"A bit odd, though," Baber said. "Right?"

"What," I asked. "A person can't want to return something?"

She flipped her pages back. "It's a very curious phrase. I'm guessing you didn't know the girl very well. Not knowing where she lived. So why go to the trouble of returning the helmet?"

I shrugged, and repeated something Charley had said. "If you met her, you'd know."

"Huh," she said. "Seems like a lot of trouble. Even for a cute girl. I mean, it's the DMV. People don't go there voluntarily."

Baber was right. Madge was not going to be on the list of those I wanted a repeat conversation with. I had spent a lot of time working myself back into shape physically. Mentally though, Baber had me. I was rusty.

"Just being a helpful citizen," I finally said.

"So let me ask you again," Baber said. "What do you do?"

"You keep coming back to me," I said. "Whatever I used to do, that's not going to help you find her."

"Maybe," Baber said. "But my gut is telling me the opposite. It's telling me to look closer here. At you. Your life. It's telling me that I'll find her by figuring you out."

"Maybe you should grab something to eat," I said. "Your gut sounds empty, to me."

Baber just kept looking at me, her head tilted, something getting added up behind her eyes.

They were focused too much on me. Not enough on Angela.

It made me a little nervous. Antsy.

"We done?" I said. "I've got things to do."

Baber snorted.

I got the feeling that I was reading this wrong. Reading Baber wrong. For the first time, I worried that maybe I had been out of this game for so long, I wouldn't find Angela in time. That I wouldn't be good enough.

Baber made a decision. "Let me show you something." She pulled her phone out of her pocket, one of the smartphones with a big screen on it. Part of me thought I had been right, she had something she could type notes in, so she was a little old school.

She held the phone out to me, opening up a video. She stood beside me as she did. I could smell soap and dandruff shampoo from her hair, and the faintest whiff of cigarettes.

The video was similar to the news report Charley had pulled up yesterday. The footage was grainy and the color wasn't great, the shot itself must have come from a security camera somewhere near the Chinese restaurant.

I saw the kidnapping again. Just from a different angle. Angela, walking into the picture, at the top of the screen. The Escalade stopping with a screech in the middle. The camera looking down and a little behind everything. The guys getting out and running to the far side of the screen to grab Angela. Throwing her in the truck. The truck peeling off.

Then me, a moment later, running after the truck. There was a good shot of my face there, angry. Jaw clenched. Eyes furious. Arms pumping as if I was willing myself to catch the vehicle. A man on a mission.

Baber paused it there, and looked at me. Waited a long moment for me to get it. And I didn't.

"I don't see a helmet there," she told me, softly.

Dammit.

I let out a breath. She was right. That video clearly didn't show a guy trying to return a helmet. It was a guy chasing down a truck. It was a guy starting on a path, at the time unaware of the journey he was beginning. A furious, angry guy.

She pulled back from me, looking at me, thoughtful. Her forefinger tapping the side of the phone.

"You're an odd one, Jim," Baber said. "You come out of that bookstore all hell and high water. You immediately find her bike, so you know what she rode. Even though you didn't know her, because then you went about trying to find her address."

My name wasn't Jim. My fake name wasn't even Jim. I guessed it was a name she used in the heat of an argument, some kind of nickname. Something from some time ago, old school, like her notepad.

I stayed silent. Frank stayed silent, though I heard each big-footed step as he moved around in my bedroom. I got the feeling the mountain was always quiet, until it erupted.

"At first, I wondered if you were angry because the girl got kidnapped," Baber continued. "Or if you were angry because your fellow kidnappers left you behind."

Our eyes locked. I knew Baber had something to say, and I let her say it.

"So I had to see you," she said. "Take a look for myself, you know?"

"Is this from the army?" Frank asked, again from the bedroom. "What do they call these, combat blues? Battle blues?"

I looked back. He was standing in the doorway, between the bedroom and the little hallway to the kitchen. His large hand held a hanger, and a uniform wrapped in plastic from the dry cleaners. My old service uniform. To me they were dress blues. Dark blue pants and jacket. Ribbons on the front.

Frank was peering at the ribbons on the front.

"Just a costume," I finally said. "Halloween."

"Really?" Frank turned and peered closer at the front, the plastic sleeve swishing in the air. "Looks real enough."

Baber gave me a look. "Halloween isn't for a few weeks."

"Isn't this the marksman badge?" Frank said, holding the plastic close to his face. "The thing that looks like the Red Baron's cross?"

It wasn't a marksman badge, but sharpshooter. I didn't correct him. And thankfully, Frank had distracted Baber.

She grinned. "Are you talking about Snoopy and the Red Baron?"

"Maybe," Frank said.

"That's from a comic strip, you know," Baber said.

Frank shrugged. "The Red Baron was real."

"Look," I interrupted the banter. "This has nothing to do with me. I tried to help someone, that's it. Your time would be better spent somewhere else."

"Yeah, you'd think so," Baber said. "But I got a good feel you're tangled up in this somehow."

"You're wasting your time," I said. Hers and mine.

"I'm still looking for her," she said. "But I'm also looking for you. For everything about you. I'm going to dig into everything in your life. Turn over every rock."

"Suit yourself," I said.

She shook her head. "You don't get it yet, but you will. I'm pretty sharp. You'll find that out. Whatever you're keeping from me, I'm going to find it."

It was my turn to grin, but I only did it inside. Anything she really wanted to know about me, she would never find. That was something she didn't know yet, but she would always only see me as Hamilton, day trader.

She leaned forward again. The two buddies conversation. "So feel free to go about your day. But if that girl ends up dead, and you could have helped me and you didn't, then I'm going to nail you to the wall."

She really believed that. I could feel it from her. A desire to do the right thing. And a conviction that she would.

Something I had felt once.

I stood there, watching her. Putting on my bored face. It was something I used a lot, the past couple of years.

"Done?" I asked her. Feeling the mountain behind me, waiting.

Baber nodded. "For now."

"Next time," I said. "Bring a warrant. Or don't come."

"Sure, Jim. Sure," Baber said. It wasn't my name, so Jim must be something she used a lot. "If that's how you want to play it."

The two of them left then, at some silent signal, or maybe none, maybe it was just two partners who had been together a long time. The big man patted my shoulder as he left. A *we'll see you again* type of pat. His paw was large and heavy, like a cinder block.

I got up and shut the door behind them. Then I moved to the phone. The cord had twisted, so I picked it up and untwisted it so the curly cable hung in a perfect U-shape. I made sure there was a dial tone, when I lifted it. Then carefully centered the phone on its cradle. And forced my hand away.

I walked to the window. Watched the street from there, until I saw the pair of them walk out the front door of my building and across to their car. A dark four-door sedan. I thought one of those big Chevrolets police departments always had.

Frank held up his hand, stopping traffic, as they crossed. Then he walked around and eased himself into the car. The sedan shifted as he got in, rocking a little back and forth. Baber opened the driver's door, but before she got in she looked up at my window. Directly at me.

And winked.

CHAPTER
FOURTEEN

Baber and Frank walked down the hallway, then the stairs. Floor after floor down. Her pumps clicked lightly across the wooden steps, but the stairs groaned at every placement of Frank's heavy feet.

She let out a big breath. These older apartment buildings always smelled like floor polish and Lemon Pledge. Something they treated the wood with, maybe.

She stumbled a bit, almost missing a step. They were both tired. They were always tired. Some murder up on westside last night, and now she got pulled into this kidnapping. Almost a day late into it. So here they were, chasing down one of the few leads they had.

At least Frank had a consistent type of energy that pulled her along sometimes. Implacable. That was the word she was trying to find, in her muddled mind.

"Haven't seen a phone like that in ages," Frank said. "Guy's got no cell phone, no laptop, no computer. Just a phone from the eighties hanging up by the fridge."

"You're right," Baber said. She still had her phone out, stopped on the video of Hamilton chasing the truck. Her other hand guided her down the stairs, lightly touching the banister. The stairs complaining as Frank came down behind her, *groan, groan, groaann.*

"Should have brought him in," Frank said.

"We couldn't hold him," Baber said as the two hit the bottom of the stairs, standing there a moment. Facing each other. "And he wasn't the type to scare easily."

"Still," Frank moved his massive shoulders up, then down. "Couldn't hurt."

"You're right." Baber looked at her phone. She had the next part of the video on a loop, it was the part that had got her gut thinking. "But there's time for that."

The camera had Hamilton standing there, watching where the truck had left. For a moment or two. She could almost see him make a decision then.

He turned then, and walked past a row of cars. Stopped at a silver BMW parked in front of the restaurant. Then kicked it a couple of quick times, until the car alarm went off. Then Hamilton walked away, the lights on the BMW blinking on and off, almost furtively.

Hamilton had picked that car out. When she first saw the video, she had backed it up to see why. Had the tech back it up over thirty minutes. Thirty-seven minutes and twenty-three seconds, to be exact, when the BMW had parked there. In a place designated for pickup orders.

There was some dark rage in Hamilton. But he had controlled it. Something had lit him off, and he had taken it out where he could.

The man was dangerous. She could feel that from him. And wondered again what it was that the man did in his life. She glanced up at her partner. "Did you see Hamilton when you picked up that phone?"

"Nah," Frank said.

"He about shit a brick," Baber said. "I thought he was going to come after you."

"Really," Frank grinned, and you could see his two front teeth had a tiny gap between them. "That would have been fun."

"Maybe," Baber said, thinking. Frank used to box, and years later still carried the frame of a heavyweight, decades after he quit. "I thought he was about to snap."

"He's an odd one," Frank said. "Guy has sheets in the dryer. A well-made bed. Hospital corners and all. But no bed frame. Mattress on the floor."

"Odd," Baber said. "If he's been there awhile."

"Definitely," Frank agreed. "I kind of feel like we'll see him again."

"I kind of feel it's headed that way," Baber said.

"Let's go see this girl's apartment," Frank said. "We can come back later and see if Jack wants to go him a few rounds."

"It's not Jack," Baber said.

"It's not Jim either," Frank replied.

"You're right," Baber said. "I'm not even sure it's Hamilton."

The two headed out the front door, over to their car. A heavy black Chevrolet Malibu. "When did we get the call?"

"Desk guy said it came through, maybe thirty minutes ago," he said. He stepped out on the street and held his hand out. Frank was the type of guy to walk and expect things to stop for him. He was large enough to get that kind of attention. "Some girl recognized her friend on the news, called it in."

"This girl just saw it?" Baber asked. Her mind always asking questions. Even if she had called it in, they would have needed to vet the tip. Make sure it was good. Anything that got broadcast on the news usually got a few hundred fake calls in. People wanting attention. Others thinking they recognized her. Something seemed off. "Who's watching news this early in the morning?"

"Some people do," Frank shrugged. He got into the car, and the Malibu rocked back and forth before setting in.

Baber opened her door. A lot of things so far felt off. Hamilton by far the largest. At least they had another lead. They'd check out the apartment and see what they found there.

She felt like she was behind though. In some race and lagging. Her gut told her Hamilton was the key to this. Baber looked up at the window. The man was standing there, staring down at them. A statue. Some kind of mystery she had to unearth.

She winked at Hamilton, and got into the car. Baber was good at digging. She'd find out what she needed to about the man. And, like she had told Hamilton, she'd nail his ass to the wall if he could have helped her, and didn't.

THE COLLEGE ON ANGELA'S MAIL HAD BEEN EASY TO FIND. The Registration Department less so. However, by asking a few questions of students at various points on the campus, I found myself at an older building, maybe built early in the nineteen-hundreds, looking rough around the edges, but with a solid paint job on it.

The campus was nice. Fredrick's Community College was old, but still had those thick lawns that lay between older brick buildings, giving a feel of history to the place. The red brick and the green grass looked good, paired together. Like they had always been that way. Always been there.

Older trees, tall American Elms, shadowed sidewalks and benches, and even though it was chilly in the air there was a fresh smell of the grass, like it had recently been cut. Smaller redbud trees, trimmed almost like tall shrubs, were planted along the wall of the registration building, the pinkish-red flowers in full bloom.

I couldn't help the bad feeling I had about Baber's visit. She should have been to the apartment yesterday. At worse, early this morning. Before seeing me. If she had found anything at the apartment, she would have seen Charley. And if she had seen Charley, things would have gone much differently this morning, with me.

I couldn't figure it. Boston was a large place, with a lot of people. A lot of tips get called in on something like a kidnapping. People who know a thousand different Angelas. People who know exactly who the kidnappers are.

People who had dreamed up the whole thing and knew exactly where she was being held.

It would take some vetting. Still, sixteen hours or so seemed like a long period of time. Especially because Charley had been pretty specific with her information. She had sounded credible. Those calls usually get front of the line.

I didn't like where my thoughts were headed. I didn't believe in things like coincidence, in a case like this. I felt like someone had delayed the tip. Had given someone plenty of time to go through the apartment. Maybe get the guy I had left there. Maybe even clean up the blood.

That meant people in power were involved. Or at least, people with access to power. So, money or someone political.

Or, if two different groups were involved, both.

I took stock of myself. Tan pants. White shirt. Brown sports coat. I was dressed, but I wasn't ready. I knew I carried an edge. I knew people sensed it in me. The anger, held in bay behind the wall I had built around it. Others sensed it and stayed away. Some people, like Charley, sensed it and stayed for a bit, until it had frightened her.

Angela had sensed it and recognized it. Understood it, even. And had stayed.

I couldn't be that person now. I had once been confident, happy. I had been the type of person people wanted around. A guy other guys drank beers with. A guy other girls were excited about showing off to their friends and family.

I needed to find some way to be that person again. Just for a bit. Until this part was done. I thought I had one chance at all of this, and I couldn't afford the luxury of being angry. At least, I didn't think Angela could.

I took a deep breath and walked up the stairs into the Registration Center. The door squeaked open to a nicely blue and white tiled hallway. I found Student Registration and ended up waiting behind a few younger kids. One wanted to know what he had to do to get his student loan so he could pay for his class, and the other was trying to transfer some credits from a night school. There were two younger students helping each, a young man and a young woman, both probably students and working part-time in the hall.

The young man finished first, but a phone on his countertop rang and he answered it. His eyes rolled up, as he began to answer questions like *what time do you close?* and *can I do this over the phone?* and *what do I need to bring?* Questions he must answer thousands of times each day.

The young lady finished up and waved me forward. "How may I help you?"

She was blond and plump, not too tall. Her lips were pale and plump like her body, though her face was thin for the extra weight she carried. Her makeup was a bit thick, maybe to hide a few pimples on her face. The nameplate on her counter read Tammie.

I let out a low breath and tried a smile. A real smile. Or as close as I could get.

"Hey Tammie," I said. "I'm not a student here, but I'm looking for some information on one. I was hoping you could help me."

"It's likely," Tammie smiled back. She had a nice smile. "I do kind of work in the area where all students are registered."

"Great," I smiled and leaned a little closer. Like Baber had, earlier. Two friends, having a good talk. "I'm not looking for much, just the names of some teachers for Angela Martinez."

"And this is in reference to?" Tammie asked.

I looked left and right, almost conspiratorially, and said in a low voice,. "I can't say much about it, these custody cases can get out of hand."

"This girl has a kid?" Tammie asked, with a slight frown.

"Yeah," I said, "and the father is really putting it to her." I gave Tammie the *you know what some guys will do* kind of shrug. "All I'm looking for is a few character references for Angie." I gave her a wink. "You know, the courts always respect the words of a professor."

"Oh yeah," Tammie nodded, like she had been part of all kinds of cases.

The young man hung up then, and looked over at Tammie. "You got this?"

Tammie looked at him, and back at me. I waited for a second, willing Tammie to help me out. Trying to relax. Hoping she wouldn't get him involved too. The more people I had to convince, the easier the lie would unravel.

She finally nodded back. "Yep."

"Great," he said. "I'm going to lunch." He flipped his nametag around on the counter and left.

Tammie turned back to me, in full gossip mode. "Is it the husband?"

"I can't really say," I said, giving her a slight nod. Bringing her into the act. "Just looking for a list of classes."

She looked confused. "If you're here to help her out, shouldn't you already have the names?"

"I know, right?" I rolled my eyes. "But that's not how it works. I'm court-appointed, you know? I didn't want to go to the list of people the lawyers provide. Just can't trust them."

"Oh, I understand," Tammie's eyes opened wide. "I had a friend, she hit someone else's car backing out of a spot. The person was going too fast in the parking lot, but," Tammie waved her hand, "you know lawyers."

"Exactly," I nodded. "Everything I've found tells me Ms. Martinez has a great relationship with her son. But some references from respected professors would be a great help."

She nodded again, looking at me. "Oh I understand. All my friend could talk about was the lawsuit."

I waited a bit then. I didn't know how much further I could spin it. The best lies were quick. The longer you told them, the easier they were to catch.

Tammie, though, might have been a little slow on the uptake. So I finally asked again, "If I could get the names of those professors? Just maybe the ones from this semester?"

"Oh," she said, shaking her head at herself. "Sure. Let me check for you real quick."

"I sure appreciate it," I said. *There's one for you, Madge.*

Tammie typed a few things in the computer to the side of her. She hummed while she worked, and I was pretty sure she was unaware she was doing it. A few times she shook her head, "Angie?" she asked. "Or Angela?"

"Angela," I said. "Though her friends call her Angie."

Tammie finally said, triumphant, "There it is—it's under Angela Martinez. Lucky we just have one of her."

"Great," I said, giving Tammie a wink.

She clicked on her mouse, and I heard a printer whir up in the background. She turned around, pulling a piece of paper from behind her, then turning it back.

"A list of her classes," she smiled.

"Thanks again," I said. "If I get a chance, I'll tell Ms. Martinez you were a big help."

"Oh it's no problem," Tammie said. "I understand lawyers and all."

"I'm sure you do," I said, and took the paper from Tammie. It was nice to have something work out for me. I wasn't a people person anymore, so even just getting the list of classes felt like a tiny victory, but Angela would need a few more if I were going to find her.

I nodded one last time at Tammie. "Have a good one."

I took the paper and headed to the bookstore on campus. I crossed a group of students on the lawn, standing with signs, telling me that a Bigger Boston was a Better Boston. One of the girls there, a young girl with blonde hair tucked underneath a cabbie hat, tried to hand me a pamphlet.

I waved her off. I thought she might have called after me, but I didn't turn around. Didn't face the crowd of accusing signs, and the young group of kids who hadn't lived the life I lived. Children who had yet to get out in the real world and discover that life was unfair, that bigger wasn't always better.

Sometimes other people wanted bigger, and their want conflicted with yours. Sometimes other people wanted better, more, not for others, but for themselves. Bigger and better always seemed to me to be a monster, a breath full of empty promises, hiding a belly hungry with need and a mouth ready to swallow you whole.

The bookstore wasn't packed. Maybe because it was a Thursday, maybe because all the students had all their books for the semester. The store itself smelled just the same as the bookstore yesterday, with rows of newly printed paper and books lined up in front of me. And shelves of notebooks and pens, all with the colors and mascot of the college printed on them. What looked like a bald eagle, with a cocky grin on its beak.

Just like the registration office, young kids worked here as well. Staff on the cheap. Nothing a crack investigator like me couldn't handle. I was just there to buy a regular manila envelope, the kind a thousand law offices had, a pen, a sharpie, and a ream of printing paper.

Outside I took a few dozen sheets out of the package of paper and ruffled them a bit, then placed those sheets in the pocket of the folder. I folded a couple, just to give the envelope some thickness. I threw the rest of the paper in the bin next to the store.

I placed Angie's class list inside the manilla envelope next, and pulled it out a hair so it would be easy to see when the folder was closed. On the front of the folder, on the top right I took the big sharpie and wrote in large, bold letters *Martinez—458-210529*. Like it was a case file I had picked up somewhere.

I found a bathroom and looked at myself in the mirror. After a moment I roughed up my hair a bit, unbuttoned the top button of my white shirt, and folded up my jacket a couple of times. Made it look as rumpled as I could. I checked the mirror again, and felt like I looked as close to a harried minion of Children's Services as I could. It should work well enough.

Angela had an interesting course list: mechanical engineering, some math classes, a Shakespeare course. Even a high level computer data security course. It was a heavy course load, but there was a still performance class nestled between computer science classes. Seeing the acting class brought back memories of Angela's picture on the wall. The one of her singing, on stage.

I couldn't grasp her major from the list. I wasn't sure where to start, so I just went top to bottom and visiting classrooms, trying to find professors who knew her. It took some time to figure out which building was the Science building, which the English, and where the Performance Center was.

I found myself crossing back and forth over the same lawn. The second time I did so I passed the same pair of students on a bench. Two guys, one with a green toboggan pulled low over his ears. Toboggan said something to his partner and they both laughed.

Maybe that was their deal, sitting on the bench and watching lost adults wander by. Maybe some of those adults still wandered the campus, lost souls trying to figure out how to pay whatever bill was due, where their kids might be, which parking lot out of the fifty surrounding the campus they had parked.

I couldn't find the computer course professor. The performance professor, a Dr. Thelisia, told me she hadn't seen Angela in a day but if I saw her could I remind her to work on her upper register for Friday. I asked her what was Friday, and she gave me an *aghast* look. Both hands held up high to her face, palms out. Wondering how I could not know.

So, no luck. Her Shakespeare class was on Mondays, Wednesdays, and Fridays. It being Thursday, I hoped maybe her instructor, a Professor Kirschke, was on campus. Maybe he had office hours. People worked those.

The English hall was a large red brick building split into two wings, and bent a little like a boomerang, each wing wrapping around me, as I walked up. Large sets of double doors faced me from the middle section, and I headed towards those.

A spattering of kids stood around the doors, some smoking, other groups just talking. I felt like there was a wide gulf between me and those students, more than the ten years or so that separated us. They lived a carefree life, where their only worry was the next class, the next assignment, or if Susan or Greg liked them.

I walked past the smokers and passed through the double doors. The bottom floor had a wide set of stairs in the middle, heading up, doubling back on itself each floor. Around the stairs were a number of tables and benches, all spaced out. A small cafeteria sat off to the side, somewhere you could grab a coffee, a pre-made sandwich, or some munchies.

Class must have just let out. There were plenty of kids walking around. Some with backpacks, some clutching a pile of books to their chests, some walking in a group, laughing together. There was a line at the cafeteria register, other kids at the tables, even more walking in and out of the hallways that led into each wing.

Next to the stairs was a building map. I found Kirschke's office on it, the third floor. Headed up the stairs, getting stuck behind a heavy kid plodding upwards, taking each step slowly, his hand out in front of his face and holding a phone.

A number of kids were heading down the stairs, the plodding kid seemed to be the only one headed up, and it took everything in me not to push past him. Phones today seemed to remove any awareness of what was ahead of a person. Or behind.

The stairs ended on the third floor. I headed left, down the hallway. The tile was all white with specks of black, polished recently. To the inside of the hallways were classrooms, to the outside looked to be offices. Kirschke's was the fourth office on the right.

The door was open. The room was square and small, as if someone had taken a cubicle and just built the walls higher. The door itself sat in one corner of the room. There were old windows in the back of it, looking down on the parking lot in back of the building, letting in the sun. A bookshelf on the far side of the room, floor-to-ceiling, thick with books.

The most noticeable thing in the room was the desk. It was a large, old, wooden thing lit by the sun's rays. It was big enough I wondered how they had even got it through the door. The desk was one of those executive types, heavy dark wood, rounded corners, big panels and delicate trim. It was as big as the room, well-polished oak, but also old, as if it had been passed down from generation to generation.

The bookshelf held a lot of books. I could make out Shakespeare's name, Milton and Browne, a few others. Thick books with Old English type on the front. All kinds of sizes and shapes, thick books of literature, thin books of what might be poetry. Even a few thin hard books that looked like comic novels.

The wall close to me was bare, and covered with a light yellow paint. Clean, but needing a fresh coat or two. Maybe what tenure gets you nowadays.

Sitting at the large desk and typing on a computer keyboard was a young man. Maybe my age, maybe younger. He had thin black hair laying back, and wire-rimmed glasses on his nose. A couple of large books lay on the far side of his desk, by his elbow. Maybe ones he liked to read often. A square monitor sat right in front of him, thin, with a black case and a couple of cables trailing from it to the other side of his desk.

No matter how elegant or fancy the desk, the cables always ruined it. Black ugly things, winding across the surface. A piece of electricity, thrumming and humming, in a place that deserved quiet contemplation.

After a moment, the man noticed me.

"Can I help you?" he said, pleasantly enough, and waved for me to come in.

"I hope so." I gave him a harried look and flashed the manila envelope. Sat in one of two chairs in front of his desk. The chairs were wooden and hard, with harder flat gray cushions on them. "Professor Kirschke?"

"The name's on the door," he said, smiling unapologetically.

"Terrific," I said. He had a little box on the corner of his desk. Something to hold cards with his name, title, and phone number. I picked it up and glanced at it, like I was verifying something, and then got on with the act.

I introduced myself, and went into my story. Looking for information on Angela Martinez for a Children Services report. Just getting background. Maybe some names of her friends, what kind of grades did she get, those types of things. In the end I pulled the class list out of my folder, like it was something official, and gave it to Kirschke.

"So I'm just going through her class list, kind of getting that background from Angela's teachers."

The whole time Kirschke watched me, and I got the same feeling from him that I had from Baber. This was a man who observed and took in things in order to make sense out of them. He was going through that now. His eyes were sharp and intelligent.

"Hmm," Kirschke said. He typed something on his computer and hit the enter key. Clicked his mouse. Then turned the monitor around.

It showed that video of Angela's kidnapping again. A third version, maybe from a phone in the parking lot. Inside I shook my head. These videos were so popular I'd have agents calling me. Asking me to star in their new thriller movie, *The Guy who Loses the Girl*.

"Want to try again?" he asked me.

I sat there for a minute. Not knowing where to go.

"Let me help," he said. Playing another video. One of them showing me running after the truck. "This is you, correct?"

I looked at the manilla envelope. Set it on the chair next to me. Nodded.

"So," Kirschke said. "Take it from there, then."

I looked at Kirschke. His face was open. He looked interested. I had been wrong, comparing him to Baber. She was digging into me to find out where my lies lay, where she could trip me up, anything that would help her get a step closer to finding Angela.

Kirschke wasn't trying to nail my lie to the wall. He was more curious as to what I was doing. The purpose to which he applied his thought wasn't in order to catch me in a lie, it was a man who listened and understood knowledge for knowledge's sake.

"I used to be better at this," I said.

Kirschke smiled.

Maybe I could just tell him the truth, and see where that got me.

So I did. I told him about sitting in the bookstore. Meeting Angela. Our brief conversation. How it started. How it ended.

"She actually quoted Spenser?" Kirschke asked, his smile growing larger.

"She did," I said. "I didn't get it at the time, but I found the line later."

"You have *The Faerie Queene*?" He was curious.

"I bought it," I said. "Read some of it last night."

"Hmm," Kirschke said again. Absorbing. He pushed the monitor back aside, it made a little scratching sound on the wood of his desk. Looking at the surface, there were plenty of etches on its surface. Things that had been polished out and brought back.

The motion revealed the two large books on the corner of his desk. One was *The Collected Works of Shakespeare*. The second was *The Faerie Queene*. That's when I knew Kirschke had something that would help me.

"You knew her," I said.

"I *know* her," he said. His eyes flashed over with sadness, hidden a little by the reflection off his glasses. He leaned back in his chair, each of his hands placed on the edge of the desk in front of him. "But I don't know you."

"Yeah," I got what he was saying. He wondered what he could tell me. Or maybe what he should tell me. A silence went through the room. It didn't make Kirschke uncomfortable, he just sat there, observing. Measuring.

I got a little anxious, though. I thought Kirschke had information he could share, that might help me. I didn't know how to go about unlocking it. And I felt my next words would be key in the attempt.

"Show what you be," I said, aloud. "That was the first thing she said to me."

Kirschke nodded. "She loved that line." He picked up the book, different than mine. Older. The full knight on the worn cover. Little colored tabs poking from the pages on the top, where he had marked passages, maybe. Then he sat it back on the desk, between us.

"I don't know that I understood what she said, at the time," I said. "It took me later. That night."

"The thing about great literature," Kirschke said, "is that it doesn't have to mean the same thing, all the time. Each person can pull something different from it. Twenty people can read the same line. It can mean twenty different things. Or forty." He leaned forward a bit. "Or one."

"Yeah," I said. "Yeah."

The quiet again. Outside, over Kirschke's shoulder, the window revealed a bluer sky than in the morning. The sun, finally up and fully awake, its rays burning away the hazy gray of morning.

"I kind of thought," I said. "She was saying be true to who you are."

"It could be," he said.

"I'd like to help her," I said.

"I see that," he said.

"I'm kind of stuck," I said. "I think things are escalating. I don't have much to go on. Yesterday, there was blood in her apartment. I don't think it's hers, but I think it means there are different people after her. Her or someone, or maybe something she knows."

He looked at me, and I looked at him. A car fired up in the parking lot outside. Something large, with an eight-cylinder engine, and the kind of muffler that made the engine rumble like a beast.

"This is kind of the last thing I can do," I said. "Dig into her background. See if there's something there that will tell me how to find her. How to help her."

The muffler grew louder, as if someone had hammered the gas pedal down. Both Kirschke and I looked at the window. He saw something in the parking lot I could not, and slightly shook his head. A motion I think he probably repeated, many times. When he turned back the rumbling of the car started to fade, as if it was heading far, far away.

Kirschke grinned then. A quick move of his lips, echoed in his eyes. "Add faith to the force, right? What kind of teacher would I be if I didn't do that?"

"So you'll help me?" I asked. Relieved.

"I'll tell you what I know," he said. "And let you take it from there."

THERE WASN'T A BELL OR ANYTHING, BUT STUDENTS started filling the hall outside the door. A last second rush to make it to class on time. Muffled sneakers made a herd-like sound on the hallway tile, mixed with occasional clicking of pumps or heels. Voices and conversations, *did you get so-and-so finished, wasn't that assignment tough, are you ready for the test,* all of that.

Kirschke got up, slid between the edge of his desk and the wall. He closed the door, muting the herd. The professor was taller than I had thought, carried the wiry frame of someone who did a lot of physical activity, and the tanned skin of someone who did that activity outside. Then he sat on the corner of his desk in a pose he seemed to feel comfortable in. The desk was large enough that he still was a few feet from where I sat.

"First of all," Kirschke said. "I don't know her as well as you're hoping I do. I've got this session I call the Late Night Brain, it's a weekly thing where I invite any student to come hang out for an hour. It's not a class, it's just a place where we can get together and talk about anything."

I waited, letting him tell me what he wanted.

"It's something I thought would help students," he said, wanting to explain his thing. "People don't get together and talk about things anymore. No random conversations. I think there's a skill lost in the world today, where people get together and talk about things, learn about each other, come to the middle ground on some random topic. I'm not sure what started it. Maybe science, with its definition of truth. Maybe math, where two plus two always equals four. I feel like there's this growing feeling today where things either *are* or *aren't*, where things are either *true* or *false*, where there can be only one right answer to any question."

I thought about what he said. Maybe he was right. Though I couldn't see where he was going with it.

"Some truths, I'm not sure they can be defined in a particular way," he said. "I wanted people to understand that. I thought the meeting was a way to do that."

"Are you telling me Angela came to the meetings?" I asked.

"A year ago now," he said. "When she first came to this school. She took my Renaissance class, I always invite my classes each semester. I found her thoughtful. She would always watch others answer, speak, about anything. She wrote things down in a little notebook. Taking in what they said. So when she spoke, it was with a deeper insight. Her comments always took their answer a step further. Something that advanced the topic in an unexpected way."

Kirschke sighed. "I liked that. It's not something many people do, anymore."

He seemed young, to have that kind of opinion. Those kinds of thoughts usually come from the elderly, the old. People who had experienced more. But he wasn't wrong about Angela. She had watched me, in the bookstore. While doing so, she had come to some conclusion. And then she had spoken, her first real words to me had been that line from *The Faerie Queene*.

Show what you be. Be not faint. Have faith. My lips twisted at the thoughts.

"I think it's something she taught herself," Kirschke said. "Not that she wasn't thoughtful. I think it was the notebook. The notes she would take, while people spoke. I think she trained herself to look past the surface of a conversation. Past the outside of a person. Past the outward appearance of a thing."

I thought I had seen that notebook. A tiny spiral thing, with a telescoping pen. I wondered if she had jotted down something about me, while I had been watching others outside. What those notes might have said.

You have that look...

The look of being uncomfortable. Of trying to be something I wasn't. Of not being able to be what I used to be. The look of someone stuck between what he had once been, and what he was becoming.

"That's not helping me find her," I said, maybe a little short.

Kirschke made a little motion with his hand, a little *hold on* type of motion. "I tell you all this because I think in the beginning, she was someone who took things at their face value. Of how people appeared to her. And I think what happened changed her. It's what brought her here. If I had to guess, that event is what this is all about."

"That event?" I asked.

He nodded. "Benjamin Whelan."

There. I had a name. Now I needed the event. "Tell me."

His hands opened and closed. When they closed, each of his thumbs rubbed the side of his forefingers. "I don't know how much I can tell you."

"What do you mean?" I asked. "Just tell me what you know."

"That's what I'm saying," he said. "I don't know much. I'll tell you what I know, but if I tell you what I suppose, or what I guess, I might lead you astray. What I tell you now, it has power. It could take many different shapes. I'd rather guide you right."

"Professor," I said. "Doctor. Whatever. I'm not interested in what you think may or may not help me. Just tell me what you know. I'll take it from there."

He laughed. His hand reached out to lie on *The Faerie Queene*. "Full of confidence," he said. "You carry a certain pride. A *see things through* kind of guy."

"Maybe," I said. At least, it was who I had been once. I didn't think I was that guy now. Not confident of anything, anymore. Except maybe that I would find Angela. That, I was sure of. I would figure out who had kidnapped her, and why, and make them understand why they should never do it again.

Kirschke nodded. He appeared deep in thought. His finger traced along the cover of the book. "Benjamin Whelan is the son of David Whelan. You may have heard of him. Rich man. His family has been in New England since the day the Mayflower arrived. Angela met Benjamin, back at Harvard."

I thought I had heard of David Whelan. Recently, in fact. But I couldn't place the name, or remember where I had heard it. Maybe the gym yesterday? The bookstore? Something I had seen or heard, maybe something on tv somewhere?

"Angela went to Harvard?"

"She is bright," Kirschke said. His face twisted a little, maybe conflicted. "She was there on a scholarship. Something Harvard created to get the right percentage of minorities into their institution."

Some of the pictures back at her place made sense then. A younger Angela, dressed up in Victorian dress, among others dressed the same. Singing. Acting. Maybe a few Shakespeare plays, maybe other performances. Well-built stages, and backs of unilluminated heads in some of the shots, as if someone had taken the picture from the back row of a seated crowd.

I remembered Angela's voice, when she first spoke to me. A powerful timbre resonating deep within. Someone who knew how she sounded, and could craft that sound to a desired effect. Someone who maybe had once thought voice, and words, and passion at one point was enough. That the performance was all. A woman who had learned things since, things that lay much deeper. That behind every performance were deceptions and betrayals and lies. That sound, as pure as it can be heard, as loud as it can be played or sung, cannot always mask the brutal truths of life.

"She met Benjamin there," Kirschke continued. "I don't think his father liked her."

"Not of the New England blood?" I asked.

He shrugged. "I wouldn't want to guess."

I got it. I understood. This was a man who collected information. Who pulled students in to talk about things. To figure out and discover, to identify and learn. To put things together in ways that made sense. It's why he liked Angela, she had seemed to be the same way. A discoverer of truth. Not someone who took things and made half-ass guesses about them.

That was more me. I wasn't great at figuring things out. All I could do was unearth a stone, take whatever information it had, try to put it together into some half-assed guess. Maybe hope I'd take an intuitive leap to where the next buried stone might lie.

"Benjamin was a senior, I think," Kirschke said. "Extremely bright guy, from what I understand. Already working for his father in one of his companies. Some kind of tech genius, maybe."

He paused.

"This is where I could mislead you," he said. "I know that Angela and Benjamin were together at the time. I know the relationship was special, because however it broke, it led her away from Harvard. I know that she didn't or couldn't talk about it. In fact, I only know Benjamin Whelan because of things I gathered from her, over the year. She never spoke directly of him. But anything else I could tell you would be suppositions. And," his finger tapped the book. "I don't want to play that role."

"It's more than I had," I said. I had thought power or politics was behind it. A rich father would be powerful. "You've pointed me in a direction. That's better than nothing."

"Perhaps," Kirschke said, his finger still lightly touching the book. "Or maybe I'm pointing you to a place no one should go."

I snorted. "Try not to think too much of it. This isn't some story from a book, doc. You're not some wizard with the only clue I need to point me forward. I'm going to find her, with or without your help. Where I'm going, it's all on me."

I thought about what I had said, and how it might sound. "Although, I don't want to sound like I don't appreciate your help."

Kirschke smiled a little smile, something that came from a memory or a thought he had. "You think life isn't a story?"

"Professor," I said. "This is life. Life doesn't have fairy tale endings. It has choices and consequences. Good and bad. These people, whoever they are, they made a choice. And I'm their consequence."

Kirschke nodded, slowly. "Perhaps."

"No uncertainty to it," I said. If there was one thing I knew, it was that these people would regret me falling into their lives. "Trust me on that."

His nod took on a little more speed. As if he had been lost along a certain train of thought, and now the train approached its destination.

Kirschke suddenly smiled. "You say life isn't a story."

"It's not," I said.

"Let me ask you," he said. "Why not let the police handle this?"

"What do you mean?" I asked.

"I mean, the police," he said. "They're trained for this. It's what they do. Find people who break the law, and bring them to justice. So why are you doing it?"

I frowned. "I told you," I said. "Choices have consequences.

Whoever kidnapped Angela made a choice. They have to face the consequence. I'm that."

Kirschke nodded. "Because you've done this before? Because you have some kind of training? Because you're just some good Samaritan, some Dudley Do-Right?"

I waited a moment, wondering where he was going with all this.

I did have a history to this. I had once served as a soldier. After that, I had been accepted into an elite organization whose sole purpose was to do the right thing. The just thing. To find enemies, foreign and domestic, and eliminate them.

But I couldn't tell him that history. And I wasn't going to go into my time growing up, my parents, my sister, the farm. Baling hay out in the hot sun, the twine cutting into my hands, the smell of fresh-cut grass. Pulling weeds from thousands of organic strawberry plants, because my parents believed in doing the right thing. Hard work. No shortcuts. The ideals I had been raised with.

At a very young age, I think second grade, one of the kids in my school had gotten very sick. I didn't understand at the time, but it had been leukemia. Or the beginnings of it.

He was missing school. I went to the teacher, after class, and volunteered to take his homework home at night, and pick it up in the morning. He lived along my walk home, five miles of country road.

The kid had been excited to see me. I hadn't realized then, the journey he was going to walk. I think his name was Nicholas. Like Santa Claus. And his face was overjoyed, each time I brought his homework home. And happy to see me, when I picked it up in the morning. It got to where I stayed in the afternoons with him, so we could work problems together.

I hadn't seen his face getting thinner. Or how he lost weight. But I noticed, when he couldn't get out of bed anymore. When tubes were stuck in his arms, and when he couldn't raise his head from his pillow.

He still smiled, when I stopped by. We still worked the homework together. We kept up the fiction, maybe because I hadn't known anything could be different. His mother met me with cookies and milk, and let me spend time with her son as much as I could.

And then, one day, Nicholas was gone. It was a lesson I had learned, with all the others instilled in me by my family. I was good at fighting. I was good at other things. But maybe, once upon a time, I had been the best at the dream.

But that had been then. This was now. In this moment, I was the person who could best help Angela. I had all the skills needed, and the determination to carry out the task. To make sure the decision these people made, that day, to make sure they never made it again. It had been precipitous timing, these people choosing that day, that time, that place, to abduct her.

Because I had been there.

After all of that, there really was only one reason I thought I was the right person for this. Because I could do it. Because I *knew* I would find Angela, faster than the law. I had none of the restrictions they had, and all of the tools and passion for vengeance.

I had the ability to keep people safe. To rescue them, if needed. And ultimately, to punish those responsible. Not many had the ability or the capability to do all three, nor the desire and will to go through with it.

I did.

Kirschke watched me. I had the feeling he had been watching for a while, and that the memory of Nick had revealed something to him. His eyes twinkled with a hidden piece of knowledge.

When I spoke, my voice was low. "Because I'm the kind of consequence these people deserve."

Kirschke nodded, but stayed quiet a moment. As if allowing me to think about what I had said. "But it's not a story," he said.

This, to me, was the difference between people going to school and people living in the real world. People in school could afford to dream about fighting monsters, quests to become better, rescuing fair maidens. People in the real world couldn't. *I* couldn't. Not anymore.

"No," I repeated.

Kirschke wanted to laugh. I saw it in his smile. Not something mean, but the laugh of someone who wanted to share the joy. As if he still knew something I didn't.

I got up to leave. My brain didn't work that way. I wasn't great at understanding the *whys* of things. So I didn't give the professor a chance to laugh, or share whatever other realization he had.

I just left. Waiting for a chuckle to follow me out the door, but not hearing it.

KIRSCHKE HAD BROUGHT UP SOME THOUGHTS, THOUGHTS I didn't like and didn't want to think about. So I brushed them off, walking quickly down the empty hall, my sneakers making tiny squeaking sounds on the floor that echoed loudly. On my right I passed class after class, full of young kids watching the front of their room, and the teacher I couldn't see in each. Most of the kids had laptops on their desks, open. Hopefully typing notes and not surfing Facebook.

I concentrated on that, and not what Kirschke said. I wasn't what Angela needed. I was a person who happened to be there. And I was a person who could do great physical harm to others. A person who could —if forced—kill.

Angela didn't want any of that. She didn't need any of that. She may have been interested in me, but I was sure it was in the way most young women were interested in the bad boys of life. Guys who radiated danger, who rode the edge of being an ass, who thought only of themselves. Guys women would force themselves on, wanting that for themselves, the power of doing something only because you wanted it, regardless of others.

I was something different. I was an ass, because now it was the nicest thing I could be. I radiated danger because I held it tight within me. Because inside was a burning hate and betrayal that would hurt others, if I let it escape.

Charley had seen that. Now she wanted nothing to do with me. If Angela really was interested, even if she had been hurt once, even if she had seen something in me that echoed between us, she would learn the same thing. And get away, as fast as possible.

I shook my head, focused on each step of the stairs as I walked down them. Past a student here or there, maybe leaving for the day, maybe coming in for a class. Maybe a conference. I got to the bottom floor and burst through the big double doors like I was escaping Kirschke and his feelings of lives and stories, knowing the professor knew nothing about me, but fleeing him as if he knew it all.

I took a couple of steps past the door and stood out in the bright light of day, wanting the sun to burn away all those thoughts, of me being a knight rescuing a maiden who needed it. Of there being a possibility of something more in my life, than the burning hate I had in my heart.

I focused on moving forward. I was good at that part. I focused on the next stone, that might lead me to another half-assed guess.

Benjamin Whelan. David Whelan the Third. I had names. According to Kirschke, rich and powerful names. People who could kidnap others, if they had reason. People who would be in the news, if for no other reason than social media demanded that kind of thing today. Stories of who got what toy poodle, or said something about another famous person, or what suit or dress they wore at such-and-such an event.

I left the English building and headed for the library. I had marked it, when I had been searching through the campus earlier. It was close to the campus bookstore. The afternoon air was chilly, but the sun was warm, and I opened my jacket as I strode across the sidewalks.

Thankfully the kids on the lawn outside were gone, with their campaign signs and pamphlets. Maybe their *Bigger and Better Boston* was taking a long lunch break. Or maybe they had found it was big enough, already.

I got to the library, a tall building of dark brick and big windows. I got to the front and walked through a large set of wooden double doors. The doors were thick and heavy when I pulled them open.

Inside a short set of stairs descended onto the first floor, a large area with a help desk in the center and little tables and computer monitors everywhere. Three floors raised above me, each floor full of rows of shelves. Each row was signified at its end by a large letter, which would be the letter the author's last name began with. The shelves were stuffed full of books, all different sizes and colors.

The smell of paper was strong, and unlike the bookstore, this place was quiet. So quiet I could hear the flipping of pages at desks. The whisper of someone's jeans, as they walked in front of me. I got the distinct feeling I was being watched by everyone, like I didn't belong in this world. Like I was reminding them there was a life outside of this. The feeling wasn't quite unsettling, but it was noticeable.

I needed information quickly, and this was where having a computer or phone would have helped me. I would just have to make do. I walked around the tables, all the computers in the library were password protected. So I started asking students if they would look up a name for me for twenty bucks. All of them said no.

I went up to fifty bucks and kept getting the same response. Some of the kids looked at me oddly. It was probably a weird question for kids today. They had all grown up with something I hadn't, little phones always connected, always online. I just kept asking and upping the amount. I would have jumped at fifty bucks back in my day. I would have jumped at twenty, matter of fact. I had mowed lawns for less.

One of the kids *shushed* me, a taller girl with glasses and curly dry hair, the kind that frizzed easily. She looked at me through her glasses, her eyebrows raised, and got ready to shush me again. She had a large book open in front of her, something about the life of animals in Africa. Something with pictures.

I gave her the stare. She didn't back down. Definitely born to be a librarian. I moved a bit further away and kept asking kids at terminals, until finally a student agreed to log on for me.

He was a short, fat kid with black hair and a pimpled face. Contacts, not glasses. He had a thing of eye drops next to the monitor, so maybe he was here for the long haul. Maybe I was interrupting a long day on a research paper. Whatever, I was thankful. I handed over five twenties and let him stand behind me as I started Googling.

"Are you a detective?" he whispered.

"Sure," I said, then looked at what came back after I searched the Whelans. The kid stayed behind me, reading over my shoulder.

A couple of searches brought up an article from the *Boston Herald*. A car crash from years ago. Benjamin Whelan found dead behind the wheel. There was a black and white picture of a nice convertible Porsche leaning against a tree, in a way no car should be leaning, front end sitting against the ground, rear wheels in the air. Top of the car braced against a large maple tree, the trunk cracked.

No toxicology report in the paper and no mention of whether or not Benjamin had been drinking, but it was a nightmare of a crash, and there's rarely a sober person who aims his car at a tree. I looked for the byline and found Sara Knox as the contributor of record, making a note of it. Then I searched on.

Not much else on the crash. The car went out of control after skidding on a wet road. The kid had been heading back to college from a weekend up in New York. Survived by his father, David Whelan III, of Whelan Enterprises. I brought up a picture of him, he was an older man, thin face, with wispy white hair and a darker salt-and-pepper mustache.

There was no mention of Angela, or any girlfriend Benjamin might have had with him. There was oddly a mention of his father, how

Whelan Enterprises had just bid on a lot of property at the warehouse district, off the shore. How his father had taken family money and turned his company into a giant of the technology industry.

The kid whistled. "That guy makes some money."

"What do you mean?"

"He's the guy trying to get the next stadium built for the Red Sox," he whispered. I wasn't sure if he was whispering because he felt like he was detecting or if it was because we were in the library. "He tried to buy the team, too."

I realized that's where I had heard Whelan's name. One of the sports anchors had been talking about him yesterday. The guy fronting the proposal for the new baseball stadium. The new place they wanted to move the Green Monster to.

"You a baseball fan?" I asked.

He nodded, vigorously. "Mookie, baby."

I was a little surprised. I thought all kids played video games today. Especially round, heavy kids. Maybe I shouldn't take all things at face value.

"He's doing something now with GPS," the kid said. "Some kind of new automation, like drones or something. He's into all kinds of stuff, but he's mostly tech."

The mention of GPS triggered a certain feel from my past. When you served in the military, it was hard not to hear certain buzzwords and think what application a piece of technology could have, when you were trying to kill others. It was part of the thoughts you had and couldn't get rid of, even long after you left. GPS was one of those words. Tech another.

I pushed the thought aside and typed in *David Whelan the Third* into the search bar. The Red Sox stadium popped up, just like the kid had said. Plenty of other things, too. Construction sites, shipping, banks, high-end real estate. The man was from old money, his family had been in Boston since the Mayflower, it seemed, but he had taken that money and built international businesses.

Whelan had to fight for the stadium deal over the past few years. The last governor had been dead set against it. It didn't matter because the new governor had locked the deal up, had pushed it through the mayor and the city council, citing how beneficial the construction would be for the city. The jobs. The new money. The new guy was really promoting the new stadium, it seemed. There were posters and flyers about it everywhere.

Maybe because it was an election year. That was the thing about politics, money always seemed to win in the end. People could only stay in office so long. I wondered if the old governor had wanted too much money, and come election time Whelan had just pumped money into the opposition. A large campaign contribution or two.

I guessed in the end it didn't matter, because Whelan got the deal he wanted. He was going to make hundreds of millions on this one. Maybe a billion. I searched a bit longer. There was nothing I could bring up, as far as what David Whelan wouldn't like about Angela. Nothing about her and Benjamin Whelan. On a whim, I googled her name.

There was a return. Something from a small paper, just one line. When I clicked on the link it brought up the picture of her in the white dress, singing on stage. The title was cheesy. *Minor-ity Legend Retires Early from the Limelight.*

I cruised through the article. It was just a few paragraphs, from the local paper. Angela had gotten to Harvard on a scholarship. She was just starting her junior year. She had done a number of plays, the paper had listed it, and had noted that she had sold out the house once. She had been in New York one weekend to do a show for the school, then had just quit.

There wasn't much to it. Apparently Angela couldn't be found to comment, or hadn't cared enough to comment. I looked at the date of the article. Went back to the date of Benjamin Whelan's death.

His accident had been a week before.

Aha. There was something there. Nothing that explained a kidnapping. Nothing in the paper that said Angela was even there. But something in my hindbrain told me I needed to follow this down.

Like I said, I wasn't good at piecing things together. I was good at hunting things down. I would follow half-ass guess after half-ass guess, until I got to where I needed to be.

I looked at the Boston Herald paper again. Got its main line from the site.

"Hey guy," the kid said. "You've been silent an awful long time. You still detecting?"

I nodded and got up. "Thanks for your time," I said, palming him another twenty.

"Sure man," he said. "Be happy to do it again, for that kind of cash."

At least some youth today still believed in the power of the dollar.

There was a set of pay phones outside the library. They looked like they hadn't seen a lot of use lately. I wondered when I would see the last one, or if I was standing in front of them right now. I picked up the handset and heard a dial tone. The line worked. I plugged in some change and dialed the Boston Herald number from their site.

A voice recording told me a few different options, none of which I liked. I navigated the phone menu by trial and error, until I was able to get an actual person.

"Boston Herald front desk," a bored female voice finally answered.

"Can you transfer me to Sara Knox's desk?" I asked.

"This is in relation to?" The voice returned, barely interested.

"She gave me her card," I said. "But I lost it. She wants some information I have."

"Concerning?"

"If I told you that, you'd be Sara then, right?" I answered. I didn't like the voice, but I wasn't sure I wanted to go back to the phone tree. It was a near thing, though.

There was a click on the line and then the phone started ringing again. After the third ring another female voice picked up, this voice a little deeper and huskier, and sounding a lot more, well, alive.

"Sara Knox's desk," the voice said.

"Am I speaking with Ms. Knox?" I asked.

"You are," she answered. "What is this concerning?"

"I'd like to ask you a few questions concerning a story you did a while back," I said. "On Benjamin Whelan."

"You mean the crash," Sara said. Her voice immediately betraying an intensity. An urgency which told me that Sara knew Angela had been abducted, that Sara was following the story, and that she had more information about Angela and Benjamin. Maybe things she couldn't publish, either because they hadn't been verified enough, or because of the threat of a lawsuit. But things, either way, that would help me.

"I do," I said.

"You have information then," she said.

"Maybe," I said. The day had gotten a late start, thanks to Baber, and it was around two o'clock in the afternoon now. "How about a late lunch?"

"Sure," she said. "You like a good burger?"

Good, bad, the food wouldn't matter. It was the info I needed. "Whatever," I said.

"Meet me at Hoopers in fifteen," she said. "I'll be in a booth, back wall. Wearing a white top, blue jeans, and a Patriots cap. You won't miss me."

"I'll be there," I hung the phone up and opened the phone book. It was old and weathered, like it hadn't been changed out at the beginning of the year. I guessed I was lucky it was there at all.

I found Hoopers and grabbed the address, then headed to the parking lot. As I walked I passed the same number of kids on campus as I had earlier, when I first had been looking for Student Registration. Like the college was some world where everything stayed the same, the same kids walking the same paths to the same classes at the same times, each and every day. A routine all their own. For a moment I was envious of it, of the constancy, the normalcy in that life.

Then I kept walking. Got in the car and pulled out of the parking lot. I tried to leave that feeling behind. The desire for comfort, for sameness. For what kept all the dark feelings at bay.

Hoopers turned out to be a small college basketball hangout. The guy who owned the bar apparently had played professional once upon a time. Maybe for the Celtics, with all the green gear on the walls. Jerseys, headbands, shorts. Banners of championships.

Other than that Hoopers was a standard pub place, dark woods, flat screen televisions hanging from over the bar, and heavy wooden chairs fitted around thick wooden tables, all scratched from long use. The place had a thick smell of fried potatoes and hot grease.

The pub was fairly empty, that time of day. A few people at the bar. Sara was exactly where she said she'd be, easy to find in a booth along the back wall. As soon as our eyes met she waved me over.

Sara was athletic, but also a little on the heavy side, with big breasts and hips, and a waist smaller than both. Her white top stretched pretty broadly across her chest, and snugged up below. Her Patriots hat was an old one, blue and white with the minuteman logo on the front. Thick black hair pulled back through the back of her cap. She had a big glass of beer in front of her, maybe three-quarters full with something dark. Maybe Guinness. The glass still was frosty with ice, like someone had just pulled it from the freezer.

I nodded and slid into the booth across from her. She tilted her beer towards me. I shook my head.

"So," she said. "Who are you looking for information on? Benjamin Whelan? Or his father?"

"Yes," I told her.

She smiled. "Both might cost you two lunches."

"As long as we eat them both today," I said. "I'm in a rush."

"Tell me, then," she said.

"Tell you what?"

"My man," she said, still smiling. "None of this information comes from the goodness of my heart. I know there's a story here. And that's kind of what I deal in. So give me."

I looked at her. I wondered what she had. I knew I didn't have much. It wasn't like I was dealing in nuclear bombs, diplomatic assassinations, or national secrets. I was a little afraid what I had wouldn't be enough to get anything in return.

An older fellow came up to take our orders. He wore a white apron, folded in half and tied around his waist. The apron was spotted with grease. He set down a couple of waters, asked if I wanted a beer. When I said no he went right on to taking our orders. Like he had done this many times with Sara, already.

I looked around on the table, there was no menu there, but there was a list of burgers and side orders on a large chalkboard above the bar. Everything that wasn't grilled was fried.

"Get the Trifecta," Sara told me, before ordering it herself. With extra cream cheese.

I didn't know that I wanted that, but in the end it didn't matter. I nodded to the waiter for the same. The chalkboard had the burger, the Trifecta. Three patties, a pile of jalapenos, onions, strawberry jam and cream cheese. I wondered why in the world would I put extra cream cheese on that. Or even eat it at all.

"It's not that bad," Sara grinned, watching my face.

"Sure," I said. It wouldn't matter, I would eat it to give my body something to go on. "Probably an acquired taste, right?"

"So," Sara said. "You decided yet?"

"I'll be honest," I said. "I'm not sure I have anything that would really interest you."

She shook her head. "Come on, man," she said. "We both know you're the guy that chased Angela Martinez when that truck took her.

It's all over the news. And now you're asking about Whelan. There's something there. You know it. I know it."

"I'm telling you I don't have much," I said. "What I do have is that someone took Angela for some reason. I don't know who or why. I'm hoping that finding out more about her background will give me one or the other."

After saying all that I took a breath. I hadn't said that much in a long time.

"So, what?" Sara said. "How do you know her?"

"I don't," I said. "I just met her, yesterday."

She frowned, sipped her beer. Her hand left little fingerprint patterns in the ice. "Then why go to all this trouble? Why's it a problem of yours?"

I shrugged. I didn't even know why I wanted to do it. Other than I had liked Angela, meeting her. I had felt something in common with her, something shared across our pasts. Like soldiers could feel a common bond between them, even if they had served in different wars. There was... a commonality there.

And if I was being honest, she had made me feel something other than anger. Than hate. Than rage, disinterest, routine. She had cracked open a door, and even though I was afraid to open it any wider, I still hovered outside. Hand on the knob.

I think Sara saw some of that, in my face. "Wow," she said. "Wow."

"What?" I asked.

"Tell you what," she said. "I'll tell you what I know. More than just what I know. I'll even tell you what I guess. If you'll keep me updated."

"Updated?" It was my turn to frown. I sipped some of the water. And frowned harder. There was a reason Sara had ordered the beer.

"Yeah," she said. "You're going after her, right?"

"I am," I said. Choices have consequences.

"Then I want a front-row seat," she said. "I want all the details, everything you find and do. Promise me that, and you'll get everything I got."

My hand drifted to the water again. I stopped it. I looked at Sara, who waited patiently. She wanted whatever story she could get. The thing was, there was no way I could tell her everything I was going to do. Especially when the consequences came calling.

Charley came to mind. How she had been afraid of me, of what I might do. Of the untapped anger she sensed in me. Part of me shook inside, in fear, scared of who I had become.

I had once been a boy on a farm. With parents who loved him. A high school girlfriend, whose eyes sparked up when she saw me come off the football field after practice. Now I was this guy, this thing, whose mere presence held a darkness that kept others at bay. Who was capable of things that made others run.

"The thing is," I said, in a rough voice. "Some of the things I might do, they aren't things people should know."

Sara's eyes lit up. They were an odd shade of blue, bright now with interest. Eyes like Angela's had been. Eyes like Charley's until she had seen me torture a guy.

"Then we need to set up some trust between us," she said. "I've got to trust that you'll give me the information you can, and you have to trust me to keep some things quiet, that you need."

I nodded. Trust for me was a hard thing now. I teetered on the edge of accepting the deal, but something held me back. Something that had begun in a small office, a few years back, and half a world away.

I wondered if I could stop now. Could I just go back to the routine? To the wait. To the payment I justly deserved. Could I do that?

In a way it would be easy. I could forget about all of this. Take the helmet out of the trunk and just leave it on the street. Throw the book away. Tomorrow would be scrambled eggs and a museum.

My mind warred on that edge, for a moment, for an hour, I couldn't say. I knew, as much as I knew anything in my life now, that if I gave up now I would be giving up a part of myself for good. The part that used to be the greater me, but was dying a slow, methodical death. If I turned away from Angela, and back to the routine, I would be plunging the final knife into that me.

My hand had clenched into a fist. I unclenched it.

Sara watched all of this, silent. Quiet. But excited. As if she knew which direction I was teetering.

"You give me what you got," I said. My voice hoarse, low. "I'll give you what I can."

She nodded once. Slowly. As if realizing the gravity of the acceptance. "You'll find me good at my word. I promise, nothing published you don't want published. But I want the story. All of it."

I nodded back. The muscles in my neck tight. "What I can," I repeated.

"Okay," she said. "Fair enough."

There was nothing fair about it. I was giving up part of myself to someone who could publish it to anyone and everyone who could read it. I wouldn't lie to her though, I would tell her what I could. Maybe in that way I could control some of what I did. Maybe in that way I could use the anger inside for good. If it came out, uncontrolled, maybe knowing that I was recording it all, maybe telling Sara would help me reign that anger back in.

I could only hope.

I hadn't had great success at it so far.

The routine had been all. But I was way off it now. In uncharted waters. Sailing a ship deep over the edge of my flat world, plunging over the edge, with no idea what waited below.

TWENTY

The old man had come back then, sliding two heavy wooden platters in front of us, holding the trifecta and fries. The platters were a dark wood that had seen a lot of use, with little scratches all over them. There was a dark green plate on each platter holding our burgers, each one was tall enough that they leaned a bit, the side revealing layers of meat and cream cheese, jalapenos and jam. Nestled to the burgers were thick, wedge-cut fries, fried to a nice crispy golden brown, and a wide black plastic cup full of ketchup.

The burgers smelled good, like hamburgers on a grill should smell. Charcoaled meat, sizzled well over flame. I took a breath and caught the heat of the peppers, the greasy smell of fried potatoes, and the faint sweet scent of strawberries.

Sara dug right into hers, wiping her mouth after every bite with a well-practiced motion. It was a messy burger. Thick slabs of cream cheese had been tucked between the patties, the cheese peppered with grilled jalapenos, and when you picked up the burger everything dribbled out the side—juice and jam and cheese altogether in a stream.

I tried it, and found the burger better than I thought it would be. Still not what I would order, but the sweetness of the jam and the cool taste of the cream cheese balanced the heat of the jalapenos nicely, and the meat was excellent.

We ate in silence. Sara packed it in, and didn't start on her fries until her burger was completely gone. After finishing the last bite, she wiped her mouth and picked up a potato wedge. She dunked that in a small cup of ketchup on her plate, and then popped it into her mouth, chewing quickly and swallowing.

I wasn't sure where she put it all. I had enough of the sweet, the heat, the cheese, it mixed all together in the mouth and though it tasted okay, the meat was good enough to be on its own. Sometimes you just wanted a burger.

"I trust you enough," Sara said. "You got a feel to you, you know. Kind of a rusty-knight Travis McGee thing going on."

"I'm not any kind of knight," I said. Maybe a bit too quickly, thinking of things like trust and betrayal and the smell of grass early in the morning on a football field, and the scent of urine when the guy in the kitchen had pissed himself.

My conversation with Kirschke hadn't been that long ago, and I mocked it. My life wasn't a story. I wasn't holding a battered shield, with a rust-colored cross etched across its surface. I wasn't that guy, at least anymore. I was the guy who did the battering.

"But you did something, right?" Sara asked. Her eyes narrowed. "You got that kind of feel. The military look."

Angela had said the same thing. *You have that look.* Why had it mattered to her what I looked like? What had sparked her interest in me? Likely that I was dangerous. That I was a batterer, a killer, hiding in the clothes of a man staring uselessly out a window.

I swallowed, only I hadn't put any food in my mouth. It was a hard swallow, like I was forcing down some hard, unrecognized truth, cold and ugly and trying to work its way back up. The force of it knotted, deep in my throat.

"What does it matter what I look like?" I said, roughly.

"You were in the military?" she said. "Some kind of soldier? A seal?"

"Whatever I was, just leave it," I told her.

"You know I can find out," she said, grinning. Maybe teasing me. Maybe not.

I shook my head. "Leave it." My voice like a growl.

"Fine, fine." Sara threw up her hands, a gesture like throwing up a white flag. "Whatever, I'll leave you alone. Just stop being so touchy."

"I'm not touchy," I said. Looking at the plate, and the mess of the burger left on it. I wasn't sure how Sara hadn't gotten anything on her shirt. I was halfway into mine, and wanted another napkin. Or ten napkins. Or a towel.

Sara rolled her eyes. "Sure you're not."

I wanted to change the subject. To get to what I came here for. I pushed my platter aside. "So tell me about the crash."

"Sure," she said, finishing up her fries. Knowing I was changing the subject. She ate one and sipped her Guinness, setting the beer down with a solid thunk on the table. The ice was gone, leaving little drips of condensation that trailed down the glass.

"There are things you can publish, and things you can't," she said. "Things you can say, and things you have to be absolutely sure of, before putting it out there for anyone to see. Before putting it in print."

"Right," I said. "You need to publish the truth."

She shook her head. "Not truth so much, as prove. You have to prove something, in order to publish."

"Aren't they the same thing?" I asked.

I didn't think you couldn't prove something that wasn't true. Though media today seemed to think little of either concept. People with posts and Tweets and Instagrams put out whatever they wanted. If enough people followed that person, that account, those posts would just be true to them. At least socially. It's why I kept away from all that. Just because a lot of people believed something, never made it true.

"Not for me," Sara said. "If *truth* and *prove* were the same thing, you could use one word for the other, right?" She reached down and grabbed another wedge, stirring it in the ketchup cup. "Proving things to me is like climbing a set of stairs. Each time you find a bit of proof, you get to take another step up. And waiting for you at the top of the climb, that's the real truth."

Said like that, I could understand it. Truth was what was left after you peeled away all the layers hiding it. After paring away the hard skin it hid behind. It made a kind of sense.

"Besides," she said, "you can print the truth, and still get sued. But if you print something you can prove, well, that lawsuit won't go anywhere."

It made a kind of sense, in the world today. Though I wasn't worried about what I could prove. I wanted the truth, and I didn't care about proving it. I just wanted to *know* it. Knowing would lead to acting. "Then tell me what step you're on now."

"About the crash?" she said.

"You have something better?"

She shrugged. As if there was plenty she could guess at. "On the surface, it was a wreck like any other," she said. "Dangerous, winding road. Steep incline. The crown of the road is inverted, meaning that the centrifugal force pushed the car outside faster, and easier, than a road that's properly banked."

I remembered the picture. It had been a black and white screenshot, a light colored Porsche Boxster face on into a tree. The trunk of the tree had made it a few feet into the center of the hood of the Boxster, and the car was leaning forward against the tree, as if its speed had lifted the rear of the car when the front of it had its final impact, and the force of it had tipped the car over to lean against the trunk.

The front bumper of the Porsche had looked like a V, when they had taken pictures of the car sitting back on the ground. Where there was metal, the metal had folded and wrinkled and lifted at the edges. Any plastic pieces looked like they had cracked or exploded. It had been a convertible, and the top had been down, the windshield shattered where the tree had slammed into it.

"What did you find below the surface?" I asked.

"A few odd things," Sara said. Ticking the points off with the finger of her free hand. The other still holding the potato wedge. "Benjamin had just bought the Porsche, the day before. Cash. When he already had one, a black Cayman he'd driven for years."

"Rich people have two cars," I said. Usually they had a lot more. All kinds of toys, things to play around with, elegant cars for daily drives, fun cars for weekend trips. Probably just wanted something new. "And plenty of cash."

She held out her free hand, like she was getting to more. Her other still pinched the wedge between two fingers. "The story was he was headed back home after a trip to New York, but that road he was on wasn't headed back to Boston."

"Maybe he was taking the scenic route," I said. Wondering now if I was going to listen to some conspiracy theory that would lead me nowhere.

Sara smiled, though. "So by scenic route, you mean northwest then, right?"

I frowned. "He was headed out of New York?"

"Like, towards Canada." Sara nodded. "Pretty scenic, right?"

I didn't know. If Angela had been with him, maybe it would have been. Maybe they were going to Niagara Falls, to spend a romantic weekend alone. Seemed like something a rich person might do, on the spur of the moment.

She finally plopped the wedge in her mouth, lost a little in either thought or memory. Thought of what she was trying to uncover, maybe. Or maybe it was just the memory of all the digging she had done.

"His father have anything to say?" I asked.

Sara shook her head, swallowing. "Nope. David Whelan the Third remained silent. The standard press release, *thanks for all the well wishes, please leave the family to grieve*, etc..."

"Is there a mother?" I asked.

She shook her head again. "Mother died when Benjamin was young. David Whelan never remarried. Hasn't really dated, either, since."

Sara corrected herself. "At least, he hasn't dated someone out in the public limelight."

"Since then he's been reclusive," she said. "But expanding, as far as business. There's talk about going into politics, as well."

"Is that something he could do?"

"He has the money for it," she said.

"Huh," I said. What Sara had told me maybe was a little odd, but nothing unexplainable. Just little coincidences. The information she was giving me was a poor trade for what I might give her, so far. "I'm not sure where that helps me."

"Slow your roll," Sara said. "I'm getting to it."

She pulled a large bag from where it had been hiding in the booth next to her. A large purse or maybe a laptop bag, with Patriots colors all over it. Blue and white and red. She dug inside, pulled out a folded piece of paper, and handed it over to me.

The paper felt warm, like it was fresh from a copying machine. Maybe it was, or maybe Sara's laptop was on. Maybe it was just my imagination, thinking it had grabbed some piece of the truth, hot off the press.

I opened it and found a police report. Dated a few years back. Whelan's accident. The top of the report had computer-generated images of two cars, each image in a separate block, as if a person was looking down on two vehicles, one behind the next. Two places a police officer would scribble and color, according to what car was damaged, and where.

Each block of car was labeled in standard font: Damaged Car No. 1, and Damaged Car No. 2.

Damaged Car No. 2 had been crossed out with a pen. There was a note hand-written to the side, saying the accident had involved just one vehicle.

Damaged Car No. 1 was all marked up. Dark solid lines heavily colored the image, all along the front, as if someone had taken a black pen and traced little short lines along the car, over and over. Like people did with a pen and a notepad, scribbling over and over.

The lines were everywhere. The car image looked half colored in with heavy hand-drawn lines scrawled across the paper. There was even a hand-drawn V behind the front bumper. The wreck had been something.

There was a grid of blocks, a section that looked like graph paper, below the Damaged Car blocks. The road was drawn on the graph, a single lane of traffic heading in both lanes, separated by double-lines in the middle. A quick sketch by an officer of the scene of the accident. The road was like one big curve, with a hand-drawn car drawn heading in the opposite direction that was labeled *Witness Feidena.*

There were little marks made, tiny black arrows, showing where the Boxster had left the road. One mark on the road itself, close to the shoulder. Maybe where Benjamin had tried to stop, just not in time. There were guardrails drawn there, representing thick metal things, a section colored in where the Porsche had flipped over the rail and headed down the hill.

There were also some words written alongside the road, right before the curve, noting the inverted crown of the curve. The slope of the road was also listed, and the length of the descent before the curve. One mile of downward slope, that right before the curve was a sharp thirty degrees.

Something in the image tingled my brain. My intuition, telling me I wasn't seeing something. Or that I should be seeing something there, that wasn't.

Sara watched me. Her eyes twinkled with knowledge. She knew what I wasn't seeing. She was just waiting to see if I got it.

I went back to the report. Below the graph section there were twenty lines, where the officer wrote down what he had found at the accident. Just the first page of what I imagined was a lengthy description, after everything was said and done. I ignored the tingling in my brain, it would tell me when it was ready too, and read on.

The police officer responding was a car buff. I could tell by the way the damage was described, some of the words he used when talking about the Porsche. Maybe I would get lucky, and the officer would describe what my intuition was telling me I was missing.

His words spoke of things like trim levels, and how the Boxster was the newer GTS. That the car had custom white bucket seats with a thick black stripe down the center and Z-speed rated racing tires. That the tires had special ceramic brake calipers, each painted black with the word *PORSCHE* inscribed on them.

Sara ate, not talking, quiet except for the munching of her fries. A little scratch of the ketchup cup against the platter. A little sound, like she hummed a little, when she ate.

Everything about that car screamed that it was built to race. To ride with the top down, hair blowing in the wind. That image tugged at me, and I remembered when I had first seen Angela on her bike. Also white. Something built to race. Something to ride the wind on, hair streaming behind her.

I got the feeling Benjamin had bought the car for Angela.

It was hard to believe something built that way would crash in the way it had. Porsches handled the road well. It was built for hugging curves, taking them tight, coming out of it with the hammer down and accelerating. Even a bend with an inverted curve, on a bad slope.

Then it hit me.

"The skid mark," I said.

Sara grinned and nodded, popping another fry in her mouth.

I checked the graph paper again. And I was right. There weren't any brake marks drawn on the road, like an officer would do in any report. Nothing indicating the Porsche had hit the brakes before it wildly caromed down the road, until it flipped over the barrier and tumbled down the hill.

It had been the calipers. The officer had specifically mentioned them. Reading on, I saw that he had made note of not seeing any signs of the brakes being engaged before the Porsche had hit the guardrail.

One sharp skid mark found at the site of exit from the road, the report read. *Many older brake marks on the road. Nothing fresh. Caliper on the front left tire looked okay. The front right was too damaged to see. It appears as if the driver was going too fast, and hit the brakes hard. Only one brake responded, possibly swinging the car into the guardrail.*

The officer went on with more detail of the wreck. There was a lot of sharp metal around, things twisted and torn off along the undercarriage. I read through it all, but found nothing of interest.

Benjamin Whelan was found dead at the scene. Whether or not he had been alive before the car had finally stopped rolling could only be guessed, because the trunk of the tree had finished him off. His blood was all over the car. Sprayed over the dash and both seats. Splattered over the windshield. All the airbags had deployed, along the driver and passenger's side, but they could only do so much.

"Passenger's side?" I mused, aloud. As far as I knew, airbags only deployed in a seat that a person was sitting in. It's why I got frustrated sometimes, when I tossed my gym bag in the passenger seat and the little light came on telling me my gym bag didn't have its seat belt on, the little alarm beeping *seat-belt seat-belt seat-belt,* over and over, until I finally pushed the bag onto the floor.

"Someone was in the car with him," I said, looking at Sara. "Angela?"

"That's my guess," she said. "But she was never found at the site."

"Tossed out?" I said, looking to see if the officer mentioned anything about the seatbelt on that side. Not finding a comment on the sheet. I waved the paper at Sara, it made a fluttering sound. "Is there more?"

"That's what I got," she said. "Funny enough, the case was closed. I've tried all my contacts, and no one can find anything else."

"No investigation?" I said.

"Nope," Sara said. "David Whelan didn't press for an investigation, charges, anything. Just put out the press release and that was it."

"And you think she was there," I said.

Sara nodded.

"But you can't prove it," I said.

"They were dating at the time," she said. "Angela was in New York, performing for the school."

I knew there was more though. I had only known her for the course of the meal, but you could tell she liked to hold something back, to wait and see if the person she was talking to would guess. Maybe even figure it out. She liked the surprise.

I just waited.

"Angela was supposed to perform the next night," Sara finally said. "She never showed."

So nothing she could prove, but a hard enough truth for someone like me.

"She also never went back to Harvard," Sara said. "In fact, she kind of disappeared, until now."

If she was in that wreck, there was no way she could have gotten out of it without some kind of injury. I would be surprised if she hadn't broken bones. I scanned the report again, there was no mention of finding a girl. She could have been thrown out, the Porsche did have its top down, but still, it would have been a miracle for her to come out of that crash alive. It would have been beyond miraculous for her to walk away.

"Did you check the hospitals?" I asked.

Sara gave me a look that said of course she did. "There are more Jane Doe's checked in over a weekend than you would think." She shrugged. "In the end, it was up in New York, and I was here."

I could tell it ate at her a bit. That she had known there was a story there, and had ignored her gut instinct to follow it.

"And then," Sara said, "it went away."

"Until now," I said.

"Until now," she agreed, frowning in a weird way, with just one eyebrow lowered, the lips on that side of her mouth twisting.

The circumstances in the report said Benjamin Whelan had been killed. The circumstantial evidence told me that Angela had been there. And then she disappeared. And now two groups of people were after her, something she knew, or something she had.

Politics. Money. Power. Always deadly bedfellows. Had David Whelan been into something, something his son had paid the price for? The kid at the school said he was into all kinds of automation, other things. GPS stuff. Something about GPS and automation made me think military. But nothing came to mind, other than the thought.

To be frank, I just didn't know enough. But I knew enough to move to the next step. David Whelan.

"It's a shame, really," Sara said. "Word was Benjamin was kind of a genius. Father must have been really proud."

I went to give Sara back the police report.

"Keep it," she said.

"I don't need it," I said, holding it out. I would remember everything there.

Her eyebrows raised, but she took it from me.

"Can you find the officer?" I asked. "The one who found the car?"

"Sure," she said. "Take a little bit."

"The faster the better," I said. Whatever was going on wouldn't go on forever. There would be a time when it would all come to a head. A time soon. I had to find Angela before that happened.

"What's your number?" she asked.

"I don't have a phone," I said. It wasn't a lie, not really. I didn't have the kind of phone most people had, where they walked around everywhere, staring at a screen.

"How am I supposed to contact you?" she said.

"I'll call you," I said.

She shook her head, maybe wondering about a guy who walked around without a phone in today's world. I could have told her it was freeing, that it was nice to exist without that kind of tether, something tying you to the world no matter where you went, but that part would have been a lie.

The old man came back then. I grabbed the check, handing over enough cash to cover everything with a tip, waving off his motion to get change. I told Sara I'd call first thing in the morning, then left.

Two years ago, Angela had been in an accident that had changed her life.

Two years ago, I had been in one that had changed mine.

Kirschke would have loved to hear that.

TWENTY-ONE

I walked out of Hoopers to rush hour. Lucky me. The pub was downtown, and it was the time of day where commuters were heading home. Boston's mass transit was unreliable at best, broke down normally, and most people drove because they liked having a job. Or, at least, they liked having something that paid them money so they, in turn, could pay other people money for things like cars, homes, college funds, therapist sessions, replacing the water heater, new braces for their kids, alimony...

Ah, the great American dream.

Boston also had been around a while. The streets from two hundred years ago wouldn't fit the same traffic that was around now. There were no city planners looking at how to move six or seven hundred thousand people into and out of an area. Roads joined at odd angles, merged in unusual ways, split when you least expected them. Even with hundreds of years of planners and builders and new construction trying to fix what had first been laid out. So there were always accidents, and if by some miracle there wasn't an accident there were always the drivers that cut across lanes, bobbing and weaving in traffic, trying to get ahead by just one more car. Then another.

It took me two hours to get home. The whole time I fought a sense of urgency. My fingers tapped the wheel. I turned on the radio, something I hadn't done in the whole time I had the car, looking for a rock station with music that would echo the driving beat inside my chest. Something that would maybe mask the constant blares of horns, other drivers letting out their frustration.

There were long periods of dead stops. Then I took deep breaths and tried not to get out of my car, especially one time, when I wanted to walk two cars up and ask that driver to turn off the turn signal she had left on thirty minutes previous. I mean, you can't turn left into a concrete barrier, though after thirty minutes I wanted her to try.

The sun went down in front of me. The glare spread through the windshield and burned into my eyes. Flipping the visor down worked for a bit, but the sun just sank lower. I ended up squinting hard, enough to give me a small headache. I didn't own any sunglasses. Part of me wanted to get Angela's helmet out of the trunk and try that on. At least it had a tinted visor.

By the time I neared my neighborhood it was dark out. The busy kind of dark, where cars still zipped up and down lanes, people still getting home. Plenty of people on the sidewalks, a blended mix of people in suits and jeans and beggars and everything in-between.

Years ago neighborhoods had been different. Quieter. Cleaner. Now there was so much traffic on the sidewalks no one took the time to clean them. Styrofoam cups, protein bar wrappers, cigarettes all littered the streets. Storefronts always needed a good wash.

I wasn't that hungry, the Trifecta had been filling, if it hadn't been what I wanted. But I had just eaten a part of it, and skipped most of the wedges. And a part of me craved Vietnamese.

It was funny. Vietnamese was yesterday's dinner. Yesterday's routine. I had missed it, though. And now I wondered if I wanted the Vietnamese because I wanted the Vietnamese, if my body was trying to get back to yesterday's routine, or if in some way my mind recognized that I was slipping over the edge a bit, that I needed to find a way to relax, inside.

Maybe it was I just liked Vietnamese. But my thoughts and cravings were never thoughts and cravings, I always needed to look behind them, to make sure they weren't steering me in a direction where the anger could take me. Like I had, back in the kitchen, with that guy, and Charley.

I snorted, jerking the car to a stop as some guy in front of me put his car in reverse, trying to work his way into a spot so small even one of those tiny electric cars couldn't fit in it. Maybe all of this inside me was just the traffic. Two hours in this would push anyone over the edge, much less someone with my... past. Background. Hate and Rage.

Whatever it was and whatever I was thinking, I pushed it all away. Those thoughts would keep until tonight. When I closed my eyes and the nightmare came.

Until then, Vietnamese sounded good. Hell, I would get it. Fuck the routine. Parking was hell in front of my building, so I worked my way down the streets towards the Vietnamese place. When I found a spot, I parked there, figuring it was close enough to the restaurant I could circle around and get some Vietnamese, then head home.

I walked quickly. The sidewalks were crowded, but most people avoided me. It made for a quick walk to the Vietnamese place I was thinking of, a tiny restaurant with a red banner across its top, white letters most people could read painted across it.

I did like the food here. I usually got a bowl of Pho and a Banh Mi. Everyone said Pho was a complicated dish, but to me it tasted just like soup. Hot soup, good soup, but still soup. A nice warm thing to have on a chill night at the end of fall. The Banh Mi was tasty and sweet and spicy, everything the Trifecta wanted to be when it grew up.

I never had to order the food when I walked in. There was a young Asian girl, thin with long black hair, that always worked the register. She always recognized me and would have my order ready almost by the time I got to the counter.

There was something to be said for routines, they made things faster in their efficiency. I paid her, thanked her and took my order. The bowl of soup and sandwich were warm, even inside the paper bag. The young girl smiled at me with a genuine smile, open and friendly, even though her two front teeth were crooked. She always smiled, and I thought she was one of the rare people who couldn't sense me the way most did. Or maybe she just ignored the *stay away* vibe I usually put out.

I headed to my apartment, carrying the warm bag of food, wondering about people who ignored that part of me. Or maybe saw past it. Like Angela. My throat tightened, when I thought about earlier, about wondering if Angela had been attracted to me precisely for the same reason others stayed away. Because I was dangerous. Because there was something in me broken, and that part could never be fixed, it only could be eased by the most boring of routines, or in quick, violent episodes. Like kicking a car. Or stabbing a guy in the leg, and making him wet himself.

I was so deep in thought that when I neared my building I didn't see the guy waiting for me until I was almost on him. I noticed him only out of the corner of my eye, and it was less of a notice and more of some predator-prey intuition that warned me to *look*.

And it wasn't who he was that caught my attention, or how he dressed, but more how he stood. Relaxed but ready. The stance of a professional, waiting for action. High and tight haircut. Jeans, white button-up shirt, tucked in. A thin gray peacoat, waist-length, on against the chill. He leaned against a black metal lamppost, directly in front of the stairs leading into my building. Like he was waiting for a girl.

The man was trying to blend in, but those of us who know, know.

I didn't see a shoulder rig. There was a good chance the back of the peacoat covered a gun, tucked into the back of his jeans. Something he would do when he wanted to have it with him, but wasn't sure he needed it. I was a few steps away. I slowed down and looked around. Across the street was a nice Lexus sedan, black with tinted windows. The driver's window was down, and a second person sat in the car, looking over my apartment with the same casual disinterest. Same high and tight haircut.

There wasn't a great chance that these guys were here for anyone but me. The guy certainly wasn't waiting for a girl, especially not with his driver. The video was everywhere, and although no one would find out who I really was, or had been, it wouldn't be hard to find out where I lived, now.

Especially for someone with resources. Someone with money. Or power.

I didn't have money, or power. But I had a great resource. Myself. And I could learn what I needed to, when I needed it.

I sauntered along to the steps leading up to my building. I turned my back on the guy watching, making sure he caught a glimpse of my face. I set my dinner on the buzzer-box next to the building. Then I took a second, patting down my jeans and jacket, like I had forgotten my keys.

The professional began to tap me on the shoulder. His voice was clipped with a military precision. "Mr. Hamilton?"

I reached back and grabbed his hand. Spun around, trying to pull him around so his back was to me, but the man was experienced enough to know the move and his hips tightened against it. His other hand reached behind him, so I folded the hand I held back at a bad angle, wrenching it.

I noticed athletic tape there, right at the man's wrist. A bit hidden, but where someone might wrap a piece of gauze, as if protecting a particularly bad cut. The stretchy tape wrapped tightly around his skin and disappeared under the sleeve of his jacket.

The man set his jaw to keep from crying out, and stood there.

"If your other hand comes back out with anything but four fingers and a thumb," I said, "I'm going to break this wrist. And then your arm."

I waited for the man to test me. Maybe the tape would hold the break together for him. He looked like the type of guy who came prepared. But he grimaced a grin at me, then pulled his hand out from under his coat. Slowly. Fingers and thumb out, showing me it was empty.

A car door slammed shut. The man I was holding waved his free hand a little above his shoulder, fingers pointed backward to the Lexus, where his partner was getting ready to cross the street to us.

"You shouldn't sneak up on people, friend," I said.

"I'm not here for trouble," the man said. "Just to talk."

"Funny way to show it, going for the gun," I said, holding his wrist tight. People walking by us gave us a wide berth. "Turn around," I told him.

The man did, slowly. Holding his free hand up. I snuck a hand out and pulled out a Beretta semi-automatic. The grip of the gun was warm where it had sat against the man's body. I quickly slid the Beretta inside my jacket, dropping it inside the pocket there, where it hung heavy.

Then I let go of the man and stepped back. The man did the same, placing his back to the car on the sidewalk, an old blue Ford Taurus with a few black scrapes against its door, and a dented quarter panel.

"You want to talk," I said. "Now's the time."

"Not me," he said, working his wrist out. "Who I work for."

"Let's go see him, then," I said.

He shook his head. "We're not doing that."

"Now's the time," I said. "Or we can do it when I figure out who it is, and come see him myself."

"You don't know who it is," the man said.

"Think I can't find that out?" I said. "The longer it takes, the more out-of-place I'm going to be."

"You can certainly try," the man said. His stance was tense, he stood on the balls of his feet. More ready now, than before. Still not good enough though.

Even if he thought he was. Even if he was good. He just wasn't me.

The man's eyes focused on me, taking in every detail. As if he had a certain picture of me in his mind, and now that he saw me in person, he was coloring over the black and white preconceptions in that picture. Changing who he thought I was into someone different.

"Fine," I said. "When?"

His lips smiled a bit, just the corner of his mouth, and the smile never reached his eyes.

"Yo," his partner called out from across the street. One hand behind him, under his jacket.

"We're good," the man shouted.

"So far," I told him.

The man nodded. He was a professional, and professionals did things the right way.

I suffered no preconceptions. Not anymore.

"Tell you what," the man said. "Tomorrow morning, come to an address. Nine o'clock." He recited the address, a place in Beacon Hill. Where rich people lived.

"What's in it for me?" I said.

"You're looking for the girl, right?" the man said. "Maybe we can help each other."

I froze then. The man did too, recognizing the motion. The part of me that diagnosed everything going on around me, that told me when to strike, and where, and how hard, was raging inside. The small part of me, the part Charley had reminded me that I still had, the part my parents had raised, held that anger back. For now.

The few people around us seemed to give the two of us an even larger berth.

"You have her?" I asked. Carefully.

"If I did, would I be here?"

"If you do," I told him. "You'll regret it."

He nodded and held up both hands. "Gun?"

I took a breath. I didn't need one. And if I did, I knew where I could get it. Borrowing someone else's piece always led to trouble. If these people actually could help me, then I wanted to stay on their good side. Or at least make the effort.

I took it out of my jacket. Quickly pulled the clip out of it, ejected the one in the barrel. Tossed the man the gun. But threw the clip across the street, letting it clatter across the pavement.

I know. It wasn't a great effort. It was what it was.

The man grinned a knowing grin. Nodded and backed up, around the Taurus. Keeping me in sight. I watched him until he looked both ways, crossed the street, and got into the Lexus. His partner stared at me the whole time, his gun tucked under the sill of the window, I had no doubt.

Then the Lexus took off, forcing its way through the traffic. I made a note of the plate, and wondered if my dinner would settle any of this down. Or if the routine was so far gone it wasn't going to matter anymore.

CHAPTER
TWENTY-TWO

I grabbed my dinner. The bag was cool, and the bottom was a little wet. I knew the sandwich would be the same. I walked into my building, with its constant smell of Lemon Pledge, and headed up the stairs to my apartment.

I entered the place. It felt as empty as it always did. The lights were off, the furniture dark outlines sitting in the pale illumination coming from the lights on the street. I clicked on the ceiling light and set the bag on the kitchen counter, dithering for a bit, looking at the takeout.

On a normal day I'd set out my single plate, grab my cheap silverware, and sit at the one chair and eat my dinner. It would be warm enough to be good, the soup would still be hot, if I ate it while I ate my sandwich.

Now the sandwich was lukewarm at best, the crisp edges of the bread mushy. The soup colder than soup should be. I could microwave it all, the machine would warm it, but it would be a fake heat. The bread wouldn't be toasty, like it had just been pulled from an oven, the meat wouldn't be seared, fresh off a grill, the soup wouldn't be steaming out, like the Pho had just been ladled out from a bubbling pot.

Instead, everything would burn with an irradiated heat, be irrationally hot. No matter the time set. Bread, meat, Pho, everything would singe or sear or burn, when I pulled it out and tried to eat it. Everything almost sun-like in its heat, as if the microwave had needed one more second from kicking off nuclear fusion and forming its own star inside.

My routine was blown. I still stood there in front of my dinner, both of my hands clenched tight, each of my thumbs rubbing the side of my forefinger, right at the middle knuckle. I took a breath and relaxed. The Vietnamese food might have been a last second Hail Mary pass from the back of my brain, the part of me hoping to keep something in place, something to keep the anger in check.

Like the microwave though, once it was turned on, I just wouldn't be able to control how hot it got. It was a switch, it was on and off, and once I hit the start button, I would have to understand how things came out were just how things were going to come out.

Once I flipped that switch, that's just the way it would be.

I ate the food cold. The Pho tasted less like hot soup and more like bad ramen. Cold, gloopy noodles. Hard thin flabs of meat that had been cooked after the broth had been poured over them, but now were just rubbery. The Banh Mi wasn't any better. At least the bread was okay, cold. It was just a bad sandwich from a bad deli.

I cleaned up after myself and wondered what I would do now. It was early to go to bed. Too early, for me. Tomorrow I would go to the address, and I would go from there. I had to call Sara, and maybe talk to the cop who had found the wrecked Porsche. I thought David Whelan ranked among the names of people I had to see, and thought maybe I'd fit that in.

It would be a busy day. One that hopefully proved fruitful. But not one that I was ready for, at least, not ready to go to sleep for.

I looked over at the television. Then the book on the coffee table, holding the drying towel in both of my hands. Thinking.

The phone rang.

For a moment I didn't understand the sound. The apartment was quiet, the people upstairs hadn't started their nightly clogging tournament, and the street outside had little traffic. So the hard, glaring ringing of tiny metal bells inside the phone broke the silence like a gunshot. And like a gunshot, it was something you never felt, until the echo of the bullet registered in your brain. That was always when you looked down, and found the stain spreading across your chest. The wound, long after the sound.

I looked at the phone. I could almost see it vibrate each time it rang, the plastic handset bouncing in its cradle, the cord trembling in the air. I forced myself over to that side of the kitchen and laid my hand on the receiver, feeling it shake underneath my skin.

Then I picked it up. Placed the handset to my ear. The receiver felt hot there.

"J," she said. The one word being everything and nothing.

I stayed quiet. I couldn't trust myself to speak. My hand tightened hard on the cradle, until I thought the plastic would crack. I wanted to say *I knew you'd call*, but of course I had known that. It's why the phone was there, after all. Then there were a million more things I wanted to say, to demand, to *scream*, but I ended up just standing there, frozen. Phone hard to my face.

"I saw you on the news." she said. As if explaining why she had called.

That was something you said to someone next door. A neighbor. A friend. Maybe a brother or sister, after they called and said they had been interviewed for such-and-such a thing. Not something you called and said after two years apart. After leaving a person to die.

She let out a long breath, not a sigh, something sadder. Longer.

"Don't say anything," she said. And a moment later. "It's probably for the best."

There was a hum in the line, something you only heard over hardline, physical connections. As if all the electricity between each phone, between those two points, had been bound into this vast potential that lay waiting between us.

"I saw you, and my first thought was, there's J. Doing the right thing. Like you always did," she said. Her words started out hesitant, but quickened in their pace, as if once she had started, she needed to get them out now, or never would. "Then I saw your face at the end, all the anger and the rage, and I didn't recognize that person. There was so much hate there, J, and I wondered if that was me..."

I didn't react. My chest was empty. My mind blank. My leg, where I put weight on it, ached out its own cry, like it always did. I wanted to demand Sam tell me where she was. I would take the first flight out. I would settle that score. But I couldn't move. I couldn't breathe. Everything I did was focused on holding the receiver to my ear.

The silence across the line grew. It swelled. The hum of electricity built into a roar. It thundered in my ears. And somewhere behind that roar, there were four tiny, tinny words.

"It's just as well," she said.

Then there was a click. Her side of the line, hanging up, dividing the hum in two. Leaving the roar to remain. Wherever she was, whatever money she had gotten for the virus, however much distance was between us now, none of that would be enough.

I stood there for a long time before hanging the phone back slowly in its cradle, as if someone else moved my arm.

———

Sleep would not come for me tonight. Not even the kind of sleep I normally got. Fitful, with the nightmare. Waking up in a cold sweat. Heart pounding. The monster had shown up before I had even laid down.

The first thing I had to do was settle down the anger. My inside was bursting with it. I think I had hung up the phone carefully, because any other motion would have had me tear the phone off the wall, throw it through another wall. Then I would have torn through the apartment, breaking and throwing what I could, until I was exhausted, or the police came.

Baber would have liked that.

So something in me had carefully hung up the phone. Something that still had a bit of control over what I did. That same thing inside went through what I knew, now.

Samantha had called, which meant she was alive, and somewhere in the world. Easy facts for people to say about anyone, but now I *knew* them about Sam. And knowing them, I could take another step.

From there, the rest of it would unfold.

I would find out who she had betrayed me for. I would find the agency, the country, whatever and whoever it was. I would find them and hunt them all down, until there was nothing an no one left. I didn't care if it was the old Spetsnaz, one of the Alpha Groups in one of the countries around the Ukraine, MI6. I didn't care what group or what country, whatever special intelligence group Sam worked for now. I was going to burn it all down.

That was many steps from now. I was still on step number one. Establishing life. Presence on Earth. No need to look that far down the road. I had built my routine to do exactly the opposite. To stay ready, until that day came.

Somehow, sometime, someway, I stopped standing by the phone. Moved and poured myself a glass of water, straight from the kitchen sink. Drank it, gulping the tepid water down in big, hard swallows.

The water was city water, supposedly indifferent to taste, yet always carrying little hints of chemicals after the swallow, chemicals that supposedly kept it clean and healthy. Hints of fluoride, maybe whiffs of chlorine. People weren't supposed to taste the stuff, but there was an obvious difference between a glass of city water and water fresh from a mountain spring. Easy to tell, once you had it.

People used filtered pitchers now, where they had to purchase a new pricey filter every thirty days, or had some kind of fancy refrigerator with a Filter-5000 inside. I had neither. I really didn't desire to pay money to drink supposedly pure water, nor try to figure out the fourteen steps in replacing a filter the refrigerator seemed to be built around.

Not that I didn't have the time to figure that out. I just didn't want to. I always found chilling it hid a lot of those chemicals, but this was straight from the tap, and I grimaced, but drank it down like I was dehydrated. I wondered what the Romans had done, after the water ran hundreds of miles in the big stone aqueducts. I wondered if they too had found the taste too limey. Or had spat it out, saying there was too much grit in it.

I drank two glasses. Then a third. One hand bracing myself on the counter, letting the water run into the sink, letting the sound of it, the *sssssshhhhhhhh* of the water rushing out of the spout, lull me to some kind of normal place and time. As I did, I looked around my dark apartment. The empty table. The clean counter. The coffee table.

The Faerie Queene.

I found myself on the couch, the book in my lap. The room dark, the tiny reading light on. The same black window in front of me. To the right of the window was the television, its screen off and black. Two portals that reflected nothing back at me.

I opened it to where I had left the story, the night before. Reading on from there. Like last night, figuring out the words initially made the poem hard to get into, but I found the rhythm quicker this time, reading each stanza at the correct pace. My mind saw and interpreted all the *thees* and *thous* and it replaced the misspelled words of yesterday with a similar word of today, and I could only hope that when I exchanged an old word for a newer one that I wasn't losing some hidden meaning in translation.

I lost myself for a bit. After leaving the cave, and all the spawn of Error, the knight and the lady found a place to rest and recuperate. A priest, or a hermit, guided them there, which seemed like a nice thing to do.

And then I saw the priest wasn't who he represented himself to be. He was someone else. Someone who could speak and create multiple truths. Someone who could create and send dreams to others, dreams that shaped what they thought and said and did.

Like the night before, I set the book down for a minute. Goose-bumps ran up and down my arms. The dim light reflected the same dark shadow in the window, me, unshaped, a formless blob that shifted and moved, a bulbous pupa with the larva of some unknown creature inside.

The lady and the knight went to sleep. In separate rooms. Maybe the first time they had been separated, in a long time. I had to read the next part multiple times. The words had a way of confusing me. Maybe I was tired. Maybe, coming down off the anger earlier, emotionally I couldn't connect with it. Maybe it was meant that way.

There were multiple ladies, each a double of the other. There were multiple knights too, copies of the first. And dreams, nightmares sent by the priest, who was not a priest, and who seemed to direct everything like it was a play.

The knight had gone to bed, the priest had tried to set him up with one of the fake ladies, but he had turned her away. The knight seemed to have some instinct that she wasn't right. Wasn't true. So the priest upped his game, sent the knight a dream of his real lady sleeping with another man. Laughing, as if when the knight turned her away, she felt free to do with her body as she wished.

I wasn't sure why the knight believed the dream. He had spent enough time with the lady that he should know her better. In the end, it seemed sad. Like what they had built together, whatever quest they were on, hadn't been strong enough to hold the two together. Part of me wanted them to make it. It hinted, to me, that even though they had left the cave of Error, that some of the spawn still clung to them, twisting their judgments, manipulating their feelings, clouding what the knight knew to be his truth.

The knight's lady woke, and finding her knight gone, continued along her task. Even if she missed him, or didn't understand what had happened. I admired her for that. She had an evil to face, and the lack of support did not deter her. She found the strength to go on.

The words got more and more thick, on the paper. Or my eyes got more tired. I started to drift off, shaking my head and coming back to the story. But it made less and less sense. The two of them continued, facing enemies, encountering more and more lies. Giants, lions, other knights, other ladies. Both the knight and the lady doing their best, on their own, and yet both of them being dragged down by the things around them. Deeper and deeper, the harder they struggled.

I finally decided to go to bed. As tired as I was, I knew I wouldn't really sleep, but it was part of the routine. I knew I couldn't start tomorrow, until I faced the nightmare today. So I walked around, making sure all the windows and doors were shut and locked. Adjusted the thermostat, wanting it colder, knowing it wouldn't help. Cleaned the counters, the table, squared *The Faerie Queene* to the edge of the coffee table. Took a look at the photo there, the prow of the gondola pointed down the canal, as if open waters lay ahead, if all I could do was push off a little harder.

Then I turned off the light, moved to the bedroom and lay down. The sheets were tight to the mattress, pinned beneath the floor, the bed, and my weight. They were slick and cool and gave me the feeling like I was trapped. I lay there in the darkness, tossing back and forth, trying to find different angles for my head to rest on my pillow. Different positions for my legs to lay, they kept moving, like they wanted to run. I had to fight to hold them still.

I tried breathing long, slow breaths. Counting to five on each inhale, then reversing and counting five exhales. Trying to stay focused on counting, and breathing, and those two things alone. But my mind wouldn't clear, it kept going back to the phone ringing, the tolling of the bell splitting the air. Me answering. Sam's brief words to me. The roaring of the line. The anger and rage and hate.

She had left me. She had shot Aaron. And then she had taken the virus and disappeared.

I never knew if I was more angry about that betrayal, or the fact that I had never guessed it could happen. Never seen it coming. Never knew she could be capable of that.

I was never mad at the torture. I was just so furious at what had happened before that. My mind went through all the moments we had together, and never did I sense that she would do what she had done.

Some lies seemed to be beyond me. And none of it should matter, now. I was on a different path. I had found something that had given my life a little meaning. Something more than the routine. When I had thought I had given that part of me up, it had risen to the surface again. I think, maybe it was hope.

You have that look.

There was something in Angela, something that called to me. Something I was afraid of. I didn't want her interested in me because of some danger kick. The more I learned about her, the more I thought we had fought similar battles. Betrayals, in our past. But she had overcome it, and I thought I could maybe learn that from her. How to move on, and become something better than what I was, now.

And then Sam had called.

My feet kicked out, toes pushing hard against the tight sheet. My jaw clenched and I jerked the pillow underneath my neck for the hundredth time. I kept hearing her voice, over the line.

I wondered if it was me...

Who the fuck else would it be, Sam? Who the fuck else did *this* to me? All I want to know is why, what made it worth it, to you?

It's just as well...

Like she hadn't done what she did. Left Aaron for dead. Stole the virus. Left me fighting off a small army. Shot. Captured. Tortured, my leg broken in little bits, over weeks.

Of course it's just as well. Actions had consequences, Sam, and one day, I'm going to be that consequence. But I wanted to know the action, first. I want to know *why*.

I had grown up on a small farm. Organic. The smell of manure and the sickly sweet smell of compost. The mooing of cows and constant working of the fields, the pulling of the weeds, over and over.

I would find this one, and pull it too.

My parents were kind, and generous, and good. I had grown up the same, believing in their values. I had played football and kissed the homecoming queen, but I had also been the guy who had tutored a fellow football player, too embarrassed to ask for help. Even younger, I had taken homework and stopped by a kid's house who always seemed sick. I would stop by and see how he was, talk about the day in class, other things. I was too young to know what leukemia really was, and hadn't understood it, when the kid had passed.

I had been *good*, dammit.

No longer. I was a guy who knew that being good didn't matter. There wasn't some karmic scale, balancing the good you've done against the person you are. Everything was a choice and a consequence. Action and reaction. And that was all.

As long as I understood that, I could accept it. Life. My life.

Though a part of me knew my parents would be ashamed.

I no longer looked for the end of the rainbow. The hidden reward of a deed, selflessly done. There were no heroes in this world. Just people living their lives the best way they knew how. Some of them thought of others. Some only thought of themselves. But they all made the choices that put them there.

I kept moving. Thrashing. When I did fall asleep, it was brief. But even brief, the nightmare was the same. Like fast-forwarding through a movie, and just getting the highlights. I had no idea exactly when I moved from the racing of my mind's thoughts into the bleakness of my subconsciousness, until it began.

Like always, with the icy chill of realization.

The block of ice, down my back.

The knowledge of something terribly wrong. Some error unseen.

I was in the office again. Or the office-cave, again. Dark stone walls, torches.

Error's cave.

The smell of dark Turkish coffee was always so strong. So strong it felt like it was trying to wake me up, or wake me to something. Torches, shifting firelight revealing the bloody letters scrawling the same word, over and over.

Aaron was on the floor, hair covering his face. This time he was dressed in armor, like a knight of old. Not in his tactical gear, and the armor was without symbol, yet polished enough the torchlight shimmered across it. A sword lay by his outstretched hand, the blade dark, with wisps of smoke drifting from its sharp tip.

I was a knight too. A copy of Aaron, maybe. At least, I wore the same armor, though mine creaked as I looked around, or when I swung my arm, surprised to see myself clad in it. Like the metal needed oil. Lots and lots of oil.

The cavern was the same as the night before. The same walls, the same scrawling word across the stone surface. The same sense of betrayal.

"Angela," I said. And was surprised to hear the change. My voice was tiny in the room, so small that the word did not echo back to me.

Tonight, a stone table lay in the center of the room. A motorcycle helmet sat at its center. A torch threw fiery light across the helmet, and the play between light and shadow made it appear as if the wings of the helmet moved, gliding through unseen currents.

This wasn't the right dream.

I corrected myself.

"Sam," I said aloud. With force. The word bouncing back at me, like a slap.

Even as I spoke her name, the helmet began to morph. Became a bright white case, with flames painted along the sides. It lay open, like it always did, but instead of the broken vials of virus, there were tiny Matchbox cars. All convertible Porsches. All bent and broken and smashed like they had been hit with a ten pound hammer.

I wanted my old nightmare back. That nightmare terrified me, but at least I understood it. Understood why I had it. If I couldn't get rid of it, at least I knew from whence it came.

This nightmare was running wild, a train without a destination, just a lot of mass moving at a crazy speed. I wanted to move to the table, to look at the case more closely, but as I moved the creaking of my armor got louder, became the squealing of a large iron gate. The metal became stiff around me, like concrete, as if it had been so long since someone had greased the joints, they had locked up.

I couldn't move. I could just look at what was in front of me. Aaron, in bright armor. The spawn of error, scrawling across the walls. And the case with the Matchbox Porsches. Fluid leaked from each of them, a fresh yellow-tinted liquid, a little darker coming out of some cars, than others.

Two spots were empty in the case, where Matchbox cars might have been. One of the spots soaked in the thick brake fluid. The other clean and empty.

The fresh blood of error ran faster and faster. The letters swarmed my feet, the metal boots hot underneath the scrawling, a coal-like cherry red. A large bell tolled then, sounding like the blaring of an old black phone, the ringing getting deeper and deeper until it became a tolling, the tolling of a large bell, like the one on Notre Dame, banging a warning over and over and over.

Go to Paris, I had said. *Better memories there.*

The nightmare train was off the tracks. It had taken too much out of my life, blending it too much with the past. Everything was confused, and the buzzing of bees behind me wasn't helping.

Not bees buzzing, but the twanging of Bowstrings. Accompanied by the light sound of sticks smacking stone. More sticks, rattling into the room, across the stone of the floor.

Arrows were being shot at me.

I screamed and pushed and swung as hard as I could, but the armor was rusted shut. So rusty I could see it. The burning of the words across my feet smelled like burning metal, a furnace of iron and oxide.

Cold pricks stabbed my back. Little pinpricks of arrows, sticking me over and over. As if nothing covered my back, it was bare to the world.

Arrows rattling. Stabbing pricks of metal. Tolling of a bell. Smell of Turkish coffee. The little cursive script of the word *error* doubling back and covering itself, smearing the words with fresh, bright blood.

My jaw hurt. It was clenched so tight my teeth cracked with large pops. The arrows became swords, large metal things that jutted out of my chest in the slow motion only nightmares had. I was being impaled.

The pain in my chest was hollow, like the tolling bell. It was also fiery hot, like the lava-like heat around my feet. And the pain was so large, so big, I didn't think I could hold it all in.

I screamed and flailed, even though I was locked in place. Nothing moved, except for the tiniest motion of my head, turning just enough aside that I could see behind me, in the furthest reach of my peripheral vision.

So many knights behind me. Thousands. Millions. Impossibly packed together, copies all. Every one of them was stabbing each other in the back, one knight in front of the other, millions of impalements of the same person, over and over and over. All of them screaming, the screaming becoming a roar, the roar growing so loud in my head it became something I could see, anger and pain and rage and hate bursting out like the mushroom cloud of a nuclear bomb, wiping out everything underneath it...

I jerked awake.

Heart pounding.

Skin pouring with sweat

Chest heaving, drawing in large breath after large breath.

My body struggling to move, enclosed in damp sheets that had twisted and wrapped around me, encasing my broken self like a wet, frigid cocoon.

TWENTY-THREE

I got up. Sheets in the laundry. Remade the bed.

Worked out, like the day before. Push-ups and pull-ups and crunches.

Lukewarm shower. The soap leaving a soft scent of honeydew melon and cucumber.

Put on jeans and a white T-shirt, plain. No logo or brand on a shirt pocket, or over the heart. Nothing fancy today. Sneakers, and a dark brown leather-like jacket.

Made breakfast. It was Friday, so scrambled eggs and wheat toast. I had one grapefruit left, so I cut it in half and wrapped one-half in plastic wrap and stuck it back in the fridge for tomorrow. Saturday was shopping day.

The eggs were bland, but eating them with the butter and toast got them down. The grapefruit was more sweet than tart, too much so. I missed the tartness. The orange juice the same. Everything tasted off, too sweet, too bland, too dry.

I turned on the television this morning as I ate. The local sports show. I felt like today, more than ever, I had to get back on the routine. Leaving it, even for so short a time, had muddled up my life. It was messing up my already fucked-up dreams. I needed to find a way to get back on track, to get back to as much of it as I could.

That meant finding Angela. Fast. Yesterday I had felt like I had some time, a few days. After all, the people holding her needed something from her. Or one of the groups needed something. That kind of bargaining took time. Power and money, and the struggle between them.

It was me that didn't have the time. The longer this went, the more I derailed. The more I moved into the unknown. Things were escalating and changing too much, and that was changing me too much. More than I could afford it.

One of the newscasters talked about the new baseball stadium again. The bill to build it was up in front of the state legislature, and the acting governor was trying to push it through. Touting how good it would be for the city, how many jobs it would bring to people who needed it, the working class. How much more money it would bring in.

The governor was really pumping it, in the news. Which was typical, it being an election year. People always seemed to celebrate the big things, and leave all the little things that really affect people forgotten. Nothing like a big distraction.

Maybe the revenue would be good. People needed money. But I wondered if any of it would reach the people who really needed it. Or if the money would be funneled to the people who wanted it, instead.

David Whelan, I thought to myself, *you are on my list.*

I was going to see him. Right after my meeting with the mysterious third party. If I was lucky enough, I would get enough to go on there. Maybe even a location of where the girl was, and if not, at least more knowledge. Maybe even enough I wouldn't need to call Sara.

Part of me wondered about Whelan. His son had likely been killed. Could he have Angela? Was he trying to protect her, from some devotion to his dead son?

A guess, at best. I finished my breakfast. Washed the dishes, with apple blossom soap in tepid water. Putting everything away as the television ran on in the background.

The anchors talked about a missing plane from a few days ago. Apparently it had left New York, on its way to London. Heathrow Airport. It hadn't been far from England when it just dropped off the map.

All kinds of search-and-rescues were being done. Rescue crafts lining up in grids and searching the ocean, like lines of people would do, looking for a missing kid in a forest.

The ocean was a big place. I thought it unlikely they would find anything. The cold currents were deep and dark and would swallow anything whole, dragging everything into murky depths that would forever hide whatever sunk into them. Leaving no trace of passage. Nothing to say *I was here.*

The news report went right to commercial. An advertisement for the upcoming election. Bigger and Better, paid for by such-and-such group and always approved by the candidate. As if the candidate hadn't written the whole thing. Probably paid for it, as well.

I turned off the television. All kinds of bad things happened in the world. Why did we always have to hear about all of them?

I was ready. The ocean may be deep and dark, but I would dive into the fathomless depths as many times as I could. I would find everything I could find, and maybe even save someone who needs saving.

It'd be nice to do that, again.

I was walking past the kitchen when someone knocked on my door. Knocking I recognized. Three hard raps of knuckles on wood.

"Mr. Hamilton," Baber's voice called out. Her voice strong, through the door. "Want to open up? Take a look at this pretty warrant I brought with me?"

TWENTY-FOUR

It wasn't a search warrant. I guess they had gotten the looking around part in yesterday. It was for bringing me in. At least, it read that way. The timing of the warrant was odd, because if they had talked to Charley, if they had been to Angela's apartment, then yesterday would have been the day to come get me.

So Baber and Frank had been delayed. Or Charley's report had been delayed. And like I thought earlier, only politics or money had the kind of power to do something like that. Someone had already known where Angela had lived, and had sent someone there, and wanted to delay any effort by the police to get there. There was likely a mole in the department. At least one. Or someone passing the order down from up top.

The police commissioner was an appointed position, they were usually appointed by the mayor. Sometimes the city council. They could be hired or fired at any time, which gave the mayor a little power over the police. Especially if the commissioner didn't have a backbone. But it was hard to see that happening here. It was more likely some money was paid to a person or people handling the calls, and something was asked like *if this address gets called in, lose it for a bit*. I just didn't know.

What the hell did Angela have?

I opened the door. Baber and Frank stood there, in the same positions as yesterday. Looking just as tired. Maybe even wearing the same clothes. Baber in a dark jacket, white blouse, darker pants. Frank with an old trench coat, tied around his waist. The cigarette smell from Baber was strong today, but she had a tiny grin on her face. Not a mean grin, just a satisfied one. As if something had gone right for her.

Frank held handcuffs. They dangled from one hand. Actually, from one thick finger of his hand. His trench coat didn't quite reach his ankles, as if he couldn't find one long enough. Or maybe he had grown, between yesterday and today. He was Black Giant.

"I'll come," I said, holding my hands up.

Frank raised his eyebrows, then shook his head. "Let's not take that chance."

His voice still had the same grumble. Like rocks sliding down a mountain. Frank turned me against the doorframe and pulled my arms behind my back. Locked each cuff around my wrists, tight enough that they pinched, the metal ice-cold against my skin.

"Want to tell me what this is about, Baber?" I said, face against the door jamb.

"We'll save that for the station," she said. Her voice measured, but soft. As if she was finishing up a long day's task, and was ready for her reward.

Frank finished up and tugged me away by pulling on the back of my jacket. The motion felt like a parachute opening in free fall. I was jerked back, and struggled briefly to stay balanced.

Baber took a peek past my door, into the apartment. A frown on her face, maybe at the starkness of it. "Want the door locked?"

I nodded. At least Baber was courteous. Even if they did cuff me.

She locked it from the inside and shut the door. The two were quiet. The hallways were quiet. There was only the tip-tap of Baber's pumps against the tile floor, as they led me down the stairs. Black Giant held my shoulder and guided me down in front of him, like I was a marionette bound by one large string. We got to the bottom and headed outside to their car, the dark four-door Chevrolet. It waited right in front of the building, engine still running.

There weren't any swat teams around. Or cops in tactical gear. I expected something like that, if Charley had talked to them. You didn't peaceably bring someone in, when you knew the violence they were capable of.

Or maybe I just thought too much of myself. Maybe Frank was enough.

The big man tucked me into the back of the car. There wasn't a lot of room, I was behind the passenger seat, and that seat had been pushed all the way back. It was close enough that the back of the seat pinched my knees, and my leg ached no matter how I angled it. I wriggled around, trying to find a comfortable position with my hands behind me. There was none. There never is.

Frank waited until I stopped moving. All I could do was lean half-forward a bit, setting my wrists on the small of my back.

"Done?" he asked, nice enough.

I nodded.

He grabbed the seat belt, ducked into the car, and drew it along my body until he clicked it shut. He was large enough that the size of him pushed me back, then the belt tightened and held me there, enough that my back pushed my hands into the seat, and I felt the tension of that position in my shoulders.

"Short trip," he said, smiling, and then withdrew. And withdrew some more.

He was a very large man.

Baber had already gotten in. The car rocked as Frank got in the passenger seat. He still had to bend his knees a bit. Baber was the type of person who seemed to like to drive, but with Black Giant as her passenger, she may have had no choice. I couldn't imagine him fitting behind the wheel.

I lived in Dorchester. Baber pulled out and circled around, heading west a bit until we picked up Melnea Cass Boulevard, and took that to Tremont Street. We were headed to the main station then. Headquarters.

It was a short trip. No music played in the car, though occasionally a voice spoke over the radio unit, speaking with various police codes and callsigns, cops in the city replying on route, or busy, or repeat last.

It was early, and traffic was just beginning to pick up steam, getting ready for the morning rush hour. Most of the vehicles heading the opposite direction of us. Those people would likely be trying to beat the same rush at the end of the day, speeding through work, clocking out quick, and driving like a bat out of hell to get home before all the roads turned into parking lots.

The police station was a large four-story building, actually it looked like two large four-story buildings with a single floor connecting the two buildings at the top. A bridge between the two. The building was made up of large gray blocks along each floor, each block lined with four-square windows, with even darker gray lines bisecting each square of windows like gun-metal crosses.

A tall blue vertical sign stood by the street in the middle of the building, with Boston Police spelled up the sign, from top to bottom. Like an old Egyptian obelisk. People and police officers walked inside the department from the street, others walked outside. A clump of people with a sign that said Occupy Boston stood listlessly at one corner, no one paying them any mind.

Baber found a place to park around the side. They got out, pulled me out, let me stand for a moment. I had to shake off a little numbness in my right leg, and Baber watched me limp a bit, her eyes curious.

Inside was an open floor with chairs lined up in rows. A waiting area. There was a large desk dividing the room from the area behind it, acting as a gate. One of the desk sergeants there waved a hello, Baber nodded in return, and we were waved through.

We walked through the area, down a hallway made from the gray-colored walls of cubicles. Cops dressed in blue uniforms were everywhere, like a small army. There was a hustle and bustle in the air, along with the smell of coffee. Cups of it were everywhere, desks, break rooms, on top of file cabinets, as if people had gotten a cup, set it down, and forgot where they put it. And then did it all again. And again.

Radios squawked and people shouted back and forth over walls. An officer brushed past us, rushing with a large stack of files held to their chest in both hands. It was chaos, but there was a current of order running through it, as if everyone understood what needed to be done, who was doing it, and where. Organized, but loud.

Baber wasn't putting me in a cell. At least, not right away. Which told me I was getting interrogated. I didn't want to be locked up today, I needed to be out. Getting questioned was something I could handle. They weren't likely to take a hammer to my leg.

We got to an elevator bank, waited for one, then took it up to the next floor. The elevator smelled like frosted donuts. The door dinged open and Black Giant guided me out to another desk. A few more sergeants worked there. They had done this part and were ready.

Frank uncuffed me. My fingers tingled a bit, and I worked both wrists with my hands. Baber asked for my things, all I had was my wallet and keys. She looked at both, then copied some things down from my license on a paper on the desk.

While she filled out the paperwork, one sergeant fingerprinted me. He grabbed each of my fingers and pressed it against a pad of black ink, then rolled the digit on a piece of paper, inside a block meant for that finger. Then he did each thumb. The ink was cold and wet against my skin. I was allowed a tiny alcoholic wipe to clean my hands with, the alcohol cool as it evaporated.

Everyone was quiet, for the most part. Everyone here had done this many times, both Frank and Baber and the desk sergeants. The process was efficient. Throughout all of this Baber would look at me, as if she had a secret she couldn't wait to share. Especially when they took my fingers and pressed them against the pad. Baber watched that, closely.

Something inside me tinged off. Like the returning ping of a ship's radar, as I sailed across the ocean, warning me of a jagged reef waiting ahead, just below the water's surface.

I didn't know what that reef could be. I had some guesses, but they felt off. If they had found the guy in Angela's apartment, they would have come with more than just Baber and Frank to arrest me. If they had gotten Charley's call, and gone to Angela's I felt like it would have ended the same way.

We finished up at the desk. Baber and Frank led me down a hallway of doors, each leading to its own room. The door opened inward. Baber went in first. Frank guided me in next.

I guessed, whatever it was Baber knew, I'd soon find out.

CHAPTER
TWENTY-FIVE

THE ROOM WAS A SMALL INTERROGATION CHAMBER. A LARGE mirrored window to my left, as we walked in. Gray concrete floor. Darker gray walls, also concrete. Easy to clean.

There was a heavy black table in the middle, thick dark metal anchored to a concrete floor with bolts. Four small chairs sat around the table, two to either side. The chairs were made of thin, shiny metal tubes, the aluminum legs curved like a giant C under the seat, so the chair would rock a little when you sat in it. Like a rocking chair. Like a subliminal message was trying to be conveyed, something like *come on in and take a load off*...

Frank led me to one of the chairs. I took it and sat down. There were metal U-shaped bolts welded to the table, but he didn't cuff me to those. He just watched me sit, then wandered back to the door, shutting it. Leaning back against the corner of the walls there, one shoulder over the mirrored window. I guess he didn't trust the tiny tubes of metal to hold him.

The room smelled cold, like the inside of a freezer. Baber pulled a chair back. The metal legs scratched lightly along the floor. She took a seat. Her face still looked tired, with dark circles under her eyes, but the eyes themselves were alive with interest.

"Hamilton," she said, holding both hands open, as if appraising the space. "It's almost like you're home."

I grunted. The corner of my mouth lifted. It was funny. "Too many chairs," I said.

"Yeah," she agreed. "Feels almost cluttered, right?"

She smiled. Black Giant looked on with disinterest. The mirrored window sat behind Baber, I could see her back, shoulders a little slumped. Hair tousled. A tiny camera hung in the corner of the room, above the window, in the corner opposite Frank, red light on and blinking.

"You look tired, Hamilton," she said. "Sleep well?"

Not in years.

"About the same as you two," I said.

Baber smiled a little. She sat there and watched me look over the room. She pulled out her pad of paper from her jacket, and a pen, and sat it to the side. Then she read the Miranda to me, quickly, but understandably. As if she had said the words many times and knew exactly how to pronounce each one.

She asked me if I wanted a lawyer, told me the bit where the court could appoint one if I wanted it. I asked her why I would need one.

Baber smiled, and waited. She wanted me to make the first move. Normally, I could wait with the best of them. I had been patient before, but over the past couple of years I had mastered the art.

However, there were a lot of things on my list today. I wanted to get to all of them. I felt like the time I thought I had was slipping, that the hourglass had tipped over and sand was running all over the place. That something had happened, and things were accelerating.

I needed to accelerate with them. More, I had to get there first. Just getting there at all wasn't going to matter.

"What's this about, Baber," I asked.

Her eyes narrowed, but still were alight. Capturing, like the camera behind her.

"Tell me what it's about, Hamilton," she said. "You came here quickly enough. You must have some idea."

"You got that wrong," I said. "If I had an idea, I wouldn't have come."

I needed to know what she knew, maybe more than she wanted to know about what I was doing. Definitely more than whatever it was she thought I'd done.

I looked at the mirror and wondered.

"Are we going to get to the point here, or just play word games?" I asked.

"I like the word games," she said. "I get a good feel for people, with how they play."

She watched me. I trusted what she said. She would be good at reading people, and she was capturing every glance I made, every facial tic, each roll of the eye, the placement and position of my hands, and putting it all into a file that said *This is Hamilton*. But there was something else behind all of it, something I couldn't pin down.

Baber leaned forward. "Let's talk about a few days ago," she said. "After the kidnapping."

"Fine," I said.

"You went to the DMV afterward," Baber said. "Where did you go next?"

This could be about the apartment. Maybe they had found it, the guy inside with a few light stabbing wounds in his leg. Maybe he had put together a story, and it was just now that they were finding me. Maybe it wasn't about Charley, and her calling in Angela's address to the police, at all.

"You tell me," I said. "If you're looking for me to tell you all about my day, you've pulled in the wrong guy."

Baber frowned. Stayed quiet a minute. I stayed quiet as well. She realized I could wait as long as she could.

So she changed tactics. "Tell me about Greg," she said.

"Who?" I asked.

Baber smiled. "Think he calls himself Trick," she said.

I got it. The guy at the motorcycle shop. The one I had interrupted when he was hitting on the girls. When he wouldn't take a moment out of hitting on a group of girls to help me.

"Tell me," I had told the kid, after he had told me he was going to call the cops on me. For holding his shoulder kind of tight.

"I'm not," Trick had finally said. "I won't."

"Won't what?"

"I won't call the cops."

I didn't move, but inside I closed my eyes and shook my head. Some guys could never take care of things on their own, man-to-man. They were born tattlers, and they would run and complain to someone in charge the first chance they got. Some people could never do things up front, could never take care of things on their own. They had some gene that pushed them to find a person who could do something about their problem, and complain to them.

No matter what word they had given.

Baber took my silence as assent. "Did you go into a store with a helmet, and accost a person working there?"

She used the word accost a little distastefully. So I figured she had met Trick. Or Greg. Whoever.

I stayed quiet and thought. I didn't know what Baber had. I didn't know if she was starting out with Trick, and leading me to the apartment.

"Am I being charged with something?" I asked.

Baber grinned, something nasty. Like she had me. She pulled a piece of paper from her notebook, something small and folded in two. On one side was a copy of my driver's license. My fake license, with its fake Thomas Hamilton name.

"I showed a Trick Munsen your driver's license," she said. "And he identified you as the person who came in and physically abused him in his store."

That still wasn't enough to bring me in, I thought. Unless they had been to the apartment, gotten the story from the guy there. Or maybe they did have Charley's call. Maybe they had talked to her, next.

"Aren't you supposed to use a lineup?" I said. "You showing him my pictures is kind of leading the witness, right?"

"So you were there?" Baber asked.

"I wasn't anywhere," I said. I wasn't going to sit through a verbal minefield, trying to figure out what Baber had on me, and what she was looking for. I needed to get moving. If she wasn't going to tell me something, then I needed to go. And there was one way to do this quickly.

"Let's speed this up then," I told her, placing both hands on the table. The metal was cold to the touch. "Charge me with whatever it is you think I've done, whatever it is your warrant has on me. Or let me go."

That was the rule. If they were going to arrest me, they needed to do it. She would have to give me whatever she had on me. Or she would have to let me go.

She set her jaw. Looked at Frank. He tilted his head one way, then another. Like he was undecided.

"That's it then," I said, pushing away from the table. "See you two later."

Before I stood the door opened. It swung in and traveled a few inches before catching Frank's foot. He glanced outside, quizzically. Someone out there said something. Frank let out a breath and moved his foot. The door opened all the way.

A man came in. A man in a carbon gray suit that framed his shoulders nicely. Hair cut tight to the head, that had once been long and curly. A tiny white scar across his temple, just a faded white line against his tan skin, a reminder of two years ago.

Aaron.

He walked in, a briefcase in hand. Small, square, and black.

"Don't say anything," he told me. Like any lawyer would. As if he really was one.

Baber stood. "Who are you?"

"This man's attorney," he said, holding out his hand. "Aaron Burr, at your service."

"He hasn't asked for one," she countered.

"He shouldn't have to ask," Aaron said, with a smile. His eyes lit into Baber, I had seen the same eyes scope out a target from a hundred yards away, deep into the night. The same eyes interrogate a suspected terrorist, a converted red-bearded man from Nevada, late at night in the back of a casino. Aaron was a man of many talents. "It's a right. One of these funny civil liberties people get all worked up about."

He glided around the table and took the chair next to me. Then set the small briefcase on the table. Popped it open. It was empty except for a piece of paper taped inside the top of the case, with four words written in sloppy Sharpie on the piece.

You know the drill.

I certainly did. I was surprised to see Aaron here. Surprised, and yet something in my hindbrain kept pinging me. The radar, telling me the ship I was on was headed into a bank of reefs, that jagged rock lay all around me, but for the life of me I couldn't figure out what that rock was.

ONCE, HAVING A GUY LIKE AARON AROUND WAS A CRITICAL part of the job. Having someone who could clean up messes. Provide a distraction. Get a person out of jail. Smooth-talk an embassy official. He was good at playing roles, and he had gotten us out of jams more often than he hadn't.

It hadn't been a perk of the job, but a necessary cog in the machine. So it felt good to have Aaron here, even with the radar hinting dangerous rock encircled me. Even if I was out, and no longer working for the same team he was.

"We've got a warrant," Baber told Aaron.

"Do you?" Aaron smiled, his eyebrows raised. "An actual *arrest* warrant?"

Baber stopped what she was about to say, and looked at him, cocking her head.

"So not an arrest warrant, not really," Aaron said. "And not a search warrant, or the two of you wouldn't be here, with my client. Right?"

Frank grunted and looked at Baber. She didn't look back. The door was still open to the room, and Frank nudged it shut with his foot. It closed with a thunk, followed by the quick tick of the latch bolt finding its place in the doorjamb.

"So what kind of warrant?" Aaron continued. "I mean, you cuffed my client and brought him in. You've got to have a charge, right?"

Baber's jaw flexed, like she was chewing gum that had turned to concrete. Her eyes no longer were excited. Baber looked worried, and when she finally spoke, it sounded like the words had been drug out of her. "It's a good warrant."

"It's a *governor's* warrant," Aaron said, chuckling. "Given rarely, right? For criminals wanted in another state?"

"It's good," Baber repeated.

"For Christ's sake," Aaron said. "What crime did my client commit in Delaware?"

"Maybe he didn't commit a crime there," Baber said. "But he's suspected of one."

"One there?" Aaron said. "Or *here*?"

Baber went silent again. I watched her, like she had been watching me earlier. I could tell Baber was good at her job, and committed. I always felt like tired cops were the best cops. They were people who kept going, long after the day was done, because they knew every second counted. They knew they had to keep going, because if they stopped, then the criminals win.

Baber had been curious about me from the start. She had come to my place wanting to learn more about me. But she didn't believe I had anything to do with the kidnapping. Or she wouldn't have shown me the end of the video, yesterday. She was telling me, without saying anything, that she understood I was searching for Angela for reasons all my own. But she was also saying she understood that I was a person who had those types of skills.

I had known then she was dangerous, her and Frank, in their way. People who can see below the surface of things always are. So I watched and took in what I could, now. Because I needed to know more about the people who were looking into me.

Baber's face contained anger. Not at me, and not even at Aaron. I got the feeling it was anger because she had been caught doing something she hadn't wanted to do. A shortcut she had taken, trying to get something faster. And now that shortcut was going to bite her in the ass, and slow down whatever she was trying to get to.

So Baber was feeling much like I was about things. That the time we thought we had plenty of was all of a sudden lacking. That for some reason, the hourglass was running short of sand.

"Okay," Aaron said. "Let me tell you why my client's really here. You wanted to fingerprint him and hope something popped up."

Both Aaron and I knew that wouldn't go anywhere. Maybe it would have twenty years ago, when people had paper records and faxed them back over the lines, but not today. As soon as my fingerprints were scanned and digitalized and fed into the databases, there were all kinds of ways to fake what came back.

Especially for someone who did the work Aaron and I did. Well, that I had done.

Aaron held up my hand. Even after cleaning them, my fingertips still were a little dark. "I see you got that."

The room went silent. I stayed silent. Aaron sat next to me, and I could tell he was happy on the inside. He had always been a guy who liked playing the role. His jaw was freshly shaved, and he had some kind of sandalwood cedar scent. Likely an aftershave he thought all lawyers wore.

Baber looked at me, her lips still pressed together. The sides of her jaw working like she wanted to say something, but couldn't. Or wouldn't. Her mind churned in the background. I could see it, in her eyes.

Frank finally grunted, again. Then added a few words to the grunt. "He's got you, Bee."

Aaron slapped the table and grinned. "That, I do."

"I can't put him where I need to put him," Baber said. "But I'll be damned if he doesn't know something about it."

"I could care less where you need to put him," Aaron said. "Unless it's directly out of this room, out of this police department, and finally, out of your sights. You've fucked this up, detective, and you come after my client again, everything better be buttoned up, or it's going to cost you your job."

Baber was so angry that her eyes grew moist. Her hand, next to her handpad, spasmed open and shut. She looked over at me, both eyes drilling into me.

I shrugged. "You going to let me go?"

She swallowed. It was a hard swallow. Looked back at Frank, who just kind of nodded. Turned back to us. "I played this wrong."

"That you did," Aaron said.

"I should have just come and asked," she said. "I let that kid convince me, and I let Hamilton get under my skin. He asked for a warrant, so I was going to goddamn bring one."

"A governor's warrant?" I asked. That wouldn't have held me. Aaron was right, it was only issued for someone who hadn't committed a crime in the state they were living in, but was suspected of a crime in another.

"Beebee's first warrant wasn't going to cut it," Frank said.

She just shook her head. "We don't know that."

"It might have," Frank echoed. His voice rumbling in the tiny room. "But it didn't. So we tried this."

"First warrant?" I asked. Only one thing could have gotten a warrant on me. The guy in Angela's apartment, either him or him and Charley's call.

Aaron looked at me, I held up a hand and looked at Baber. "What was that warrant for?"

"You know," Baber said, looking at me, still angry.

I was beginning to think I didn't. That I was way off. Something about Baber screamed it at me, some injustice she had witnessed or been a part of, and even now harbored. "Maybe I don't," I said, cautiously.

"You *fucking know*," Baber said again, leaning forward, pointing her finger at me, then Aaron. "I don't care what you fucking walk on today. I don't give a shit about what your lawyer says, or even about my job. You fucking know more about this and I will get that warrant and I will come after you again, Hamilton."

"We're done here," Aaron said, like he had seen in a thousand criminal television shows. Playing that role. "Come after my client again, Detective, and that'll be the last time someone calls you that."

"Fancy words don't scare me," Baber said.

"Beebee," Frank warned.

"I don't give a shit," Baber said. "You know it too, Frank. That girl *knew* him."

Knew. Not *know*.

I stayed sitting. Had they found Angela? Was she already dead? Was the feeling I had today of running short of time, was it just my subconscious telling me time was already out? That I had failed?

Aaron looked at me, eyebrow raised. I ignored him and leaned forward. "Who are we talking about here, Baber?"

Maybe she wanted to see what happened, when she said the name. Maybe she was still watching and recording, on the inside, putting everything into the Hamilton file. "Charley Taylor."

She looked at me. "Her last words were, *That fucking guy with the helmet.*"

TWENTY-SEVEN

Charley Taylor. Not the name I expected, but a name that still hurt. She hadn't even looked at me, when she had left the car. Angry at me, for doing what I had done. Angry, because she had to try to stop me, with an empty gun. Scared that the guy I was torturing would be her, next.

"You can't do this." She held her empty gun on me, as I knelt in front of a guy, about to cut under his kneecap.

"You're wrong," I had told her. "I can do this. He can do this. He has done this before. Look at him."

The guy was a killer. I knew it, because like recognizes like. But even angry, I could tell he was different. He was a guy who killed because he liked it. Maybe the spray of blood in the kitchen hinted at it.

I now thought he had gotten out of Angela's apartment. And maybe had found Charley, and taken his vengeance out on her. Some people prey on the weak, when they are scared of the strong. It made them feel tough.

That guy felt like that kind of predator.

My intuition was telling me I was on the right path.

Charley's last words told me the same. He had come after her, because of me. Maybe I should have killed him, at the apartment. Or called the cops and waited for them, instead of working the guy for information.

But all of that didn't matter now. All that mattered now was that Charley was dead, because I had asked for her help to find Angela.

"Give me a chance to help her," I had begged.

And she had. She had come along, wanting to help her friend. Giving me a chance. And, if my gut was right, I had repaid Charley by getting her killed.

I was lost in the woods, trying to figure out why all this was happening. It had started with a search for Angela. She was out there, I just couldn't find her. Just like the lost knight, after leaving his lady.

And with every step I took, more and more things shook loose around me, more and more information buried me, none of it made sense, and I sunk deeper and deeper in the hole I had begun in.

A hole like a grave, with Charley underneath my feet, and someone tossing in cold, wet dirt on top of us.

Lines were blurring, between reality and my dreams. My usual nightmare had intertwined the past with the present and morphed into something more, something different. It seemed like my real life was doing the same, blurring fantasy and reality, past and present, mingling it all together into something out of a story.

I'm sure I sounded surprised, when I finally spoke. "Dead?"

"You made sure of it," Baber said.

I shook my head. "Baber, I didn't do anything to her."

Nothing except torture a man in front of her. That was it. And maybe that had been bad enough.

Baber sneered. "Sure, Hamilton. Sure."

"Beebee," Frank warned from the door, again.

"The lawyer's right," Baber said. Her face was still angry, but I could see her trying to control it. As if it was something she had to fight, all the time. She looked up at the ceiling for a few moments, and then back to me. "I'm not going to get that warrant now," she said. "But I'll be after you. You should know that."

I didn't like how I felt, now. I was surprised, and sad about Charley, but I didn't feel enough guilt... What I felt washed over me and just left me a little sad. Charley had stopped me because she had believed in people being better. I had known they could be much worse.

I hated to be proven right.

I could have done more to make sure Charley knew she was safe. At least warned her. But I hadn't even thought about it. Not really. So there was some regret there, too. But not enough. Not near enough.

"Baber," I said, quietly. "What happened?"

She told us.

Early this morning, people reported a break in at Charley's store. The first uniforms found her, lying in her store, battered. Jaw broken. Teeth knocked out. One eye wide open, staring straight ahead. Still alive, though she would die a little later. After Baber had gotten there. After Charley had said what she had said. As one of the first responders was still trying to get her on a gurney.

Concussion, I thought. Or just so much brain trauma, nothing was left. I wondered if they had tortured her to find out more information about me. What I knew. How I knew Angela. Where I was.

Nothing that Charley could even answer.

So they would just beat her more.

So that I could be the one to save Angela.

I shook my head. Charley had said something, headed back to her store, that had rung both true and false to me at the time.

"You're not doing it for me, anyway," she said, her voice thick, low. "Or even for her. You're doing it for you."

I had let those words go, then. But now they came back and haunted me. Was I going after Angela to save her? Or was I going after her to save myself?

Lines were blurring, in my life. Between dreams and reality. They had blurred, with that stupid book and its story about knights and dragons and ladies. The actions of the knight and the lady, after they separated, seemed to echo what Charley had told me. I had sensed it in Angela, a pained past she had somehow overcome.

Just like the lady in *The Faerie Queene*. She had continued her quest, even found others to help her. She persevered. The knight though, got more and more lost. He had spun out of control, after his first encounter with Error. He had struck out on his own, killed other knights, tried to save other ladies, going up against harder and harder opponents and getting more and more lost. As if nothing remained in the knight but confusion and a death wish.

I had to wonder if I was the same. Was I just going after Angela, because if I didn't I would end up like the knight. Lost? Nothing but anger and confusion? Would I just keep going the way I had been, because I couldn't see any other way out? Would I just keep getting more and more lost, until I found something too big for me, and it killed me, or changed me forever?

It was quiet in the room. I don't know how long it had been that way. I let out a breath that felt like my first one in a while. Baber watched me. Frank watched me. Even Aaron watched me.

Charley had asked me to stay away, and I had. Mainly because I hadn't needed her any longer. And I wondered if that careless decision, the fact that I had moved on like she wanted, had cost Charley her life.

I had warned her. I had told her to load her gun. She had bitterly laughed that off.

There was rock ahead. Large jagged stones. I could feel them, dark outlines under the ocean. I could see the shadows they cast, in the depths, and began to understand the water here was much deeper than I knew. The reefs, much bigger than any reef could be. Like subsurface mountains, clawing to the surface.

Baber just looked at me, fighting whatever emotion was inside her. Frank was more stolid, glancing at all of us, or none of us. Either way, he didn't say anything, either. They both watched me process all this. It felt like it took forever.

Dammit, through it all, I found I liked Baber. She was just trying to do the right thing. Trying to help those who needed help. She was dogged. Determined. It was a quality I could admire.

Finally Aaron sat back down. Gave me a look, as if asking what was going on. Letting me know he was here. Like we were back on the same team, on the same mission. He was letting this play out, and I needed it to.

Baber was a good cop. Like me, she had some of the information, but not all of it. And if I was right, and time was running out, then we needed to share. At least a little. Things were racing, things were jumbling together, and although my subconscious had sensed it first, the feeling had grown larger and louder.

I wanted to find Angela. I wanted to be the guy who showed the people who had kidnapped her their error. Actions had consequences, and I wanted to prove that. And I was, but in the wrong way. Things I was doing were coming back and hurting others.

I wanted to be the hero, the knight, the rescuer, but maybe that wasn't me. Maybe I wasn't meant to be the hero. Maybe that would be Baber.

Maybe I needed to start thinking less about what I wanted, and more about what was best for Angela.

Or I might find her body, instead.

TWENTY-EIGHT

I ended up telling Baber as much as I could. How I found Charley. The incident with Trick. All the way up until getting to her shop. About our ride together, as we headed out to Angela's place. I told her that the place had been tossed, but I did not mention the mercenary. Or what I did to him.

Which is where Baber perked up. "When was this?"

"Later that day," I said. "The day of the kidnapping."

Baber jotted some of this down. Baber's hand was neat, precise. She glanced back at Frank, who grunted.

I wondered again when they had gotten to Angela's apartment. Charley had called them, that same day. I paused. Looked at the mirrored window. The camera, watching over us.

"Baber," I said. "When did you go to Angela's apartment?"

Baber pulled back a little, surprised with the question. I didn't think she was going to answer. In the end, it was Frank who spoke.

"After we left your place," the mountain rumbled.

Almost an entire day after Charley had called. Not quite twenty hours. I frowned.

"Is that when you got the call?"

Baber was still quiet. I could see her thinking.

"That's when we got the call," Frank said. "We were headed your way. Stopped by your place first."

Someone had withheld Charley's information, and that she had called the day of the kidnapping. That person would have her information, her name, number, address.

"Anonymous call?"

Frank's massive shoulders moved up, then down. "Tip line. Didn't leave a name. We were just checking it out, after you."

So Charley's call didn't even exist, in the department

Money and Politics.

Someone had killed Charley. Someone she had recognized, and linked to me. That could only have been the guy in the apartment. And the only way he could have found Angela, was from her call to the station.

The same department that had somehow come up with a warrant to bring me in. Which told me someone there was someone in on this from high above, a person with enough clout to get a warrant out on me. A ridiculous one, but something that would get me off the board.

Maybe using one stone to take out two birds, because Baber was off the board now too. For a little bit. Investigating me, instead of finding Angela. She had almost been pointed at me.

And now that I thought about it, how had a complaint from Trick made it to Baber to begin with? It felt like a senior detective was a little high on the food chain here for that kind of complaint.

I knew Baber felt like I did. There was something happening. Soon. We both felt the urgency, the time slipping.

I looked at Aaron. He had read the room, same as me. Read me in the same motion. Like old times. I nodded to the mirror, arching my eyebrow.

He got it. He got up, walked out. Frank moved his foot, so he could leave. Then we all heard a door open and close, quickly, next door. Then

Aaron came back in. Shut the door to our room, then moved over to the camera, unplugging it from the back.

Baber and Frank watched him. Her face was puzzled, but she was catching up.

"What do you think you're doing?" she asked.

"Protecting my client," Aaron said. "Maybe you, too."

"They'll just come in," Baber said. "There's someone watching all of the cameras, all the time."

"Better make it fast, then," Aaron told me.

Baber rocked back, as if a thought had hit her, and surprised her with its force. "You're not a lawyer."

"Funny," Aaron said. "I have a card that says so."

She looked at both of us. "Who are you guys?"

"Look," I said, leaning forward. Closer to Baber, hiding from the window behind her. "I was with Charley, day before yesterday. I was in the car after we left Angela's apartment. I watched her call the police station and report it. Leaving her name, and her number."

Baber sat still for a moment. "Bullshit."

"You'll find out it's true," I said. "You've got her phone, right? Look at the history there. Pull her records."

I watched her absorb that. Baber looked a little unsettled, and then even more so when she realized. As if it was a state of being she wasn't used to.

She looked over at Aaron. Took that motion and used it to glance at the mirror. The unplugged camera. Her skin paled, just a bit. Baber took a breath, and then found Frank.

"You haven't liked this from the beginning," he told her.

"Neither of us have liked it," she said.

"True," Frank said. "But you're the one, can't let stuff go."

Baber shook her head. Still trying to put what I told her in place. She latched back onto me, her jaw set. Still angry. "You and I know you're capable of it, Hamilton."

"We're wasting time, Baber," I said. "You're going to see the truth, five minutes after you walk out of here. You're going to see she called, and then you're going to *know*."

"What you're saying, it doesn't make sense," she said.

"Sense or not, I'm letting you know," I told her. "You got someone in the department involved in this."

"A cop wouldn't beat up a girl," she said. "They wouldn't kill her."

"Maybe not," I said. There could be bad cops just like there could be bad soldiers. People were people, in the end. "But they can let someone know where that girl is. They can dismiss a report. They can do all kinds of things, for money."

Her hands clenched on the table. Baber forced them open. "I can't trust this," she said.

"I'm not asking you to trust me," I said. "This is me warning you. Because if people are getting silenced, then you got to wonder if you're going to be on that list."

She snorted. "That's ridiculous," she said. "This kind of stuff doesn't happen. Not in real life."

I looked at Aaron, who had one of his smirking grins on. The one that said, *if she only knew.*

"Maybe not in your world," I said.

She still made little motions with her head. Little shakes of denial. I wondered if she was aware she was even doing it.

"Baber," I said. "We can help each other here. Find Angela. But if you keep going, you got to know you'll be on the same list as Charley. It's going to be you and Frank here on your own. Especially after I walk out of here."

"So you want me to trust you?" Baber said. "Over cops I've worked with, my whole life?"

"Someone deleted Charley's call," I said. "Someone sent her information to the person who killed her."

I leaned forward and lowered my voice. "You don't have to trust me.

Dig into what I'm telling you and see. Just be aware of what could happen, if you do."

The hallway door jerked open then. It slammed into Frank's foot, so it only opened a few inches. Frank growled, a low rumble, and stared outside, the implacable mountain stare, hinting at landslides.

It was nice to see the power of Black Giant used for good.

Someone spoke outside. An urgent, low voice. Fingers appeared, wrapped around the edge of the door, as if that person was trying to push their way in.

"It's fine," Frank told them. Two rumbling words.

The person outside said something again, louder. The word camera, repeated a few times.

"You deaf?" Frank finally interrupted. The grumble deeper, a prelude to a roar. "I said it's fine."

He pushed the door shut with a massive hand. Whoever was on the other side tried to hold it open, but their fingers disappeared right before the door thunked shut.

Frank then slid his foot all the way up against the door. He looked at me, his eyes slightly narrowed. Pondering. He hadn't said much, this whole time, but he had taken it all in.

The mountain was older than Baber, likely by ten years or so, and looked like he had been on the beat back in the days before digital imaging, internet cross-searches, and electronic warrants. He had done things the old way. Which is maybe why he and Baber got along. She was a little old school as well. Trusting her gut, her intuition, to put her on the right path.

Both of them had trouble believing what I had said. But both of them couldn't flat-out deny what I told them. Which meant the two of them would be digging into Charley's phone record as soon as I left.

Which was good. What they found there would bring me closer to finding her. They had slipped up with the warrant. I would backtrack that to its source.

Provided I could get Baber on my side, and give me that information.

Aaron had stepped away from the camera after the door had opened. He glanced at me, made a little motion to the mirror. We all knew that someone was in there now, watching us. I stared at my reflection there, right over Baber's shoulder, and wondered who stood behind the image of angry me.

Baber kept her eyes on me. Her mind raced to catch up. Thinking of cops she had talked to lately, maybe in passing, maybe wondering if it had been something she had said that had started the chain of events leading to Charley's death. Calculating.

"We're out of time," Aaron said, back to his professional lawyer voice. Playing the role. "I hope you're satisfied with my client's information, Detective. Next time maybe don't pull a shit warrant to get it."

He took a few steps around the table. Snapped his briefcase shut, tapped me on the shoulder. I stood, focused on Baber, who was still focused on me.

Her mind still working.

"We may have some follow-up questions," she said.

"All that will have to go through me," Aaron said. "My client's been harassed enough."

Baber kept her eyes locked on me. Ignoring Aaron. "I don't give a shit about you or your client," she said. "If I need him, I better be able to find him, or it's going to be both your asses."

Aaron looked at me. I shrugged. I could tell he liked Baber.

Aaron grinned. "We'll see what we can do," he said.

I stood then, nodding at Baber. I knew she would follow the path I had laid out. Backtracking Charley. If only to eliminate what I had told her as a possibility.

Aaron followed me out of the room. Frank moved aside to let us pass, but touched me on the arm as I walked by. A single hard press. Letting me know he was still there, with Baber. Watching me.

They could watch all they wanted, I thought, heading down the hallway to the elevators. As long as they checked what I told them. The door to the mirrored room remained shut, and I wanted to yank the door open and shout *ah-ha!*

I didn't though. I didn't want to let them know I was on to them. Or that Baber was. After all, that person likely was at the very bottom of the chain. I needed to trust Baber to follow that up.

We got to the elevators. Aaron stood next to me. I could tell he wanted to say something, he looked uncomfortable, and there was enough traffic around that he didn't.

The light above the elevators got to our floor. The doors dinged open. It was the same one as earlier, with the same sugary scent of donuts, just more faint, now. Aaron followed me, and a couple more cops got in with us. One of them, a heavier older cop with love handles overlapping his belt, pressed the second floor button.

I guess no one took the stairs anymore.

Aaron stood there. Not fidgeting, but part of him felt that way to me. The two of us had known each other a long time, and when you're around someone that long, you get to know a lot about them.

Even when they weren't moving. And especially when they had something to hide.

It was then that I understood, finally, what my subconscious was trying to tell me.

Aaron wasn't here because he was a friend. He wasn't here to bail me out because we had once worked together, or because I had saved his life, or he had saved mine.

We didn't owe each other. Friendships went deeper than that. There was no owing, no tallying of a tab. No *I saved your life there, so you owe me here*.

Aaron and I and Sam had been part of a team. We had worked for an agency, for lack of a better word. Not an agency like a bureau, but an agency, like a *force for good*.

We had rescued hostages that needed rescuing. We had killed terrorists that other specialists couldn't reach. We monitored the black market, and took out new weapons before they made the sale.

Like a virus. Or maybe like something using automation. Global Positioning.

David Whelan's company worked in the forefront of both. I had dismissed the military feel of it, back in the library, on the college campus. But my hindbrain had known. Whelan was involved in something that would have pulled me and Aaron here, back when we had worked together.

No surprise Aaron was here, now.

David Whelan was involved with a piece of technology that could kill people. It was what people wanted today. New and better and faster ways to kill. More efficient ways to war.

I didn't know how Angela could be wrapped up in this, though. Her only connection was the son. Ben.

Aaron would know. Because if he was here, others were, too. For a reason.

The elevator stopped at the second floor.

Aaron looked at me once, twice. The movement, between people who had saved each other's life, told me everything.

Both cops got out. We both waited for the doors to shut. The metal doors closing us in a square box of a gray world. It seemed like forever before the elevator lurched, and the world began moving down.

He spoke first. "You look like hell, brother."

I probably had looked better. We hadn't seen each other since they'd pulled me out of the torture cell I was in. I guess two years of rehab hadn't turned me into a male model.

It didn't matter. I wasn't interested in pleasantries. I didn't want to know if Aaron was worried about me. I didn't need that.

"What the fuck are you doing here, Aaron?" I asked him.

Aaron was always good at playing roles. So he gave me hurt.

Opening his eyes and hands. "What do you mean?" he said. "I'm bailing you out."

He wasn't bailing me out. There was no need. Baber couldn't have held me. She had been angry, and wanted to arrest me, but I hadn't killed Charley.

And the fingerprints they had taken, I wasn't worried about those. Like any other information about me, those fingerprints would be routed electronically to a database. A database the organization I had once worked for was already tapped into, because they had helped build it.

That database would see my fingerprints, and substitute in Thomas Hamilton's fingerprints instead. A clean set, with a clean record. The record of a guy who lived in Dorchester. A guy living an uneventful life.

The electronic, digital world today was a beautiful thing. Everyone could be connected to anything and everything. It's why I tried to stay off of it. It was too easy for any lie to be presented as the truth.

I snorted. "Give me a break," I told Aaron.

"Brother, you're still one of us, you know?" he said. "And *we're* here, so I thought, why not kill two birds with one stone?"

I looked at him. He felt the weight of the stare, but held up under it. As much as I knew him, he knew me.

"Why are you here, Aaron?" I asked, again.

We had been brothers, once. Maybe brothers still. Hard to lie to someone who knows you like that.

Though Sam had. She had lied to both of us.

My jaw set at the thought of her.

"Aaron, I'm not going to ask you again," I said.

"Look, you're *out*," he said. "If you were in, it'd be different. But you're out, and you know I can't say anything. You *know* it, bro."

Charley was dead. She had been killed, likely because I had involved her in what I was doing. Or because she had chosen to involve herself. In either case, she might still be alive, had I not gone looking for her, so I could help a girl I barely knew.

Somehow, Angela was tied into this Whelan thing. I wasn't good at figuring this stuff out. That had been Sam. I was just a guy that could get things done.

Charley had been killed. But Angela was out there, somewhere.

What was one life balanced against another?

I didn't like the answer. But someone else had made the decision to kill her. So I would do what I did best, and even that score. There was always some redemption in that. When the consequence found the action that had created it.

Charley deserved that, I thought.

I was good in a fight because I could always tell when the first blow was about to be struck. I could sense that moment, then strike before that blow. And those that struck first, usually won.

Out in the field I usually sensed it like the current of an electrical charge, like the invisible hum of a transformer with thousands of amps pulsing through its windings. Like the thrumming of a bass note so low you could barely hear, just feel the power of the sound, as the hairs on your arms lifted off your skin.

I could always sense that current, feel that sound, and I always knew, *always*, when the note was about to change. I could always land the first blow.

But I had missed it this time. I had missed it, with Charley. Because I hadn't been looking at the whole picture. I had been focused on a tiny piece, on Angela. I hadn't been aware of everything else in play.

I kept telling myself, money and power were part of this. Both things would always raise the stakes. Increase the pressure. Ramp up the intensity. Money and Power never moved with surgical strikes, they shifted events in broad sweeping strokes, strokes that caught up everyone and washed lives away.

Like Charley.

The first shot had been fired, and it hadn't been me. I hadn't struck first. I hadn't even known where to strike.

It was why I had woken up today with an urgency. The charge had been in the air, the transformer had been ramping up, someone had struck the first note of a song, and my hindbrain had known it.

It just hadn't made it to conscious thought. And Charley had died for my mistake. I couldn't let Angela join her.

The elevator slowed down and stopped, the heavy feeling of momentum pressing me down onto the floor. The elevator dinged open, the doors opening our square box into the world around us. People waited for us to get off, so they could get on. Cops in uniforms, lawyers in suits, other people in handcuffs.

Aaron and I remained staring at each other. One of the lawyers coughed into her hand. Both of us turned away at the sound.

We walked out. Back down the crowded hallway of police officers rushing back and forth, of radios squawking and coffee cups everywhere.

Aaron was silent, all the way until we reached the front desk. Then he grabbed my arm and leaned forward, whispering.

"I'm still your friend, man," Aaron said. "I'd be here, no matter what."

"Yeah," I said. Staring at his grip on my arm. Staring at his arm.

"No matter *what*," he insisted.

"I don't trust people anymore, Aaron," I said. "You should understand that."

Sam had betrayed both of us. She had left Aaron for dead. Me for worse.

"Brother," he said. "Sam betrayed us *both*."

I didn't want to hear her name. Not out loud. And not from Aaron.

I glared at him. Spoke softly, but with menace. "Don't you mention *her* to *me*," I said.

He looked hurt. His grip tightened on my arm. "Both of us, man."

I stared at his hand. He finally let me go. But he stayed close. Shook his head. He had been the person to joke about it. About Sam's interest in me. I wondered if he blamed himself, for getting us together. For everything that had happened since.

Maybe we were alike, that way.

"Dammit, J," Aaron said. A name I had once been, before I had been Hamilton. He and Sam both thought I was still that person, part of the team we had once been. And while Sam knew better, Aaron might need the same lesson.

"I'm not that guy anymore," I said.

"What?" he said. "Who?"

"You should know, Aaron," I said. He had led the team that had found me. Broken. Leg shattered, not knowing what I had told the people who had done the breaking. It could have been anything. I had been feverish, in constant pain, delusional for a week. "That guy's long gone."

"I can't call you J?" Aaron said, eyebrows raised. "It's who you are, man."

"Not anymore," I said.

"What the hell do I call you?" Aaron said. "Man, we're friends. We're *brothers*. We've been through shit together. We went through *her* together."

He knew better than to bring up her name, at least.

"If you want to call me anything," I said, pulling a name out from the book. Something Kirschke would have loved to hear. "Call me Crosse."

Aaron looked hurt. Really hurt, not acting.

"Whatever I call you, I'm still your friend. Still your brother," Aaron said. "I'm trying to help you here, man. Don't be like this."

"Don't be like what, Aaron?" I said. "You want to help me? Then tell me why you're here. Tell me about David Whelan. Angela Martinez. *Tell me.*"

Aaron glanced around. We stood in the front of the lobby, and the people close to us were staring at us. Like we were in the middle of a street in the wild west, a clock tower about to strike twelve, the crowd lining the wooden sidewalks around us. I was about to face some gunslinger, and Aaron was holding me back from my appointment at high noon.

Most of the cops had seen worse than an argument in a lobby, though. The sergeant at the desk was on the phone. Writing something down. Not paying any attention to us.

Even if our voices were raised.

"I can't tell you man," he said. "You chose to leave us. You told him you're out. You should be happy he's keeping you that way."

"Aaron," I said. "I'm going to find out. You can help me, or you can be in the way."

"You're mixing into some things here," Aaron said. "You know the things I'm talking about."

"Yeah, I'm late to that party," I said. I hadn't known Aaron was here. That who we worked for would have an interest. "But I understand now."

"Stay out, man," Aaron said. "Let me handle it."

A small part of me wanted to. I wanted to get back to my routines. This was a world I had left. I didn't want to know about all the horrors and the abuses. I didn't want to save anyone, anymore. I didn't want to know how much evil was in the world, because I had tried to fix it all once, and I had broken in the attempt.

But I couldn't leave it to Aaron. No matter how deep our friendship ran. Trust wasn't something I had in me, anymore. I couldn't trust Aaron any more than I could trust Sam. Or the guy standing behind Aaron.

If a thing was going to be done right, there was only one way, one person to do them. Me.

"Tell me, Aaron," I said. "Do you know who has her? Do *you* have her?"

Aaron was silent. His jaw worked a bit.

"Dammit, Aaron, you tell me," I said. I wanted to keep my voice down, but I couldn't, and my voice got loud enough that even the sergeant looked at us, phone held loosely in one hand.

Aaron's face changed. It got bitter. Like I had been the one who had betrayed him, and not Sam.

That face hurt me some. But not enough.

"Tell you what?" Aaron fired back. "You're *out*, brother. And out is out."

I stepped close to him. So that we stood nose-to-nose. I wanted him to feel the weight of what I was about to say. "You tell me Aaron. Because if I find out you're in it, or you have her, I'll be coming through you to get her. However many of you are here."

"Fuck you, J," Aaron told me. Staring right back. He had made a decision. His face hard, but also sad. "*Crosse*. Whoever the fuck you want to be. You're messing in things you shouldn't. You *know* the types of things I'm talking about."

I did. Aaron was angry. And stressed. I was a wrench in his works, and I likely understood how he felt.

Back in the day Aaron and Sam and I had done a lot of good, with who we had worked for. We had saved people. Killed others. Saved the world, maybe.

Most of everything we had done had been about weapons. Guns, bombs, viruses, global positioning, whatever, in the end it was always about killing. New ways, old ways, it didn't matter. Tensions always rose, fast and hard, whenever things that killed people were in play.

"Stay out of it," Aaron warned. "Just stay out of it, man. *Please.*"

One side of my mouth curved up. My heart raced, furious. My eyes watered a bit, maybe in frustration. I held a long moment, taking slow breaths. I was angry because I was late to the understanding, and it had cost someone their life.

That wasn't Aaron's fault. It was mine.

He wasn't telling me everything. He wasn't telling me anything. Both of us still knew how it would go down, if he had Angela. I would have to trust that knowledge would be enough, between us.

Aaron wouldn't want me coming after him.

He knew I wouldn't quit, until I had found Angela.

So I had to trust that he didn't have her. Still, Aaron was involved. He had knowledge that might help me. And he was keeping that knowledge from me.

Our eyes stayed locked.

Both of us knew where this stood. Where it would go.

"We all got to do what we got to do, Aaron," I told him.

I walked out, shrugging past a person at the door, trying to come in at the same time. Out into the open air, smelling brisk and chill. Out into the outside morning, with the dark gray skies over the horizon, the sun still coming up in the east, over the cold, restless waters of the Atlantic.

Today, I had woken up more anxious than in the past. The reason hadn't been the nightmare, or poor sleep. I was anxious because I was behind, and the back of my brain had known that. It had sensed the slow build-up of pressure, had known when the bubble would burst, and had tried to warn me.

Someone had fired the first shot. I was in the middle of a fight I knew very little about. But I was learning the players. And my body was ramping up. Adrenaline was firing. The back of my brain was spinning up the front. Accelerating. Getting me ready for a fight. Because it knew one was coming.

I had missed all the signs, small and subtle, things that had creeped along the backside of my brain, prickling along my intuition. My subconscious had known it, had tried to warn me. I had just missed it.

And missing it, I had left Charley out there. And she had paid a final price for that mistake.

I wasn't good at this stuff. Turning over stones. Piecing things together. I was good at other things, at getting in the first shot. At sensing the moment to strike, and striking first.

I had been out for too long. And someone had beaten me to it. But I didn't always have to get the first shot in, to make sure I got in the last.

People were getting killed now. That was on the table. Which made finding Angela harder, especially with the sense of urgency I felt, but also simpler. It was much easier to find a muzzle flash in the dark than a needle in a haystack.

CHAPTER
TWENTY-NINE

Baber leaned back in her chair. She was at her desk, and the chair was old, wooden, rocking back further than it should on the little hydraulic cylinder holding the chair up. Like bolts were loose, and slipping just a bit. It was uncomfortable and hard, the seat was a thick yellow cushion almost glued on, but she couldn't remove it, and, well... The chair was *hers*. That explained it enough to her. If not to anyone else who sat in it.

Her desk was like every other detective's desk, metal, black drawers that hung up when you tried to pull them out, squealing sometimes when you yanked them hard enough. A cold cup of coffee sat off to one side in a white Styrofoam cup, and she sipped it, then made a face. The fake sugar she put in always tasted more chemical when the coffee got cold.

"You sure?" she asked Frank, setting the cup down off to the side. Away from the papers and keyboard.

Frank nodded. His desk was directly across from her, like all partner's desks were. He was sitting in his own chair, a big metal thing large enough to hold him. Custom-ordered, after enough of the regular office chairs had broken underneath him.

"Hamilton was right," he said, holding up a sheet of paper in the air. The fluorescent lights made it easy to see black outlines of words, through the page. "Her phone records show Charley calling and talking to the precinct here for a couple of minutes. Five minutes, seventeen seconds, actually. Plenty long enough for her to wait on the line, get transferred, and pass along what she knew."

"Dammit," Baber said. Her gaze went over Frank's desk, to the corner of the room. Where their Investigations Captain sat in a windowed office. The Detective Sergeant was in there, and the two men were talking. The Sergeant standing over the desk, his bald head gleaming under the lights.

It was always too bright in here.

While Baber watched, her captain glanced over the two of them. Baber and Frank. She looked away. Not quickly. Not slowly, either. Her hand grabbed the paper from Frank, the page fluttering in the air. She looked at the calls, finding the one he was talking about. Definitely their precinct.

"Don't have to trust him," Frank said, "to trust what he's told us."

He meant Hamilton, but an image of her captain flashed before her eyes. Her lieutenant. Both people she couldn't trust, now.

Baber sighed. She put those thoughts away. "I know." An urge to smoke came over her, something she fought all the time and lost. "I can't figure him out."

What kind of name was Hamilton? She knew it was fake, though the man was real enough. Who picked a name like that for an alias?

"What's there to figure?" Frank said. "He's using you to backtrack what happened to Charley."

"Yeah," she smiled a bit. A nasty curve of the lips. "He is, isn't he?"

Both of them were quiet for a moment. "That's not normal for a person to do, or think." Baber said. Meaning Hamilton.

Frank knew it. "Nope. He's not normal."

"What're we going to do?"

Frank shrugged. "I guess what Hamilton wants," he said. "Backtrack."

"You think he's right?" Baber said. "About the danger?"

She waved her hand in a flutter, capturing the precinct around them. She didn't know what to think about that. His warning. A cop holding a call might be one thing. A cop providing information to someone, like Charley's address, another. But killing another cop, like her or Frank, that was miles above all of that.

Or so Baber thought.

"Eh," Frank said, his massive shoulders moving slightly up and down. "It is, it isn't. Whatever."

"Going to be hard to dig into things," she said. "If someone's watching."

"Got to trust someone," he said.

"Well, there's you," Baber said.

Frank shrugged again, as if some things didn't need to be said.

"I guess I'll pull up the call rotation," Baber said.

The police had a rotation of officers, with things like kidnapping, that helped out on the phones. She would figure out who was on that rotation, and at what time. It'd be easy to figure out who took the call that day.

And easy worried her. It was sloppy. Same, like Hamilton said, with the warrant. Baber had hated taking it, but she didn't have enough for an arrest warrant, she was tired, angry at the girl's death, and ready to take it out on a guy that wasn't who he appeared to be.

That mistake was on her. For the same reason though. Angry. Rushed. Pressured.

If Hamilton was right, she couldn't afford another. She would have to be careful. Because if the pressure was high enough that sloppiness was now allowed, then maybe she would be in danger. Frank too. Killing cops brought around a price. Maybe these people were okay with paying it.

"Don't have to give 'em anything though," her partner said.

Baber smiled. She agreed with Frank. Some things didn't have to be said. They would dig into this, but Hamilton would be surprised if he thought he'd get information from Baber. She would keep it from everyone, until she *knew*. Including her lieutenant. And her captain.

The urge came along again, strong. Saliva flooded her mouth at the thought of a cigarette. It would only get stronger, the longer she waited.

So she got up, grabbing a pack from her purse. And a lighter.

"Finally?" Frank said.

"Be back in five," Baber said, pulling out one cigarette, holding it in her fingers. Letting the craving know it was about to be fulfilled. At least, for a brief time.

"Those things'll kill you," Frank told her.

"How many times are you going to use that cliché?" Baber said.

Clichés were there for a reason. Cops worked long hours, for little pay. They had to do something to get by each day, after the things they saw, or after the people they dealt with. People who would cuss a policeman up and down all day long, then complain they weren't around when so-and-so did such a thing.

Frank knew the same thing. He grinned. "Don't make the cliché any less true."

So Baber had a vice. She dealt with it the way she knew how. Hold out as long as she could, until she broke, then start the process over again.

She slapped Frank on the shoulder as she passed and walked down the hallway. It was quiet, here on the third floor. Most of the detectives had EarPods in, listening to music, their phone within sight in case it rang. A lot of them looking through files on their desktop, getting what they were going to do for the day in place. Or typing up reports from yesterday.

She pushed in the thick metal bar on the door to the stairs, feeling the door give, and pushing it open with a grunt. The stairs were concrete, and as new as the building was, the steps were stained with coffee spills, cigarette butts, and hard dirty wads of gum that had been stepped in over and over, until they had become part of the stairs, hard dirty bumps melded into stone.

Baber got to the bottom floor. Pushed the same kind of thick metal bar on the door there. Opened it and walked outside, where all the police cars were parked. Off to the side of the lot, away from the door and where people would have to walk, was a designated smoking area. A long side of it rested against a tall concrete wall. The rest of it was a painted square on the pavement, three sides of the square, a pen made to hold the nicotine addicts in their place. They called the smoke pad *The Pen*, in the self-deprecating dry humor some cops had.

Sometimes the pen was packed. Today it was quiet, other than the occasional firing up of a police car, or the random slam of a vehicle door shutting. There were just a few fellow smokers out. Some regulars, staked out in their regular corners. Others, like Baber, giving in to the vice in a moment of weakness. Standing in a place, smoking and staring up into the sky, like they didn't know what else to do.

Someone else was here today though. Hidden in the corner of the smoking pen. Off to the side, like he was waiting. Or brewing.

Hamilton's lawyer. Or pretend-lawyer. Aaron.

She snorted and headed right over. He was already smoking, a cigarette casually held in one hand, a plume of smoke billowing from behind a flash of white teeth. He had tanned skin and dark, curly hair, the curls a little too long and hanging over his forehead. South American roots. The man could be on the cover of a magazine.

"Detective," he said, holding a lighter out, the flame dancing in tiny gusts of the morning breeze.

"I'd say *lawyer*, but we both know that's a lie." She leaned forward to let him light her cigarette, inhaling deeply while the end grew cherry red, feeling the harshness of the smoke hit her lungs. It wasn't the healthiest habit, but it brought a great rush. A little juice, after a long night.

Aaron smiled. "It is what it is."

"What are you doing here?" she asked.

He waved his hand. The cigarette traced a figure eight in the air, the smoke dissipating quickly. "I think it's called smoking."

"You know what I mean," she said.

The man shook his head, as if he was thinking about something recent, or reflecting on something in the past. "So many people think I know more than what I do."

Then he took a deep drag, again blowing the smoke out of his nostrils. Maybe he was exorcising a demon, the twin plumes jetted out like a dragon. "Perhaps, just this time, it's only about the cigarette."

Baber rolled her eyes. She got the feeling this man was never just one thing, but many. Attractiveness was one, though. Dangerous would be another. "Sure," she said.

They both sat that way a moment, smoking. Staring up into the sky above, gray and dark and thick with clouds. Tiny patches of sapphire poked out, glints of deep blue among the gray, as if the sky was a dark shroud wrapped around a storm, hiding it from those below. A storm the blue heavens wanted nothing to do with.

Thinking of things hidden...

"CIA? FBI?" Baber asked Aaron. "Homeland?"

The man didn't reply. The man leaned his back against the wall, slouched just a little forward, as if taking a load off. He finally looked at her, and Baber saw his eyes were a brilliant emerald green. His stare caught her and held her, as if it looked like he was measuring something inside her.

"What do you think about our friend?" he finally asked.

"Hamilton?"

His shoulders lifted up and down, a small motion. "Sure."

"I think he's dangerous," she said. *Just like I think about you.*

"You know he didn't do it," he said, then clarified. "Kill that girl."

Baber took a quick drag on her cigarette. Let her own plume out. Then shook her head. "I wanted to. It'd been a long day. If you'd seen the girl," Baber shuddered.

Charley Taylor had not died well. Hematomas had been all over her body from the beating, protruding in ugly black and purple lumps of skin that had stretched until the skin was tissue-thin. Some had burst.

She pushed that memory from her mind. All it got her was furious. She took things like that personally.

"And Hamilton had gotten under my skin. Then the bike guy, with his complaint. When my warrant fell through, and the lieutenant came back with a governor's warrant," she kept shaking her head, admonishing herself. "I just took it."

Now she had to wonder about the lieutenant. Was the man part of this? Was he why Charley Taylor was dead? How had he gotten that warrant, was it from the captain, the mayor? The actual governor? Who was in it, and how far back did it go?

She even wondered about Hamilton. She needed to see who had given her that task. Had that come back from the lieutenant as well? She'd need to review every conversation between them, to see if she could get a better feel for it.

That was the worst thing about this. Once you saw even the tiniest bit of a conspiracy somewhere, you saw it everywhere. Baber blew out a deep breath, empty of smoke. Trying to settle her mind down. Too much was going on.

"Fuck," she said.

"If you knew Hamilton like I did," Aaron said, then the man corrected himself. "Like I had, you'd have never believed it. You'd have gone to the fences for him, screaming denials."

"Hamilton?" she asked, sure her face looked incredulous.

"Yeah," Aaron said again. Sadly.

"Maybe we know different guys," she said.

"Maybe," he said, taking another drag. "Maybe."

The man smoked some more. The cigarette was just a stub, he'd been out here a while. And he seemed troubled. Troubled men talked.

Baber pulled a fresh cigarette out, and offered it to the man.

Aaron raised his eyebrow and smiled, something out of the corner of one mouth. Like he knew what Baber was doing. But he still took it, flicking his used butt into the bucket of sand a few feet away. A tiny splash of red ash puffed out, and then it died.

Baber watched all of that, the casual way he lit the new cigarette, the way he kept looking up at the sky. Waiting.

"None of the three," he said, finally answering her question.

"Mercenaries?" Baber asked. Wondering if he was part of some hired force.

Aaron laughed, the sound was light and quick. "You've already struck out."

"Humor me," Baber said. "Don't make me dig."

He glanced out of the side of his eyes at her, and Baber found herself caught by the emerald green stare. The man didn't seem worried about her digging into his past, and she wondered who he really was.

Other than dangerous.

Then Aaron shrugged. "You know when those departments were formed?"

"Which ones?" Baber asked.

Aaron waved one hand. Baber thought he was a guy who liked to talk with his hands. "The ones you mentioned."

"Homeland was formed after the twin towers attack," Baber said, narrowing her eyes in thought. This conversation was going in a way she hadn't anticipated. "CIA, wasn't that Truman?"

"Nineteen forty-seven," Aaron said.

"And FBI, I think that was right before the world wars, right?" Baber said. "Early nineteen hundreds."

"Close enough." The man took a puff of the cigarette and looked up at the sky, as if the man was still deeply thinking about something. Maybe what to tell her. Or maybe he was just wondering about the storm.

"Where are you going with this?" Baber finally asked.

Aaron looked at her out of the side of his eyes. "The country's been around for over two hundred years. Almost two hundred and fifty." His lips curved, slightly. "Who did all that CIA and FBI stuff before them?"

Baber froze for a moment at the question. She hadn't ever thought about that. There were militias, the army, the navy, after the country's birth. The Secret Service had been around a while. Sheriffs and deputies, out in the west. The CIA and FBI, those agencies had been formed when something came around that had required them. Like Homeland, after the attack.

There had been marshals, too, Baber thought. Like Wyatt Earp. She knew she was reaching, but she wanted to keep Aaron talking. "A marshal?"

She knew she was wrong, if he had been a marshal, he wouldn't have needed the secrecy.

Aaron shook his head. "You going for the whole side?"

"The army?" she said. "NCIS?"

"Six," he counted. "Seven."

"It's got to be one of them," Baber said. Frustrated.

"Maybe," Aaron said. "Or maybe it's something else. Something that's been there from the very beginning."

She wondered what he meant by something else. But she felt like asking him would be pushing it. So Baber let him keep looking at the sky. Smoking. Thinking.

His words got to her. Something else. From the beginning. She wondered where he was going, and felt like people did on a rollercoaster. Like she was going up a big hill, the clicking and the clacking of the carts on the rails, nervous and anxious, waiting for the realization of the precipice at the top.

"From the beginning?" she said. "You mean in the Constitution? Like when it was written?"

"Around that time," he said. "But nothing written."

He took a large inhale, let out a smoky cloud that swelled and drifted up into the air. Baber waited, curious.

"A few of our forefathers were pretty smart," Aaron said. "They set up a framework so they could build the greatest country in the history of the world. They also left the framework bare, like the skeleton of a house, so later people could flesh it out. They devised a system with three legs," he looked at Baber, and she knew this was the point he had been moving towards. "Executive, the Legislative, and the Judiciary."

The man took another hit of the cigarette, let the smoke come out gradually in a deep, slow exhale. Like people did, when the last piece of resistance left them.

"The thing about a chair with three legs," Aaron told her, "is that if a leg breaks, the chair topples over."

He smiled at her then. A friendly smile. Waiting for her to get it. But Baber didn't. She was lost. The president led. Congress was there to give the people a voice. And the Supreme Court regulated the interactions between the two.

It was what she had been taught. It was what everyone had been taught. This thing with Aaron, the history lesson and the legs, it wasn't going anywhere, that she could see.

"I don't get it," Baber said.

Aaron shrugged. "I didn't either, at first. I laughed when it was explained to me. Laughed and laughed and laughed."

His eyes grew unfocused, as if he was reliving the memory. Then one of the police cars in the lot started alarming. The twin lights on the top flashed red and blue. The blaring siren whooped up and down, over and over.

Baber looked across the lot. In the blaring car a young officer was frantically hitting things on the dash, trying to get the alarm to stop. An older man in the passenger seat muffled a laugh behind his hand.

Rookies, Baber thought. Hated that it interrupted Aaron. She worried that would be the end of it, and that the man wouldn't give her the information she needed.

He was still standing by her. The cigarette smoking in his hand, loose, forgotten. As if the alarm had startled him into another memory. He smiled, something to himself, and she was sure Aaron was unaware of where he was in that moment.

Two doors shut. The rookie and the older cop, getting out. The rookie's face red. The wind picked up and blew across the lot, stirring up a Styrofoam cup from under one of the cars and tumbling it across the pavement.

When she looked back at Aaron, he was watching her.

"A three-legged stool," he said, "is a pretty stable place to sit."

"It is," Baber agreed.

"But four legs," Aaron told her. "That's probably better."

I walked down the street, looking for a pharmacy or store. It took a couple of blocks, a lot of pushing through the early crowds of morning, a lot of hearing various people walk by talking loudly on their cell phones, a lot of listening to various vehicles passing down the street. Rumbling roars of eight-cylinder engines, low-pitched whines of the four-cylinder cars, the burst of air from the brakes of a large white bus, a yellow stripe down its side, its next stop scrolling across the front of it in dotted LED letters.

Lines were blurring everywhere in my life. What had been my past, and what was now my nightmare were wrapped altogether in my present. My life had been twined with the book, so that my past entangled everything: the nightmare, the book, my old life, all of it was somehow connected to Angela.

Maybe that, most of all, was what stirred up the concern. The worry. There was something out there I didn't know. Something dark hiding in the shadows, standing behind me, waiting for the right moment to dig its claws into my back.

Something sharp danced along my spine. The muscles on my back tightened, even though there was no knife behind me. No monster. No pointed claws.

A store finally appeared, a corner pharmacy with a big white sign over its top. A curved red *W* in the middle of the sign, a tiny hook to one of the sides of the letter. I passed a group of people standing in front of the store, waiting for the walking signal at the crosswalk. Commuters headed into work.

The pharmacy was old, in the way that even new stores aged quickly in the heart of the city. It saw a lot of use, the white tiled floor was dirty, the aisles were somewhat bare. Like the shelves had been picked clean, and the people working there couldn't be bothered to restock, or re-sweep.

I walked and found the prepaid phone section. All of the phones were locked up behind a plastic window, and I had to find an attendant to unlock the case and free one for me. While I was there I grabbed a prepaid card with plenty of minutes. Probably too many minutes, for me.

I paid in cash and headed back out. A new group of people waited at the corner. The same kind of group, just dressed up in different clothes. Different jackets and bags and briefcases. Different hats, one of the girls had a blue scarf laying like decoration around her shoulders. It was like the group of people standing there before had quickly changed while I was in the store.

The little white man in the crosswalk signal blinked into existence, and the group started shuffling across the street. There was a coffee shop there. I followed, breaking the phone out of its package, throwing the hard plastic away in a trash bin on the other side of the crosswalk.

The trash bin was a brownish round can. It had a metal cage around its top, something to funnel garbage into its mouth. That cage dripped with tacky syrup, probably from half-drank lattes that had been tossed in. How hard was it to drink a coffee? Or throw something away properly?

A car horn beeped behind me. A tiny, punkish-sounding horn. I had paused, looking at the trash can, one foot on the sidewalk, one still on the road. I stared back at the car, a tiny silver Ford Fusion with a tinier man in it. He grinned a nasty grin and beeped the horn again, waving at the light.

Some men were always braver, behind a thousand pounds of metal and a clown-like horn.

I walked to the corner of his car. Stepping off the sidewalk, and standing there. More horns started to blare, from behind the Fusion. The man looked at me, then behind his car, holding his hands up like there was nothing he could do. Back and forth, back and forth, more and more frantic. Then laying on his horn, adding his blaring beep to all the others behind him, but not looking at me now. At least, not looking at my eyes.

I stood there and waited. Staring directly at the little man in his little car with his clown-like horn. Until the light changed back to red. I took a deep breath. Then another. Then got off the road and turned back to the coffee place.

Was I being petty? Maybe. But the time had come and gone where I would suffer people who hid behind things. Whatever they did or said, their actions always revealed who they were. And like I believed, all actions had consequences.

The coffee shop was on the corner as well, opposite the street from the pharmacy. A little cafe with outside seating, tables and chairs that hugged the wall in either direction. The tables were made of an iron-like grate, the diamond-like holes creating a see-through tabletop. The chairs were made of the same, hard to sit in, and still wet from the morning dew, so they were mostly empty.

I took a seat, ignoring the chilly wetness that quickly soaked into the back of my pants. Things dried. A waitress came out. A young girl, heavyset and thick around the waist. Her white blouse rolled over her belt and around her belly like a donut. A heavier, darker vest draped over the bulge, too short to really hide the weight, and she had a white bandana with a crisscrossed pattern on it wrapped around her head. The bandana held thick dark hair back in place.

What did you call a waitress in a coffee place? Usually baristas would make the coffee inside and hand it to you there. Did they also serve?

I guessed it didn't really matter. My mind was doing funny things, going off in tangents. Rapidly, and in any direction. Maybe to distract me from what had happened to Charley. My subconscious was fleeing the scene of the crime and driving all over the place, getting as far away from her death as possible.

The girl waited in front of me. Her eyes looking at something over my shoulder. She had a large phone or a small tablet in her hand, holding it with one finger above the screen. Ready to press my order in.

Sooner or later, it would just be machines. Taking orders, taking payment, producing a product. Hell, it was already happening in stages. Someone would put it all together, something automated that would stare just over my shoulder and press whatever button was needed.

"Help you?" she prodded me. Disinterested.

"Coffee," I said. "Some water."

"Sure," she said, her finger still above the screen. Her gaze still roved over the street, maybe like me, her subconscious was looking for something with real meaning. "Something to eat?"

"No," I said.

She waited, I waited, and then she finally pressed something else on her pad and left.

Whenever machines came, they wouldn't have to worry about providing good customer service. That was getting weaned out already.

I got the phone working. Took the coffee and a bottle of water, when the girl came back. The coffee was weak and thin and I immediately hated it. The cup wouldn't sit straight, the bottom edges of the thick paper bottom caught on the diamond-shaped holes of the table, causing the coffee to tilt.

The bottle of water, with its round bottom, just kept tipping over.

Just sitting here was pissing me off. I took a breath. I positioned the bottle where it wouldn't roll into the coffee and held it there, watching the cup. I thought the water would stay. If it didn't, it was going to end up in the trash.

I chanced letting the bottle go, and it stayed. Rocking just once before settling. With a careful eye on the bottle, I dialed Sara's number and put the phone to my ear.

She answered on the first ring. "Knox."

"Sara," I said. "Me."

"Hey," she said, her voice teasing. "Look who moved into the twenty-first century."

"Sure," I said. My voice rough.

"Wow," she said. "When you wake up on the wrong side of the bed, it's a really bad side."

"I get it," I said. Wanting to push past the normal banter normal people did on the phone. "You find that cop yet?"

"Not that my job means anything to you," Sara said. "But yeah, I managed to find him, among all the other things I'm doing. We're playing phone tag."

"Okay," I said. "I'm going to need something more from you."

"Seems fair enough," she said. "Me giving you all the information you need. You giving me nothing."

"I get it," I said again. "Still, I need it."

There was a bit of silence over the connection. A deep breath. A tapping sound, like she was drumming the end of a pen against a desk.

"Look," I said. "People are dying."

"Yeah?" Sara said, her voice perking up. Her tone angered me, but that was my guilt coloring Sara's voice. Not anything she did. Sara didn't know Charley. Didn't know me, or what I had done to bring death to Charley's door.

She was a reporter. Death was interesting. I understood that.

"Yeah," I said. "So I need what I need. But I also am calling to warn you. To let you know, people are getting killed. So when you look for what I'm telling you, be careful about it."

The line was silent for a moment. When Sara spoke next, it was less playful, and serious. "You know how a reporter would react, telling them something like that."

"I know," I said. It would be like a drug. Get their heart racing. Get them addicted to the story. Maybe I was playing her with it. But I was still warning her. "But I'm still passing the warning along. Think hard before you help."

I hadn't warned Charley. A quick comment at the end, about making sure she kept her gun loaded. That was it. And it hadn't been enough. I wasn't making the same mistake twice.

"Fine," Sara said. "Consider me warned. What can you tell me?"

I did like Sara. She understood there were going to be some things I kept silent. It's why she used the word *can*. She was giving me freedom to choose what to tell her, and that implied some kind of trust.

Part of me didn't want to tell her about Charley. But I had told Sara I would keep her updated. That was part of the deal. So I told her about the arrest warrant. Getting brought in. And about Charley. Not specifically what happened at the apartment, but that Charley had helped me, and the next day someone had beat her to death for it.

"I don't understand," Sara said. "How'd they connect her with you?"

I swallowed something hard down. It tasted worse than the coffee. Because I had taken a knife and stabbed a guy in front of her. Because I had caused that man to piss himself in fear. Because I had been too angry to control what I felt in that kitchen, and I had angered someone else who killed for a living. A person who enjoyed the killing, and was nasty about it.

But I wasn't telling any of that to Sara. Not that, and not about Aaron. "They probably saw me with her," I said.

"Huh," she said, in a tone that told me she knew I wasn't telling her everything.

And I wasn't.

I was okay with that. I had given her enough. And she knew it.

The tapping of the pen started up again. Like Sara had drank too much coffee, or was too excited, and was drumming out the energy.

"Okay," she said. "What do you need?"

I remembered the driver's license plate, and asked her if she could get me anything on that.

"I got a guy," Sara said.

"And I'll need more on Whelan," I said.

"Like what?"

"Things his business is into," I said. "How he made his money. What he's doing now."

"He's old money," Sara said. "He's had money since the day he was born."

"Yeah, but he's doing something now," I said. "He's got something going on."

"You think it's tied up in what happened to Angela?" she asked.

"I don't know," I said. But with Aaron here, the Branch, Benjamin Whelan's death, money and power and politics were all over this. "I don't believe in coincidences."

"Okay," Sara said. "I can have something to you in the next day or so."

"I'll need it in an hour or two," I said.

"Ummm, dude," Sara said. "I've got other stuff to do."

"By lunchtime," I told her, looking at my phone. It was just after ten in the morning. "I'll need where he works during the day, too."

"Whelan?" she asked. "You know he's not just going to see you. He's like a recluse. Not to mention he's got all kinds of security."

"Sure," I said. I would worry about that. "Just get me the info."

"What are you going to be doing, while I do all this?"

I took a sip of the coffee. It was thin, not bitter enough, and already cool. I was starting to believe there was a reason people weren't sitting here at the tables, other than the dew. A reason half-tossed lattes coated the trash can.

What would I be doing?

What I was going to do, before this day had started.

I was late for an appointment.

"I've got somewhere to be," I said. And a thought came to me. Just something I threw in, because my mind brought it up. Nothing important. "Whelan is the thing, now."

"Sure, massah," she said. "Anything else? Need me to hold your calls? Run your dry cleaning in? Pick up any prescriptions?"

"That's it," I said, and almost hung up the phone. Brought it back to my ear. "Sara?"

"Yeah?"

"Thanks."

CHAPTER
THIRTY-ONE

Baber knew her jaw had dropped.

The man before her looked so serious, in front of her. Maybe a little sad, as well. Like he had come to a decision, something he didn't like, but had made it anyway.

She had been talking three branches of government. He had been talking three legs of a stool. What did he mean by four legs?

Baber knew, she *knew* that Aaron was a guy who played a lot of parts. A lot of roles. He was this GQ lawyer now, but she got this feel from him that this wasn't all he was. He was many things, and he chose what he was and when, and Baber thought she had understood that the moment she had realized he wasn't a lawyer.

It was always hard to trust something coming from a man like that. So Baber laughed. "You had me, for a moment."

Aaron didn't laugh with her. His eyes told her he got it. Knew what she was thinking. But he kept going.

"The founding fathers had just witnessed tyranny. Not just of a king. Of a *system*. Nobles. Aristocracy. They were smart enough to understand what power does, they had seen it through history. Power corrupts, and the founding fathers knew sooner or later, whatever country they built, power would corrupt it too."

"But that's why we have all the checks and balances," Baber said. "So that one side can check the other two."

"Three-legged stool, Detective," the man said.

"What's that mean?" she said. "There's some agency out there, keeping the legs strong?"

"Not an agency," Aaron said, shaking his head slightly. The cigarette forgotten in his hand, the darker end growing longer with gray ash. "A branch. A *Fourth* Branch."

She had trouble saying anything to that. Other than the idea sounded crazy.

"I understand how it sounds," he said.

Baber looked at him, really looked at him.

"I don't think you do," she said. "Or you wouldn't be telling me this. It's crazy."

Still, everything about the man told her he was telling her something he really believed. His relaxed stance. His calm acceptance of her disbelief. His quiet confidence that what he was telling her was the truth.

It wasn't crazy. It was insane.

She shook her head. "Nah. I don't buy it. There's no Fourth Branch."

"Not one people know about," Aaron said.

"It's ridiculous," Baber said. "This isn't some movie, where some secret agency comes in from out of the blue with all these toys and gadgets to save the world."

"Nope," Aaron agreed. "It is not."

He finally realized he was still holding the cigarette. Went to smoke it, but the movement caused the long edge of ash to fall off. Which the man looked at, the tiny gray dust dropping to the ground.

Then he flicked that cigarette into the sand bucket.

Baber worried that the conversation was coming to an end. Aaron reached into his jacket, pulled out a phone. Did something on the screen for a moment, then showed it to her. Holding the phone in an open hand, laying it in his palm, so she could look down at the screen.

He had opened a photo. A soldier, in uniform. Laying outside, back against some rock. A flap of a white and tan tent in the picture next to him. It was a sandy place, with tan rocks and clayish ground, wisps of dust carried by an unseen wind. The sun was bright in the picture, and the sky was blue. There weren't any clouds.

The soldier's uniform was dirty and blackened. There were holes in it, tears, as if he had been standing close to something that had blown up. His left shoulder was duct-taped, as if someone had taken a roll and wound it around where the arm met the shoulder. The tape was grimy. The soldier's face was dirty as well, streaks of black down his cheeks, and the soldier's eyes were closed.

He looked like he was sleeping.

He was also Hamilton. A younger Hamilton. His camouflage would have blended in with the rock behind him, if it hadn't been so torn up and burned. One of his hands lay across his lap, another on an assault rifle, on the ground next to him, and the skin on both hands was red and blistered.

"You recognize him?" Aaron asked.

Baber nodded. Wondering about Hamilton. A man with a ranger uniform in his closet, but no ranger history on his record. "*Who is he?*"

"A man who saved my life," Aaron said. "More times than I can count. This one though, this one was in Afghanistan."

He opened his jacket with one hand. Unbuttoned his white shirt with one hand. Pulled a flap aside, so Baber could see a jagged scar there. A torn, ripped thing across his abs. As if a burning piece of metal had been pushed into his stomach, right above his belly button, and shoved violently to the side. The man held his shirt open long enough for her to see the scar tissue winding across his stomach, a little line, pale and lifeless. Once, it would have been red and swollen and angry. This wound had happened long ago.

Then Aaron closed the shirt. Baber wondered how many more scars this man had, and swallowed, quickly.

"J–" Aaron started to say, as if he was saying a name, then he shook his head and smiled. As if at himself.

"Hamilton carried me miles. You can't see it in the picture, but something had punched into his back as well."

Aaron touched the back of his own shoulder, where the duct tape was, on Hamilton.

"He bound up my stomach the best he could. Yanked the tape tight around the wound, keeping that friggin' piece of metal there, so my guts didn't empty out." Aaron's lips curved even more at the memory. "Man that bastard hurt."

Then he buttoned the shirt back up. Still with one hand. Keeping the story going.

"Then he carried me back," Aaron said. "Fought off the group following us. It was a mission that wasn't supposed to go south, but had. One of those peacekeeper talks some terrorist group got wind of. Our vehicle blown up. The comms, too. So Hamilton drug me miles. Stopping occasionally to go back and hunt those who were hunting us. Got us to a backup extraction zone and waited there. Set me up safe, went out and hunted those fuckers until every one of them was dead."

Aaron took a deep breath and let it out. Baber saw that his eyes were wet. His voice shaky. "But this picture says it all about him. We got back, and he wouldn't let anyone work on him. He waited here, outside the tent, while they were inside patching me up. Only when I was out of the woods, did he let them take him in."

The man was crying then, and wiped both cheeks with the back of his hand.

Baber had tears in her eyes too, and looked away. Took a shaky puff of her cigarette and let the smoke ease out of her lungs. Whatever and whoever Aaron was, whatever lies he told and whatever roles he portrayed, that story had been real.

She wondered, if Aaron had been in the tent, who had taken that picture of Hamilton.

Aaron put himself back together as well. Fingers on his free hand twitching. The man sniffed the air, the sniff something long and drawn and wet. Wiped his eyes a few more times. Then he took a deep breath and thumbed the screen of the phone, so another picture showed up.

This one was of a cave. Or a dark room. So dark Baber couldn't see the walls, so maybe that's why she thought it was a cave. The floor was dark and wet and maybe a little muddy.

A man sat in the chair there. A bright light hung above him, like all the scenes in all the movies where someone is a prisoner, where they are being interrogated. He had on a simple T-shirt and pants. The shirt was too big for him, it hung like a drape, like it was something someone had found a shirt somewhere and put it over him.

Things were in the background of the picture, over the shoulder of the man. Tools and instruments. What looked like a bag for intravenous solutions, hanging from a pole. Some bandages. A pack of syringes. Items to keep the man alive, maybe. Or to bring him back?

The man's hands were wrapped around the back of the chair, like he was a hostage. The pants looked like dark camouflage jeans that kids wore at night, or maybe it was something tactical. Black and dark grays.

The legs of the pants looked funny. Or, one side did. The man's right leg in the picture laid off to the side. It hung like a piece of rope. Like there was no bone inside left to support it. Just a piece of chunky meat. It made Baber think of the necklaces made of macaroni noodles she had made as a kid.

Baber realized the jeans had been cut off that leg. No pants there. The leg was so beaten, so mottled, it just appeared to be the same color as the pants on the man's other side. The leg itself bled out of dozens of tiny punctures, like a little tool had hammered into the leg, over and over.

The man's face was gaunt, way too thin. Ashen. Dark liquid lay over the skin of his face, like blood. His hair was matted and grimy, hung in loose strings around his scalp.

She recognized his eyes though. They burned feverishly. They burned with something she still saw in him today.

Hamilton.

"Jesus Christ," Baber finally said, stepping a little back. She looked at Aaron. "What are you showing me this for?"

He shrugged a little. "He was the best of us, once," he said. "I thought... I thought you should see both sides."

"The best of who?" Baber said. "This Fourth Branch?"

"Yeah," he said, pulling his phone back, thumbing the screen off. "But then this happened."

"When?" Baber asked.

"Not long ago," Aaron said, his voice almost a whisper.

They both were quiet. Aaron looked at his free hand, let his fingers wiggle a little. Then finally spoke. "I think, maybe, I showed you so someone else would know. What he once was."

"He's not that now," Baber said. Thinking of the eyes. The fury, behind them.

"No," Aaron said. His voice grew stronger. "But he's not the other thing, either. He's not a man who goes around hurting innocents, Baber. He's not someone who beats a girl to death."

Baber saw the man in the picture. The second man. Eyes burning with hate and anger. Pain. Rage. So much rage.

It was hard to put the second man with the first. The soldier. The man napping outside a tent. Face exhausted, but relaxed. A pinch of worry on his brow, as his friend inside was being operated on.

She closed her eyes. One image superimposed itself on the other, and became a big jumbled mess in her mind. As if the two pictures were so diametrically opposite that, when put together, they annihilated each other. Like matter and antimatter, this man had exploded, and whatever was left, wasn't much of either.

Baber finally opened her eyes. Looked at Aaron. Who stood there, waiting for her verdict.

"This is crazy," she said. Not wanting to believe the man, but finding herself leaning that way.

"It's a crazy world," Aaron said. "It's not a place where people could read old books and ponder and think. Put a quill to paper and order their thoughts. Debate for years and figure out the best way to tackle a problem. Or even if a problem exists."

His jaw set to the side. "It's a world of the internet and videos and fast cars. Where digital ones and zeros go everywhere and can say anything. At any time. Where people will believe something written in a hundred and forty characters, but not something right before their eyes. Not something they *know* to be true."

Baber sensed out of all of this, he was about to get to the thing he wanted to tell her most. What he might have wanted to say, when he wandered out here and lit his first cigarette. Waiting for her to show.

"Tell me," she said.

"The three-legged stool, it's breaking," Aaron said. "The legs are weak. Have been weakened. There's just not much left, to hold anything up." He shook his head, which he kept doing, as if there was a truth out there, over this whole conversation, he didn't want to be aware of.

"And the Fourth Branch," he looked at her, his emerald green eyes still wet from his tears, worried. Sad. Like he had come to an unacceptable truth. "The fourth leg is breaking, too."

THIRTY-TWO

I held the phone in my hand. The speaker was silent. Sara was already gone, working on the information I had asked her for. The only thing I heard was the rumbling of engines, the purring roar as the light turned green and the cars took off. The slight squeal of brakes, of tires sliding on the road, when the light flicked back to red.

I looked down at my coffee. Winced at the weak taste. Looked at the trashcan on the cover and its latte-covered lid. All the people walking by it, crossing the street. Some people walking inside the cafe, walking back out with their own specialty coffee with fancy syrups and non-dairy milk blends.

I forced myself to take a big sip. Then another. I wondered how this place stayed in business. Weak coffee had none of the caffeine stronger coffee had. None of the bitterness, either. Nothing frothed milk could offer its warm sweetness too. Maybe these people walking out liked the sugary flavors, instead of the bitter coffee. The caramels and the white chocolate and the hazelnut flavors.

I could ask them, or I could concentrate and keep going. I dialed another number. One I had gotten off a card. The person there answered after a few rings.

"Kirschke's office," the professor said.

"Kirschke," I said. "It's me."

It didn't take the man long. "The knight, calling in from his journey?"

"Sure," I said.

"How's that going?"

"Not good," I told him. "People are dying."

There was a little quiet. "Well, like you told me," he said. "This isn't some story."

"No," I said.

"Was it you?" he asked.

I should have thought he'd ask that. One time, he might not have thought about it.

"No," I said again.

"Was it Angela?"

"No." The third time was the charm. "But I wanted to warn you. Just in case."

"Hmmm," Kirschke said. His tone was curious, but also had a hint of a grin. "So are English professors on some national hit list, somewhere? Is it the Libyans?"

"I don't know," I said. Then corrected myself. "Probably something that I'm doing."

I didn't need to warn him. That had been in the beginning of my search for Angela. There had been no one following me. No cameras catching my wandering around lost on a college campus. No angry man in a kitchen with urine-stained trousers and a knife in his leg.

In my mind I had made that pretense. But I knew I wanted something else. I just wasn't sure what.

"I read the book some more," I finally said.

"Good," he said. "More people should."

I knew both he and I were thinking of his last comment to me. His question, actually. Whether I was doing this because someone had made a mistake, and I was the guy who could correct that mistake.

I liked that side. Maybe because I could control the outcome. After all, if I was some knight that carried out justice, then at the end I would save the girl. Walk away a hero. And if I did that, maybe some forgotten part of me could be reclaimed. The person I used to be.

But Charley's death had changed that. I had been foolish to think I could walk through a city doing whatever I wanted, with no consequences to those actions. Not foolish. Ignorant. Uncaring. Maybe even stupid. What I had done in that apartment had led to someone killing Charley, I was sure of that, and that meant to me I had no control.

Which meant I couldn't be the hero.

Still, Kirschke had said that I might be the right person, in the right place, to correct some mistake in Angela's life. Or to help her, when she needed help. She had made a choice, at some point, and maybe I was what had come back to her.

The lady in *The Faerie Queene* was the real hero. She was constant. Good. She persevered no matter what happened to her.

The knight was just some guy. He did some good, maybe, but I was starting to think the crosse he bore was the red stain left from all the mistakes he had made, the blood of wounds that couldn't or wouldn't close, because he kept re-opening them.

In the story, things kept happening to him, leading him further and further astray. Maybe he took a step forward here and there, but usually that was so he could take two steps back. Dropping further and further into despair. Getting more and more lost.

The lady was the truth. I was a bit player in her story. Which meant there was no saving me. There was no happy ending, no place where I could become the hero. Reclaim who I had been. Walk away feeling proud, for what I had accomplished. Helping another.

All I could do was cause more death. But I was good at that. From there, I couldn't control what happened, any more than Spencer, when he had first set ink to paper.

If I was the answer to something Angela had done, some choice she made, I would be the best damn answer there could be.

Then I would go back to being lost. The routine. The black phone and the hate and the rage. Waiting for a day that may never come.

"The knight," I said. "He doesn't do a lot of killing."

There was a little more silence over the line.

"Well," Kirschke said. "He killed Error. He kills other knights."

"I don't think he killed Error," I interrupted.

"No?" he said, leaving the question open. Like anyone who was interested in a discussion, he wanted to hear what I had to say. Maybe as much as I wanted to say it.

"No," I said again. Thinking of all the little worms, the spawn, that had left. "I don't think something like that can be killed."

"Interesting," Kirschke said. Still with the curious, *what else* tone.

"You can't kill something like Error," I said. "You can only bring it out into the open."

"Maybe killing isn't always the answer," Kirschke said.

Death was always the answer. There were very few finalities in life. Few things that meant something to a person like death. A few points more or less on a credit report, the difference between an *A* or a *B* on some exam, blaring a car horn, none of those sharpened the knife-like edge of a decision like the hard, unyielding stone that was death.

I told Kirschke that. Not in so many words, but enough so he got the gist.

"That's an interesting take," Kirschke said, his voice carrying a different tone. Not a *what else* tone, but something that wanted more. Maybe what he sounded like when a student said something that caught his interest, and he wanted to dig into it. "You should come by, one evening."

"Come by?" I asked.

"Yeah," he said. "Wednesday evenings. The Caffeinated Brain."

"Yeah," I said.

My mind had gone back to what I had said, at first. It was back in that cave, with *error* scrawling across the walls. The tolling alarm of the bell echoing in my mind, counting down. The rusty armor, locking me in one place. The case of broken matchbox cars that had turned into the helmet that had turned into the empty shell that had once held the virus.

"Maybe," I said then. "Maybe when this is done."

"You're invited," Kirschke said.

I wondered what he thought I would get from a group of people sitting around talking about video games. Or elections. Or anything. Maybe the professor wasn't asking just for me. Maybe it was about what other people might get, if I went.

He laughed then. "You know, when you're not busy hunting down kidnappers."

"Thanks," I said.

Twice I had said the word in the past ten minutes, when I hadn't said it for years. Then I hung up the phone and stood. Finished my coffee and tossed the empty cup in the center of the trash bin. Left my water, still precariously perched on the table.

Then I walked to the corner. Waited for a taxi to drive by. One of those classic yellow cars, or the newer looking whiter sedans with a weird green diagonal stripe leading across the passenger door from its rear window.

I saw neither. I guessed taxis didn't expect to make a lot of money around the police department. The people here looked like they lived here, walking back and forth. Not a lot of people leaving there ready to pay someone else money to take them somewhere, maybe.

The bus stop wasn't far. But I didn't want to have to make a lot of connections. I didn't want to stop and start. I wanted to *go*, to get to the address the guy gave me, and I wanted to go now. Not after a bunch of stops.

Maybe the knight in the story wasn't the hero. Maybe he was lost, and struggling to find out his purpose. But I thought now that he was just a side part of the tale. The real story was with the girl. She had been his purpose, and when she had disappeared, he hadn't known what to do.

I felt like the knight had gotten one thing right, though. Even lost. It was something we were both good at. When all else failed, it was time to start swinging. Going after bigger and badder enemies, climbing that ladder, until he toppled them all, or a giant put him down.

That was something I understood.

Cars *whusshed* by, the currents of air they left behind fluttered around me and highlighted the acrid smell of exhaust. Still, no taxis. But the light turned red, and one of the cars with a purple light on the dash stopped in front of me. One of those services people with phones used an app to call for a ride. I tried to look as friendly as I could and knocked on his window.

The kid inside, a young thin man with a nose ring and spiked blue hair, cracked the window the smallest of bits.

I guess I wasn't great at friendly.

"Yo," he said. Cautiously.

"Need a ride," I said.

"Use the app, bro," he said.

"Don't have an app," I said, but opened my wallet. "But I do have a hundred dollars cash, if you take me here." I gave him my address. I had decided to get my car. Having something to drive always beat depending on someone else, or a public service to take you there. Even with the traffic.

It wasn't far. No place in Boston was far. And a hundred dollars off the books appealed to a lot of people. Maybe not kids in a library, but definitely to one driving for change.

The kid reached down to his phone. It was in a cradle on his dash. He tapped a few things and the app closed.

"Done," the kid said. He rolled down his window. I handed him the cash. There was a thunking sound of unlocking car doors, and I got in the back of the car. It smelled like vanilla, and the thought made me think of Charley, who had at one time found that scent and me funny.

No more though.

I set my jaw.

The kid looked in the mirror and maybe regretted picking me up.

Whatever, I thought. It was time I started swinging.

CHAPTER
THIRTY-THREE

Baber watched Aaron. They had been out here a long time, longer than a smoke break usually took. The cops around them had changed out, become new faces standing in new places. The smell of smoke still the same, acrid whiffs blowing across her face, as the wind stirred through the parking lot. Frank would come looking for her, soon.

She wondered what he meant, about legs breaking. About the branches of government, breaking. It wasn't like she was happy with some of the decisions made by those in charge, over the years, but it was still a great country. The greatest.

Baber focused on something else though. Something she found more interesting.

"Why are you telling me all this?" she said.

Aaron smiled, the smile where his green eyes radiated a hidden interest. Baber felt her stomach tingle a bit, and pushed that feeling down. She was too old for a crush.

"Maybe I know you won't believe any of it," Aaron said. "Maybe I just needed to vent. People do that, right? Maybe I had a bad day and have a bad decision coming up, and just wanted to talk some nonsense with someone I feel a certain level of attraction for. Maybe a good feel for."

Baber rolled her eyes, and the man saw it, keeping his grin up. But a forced grin, now.

"Or maybe I just have a bad habit," he said, flexing his first two fingers. "Something I had a hard time quitting."

"It's a bad habit," she admitted.

"They'll kill you," Aaron echoed the words everyone said, the hidden joke among smokers. Even Frank had said them, understanding that those three words were told to every smoker millions of times a day, by millions of non-smokers. People with their own addictions and bad habits, if not cancerous ones.

The edge of her mouth curved. Some things were hard to give up, even if they would kill you. Because getting through the day was more important, than the rest of your life.

"Hamilton was one of the best of us, Baber," the man said. "He would have been the guy who led the Fourth Branch, one day. The guy who makes the decisions for what we do, where we go. Where the ship that drives this great country sails."

In her mind Baber could see both pictures Aaron had showed her. The man, exhausted and waiting outside for a friend he had saved. Another man, in a chair, leg shattered, eyes burning with a feverish rage.

"Hamilton?" she asked.

"Yeah," he said. "He was the best of us, once. Some small part of that guy remains. I kind of would like to see that part grow back. I feel like I owe him that."

"And you think I'll help that?" she said. "With this mythical tale of government branches and secret agents and breaking chairs?"

Aaron shrugged. "I looked up your record, Baber. And I got a good feel for you. It's my talent, reading people."

"So you know I meant it, then," she said. "About nailing his ass to the wall."

"You meant it," he agreed. "You just don't know Hamilton like I do. You'll get to, though. So you'll see. And when you do, maybe you'll think about this talk with me. This mythical discussion of government branches and secret agents and breaking chairs. And maybe that'll influence what you decide."

"I doubt it," Baber said.

"Good," Aaron said. "In this world, today, people should question everything they hear. They should find out, really find out, if something was true before blasting it across social media. People should know the truth, experience it, before they can trust it."

The man looked at his watch. Not because he needed to know the time. He was letting her know he was leaving.

"Taking off?" Baber said, letting him know she knew what he was doing. "And the movie was just getting interesting."

"I got to do something for a friend," Aaron said. "Help Hamilton. That's really what I was here to say. The rest of it," he shrugged. "Is just the rest. Believe it, don't believe it, I'm not sure that matters anymore."

Baber's fingers got suddenly hot, right behind the knuckles, and she flicked them, quickly. Her cigarette went flying, a long cylinder of ash breaking off of the end. She had let it burn down, listening to Aaron.

"Bad habits, right?" Aaron said.

"They'll kill you," she agreed.

He left. She watched him walk away, narrowing her eyes. He slumped, though most people wouldn't be able to tell, because he also walked like a big cat, the tail of his coat swaying just a little back and forth after each step. A predator. A predator with a bad choice in front of him. A bad choice, or a great weight.

The door opened before Aaron got there. Frank. He held it open and looked at the man with the face he used when the shit hit the fan. The blank face, implacable, waiting for what happened next.

Aaron had to shift sideways a bit to get by the big man. Flashing Frank a grin, too. Like they were old buddies. And then he was gone.

Frank looked at Baber, one eyebrow raised.

"Yeah," she said. "I know."

"You get anything?" he asked. His voice, the low rumble, carried from the door.

She looked at Frank, then at where Aaron had disappeared. And laughed a brief laugh. "To be honest, I got no fucking idea what I got."

"Well buckle up," Frank said. "We got a body."

The way he said it, made her feel like it wasn't a regular call. "Martinez?"

Frank's shoulders moved up and down, taking his trench coat up and down with him. "Young girl. Hispanic or Latina. Hard to tell more than that," he said. "Harbor."

She understood then. They wouldn't be able to tell. Water-logged corpses were the worst. Bloated, all kinds of sea life nibbling at the body.

"Coming," she said, bending down to pick up the butt of her cigarette, tossing it into the bucket. Thinking about the lawyer, or the fake lawyer, and everything he had said. About the picture of Hamilton, the one where he was strapped to a chair.

Baber had seen a lot of evil, in her job. A lot of bad things happen to others. Most of them kept her up at night, were likely behind her smoking habit. And maybe her drinking. But people coped how they could, today.

Now she had to wonder if the corpse they were about to see was Angela Martinez. Or if it was someone else. And she had to wonder if her and Frank were getting sent out there for a specific reason, by their lieutenant, or their captain, or the mayor or the governor. Was it just another body, or something to get them off the board?

All because a guy had chased a girl.

Maybe water-logged corpses weren't the worst. Maybe it was better for the dead person to be dead. Sometimes that was better than the alternative.

CHAPTER
THIRTY-FOUR

The ride wasn't long. It was just past rush hour, and we headed east on Melnea Cass Boulevard until we got close to Dorchester, then navigated smaller streets there. There was a little traffic there to fight through, but the kid navigated it all with the practice of someone used to driving all day. Patient when he had to be, accelerating when he needed to.

He dropped me off in front of my place. I decided to run up and use the bathroom real quick before heading out to my car. Bathrooms in cities were a mixed bag at the best of times, even when you could get the code from the barista, or the store manager. Easier to take care of business that way.

My door was open. Pushed inward. Just enough to alert me. Baber had locked it, and like Angela's apartment, the jamb was split where the deadbolt went.

My body was instantly alert. Heart racing. Breathing rapid. I slid down the hallway in little steps, quiet. My hands itching for a gun.

I opened the door. My place was a mess. Tossed. The couch flipped over and cut open. The cushions torn into, yellow blocks of stuffing lay scattered across the floor. The television tipped over and broken. The coffee table sat on its side, missing a leg.

I hadn't much in my kitchen. Just a few things, but they had all been torn out. The few cheap ceramic plates I owned shattered, the drawers emptied of the few utensils I owned. The toaster upside down, with burned crumbs of toast spread out on the counter.

And the black phone, torn off the wall.

I froze. My heart thudded in my chest, beating out a rage of anger and pain. The phone connected me to that, connected me to Sam, and although a lot had changed for me in the past couple of days, I needed that, *needed* that connection to remain.

I stepped into the apartment, staring at the receiver of the phone, the cord cut or torn or ripped, the handset buried into the drywall of the hallway.

It's just as well...

Beyond the hallway I saw my bedroom, the door there was open, the mattress flipped upside down. Sheets ripped off. The mattress given the same treatment as the couch.

The warrant had been a sham. It had always been a sham. It had been something to pull me off the board for a known period of time.

Now I knew why.

The realization hit me quick. That could have been the reason I didn't hear the guy behind me. Or maybe I was just too distracted by the phone torn off the wall, my broken connection with Sam.

Either way, I missed him. I didn't feel or hear a thing, until something heavy hit the back of my head. Then I felt a sharp, hot pain explode in my skull.

And then nothing.

———

I woke up in a familiar place. Well, a familiar position. Even if the roles were reversed.

I kept my eyes closed while I took a quick survey. My head throbbed. But I had been hit in the head before. I could get past the pulsing pain echoing in my skull, the pulsing of someone tapping my brain with a rubber mallet, tapping in a nice, steady rhythm, inline with the beating of my heart.

There was blood in my mouth. I could taste the warm, liquid copper flavor of it. I must have fallen forward, maybe my teeth bit my tongue when I hit the floor. I probed my mouth, there was a tender area on my tongue, near the tip. No broken teeth though.

My arms felt tight behind me. *Tied* behind me, at the wrists. I had been out long enough that my fingers tingled with numbness. I sat on a floor, my back against a wall, my legs laying out before me. It felt like I was sitting on a towel, or a blanket.

I opened my eyes.

I was in my kitchen. Back against the counter. Hands tied behind me, legs tied together with the phone cord. The black curls stretched thin with tension.

I was laying on a towel. A towel laying on top of a shower curtain. My shower curtain.

The mercenary squatted before me. A familiar knife in his hand. A nasty smile on his lips. The knuckles of the hand holding the knife bruised. He was dressed in jeans and a light colored T-shirt, something with a compass or cross logo on the pocket of his shirt, over the heart. And a dark leather jacket.

We were dressed very much the same. Though he was smiling, and I wasn't. But people don't really have real smiles, anymore. Just what they show to others. So maybe we were the same. He just had a front.

"Hey," he said. "Remember me?"

I remembered him. Remembered what I had done to him. And

knew, deep down, what I had done had angered the mercenary. And he had taken it out on Charley.

Merc stabbed my leg. The bad leg. Right in the meat of the thigh, much like I had done with him, in Angela's apartment. A sharp pain shot through me, and a hot wetness soaked into my jeans, spreading out in a ragged circle from where the merc held the knife.

The joke was on him though. That leg always hurt. He should have stabbed the good one.

"Yeah," I told him. "I remember."

"Good," he said. "Let's catch up quick, then."

He pulled out the knife, and stuck it in again. Just in a different place in the leg. One with a little more scar tissue, so the knife angled in just a bit oddly. Like cutting through gristle on a piece of steak.

I winced, and that motion made my head ache more. The skin around my skull felt too tight. Blood leaked out of my leg and was soaked up by the towel underneath it. The mercenary wiggled the handle a bit, feeling the hardness of knotted tissue against the flat of the blade. He arched one eyebrow in thought. Then he looked at me again.

"I'd have taped up your mouth," he said, one eyebrow raised, looking around at my place. "But I can't find any packing tape. Or duct tape. Or anything, really."

"That what you came to say?" I said.

"No," Merc shrugged. "Just wondering who's paying you, I guess. Either you're cheap, or they are."

I laughed. "Not doing this for money."

Merc smiled. "Pro bono?" His head tilted left and right, his eyes looking up at the ceiling, like he was thinking. "Maybe your guy's getting what he's paying for, then."

"Just like you got *paid* to kill Charley?" I asked.

The mercenary stopped moving his head, leaving it tilted. Staring at me with the question.

"The tattoo shop girl?"

His grin widened a bit. Nastier. "Well, some things I do for free, too."

Like I said, smiles weren't real anymore. They were just fronts. Just what people wanted to show others.

I showed him mine. The dark one. The glint of a predator's teeth.

"You made a bad choice," I said.

Merc matched my smile. "Life's full of 'em."

"You're making another," I said. "If you leave me alive."

He nodded. "I know," Merc said. "But, unfortunately, it's not what I'm getting paid for." Then the mercenary got up. "Hopefully in the near future."

He wandered back to my bedroom. I heard him digging in my closet. Then he came back out with the plastic dry cleaner's bag, the one holding my old uniform.

"This you?" he asked.

I didn't answer.

"Thought so," he said. "You rangers always thought yourselves so special. Look at these ribbons, what the hell do they mean now? What the hell kind of good does a sharpshooter badge do you, here?"

Merc snorted. "Always the hero, right? How heroic you feeling now?"

I looked away. I didn't know why I had kept the uniform. My eyes found the black phone, the handset, lodged into a hole in the drywall.

I know why I had that. I knew why I had my routine. I was staying ready, just in case. Keeping the tool sharp, for a time when Sam would call. When I would hunt her, and find out, *why*.

The mercenary pulled the plastic bag off the uniform. It made the crinkly sound all plastic does. He let the bag drop and walked back into the kitchen, throwing the uniform into the corner across from me. Right by the fridge.

Then he unzipped his pants and pissed all over it. The stream hit the uniform with a padded, wet sound. His aim wasn't great, and the urine went everywhere. The smell of ammonia was strong. Like he had eaten asparagus, before coming over to my place. Like what he was doing now had been his intent, all along.

This was yours once, the action said, *and now it's mine.*

Part of me wondered if this was the merc making up for pissing himself back in Angela's apartment. Trying to build some part of himself back up from the fear he had felt back then. Maybe this was just who the man was.

He finished and zipped back up.

"There," Merc said. "I am relieved."

I snorted. Understanding the double-meaning of the words. We had both been in the service.

"That all?" I asked him.

"Of the free stuff?" he smiled. "For now."

He squatted next to me, reaching inside his dark jacket. Pulling out a folded piece of paper, and placing that carefully on the counter above my head.

"Here's a number," he said. "Call it when you find the drive."

"The drive," I said. Blankly. That's what all this was about. I had no idea what he was talking about. "What drive?"

The merc frowned. "The USB drive."

I grinned a big grin. I wasn't looking for that. And the last time I'd seen one was...

Angela putting one into her laptop.

I held my grin, though it felt like slipping in the realization. They would have that drive, though. Right? It would be in her bag, and they had taken that. Whatever Angela had, whatever drive they wanted, they already had it.

Though tossing my apartment, Angela's apartment, told me different.

"I have no idea what USB drive you are talking about," I told him. "Why don't you give me the girl?"

"Look," the merc said. "I'm not here to play games."

"Really?" I said. "Playing Doctor's not in your toolbox? Maybe Operation is more your thing?"

He didn't get it. Maybe he had never played that game. I had never been good at pulling the leg bone out of the tiny hole it sat in. The red tongs had been too big, and I had always hit the side of the wall, in that game.

Not that I could use those tongs now. My fingers had gotten so swollen and numb they ached. I tried bunching my hands into fists and relaxing them, behind my back. Just to get the blood flowing.

I could keep up this chatter for a while. I knew how long it took to break me. I knew it, because two years ago someone had done it.

This guy didn't have that kind of time.

"Interesting you'd say that," Merc said. He pulled something else out of the pocket of his jacket. Something he pulled out of a sandwich bag, folded up in a paper towel, the thin cotton dark and red.

Unwrapping it, he showed me an ear. The bottom lobe, with a stud in it. The elegant and thin curve around the outside of the ear canal. The skin a tanned color, where dried blood had flaked off.

"Maybe Doctor is in my toolbox, eh?" Merc said. "What was the game? Operation?"

I froze, actually consciously stopped myself from moving. Stopped my wrists from tearing against the cord that bound them. Stopped my chest from swelling in a deep breath, from anger flooding my body, inhaling as much fury as it could.

I forced myself to be still. As still as I could possibly be, because if I tried to move, all that would come out. There was nothing I could do. Nothing, right now. "You said you didn't have the girl."

"I thought this might get your attention," Merc went on, as if he hadn't heard me. "Some people like using fingers, or even toes. Personally, I think there's too many of those. A person can get by with nine fingers. Or eight."

I kept trying to breathe normal. To not move much. To hold the anger in, even with my head pounding to let it all out. So as much as I measured my words, they still came out dark. With an underlying current of anger, a raging river of it. *"You said you didn't have her."*

Merc shrugged. "Maybe I didn't have her then, but have her now. Maybe I had her then, and was just lying." He held the ear in front of me. The fluorescent light of the kitchen highlighted the patches of blood over the skin, outlined the clean slice where a blade had parted lobe from flesh, the dark stud in the lobe. "Maybe it doesn't matter to you what I said then, as much as what I'm saying *now*."

He leaned closer. His breath blew over me. He had eaten asparagus lately. "The thing is, don't take the fucking risk with me. You have the drive. Or you're looking for it. So get it, and call that number. *Soon*. Because I'm gonna run out of ears real quick."

I remembered Angela's smile. Her leaning over the table, interested in me. Tucking her hair behind her ear. Maybe *that* ear. An old pain, hidden in her eyes, that her laugh had covered up.

And Charley, trying to help me. Well, trying to help a friend. Before realizing she had entered a world she didn't belong in. Before stopping me, back in Angela's apartment.

I might have killed him, back then. Something had come over me, released from the prison-like routine I had built around it. A rage and anger that would have changed me forever. Killing the man then likely would have killed the small part of me left, the part of me that had kept my old uniform, the part of me that had chased the truck, the part of me that wanted to read about a lady and her knight.

I knew this guy. I had known what he was capable of from the moment I had gotten the drop on him. I had told Charley that I was glad she had stopped me from going any further. Now I wondered how this would have played out, had she let me go on. Maybe she would be alive. Maybe Angela would still have an ear.

The small part of me would have been gone, sure.

But this guy would have been gone too. Charley would still be alive. Angela still would have an ear.

I thought the trade would have been worth it.

Guys that walk into shops and beat girls to death always were willing to hurt another person who was weaker than them. They started there, and graduated to things like cutting off body parts. It was how they built themselves up into the monsters they became.

I had rid the world of monsters, once. Slayed giants. Fought dragons.

It was time to pick up that sword again.

The routine I had built, it hadn't prevented any of this. The anger would have. I told myself I had been sharpening a tool. Staying ready. For the time I would find Samantha, and take my revenge. It was the only thing I had lived for, after breaking, in that cave.

"Get the drive," I repeated.

"Yeah," he said.

"Call the number." That was next.

"Exactly."

"And even the score," I finished, staring at the mercenary with eyes I knew looked dead inside. Because eyes were the window to the soul, and that part of me was empty.

I had tried to do the right thing.

And I had failed.

"If that's your choice," Merc said. "The way I look at this, we're even now."

He smiled then, something quick and light. As if he had a happy thought.

"The next time we meet though, that one will settle things."

I agreed. Behind me I bunched my hands into fists, feeling the cord cut into them. I didn't relax though. Not even when I felt a wet warmness spread across my palms. I kept the fists tight.

CHAPTER
THIRTY-FIVE

The mercenary left after that. He was nice enough to cut the cord binding my wrists before he did. Making a snarky remark about the blood there. I had to wait a bit for feeling to come back in my fingers. They were swollen and pale and numb.

One wrist still dripped some blood from where my skin had split around the cord, but it was more of a scrape than a cut. It wasn't deep, and stopped bleeding fairly quickly. I had always been a fast healer.

Feeling was slow returning. I flexed my fingers a bit, watching the blood travel underneath the skin of my hand, and up into each digit. Dark and angry under the surface. There was the tingling of feeling as the nerves woke up. I shook my hands a bit. I didn't like the sharp prickling feeling running up my arms. The sensation felt a lot like my brain, trying to stab out and penetrate a fog surrounding it.

The mercenary wanted a drive. A USB drive he believed Angela had. He thought I was looking for it too.

I was really just looking for her. When this began, I had found myself running through the parking lot, without understanding why. It had been an instant response, like catching a baseball that was thrown at you. Just something you did, without thinking.

Now I was in deep. I had learned a few things, over the past few days, but nothing concrete. Just little pieces of information, here and there.

Still, the back part of my brain had been working on it all. Taking each piece of info and testing it next to another. Like a jigsaw puzzle, testing all the pieces, placing the fragile knob-like end of one cardboard piece into the hole of another. Then testing another. Seeing which fit.

The Fourth Branch was here. *Aaron* was here.

David Whelan owned a company heavily invested in global positioning and automation.

Benjamin Whelan had worked for his father, and according to Sara, had been pretty bright.

One cardboard piece after another started clicking. The puzzle had no box, no picture I could look at, to see what the pieces would look like when I was done. All I could do was keep assembling them.

Angela was the next piece. It was hard to see where she fit, in all this. Except that she had been close to Benjamin. That was the only link.

Benjamin had died in the accident.

After which Angela had left Harvard.

After the accident, David Whelan had become a recluse.

Would it be a stretch to think the accident hadn't been an accident at all?

The one thing obvious to me was whatever was on that USB drive, it would have a distinct military application. If it didn't, it at least incriminated people who did. There wouldn't be a reason to kill Benjamin, unless one of those two things were true.

Or if both of them were.

All of this felt thin. It stretched, in front of me. But all the pieces felt right, the way jigsaw pieces should feel, as each piece clicked into the one next to it.

The world today was always looking for faster, more efficient ways to kill people. More *accurate* ways. David Whelan's company moved in those spheres.

What if Benjamin had found something. Something that had scared him. He had bought the Porsche the day before. He had paid cash for it, then run up to New York.

Not to see her. But to grab her and flee. Maybe he had picked her up, and told her about what he had found. Showed her the USB drive that held the information he was telling her. Maybe Angela had even held it, as he was driving.

Then the accident. Looking at it now, there was an ominous overtone to the crash. A brand new car. Sara and I had thought maybe he had bought it for Angela, but what if he had just bought it because he couldn't trust what he was driving?

After all, every new car had a global positioning system installed in it, now.

Benjamin had been trying to get away.

And he had been killed. By his father? That seemed unlikely. Benjamin had worked for him, after all. Maybe even had been the brains behind the technology his father was peddling.

So another player. Two sides. Money and Power.

All of that was thin. Guesswork. A lot of suppositions. More intuition than anything. But I also felt like I was close.

I rubbed my thumbs on each forefinger, watched the skin turn pale, and then red as blood ebbed and flowed underneath. They were good. I found a knife on the counter, the handle tucked under a cracked white plate. Used that knife to cut the phone cord binding my legs. Then doing the same thing to my legs as I had to my hands. Moving them up and down a bit. Holding a towel over where the guy had stabbed me.

The stab wounds kept dripping. I held the towel to my thigh and limped to the bathroom. Saw the shower rod on the floor, where the mercenary had ripped off the curtain. I opened the cabinet and pulled out the med kit, a blue box with a white label and a red cross. Something I had purchased from the local pharmacy.

I opened it. There was a card inside the lid, listing ways to treat insect bites, Band-Aid a cut. I checked it back and front, but there was nothing listed for how to treat getting stabbed in the leg. No Neosporin cream, no needles and thread, just a couple of cheap wipes that had the words antibiotic on the label, some medical tape and cheap gauze.

I went old school, washing out the wounds and running the wipes over each. Wincing a bit as I rubbed the edges of each cut. Both of the wipes turned red immediately.

Well, that was that.

I sat on the edge of the tub, the plastic flexing a bit underneath me. I bunched up all the gauze in the kit and held it against my leg, waiting for the blood to clot. When the wounds stopped leaking I took some cheap scissors from the kit and cut up parts of a towel, wrapping that around my leg. Then I took the medical tape and wrapped that around the towel, as tight as I could. Until I was out of tape.

After that I stood, testing it out. It wasn't going to hold long. Maybe long enough for me to get it treated. Or get some duct tape.

Time for the store, then. I threw on some jeans and walked a few blocks away. It was midday, most people were at work, so the sidewalks weren't incredibly crowded. The sun was out now, drifting along clouds that held hints of gray, a shadow of a storm flowing in from the east.

The corner store had enough of what I needed. I took a minute and grabbed as much as I could think of. Duct tape. Rubbing alcohol. A sewing kit.

I thought about it, and picked up a few more things. More gauze. A box of trash bags. A tube of antibiotic ointment. The thick kind, the ointment. Not the cream. I walked around the aisles putting what I found into a blue handheld basket. I had to squat a bit to grab the gauze off the shelf, and when I did the medical tape wrapped around my leg snapped. A warm wetness began to spread out there.

I winced and transferred the basket to my other hand. Then used my right hand to hold the towel against my leg. I limped up to the front, past an electronics section, and I grabbed a new phone cord. Not the curly kind, the straight gray cord.

I kept the limping up, one hand on my jeans, and got to the lady at the front register. She was behind a plastic cover, a wall of cigarette boxes behind her.

The cashier looked at my basket with a puzzled face. "You get shot or somethin'?"

She was smiling a bit when she said it. Like she was joking. I opened my wallet with my left hand, thumbed out some money, and handed it over. She took it and then looked at the hand holding my leg. Her eyes opened.

"Thanks," I said. I motioned for her to put the change in the same sack with the items I had bought. Then I grabbed the thin white handles of the plastic bag and left. Walking, well limping faster back home than I had walking to the store. Pressing my jeans tight, where the towel now hung loose.

The stairs were a little effort, but I got up them. My apartment smelled like urine. Maybe I should have bought an air freshener at the store. Or one of the smelly candles.

The front door wouldn't lock. The deadbolt had fully split out the door jamb. So I just shut it, letting the latch of the knob click in place. I grabbed a third pair of jeans and went back to the bathroom. Repeated what I did earlier, just doing it better this time. Washing the wound with real rubbing alcohol, gritting my teeth at the sharp piercing sting as I poured the liquid over the wound.

After I had cleaned them well enough, I liberally coated both wounds with the ointment. I sat on the lip of my tub and sutured both wounds closed. I used thick thread, and pulled each suture tight, the thread tugging hard against my skin and making a funny zig-zag of each cut. Just two more knotted lines of scar tissue, two more ugly flaws, to add to the rest.

I pulled out the boxes of gauze. The kind that had a non-stick pad on one side. A few dollars fell out and lay on the bloody floor, one bill crossing over the other.

Money and Power. I had thought that from the very beginning. I just hadn't known the players. Maybe, knowing Whelan was one, I could now guess the other. Someone who could put political pressure on a police department. A fast riser, new to the office. Someone who had an election coming up, and maybe skeletons in a closet.

Someone who was pushing through a stadium bill for Whelan.

I grabbed my phone from where it lay on the sink. Flicked it open with my thumb. Tapped the only number I had called.

"Sara Knox's desk," a voice said.

"Hey," I said back.

"Oh good night," she said, her voice half-teasing. "You got more errands for me?"

"Well, one of the two of us is sitting with two stab wounds in their leg," I said. "Thought you might want to hear about it."

She was quiet a moment. "You certainly know how to get a girl's attention."

I went over briefly what happened. Highlighting it. Then asked her the question I had. "Tell me about the governor."

"Which one?" she asked.

"What do you mean, which one?" I said, almost adding *the one all over the news lately, pushing the stadium bill through for Whelan.*

"The *acting* governor," she said, pronouncing the word, "or the one that died?"

I froze.

Money and Power.

"Died?" I said. "How?"

"Car accident," Sara said. Then she froze too. I could feel the realization hit her, at the same time it hit me. "Holy shit."

There was tapping of fingers over a keyboard, from her side. Furious, fast typing. Then another pause. "No way."

I waited, knowing she would tell me.

"Two months before Benjamin Whelan," she said. "He was driving home from a late night engagement. Had alcohol in his system, right at point oh-seven, and ultimately that's what the police attributed the crash to."

"Have the details?" I asked.

"State road twenty-four," she said. "It's a known hot spot for accidents. Bad merge lanes, too fast drivers. It's a straight shot, not really any bad turns. He was just going too fast and lost control."

"How fast?" I said.

More tapping, and Sara's heavy breathing came over the line. Big large breaths, like she was excited. I waited a few minutes, this time.

"They could only estimate it by impact," she said. "The police said the black box had been too badly damaged, and didn't record anything. So they put the crash on one too many drinks, and driving on a road known for people going too fast."

She waited, like she was reading it all. "No brake marks."

There it was. Two wrecks, months apart. Different, but same in the important ways. The ways that mattered.

I wondered if those were the only two. Or if there were more "accidents" which could be explained differently, with this knowledge. Explained by something that could grab the name of a person from a database somewhere, use a global positioning system to find them. And somehow kill them.

Assassinations on demand. Killings that looked like accidents.

"Is that even possible?" Sara said.

"It's the twenty-first century," I said. "Anything's possible."

They had companies now that cops could call, to stop stolen vehicles. Other companies, making cars that could drive themselves. Ways to find who owned what car, and other ways to wreck that car. In the digital age, with all the ones and zeros flying everywhere, being commanded to do anything, it wasn't a large stretch of the imagination to see where all that could head.

"It's just... crazy," Sara said.

New ways to kill people usually were. Until they became almost normal. Then, a while later, another new way would be found.

Sara kept talking, wondering her thoughts aloud. Processing. "Why wouldn't they hit the emergency brake?" she said. "Or turn off the car?"

"There's a GPS component to this," I pointed out. The car location could be tracked, and the accident planned at a particular, dangerous point of the road. Or at a certain speed. Or both. "Punch the gas at the right location, and that would be it."

"Like on a crowned curve, at the bottom of a steep hill," Sara mused. "Or a dangerous piece of highway."

"Especially if the person was speeding to begin with," I said.

"It wouldn't take much," she agreed.

Not at going eighty miles an hour. The car would travel over a hundred feet a second. By the time the driver realized what was going on, it would be too late.

"Have you heard back from the cop?" I asked.

"Later today," she said.

"Get a feel from him about this," I said. The guy had been a car buff. He'd have a feeling for it, something not mentioned in his report.

The Porsche had been brand new. It likely would have everything needed to stop the car, even if it wasn't turned on, or wasn't part of the package. Automobile companies today would include it, the technology was too hard to put in after the sale, and then charge a buyer just for turning it on.

I paused there, knowing I was missing something. A large piece of the puzzle, missing right in the center. Something that would tie everything together, and bring the Fourth Branch here. I didn't think two killings would be enough.

But whatever it was, it lurked right outside the edge of realization for me. I couldn't figure it out.

"Yes, massah," she said.

"I need to know more about the governor," I told her.

"What, like his political platforms?" she said.

"No," I said. "Just where he's at today."

Sara paused then. "Oh."

"Yeah," I said. "Oh." Then I added. "Whelan too."

We both knew that when she published this story, it would be big. But maybe she didn't understand how big. I certainly hadn't.

But I had a target now. Two of them. And I would see them both. One of them had Angela. Both of them wanted the drive. The USB drive Benjamin had fled with.

"I got Whelan already," she said. She gave me an address. "He's in his office today. Goes to lunch in..." There was a pause, like she was looking at her watch. "An hour or so. It's Friday, so it'll be Strega's. He likes the harbor."

"The Italian place?" I asked.

"You know it?"

"Yeah," I said. "It's in Waterfront."

"South Waterfront," Sara corrected me.

"Does that matter?"

"Only if you're from here," she said.

"Whatever," I said. "Find me the governor."

"You got it massah," she said, and hung up.

I sat on the edge of the tub, looking at the phone. Assassinations were dangerous things. If Benjamin had learned of the plan, especially if it was part of some program or technology the younger Whelan had been working on, that information would be particularly dangerous to him.

Enough to kill him.

He had bought a new car that day. Had fled the state. Had stopped to pick up his girlfriend. Heading north. Not to Niagara Falls, to spend a weekend with Angela. But fleeing. To Canada, maybe.

There was something there with the GPS. There was no reason to buy a new car, with cash. No matter what I thought rich people did with their money.

How long did it take for a car to be registered to a new owner? As soon as you drove it off the lot? How fast, after Benjamin had bought his Porsche, could that car be linked across all the digital ones and zeros of the internet to a Benjamin Whelan?

Pretty fast, I thought. Faster than Whelan thought it could be, that was for sure. No matter what he thought, or what he might have put in place to prevent it.

I sat the cell phone down. Tested my leg again. It looked like the sutures would hold.

It was time to get going. I placed thick pads of gauze on top of the wounds, then rolled wide athletic tape around my leg, circling over the pads, pulling the tape tight. Then I did the same thing with duct tape. After that I stood. Flexed my leg. Felt like I could move around fine, that the tape wouldn't restrict me, and wouldn't break like before.

Good enough.

I cleaned up the bathroom, stuffing everything into a trash bag. I washed myself the best I could, splashing cold water on my face. Tousling my hair a bit. Prodding the back of my hair gingerly.

I couldn't tell, from the mirror, what I was feeling. My face was sharp, my jaw and cheekbones protruded prominently. My hair was loose and a little wet. A few drops of water ran down my cheek.

My eyes were empty. There was no hint of emotion behind them. No fury. No righteous anger. No calm acceptance. Just... empty. If they were a window to the soul, I wasn't sure if mine wasn't a blank canvas, waiting to see what was next. Or maybe it was just gone. Maybe if a person suffered enough, had done enough wrong or had enough wrong done to them, the soul just checked out, waiting for its next turn at the wheel.

Leaving an incomprehensible, empty reflection behind.

I toweled off my face. Scrubbed my hair dry. Walked out to my kitchen and looked at the mess. The urine soaked uniform. The bloody towels, the shower curtain. The dark yellow puddles of piss staining everything.

Broken plates and silverware lay strewn across the counter. The contents of my refrigerator had been taken out and thrown around. A carton of eggs lay open, and the eggs smashed, leaving globs of yellow, yolky splats amidst white shells.

I didn't have time to clean any of this. Not now. It'd have to wait.

I got a different shirt on. A white button-up. I thought Seaport probably had a dress code against splatters of blood. Picked out a different jacket, a dark blue sports coat, pairing that with the light blue jeans I wore. I kept the sneakers, a pair of dark gray shoes, with a dark pattern on their sides, and a darker sole.

I did two more things before I left.

I yanked the gray phone cord out of its hard plastic package, tearing it out from the thick cardboard backing. The handset still lay in the hole in the drywall. I found the receiver and plugged the cord into both it and the handset. Then I placed it back in the cradle and left both there, the thin gray line tying the two together.

I also found *The Faerie Queene* under the couch. It was heavy when I picked it up, thick in my hand, and I laid the book on a clean spot on the counter, right by the front door. The cover had been folded over, and some of the pages were wrinkled. Like the mercenary had flipped through it quickly and tossed it aside.

I left my hand on the book, for a second. Right by the picture of the shield. A red cross on the shield. A thin red line across my wrist. My finger tapping the shield, lightly. Maybe waiting for the hollow ring of metal.

Around the book was the mess. The counter. The broken eggs, the phone in the wall, the cut up mattress and torn apart couch. The bloody bag of trash that carried the light lavender scent. The thick ammonia smell of urine.

The apartment had been a place of routine for years for me. A safe place. A place where I thought I had been building a new me. A different me.

Now it was *this*. I didn't know if I'd be coming back to it tonight, or tomorrow, and if I did, I didn't know what I would be coming back *to*. Or *for*.

For years I had scheduled every day out, so that I knew exactly what would happen that day. Now I didn't know what tomorrow would bring. Or tonight. I didn't even have an idea what would happen in the next hour.

I didn't know who I was anymore.

Maybe Kirschke was right. Maybe life was a story. Maybe we all flipped through the pages of our lives, trying not to skip ahead to see the ending. Sitting up late at night, trying to puzzle out what might happen next. Worried and hoping the girl could be saved. Wondering if the hero was strong enough. Wondering if the hero was even a hero.

Wondering, maybe, at what we were. If we were becoming something else. Or falling back into something worse.

Was I just an angry man, left and betrayed, building a routine to hold back a dark, monstrous rage?

Or was I a knight, lost, trying to find his way back?

I guess I was about to find out.

I had a little time, I thought. The mercenary would give me that, to find the drive. I just wasn't sure how long. A day or two? An hour or two?

I'm gonna run out of ears real quick…

I would use that time efficiently. First was Whelan. I'd find out more about what he knows. Then the governor. One of the two was at the very top of this.

I shut my door, let the knob latch hold it shut. I'd fix the deadbolt later. If there was a later. Things were coming to a head, I could feel it, and I didn't know where they would end.

I just knew that I would try.

My leg throbbed a bit going down the stairs, but my leg always hurt. This was just a different kind, and in fairness the pain echoed the ache in the back of my skull. Maybe I should have bought some ibuprofen or aspirin at the pharmacy, but I hadn't.

I didn't stock that stuff at home. Didn't like meds. I had seen people get hooked on them before, it was too easy to get used to something that helped you get through the day. All of a sudden that same thing was getting you through weeks. Then months. Years.

I was used to all kinds of pain. I would get through this. I was more surprised at the times when I wasn't feeling any. Those few times, I didn't know what to do, or feel.

My first thought was to grab my car, but it was still parked a few blocks away, and a yellow taxi had just stopped in front of my building to drop a couple off. A young couple, dressed nicely, maybe coming home early from work.

Or maybe coming back for something else, the way they leaned on each other and grinned, getting out of the cab.

I waved at the driver. An older man, small in the front seat. Dark-skinned and dark, thinning hair. He nodded and hit something on his dash. I got in.

"Stregas," I said.

"South Waterfront?" he said, with an Indian accent.

I guessed he was from Boston. I nodded. He took off.

That was all each of us said.

The drive was quick. Seaport wasn't that far from Dorchester. The driver got onto I-93 quick and headed north until it crossed I-90, where he took a ramp and merged going east.

There were still some clouds in the sky. Dark gray thunderclouds, single and alone, making their way westward. The sun was there too, among patches of blue sky. The blue and the gray were a fifty-fifty mix, and the promised storm of the morning seemed to hang in the balance of the afternoon.

We crossed over Fort Point Channel, the dark water glistening under the midday sun, tiny sparkling diamonds at the crest of thousands of waves, the channel's surface appearing like a shimmering blanket underneath me.

Blue and red lights flashed north of us, across the channel. Far to the north, around Summer Street Bridge. A police car, not moving. It was tucked in on the south side of the bridge, where the bridge headed south over the water, right in front of the big buildings there. It was too far for me to see anything other than that.

Maybe there was a difference between north and south.

The taxi driver headed out over the water, until we hit the interchange. There we got off I-90, heading over a quick ramp that rose and crossed over the interstate, and east on Four Point Boulevard. Just a few stop-and-go blocks later we hit Seaport Boulevard, and the stop-and-go got a little more stop than go.

I knew where we were. "This is good," I said.

The driver looked at me and shrugged. Told me the fare. I handed him the cash and got out.

The air was colder here, near the harbor. A stiff breeze blew in from the east, and I tugged my jacket tighter around me. The currents of wind from the ocean brought in the thick smell of salt, which always reminded me for some reason of crabbing in Chesapeake Beach, Maryland. The crab cakes there, thick and juicy, topped with coleslaw and hot sauce. Some smells, like some sounds, or a song, brought back the oddest memories at the oddest times.

I headed east. Seaport was crowded, with both vehicle and foot traffic. I think the area used to be home to the Irish community hundreds of years ago, but it was full of millennials now. Young people, dressed in nice suits, sporting gray overcoats, businessmen and women heading to and from lunch. Most of the men wore something on their heads against the wind and the cold. A five-hundred dollar cabbie hat, or a thousand dollar Stetson.

Maybe that was why there was a difference between North and South Waterfront, but I thought the difference wasn't that much, anymore. North was old money, south was new. But it was all still money.

Strega's was ahead. I wasn't quite dressed for it, but I wasn't quite not dressed for it, either. I went through the doors, the thick warm tomato sauce scents of a good Italian restaurant surrounding me. I brushed past the host before the girl could comment, a young girl in a nice pair of black pants and white blouse, telling her I was finding a seat at the bar.

Garlic hung in the air, weaving among all the conversations between people having a nice end-of-the-week business lunch. Baskets of thick slabs of buttered bread at each table. I ignored the tinking sound of silverware hitting plates.

It was warm enough inside that most people had their jackets off, and they relaxed casually in their chairs. A glass of wine, or a cocktail, in most hands. Talking to each other about weekend plans, or a business deal, or whatever.

I walked by the bar, not looking back at the host. The windows outside highlighted the Boston skyline, tall buildings rising in the north, across the harbor. I found the door to the patio and stepped outside, to the cold brisk wind again. It felt colder, after having been inside.

I searched the tables. Whelan wasn't hard to find. He was at a table, by himself. Facing the skyline. He looked much like the picture I remembered, thin white hair, salt-and-pepper mustache. A dark jacket around his thin shoulders. White shirt, and no tie.

So maybe I wasn't underdressed. Though Whelan had a nice pair of slacks on. Something that cost thousands of dollars, I was sure. I thought fifty dollars was too much for a pair of jeans.

Ships moved in the harbor, of all different sizes and shapes. A few tug boats hung around a larger cargo vessel, the ship had massive, cavernous stacks on it, the mouths of the stacks blowing large trails of gray-black smoke into the sky. There were other vessels as well, large and small, circled by all kinds of fishing boats. Some sail craft too, maybe more than usual, it being a Friday. Tiny two or three-masted vessels heading out into the open water.

The water here shimmered less. It was a wide open field of gray, swelling with mounds of waves that rolled to either side of the channel. Maybe the Fort Point Channel was choppier, with more edges the sun could catch. Maybe the harbor was just too big, held too much, that the water couldn't crash against everything and sparkle in the sun. All the water could do here was rise and fall. Breathe and let go. Live and die.

Whelan watched over all of it. A plate of food before him. Lasagna, barely touched. A glass of red, also barely touched. Two men stood behind him, one to the north and south sides of his table, keeping the tables next to his empty. And keeping everyone else away.

The privileges of money.

I went to walk by. Both of the guards were well-dressed, in form-fitting suits. Tight enough to reveal shoulder rigs inside each of their jackets. Each rig was on their left side, so each of the guards was right-handed. Both looked like they worked out, but they weren't the most alert. People just weren't expecting things like me, at a Friday lunch.

The south man looked at me. I acted like I was heading for a far table. He was good enough to look at me funny, tilting his head like he was about to ask me a question. Or maybe about to motion me away.

I looked past him. Over his shoulder, to the guy standing on the north side of the table. Opened my eyes, wide. It froze the south guard, not much, but enough.

It was over then.

I took a large step, stomping down on the guard's foot closest to me. At the same time I slipped my left hand into his jacket, angling my left arm out to hold his right arm up and away from his body. My thumb clicked the strap off the rig, and my hand was pulling the guard's gun out before he realized everything that was happening.

Then I had his gun. I dropped it from my left hand, letting my right catch it. Still holding his right arm up and away. I pushed the barrel of the gun into his ribcage.

It was a Glock 9mm, with a trigger safety. I knew the gun. Easy to use, in a pinch. Nothing to click off, in order to shoot.

All this had happened in a quick moment of time. The guard's eyes had just started to focus on me. His right arm started pushing down on my left, at least until he realized I had his gun.

"I want no trouble," I told him, keeping the gun tight to his ribcage. Keeping my left arm locked against his right. "Yet."

His right hand had bunched. He almost felt like he was going to take a step back. My eyes narrowed. I got ready to swing him around to face the other guard. I didn't have a plan, other than that. I didn't want to have to pull the trigger, but I would.

I was going to find answers. Now. Not tomorrow.

The guard saw that in my face. His arm immediately relaxed, even though his jaw set, like he clenched his teeth. His chest swelled out with a deep breath.

The north guard called out. "Hey." Took a step around Whelan to get closer to us, one hand in his jacket. I moved to keep the south guard in between us. I turned him to face the other guard, holding the back of his suit in my hand, so I could sense what he was doing.

Then I pulled the Glock back to my body, holding it low to my waist, keeping the one guard facing the other. The south guard held his hands up a bit, as if telling the other guy to stand down.

The other guard paused.

"Everyone hold still," I said. "And this can still be a nice lunch, for everyone."

I took the chair next to Whelan, who looked at me with a faint curiosity, as if he was weary, and maybe barely interested in what went on around him. His eyes were a pale blue, resting underneath thick bushy white eyebrows.

The man wasn't worried, none of that showed in his face. It was like he was on pause, as if the world around him had stopped. He sat like he was enduring a vigil, and his eyebrows lowered only a bit when he saw me take a seat. When he saw the gun, all he did was purse his lips, and that in the tiniest of motions.

"David Whelan," I said. "It's about time you and I had a talk."

His frown remained. Deepened. His gaze wandered over the harbor for a moment. He took a breath in, maybe of the salty harbor air. When he spoke, his voice was surprisingly deep and powerful, for a guy so thin. "Do I know you?"

I shook my head. "There's no need for you to know me," I said. "I just want to ask a few questions. But before we do, we have to decide how all this is going to happen."

"Oh?" He looked at my gun. I couldn't get a read on what he was thinking. "You taking me somewhere?"

"I don't want to," I said. "Like I said, I have a few questions. If you'll answer them, I'll just leave."

Whelan watched me. "And if I don't?"

"Things get messy," I said. "I'm probably going to have to shoot these two gentlemen. Then I'll have to take you somewhere else. Find out what I need to know there."

I looked out over the water. A large cargo ship was moving east, bow cutting the water. The bottom of the hull was a dark red color, and a few feet above the waterline the color became a steel gray.

"Needless to say," I said. "Where we go, the view won't be the same."

I was bluffing. Kind of. At least, as far as taking Whelan somewhere too far away. I felt like I could take his guards, but after that the restaurant would explode, people would run, and it would be tough to take the man anywhere.

Which was an obstacle, but not a large one. I'd still take him. Maybe we wouldn't make it far, but it'd be far enough for me to get what I want.

Watching the man, Whelan didn't seem the type of guy to worry about much. His face didn't hold a lot of emotion. He seemed like he was one foot in the grave, and was just waiting for the other shoe to drop.

The guard in my grip tensed up. I jerked him back a little, placing the heel of my left shoe against the back of his shoe.

"Settle down," I told him.

Whelan watched the cargo ship. I couldn't tell what he was thinking about. Finally, his head bobbed slightly up and down on his thin, weak neck. "Let's hear your question, before I decide."

"Fair enough," I said. Making sure I pulled the guard's jacket back slightly. It was buttoned, so by pulling the jacket back, I was pulling him back. His center of gravity would be slightly off. I would sense it, between my hand and my foot, if and when he wanted to make a move.

I didn't think talking about whatever military technology Whelan had created would get him to answer my questions. He moved in a world where that kind of thing was normal. He had created something that could kill people, and used it, or sold it to people who did.

But I did have one card I thought would get Whelan to talk to me. So I played it. "Why don't you tell me what your son found, that got him killed?"

Whelan's emotionless face froze. He might have paled a bit, although his face was old-guy pale to begin with. He wasn't a man that saw a lot of sun.

Whelan's eyes though, seemed to get darker. A deeper blue. As if I had woken some emotion in the man. They flicked from me, back to the cargo ship, then back to me.

"You're the guy," he said. "The guy who chased the truck."

I guessed my video was everywhere. I knew Whelan knew what I was here for, then. He recognized me, and recognized Angela.

Which told me, he knew everything I needed to know.

"I'm that guy," I said.

"You're not looking for answers," he said, with conviction. "You're looking for something else."

I was looking for something else. *Someone* else, actually. And I didn't need to find a drive to get to her.

I hoped.

"Tell you what," I said, waving the barrel of the Glock at the north guard. "Have that guy carefully, with one finger and thumb, place his gun on the table. I want their earbuds, too. Once they are both seated at the next table, hands flat on the surface, we can talk."

Whelan's cheek moved up and down, like he was working his jaw on that side. Maybe it was something he did while he was thinking, or maybe he just still had a single bite of lasagna in there somewhere.

"I like my lunches here," he said, finally.

It was a great view. One a previous me wouldn't have minded fitting into a routine, somewhere. Or somewhen. Some other life. Staring at the water and the boats. Watching people come and go around me. Listening and hearing and watching but never really being a part of anything.

"You know why I come here?" he asked.

I wasn't sure I cared. "I'm not sure that matters," I said.

"Humor me," Whelan said. His hand waved over the plate, the glass of red. "This was my son's favorite place to eat. His favorite meal. Wine."

The old man *was* standing a vigil. A remembrance of his son. Maybe wondering if he could have stopped whatever it was that happened. Whelan seemed to be a man of routines, too. Maybe this lunch thing was something he built after his son's death, something to hold other emotions, other actions in check.

There was little emotion left in either of us. No joy or happiness. Deep in my core there was only anger. I wondered what he held in his.

"Here's the deal," I said. "Tell me what you know. Don't make me come back. And you can be doing this next Friday, and all the Fridays after that."

After hearing me, the guard I wasn't grabbing took a step forward. I waved at him and raised my eyebrows. A brief moment of tension crested over us. Then a breeze picked up, a napkin fluttered across the table, tumbled over the patio, and took the moment with it.

"You'll really shoot, won't you?" Whelan said.

"I'd rather we all didn't have to find out," I said.

The old man smiled. It was fake, as if the man was telling me he understood what I was telling him. The man had built a good facade, revealing only what he wanted. I couldn't tell if he was angry at the guards for what was happening now, or didn't care one way or the other. Either way, he motioned them to the table next to us.

The north guard carefully reached into his jacket, with just one finger and thumb. Pulled the gun out, shielding the restaurant from the view, and then placed it on the table. His face promised payback. His friend wasn't happy either. But both took their earbuds out and placed them on the table as well, right by a basket of bread.

I grabbed the second gun, another Glock, and put it on my chair, under my leg. The right one, so there was a twinge of pain as I shifted the leg around, and the metal of the gun was cold under my jeans.

I left the earbuds on the table. They sat next to the bread, the faint smell of toast in the air. Each slice had a pad of half-melted butter on it, a soft yellow blob laying over crusty white grain. Too cold outside, for the patty to melt.

Whelan watched the process, but his gaze always wandered back to the harbor. As if some thought rested there, something that drew his attention. Pulled him, from the here and now.

"What now?" he asked.

"Let me tell you what I know," I told him. "We'll go from there."

I outlined it, at a high level. Told him what I had put together so far. His company. The automation, and the global positioning systems. How that technology could be of interest to the military. How what he had come up with could even be interesting to other countries, people who wanted to kill others.

I told him about the governor. The old one, and the oddity in the accident he had been killed in. How the same oddity had appeared in Ben's accident. How his son had bought his car, and looked to be fleeing north.

Then I mentioned the acting governor. How he had stepped in for the old governor and pushed the stadium bill through. Maybe an apology for having Whelan's son killed. Maybe a payoff to keep him quiet. How the acting governor seemed to be on a trajectory for something more.

His eyes might have opened, while I talked. When I finished, he spoke, his voice strong. "You've put together a good story," Whelan said.

"I've made a guess here or there," I said. "But it fits."

After what I said, Whelan didn't look worried. I thought he should have been, if I had caught him out on selling some murder-on-demand technology. Maybe he didn't think I could prove anything, but I wasn't worried about what I could prove. I was just worried about what the truth was, to me.

Whelan wasn't tense, but he wasn't relaxed, either. Still, I got the feeling as if something I said comforted him. He was hard to read, and I couldn't be sure. Like I said, it was just a feeling from the man.

Even now his face was placid. Like the water in front of us. He glanced back over the harbor, at whatever pulled at him, then back to me. Maybe measuring what to say or not say. Maybe thinking about my story. Maybe thinking about his dead son and his favorite meal.

I didn't have forever, but I waited him out.

"You think I'm selling something that can kill people," he said. "Some technology that I've put on the black market."

"I think you've sold it already," I told him. It was how his son was killed. Once you let a weapon out of your hands, you couldn't control what other people did with it. "Maybe your son came up with it. Maybe he helped contribute. In the end, it ended up killing him."

A flicker of emotion from Whelan, then. A cold anger, deep inside.

He was a man of routines. He had built something in his life to hold back a monster. Like me.

"Hard to sell something," Whelan told me, "if someone else already owns it."

I froze. The revelation was large enough that for a moment it doesn't compute. Couldn't compute. One little fact had, all of a sudden, changed my worldview. It felt like someone had dropped the floor I was standing on, that I was falling, with no wall around to catch myself.

I went to say something. Whelan watched me, a tiny smile on his mouth. I went to say it again. The smile on his face grew larger.

Finally, I said the words I wanted to say. Though I wasn't sure they held the conviction I wanted them to hold. "If you're lying to me, I'll figure that out."

He waved his hand over the table. At the barely eaten meal. At the globe of wine, barely sipped. At the cold harbor waters, the cargo ship headed out to sea.

"Tell me then," he said. "What do I have to protect, by lying? A paltry deal to build a stadium? Whatever money you *think* that gives me, whatever payoff you believe that could be, trust me, it's nothing to the wealth I already have. Nothing compared to what I've already *lost*."

I watched the man, trying to figure out if what he told me was the truth or not. He was wealthy, having inherited money from a family that had lived in Boston all the way back to when the Mayflower had landed on the coast. But people who had money always wanted more.

"My son was brilliant," Whelan said. "And yes, he did work in my company. And he had some ideas, about automating cars, travel. All the traffic here, all the accidents and the logjams, the people not coming home anymore."

Whelan's fist hit the table. Hard enough that silverware rattled on the plates, a shiver of metal against china. Hard enough that the wine in his glass sloshed over the edge of the rim.

The monster, unleashed.

"Ben wanted to help people," the old man said. "Automate travel. Have a person get in and know their trip would take just so long. Have a person know that when they got into a car, it was safe, and that they'd make it home."

My mind was still in free fall, but I started to believe him. The monster convinced me. The thing caged inside the routine Whelan had built.

Like, calling to like.

"Ben was curious about the governor's accident," Whelan said. "It was something he thought he could prevent. He was coming up with a way to use GPS to connect all the cars together on the roads."

He shook his head, as if wondering if this was the moment the old man could have prevented it all from happening. As if the old man wondered if Ben would still be alive, had he just told his son no. The choice Whelan had made, that had brought around his son's death.

Innocent, when Whelan had made it. Catastrophic, as Whelan looked back. As Whelan gazed out over the harbor.

The old man settled down some. "Ben dug into it. He must have gotten into the car's black box, and downloaded everything there. Went through the code. Everything the governor's car had been told to do."

"He found out who killed him," I said.

"He did," Whelan said. His voice quiet. "And they killed him for it."

The new realization settled around me. Ben Whelan had found out who had killed the governor. I knew the drive that the mercenary wanted had something on it, and now I knew what. Really knew. Evidence of the governor's crime.

"You never knew?" I said.

Whelan's gaze returned to the harbor. "He never told me about it. The accident was an accident, as soon as I heard about it. Until someone stopped by, later that same day."

"Why did your son run?" I asked.

Whelan snorted. "I'll never know. Maybe he wanted to do the right thing. Maybe he thought he was protecting me. Maybe they threatened him, first. Maybe he thought he could get away."

It was a lot of *maybes*. Whelan didn't know, could only guess. Which maybe he did, every Friday, around lunchtime.

The free fall in my brain came to a halt. The governor was the linchpin. I had thought Whelan was the fulcrum. I had been wrong with one, but not the other.

Still, money and power. It wouldn't be hard to find one, without the other. Now that I knew.

"What's Angela have to do with it?" I asked.

Whelan's smile was still wide. As if he knew he had thrown me off. "Ms. Martinez?" He shook his head. "I never saw her, either, after my son died. Not until this week."

He meant, not until her kidnapping had been shown, all across the news. Part of me wanted to tell Whelan about the drive, but I didn't. I would be patient, with that information. The fewer people that knew about it, the greater the chance I'd find it first.

And that would give me a chance to revisit the mercenary.

A waitress came out of the restaurant and headed our way. She wore a dark jacket against the cold, wrapped tightly around her white blouse. One of the guards waved her away.

She paused a moment, the breeze stirred a little of her hair, and looked at Whelan. Then me. Maybe she was used to Whelan being here alone. Maybe she knew about the vigil, and wondered who I was.

I smiled at her. Tried to make her more comfortable with me being around. I didn't have that kind of smile.

Her face looked confused, and her eyes went to Whelan.

"Would you like your dessert, sir?" she said. As if wondering why he hadn't ordered it yet. "The torta cioccolato?"

She was Boston, with the native Boston accent, but when she said the last two words her accent shifted into Italian. As if she had heard them so many times in the restaurant, she had picked it up.

A little dessert menu sat to the left of the basket of bread. It stood like an inverted V, with pictures of ice cream, cakes, and pieces of pie. The torta cioccolato was some kind of hazelnut and caramel concoction. Something warm, sugary, and a special of Stregas.

This must have been part of Whelan's routine. Maybe his kid's favorite dessert. If Whelan had been doing this for two years, and the waitress had been here most of those Fridays, no wonder she was confused.

"Two, if you will," Whelan nodded at her. She smiled, back on track, and left.

Someone opened the door for the waitress, as she went back into the restaurant. A man in a nicely tailored suit. The professional. I guessed the lack of communication from the earbuds had gotten him running, from wherever he had been.

He stepped outside, looking at me with cautious eyes. At his two bodyguards. That was the thing about caution. It built a stable wall, got a person comfortable in what was going on around them, until, when the time came to act, they were a step slow in recognizing it.

I gave a small wave to the professional. Showed him the Glock, under the table. Gave the man a wink. A minor thing, maybe, between the two of us. But also a tally, between two people who kept such things.

Whelan noticed, turned to look at him, and gave the man a hand motion as well. His meaning something entirely different.

The professional stayed where he was. His eyes neither narrowing, nor opening wider. He remained, unmoving, not quite uncaring, more... just like his name.

"You said someone came to tell you," I said.

Whelan nodded. "A man came by. He told me everything. What my son had found. That they had killed my son, and would kill me too."

The old man's fist tightened on the table, then released. "And then he told me never to speak of it again, if I wanted to live."

"The stadium deal?" I said.

"A consolation package." He shrugged. "No real purpose, I don't think. Something given by little men, for little reasons."

Like flowers being sent to a patient, telling them they were sorry they had cancer. No real purpose to them, other than letting that person know someone else thought of them. A little gesture, more to satiate the guilt of the person sending the flowers, then helping a person being eaten by a disease.

The hospital would do that. Drugs for the pain. Changing out the catheter bag. Place a vase of flowers on the table, to wither and die like all the other vases of flowers.

"This technology," I said. "Do you know who has it?"

Whelan shook his head. "I tried to look at it once. Almost immediately after the man had stopped by. Right after my son had been killed."

He smiled a sad smile. "The next day my driver had an accident, on the way in to work."

That explained why Whelan was a recluse now. No travel. No engagements. The man was limiting the possibilities of getting killed.

"I've taken some precautions, of course," Whelan said, glancing at the professional, who still stood by the door of the restaurant.

I wondered if those precautions involved paying people in the police department.

"Do you have someone in Boston P.D.?" I asked.

Whelan shook his head. "I keep tabs on things, gather what I can. But never using computers. Never using phones."

The old man was playing it cautious, then. Maybe the professional was steering him that way. If I took him at his word, then he wasn't behind the warrant. Which made it more and more likely, it was just one person.

"Tabs? You mean on the governor?" I asked. Making sure there would be no misunderstanding between what Whelan told me, and what I heard.

"He's the one that benefits," Whelan said. His cheek twitched. "He's young, with great charisma. Good in front of the press. There's a chance he could be President, one day. With enough backing. Enough guidance. The right amount of steering."

Political careers were like that today. It was never about a person who wanted to do the most good, for the people they represented. It was about the career. Where they went to school. What they volunteered for. What their wife or husband did.

A bigger and better Boston. Brought to you by a man who just wanted a bigger and better career. Something big enough to carry him to the presidency, one day.

"Is he from here?" I asked. Not knowing anything about him.

"California," Whelan said, with a rueful grin.

It's what someone wanting a career in politics did. They would graduate from the right school, then move to the right state. A state with a weak incumbent mayor, congressman, or governor. That was that politician's *in*, and after they made office there, they would plot their next move.

Carefully crafting how they would grow in power. How they would be represented, to the people. The ads they would run.

It was never about the people, anymore. How to represent them, best. How to plan for their state's future. Never looking at the long term.

After all, the mayor/senator/governor would only be there a short time. And who looked back, four or eight or twelve or twenty years ago, to see what caused the state of society today? Voters were into immediate fixes and politicians were into a rotating blame game. It was more about the ads and how the news reported on a person, than what that person actually did in office.

Whelan understood that, as much as anyone. "Part of the deal is for me to back him, publicly," he said. "Contribute to his campaign, attend some functions. All the things wealthy people do, around people with power."

It was the voting season.

"Bigger and better," I said.

"Bigger and better," Whelan agreed.

Everything the old man was telling me fit. I had come here thinking he had been behind it all, but it was more sinister than an old man and a weapons deal. It was politics, money and power, just not Whelan's.

I felt the truth, deep in my gut. I had likely known it as soon as I saw Aaron. Even though the revelation was almost too big to swallow. And while I didn't know Whelan, I believed him. I understood him. The two of us were men of routines. He had built something caging his monster, just as I had.

And like calls to like.

I had come here for answers, and I had gotten them. I had the governor, a man who, if Whelan was right, was on the path to the presidency, one day. A man who had killed, and had kept killing, to get there.

It was why Aaron was here, after all. The Fourth Branch existed to stop these people, before they started. To allow a democracy to be a true democracy.

The governor had Angela. He had hired the mercenary, likely a group of mercenaries, to get her. Maybe the soldiers were even his own security staff.

Those people believed Angela had information that Whelan's son had discovered. A drive Angela had kept hidden, knowing it was too dangerous to keep, but also that it was too dangerous not to have around. It was likely the only thing keeping her alive, the fact that she didn't have it on her.

At some point, I did need to find it. Right now I was swinging at ghosts. Tilting at windmills. Battling dragons.

But... if the acting governor had really kidnapped Angela, if he had been behind the killing of the previous governor, of Whelan's son, and even Charley...

Well, that dragon I could slay. I *would* slay. No office on earth could hide him from me.

Whelan's eyes left me. Like him, I turned to the cargo ship. The rust-red bow, splitting the harbor water, pushing waves to either side of the vessel. The swells rolled away from the ship, large rows of waves full of energy and promise, each row sinking slowly back into the water the further the wave traveled, until all that was left was the dying of a wake, far behind the passage of the vessel.

There was nothing left on the surface of the water, to show the monstrous ship had passed. Nothing left of the rolling, roiling, waves. Just the dying waves of a deadening wake.

The waitress had brought the torta cioccolato, and the warm smell of hazelnut and chocolate stirred something in my stomach. She set tiny white plates down in front of each of us, placing a fork beside my plate, and a white cotton napkin as well.

Whelan nodded to me to eat, but left his plate there. Untouched. The old man stared out at the cargo ship, watching the vessel's passage through the harbor, what was likely Ben's favorite dessert cooling on the plate before him. Maybe back to thinking on the moment where he had his son.

The plate had been heated, and was warm to the touch. The thick chocolate scent smelled wonderful. I ate it. It was wonderful. The cake was warm as well, the chocolate flavor moist. The hazelnut aftertaste strong.

The cargo ship powered on, the split rows of waves rolling away from the hull. I understood Whelan's thoughts. Each of us was the sum of what we chose to do, the swells of those choices ran alongside us, were pushed out into the world, and died slowly behind us, long after we left the earth.

We all wondered what would be left, long after the monster passed.

Long after the decision had been made. Long after the final wave of the deadening wake slowly sank back into the ocean.

Whelan smiled then. His eyes stayed on the harbor. The flash of teeth was quick.

"Am I to understand you no longer are after me?" he said.

I looked over at the guards. Both still were angry at me. They didn't blame themselves, for me being here, at the table, with their guns. Funny how people thought that way.

The professional was better. He knew to be cautious. If the professional swam with sharks, he knew it wasn't the shark's fault if he got bit.

I had a certain level of comfort with the man. The professional wasn't the mercenary. I couldn't trust him, or Whelan, but I could trust how I felt about that.

And, like I said, like calls to like. There was a power in that recognition. Perhaps a shared meaning, or purpose.

"I think we agree on that," I told Whelan.

"You're going to continue, though," he said. Another statement. "If not me, then you're going to find out whoever has kidnapped her?"

I set my fork back down, next to the plate. The chocolate left on the tines stained the napkin. "Until I find Angela," I said.

"Well then," Whelan said, his gaze turning to me, his voice stronger than it had been throughout our conversation. "I'm an old man with a lot of money. A lot of resources. Is there a way I can talk you into something more?"

CHAPTER
THIRTY-SEVEN

Baber remembered her younger days. When traffic was the normal flow of people heading to work, then heading home. A normal amount of cars, flowing in the same direction, then flowing back. Not the crowded mess, the stop-and-gos, the parking lots that the roads were today.

Traffic was brutal. It was always, around the Waterfront in North Boston. The roads were too small, and the number of vehicles too much. Too many cars wanting to cross the small bridges. Too many people not wanting to take the chance on failing public transportation to get to work, or wherever it was they needed to go.

Like a crime scene.

Baber swore as she drove. She stomped the gas and then stomped the brakes. She beeped her siren and put the bubble on her dash, over and over, because people weren't getting over.

Not like there were many places for those cars to go. It wasn't like they could just pull onto the sidewalk.

Frank took all of it in silence. He was used to it. Not just the traffic, but her impatience getting to a scene. Especially this scene.

The body found had been of a young, Latina girl.

They were looking for a young, Latina girl.

Baber swore again. Bleeped her siren. Hammered the horn. And finally, the car in front of her moved aside, enough for her to get by.

Just to have to almost stop, behind the next car. A blue minivan, with the stick figure family on the back window. This one had two mothers and three kids.

Baber flashed her lights, her siren, and her horn, until the minivan found a place to move over.

Then she did it again. This time, a black Ford F-150.

And again.

Again.

In this way, they finally made it to their scene. Where Summer Street Bridge crossed over Fort Point Channel and met Dorchester Avenue, right in front of the large United States Post Office center there. Traffic was even more packed there, a patrol car sat on the corner with its lights flashing, people were bundled around both the black-iron fence of the bridge, and the garish yellow fence along Dorchester. All of the people were looking into the water.

Baber swore again, pulled the car over. Left it blocking the road. Looked at Frank. "Will you call someone in to handle the traffic?"

Frank grunted. Which meant yes.

Baber got out and swung around the car. Dodging an oncoming vehicle in the other lane, moving a little too fast for the congestion and people standing around. A silver Prius trying to flee the scene. Or maybe just trying to save the world from using more of its resources.

Even though the electricity that powered the car likely had come from those same resources.

Baber gave that guy a look as he passed. The guy didn't look back, but the car slowed down.

She walked over to the police car. It was backed so that most of it sat over the sidewalk on the bridge, right behind the bronze stoplight post. A cop she recognized sat in it. An older man, heavyset, the kind of guy who liked riding around and eating. A stereotypical donut-eating cop.

"Pollard," she shouted.

"Yah?" he said, sitting with the car facing out, looking north down Summer Street.

"Get the fuck out and start handling this mess," she said, waving to all the cars packed up at the light.

He rolled his eyes and began maneuvering his bulk out of the car.

"And Pollard?"

"Yah?" he said again.

"Turn the lights off," she said.

She thought Pollard would have rolled his eyes again, but he was straining to get out of the car, and maybe doing those two things at once would have been more complicated than he could handle.

He did turn the lights off, though.

"Where's your partner?" she asked.

Pollard usually rode with Wesleyan, which wasn't the man's real name. His partner just read a lot.

The wide man didn't answer. He focused on working his way out to the trunk. There he pulled out a large yellow vest, almost like a tent, and draped himself with it.

"Pollard," Baber said another time.

"Yah?" he said, frowning at her.

"Wesleyan?"

He pointed a thumb behind him. On the other side of the bridge. Where more people were congested. Then Pollard waddled out to the street where he started trying to take control of the traffic.

Jesus, Baber thought. They didn't have tape up or anything.

Frank walked up. He didn't have any trouble with oncoming vehicles. It seemed like people could recognize objects the same size as their car.

"Patrol coming," he told her.

"The scene is a mess," she said, waving her hand at all the people. "They don't have a logbook or anything Frank. No tape, nothing."

He did his standard thing. Which was to say, lifted a shoulder and let it go.

Baber waited for Pollard to stop the traffic at the bridge. Then she walked across, telling everyone there to move back. A lot of people there had their phones out, and were taking pictures, or videos. She resisted the urge to pull her gun out.

What a clusterfuck, she thought. There's no way this will end up in a courtroom. There was just too much going on, too many bystanders around, too many ways to contaminate evidence. If there was any evidence left, at all.

Pollard would have been the worst cop to send here. And she hated where that trail of thought led her. She hated Hamilton, for bringing the idea up. That someone above her was maneuvering her case, *her*, in ways to make sure no case would ever be brought forward. Could ever be brought forward, against whoever.

She shouted at the bystanders, louder. Some of them looked back, but they didn't start moving until they saw Frank. She could always tell that moment, at the lift in their eyebrows.

Baber got to the railing. It was rusty on this side of the bridge, and red. The fence along the street the same red rusty color. Both railings different, older, than across the street on the other side of the bridge. She wondered why. Likely whoever painted them was told to paint to this exact point, and no further. And that person had done exactly that, hadn't looked across to the other railing and decided that it should match.

She leaned over the railing. Wesleyan was down there, squatting on a wooden platform. Old planks, dark in color, stretched a few feet out into the channel, and ran alongside the brick for about ten feet or so. The boards were weathered, curving up at some of the edges, and the platform was attached in some way to the brick wall of the channel. Right beside the bridge.

Wesleyan knelt on the platform, one hand on the brick wall. He was thin enough that a slight burst of wind could blow him off. His other hand held a body that was half on the platform, half in the water.

He didn't look thrilled about it.

Baber wouldn't have, either.

"You got it Wesleyan?" she asked.

"I've fucking got it," he said. "I've had it for an hour. Where the hell is everyone?"

"Your partner looked comfortable," she told him.

"Yeah, well, I was pretty sure this platform wouldn't hold him," he said.

"Should have sent him anyway," she said.

Wesleyan snorted. "Been wanting to do that a while."

There was a yellow nylon rope on the road side of the railing. Huge knots every two or three feet. It was tied around the base of the railing, where a rusty pole was lodged into concrete. Something Wesleyan had come up with to get down there.

"I'll be down in a second," she said.

"Good," Wesleyan said. "This thing isn't pretty. And it smells."

"Hey," she said. "The thing is a girl."

Wesleyan shook his head. "Maybe once," he said.

Baber walked back to her car. Frank was moving people away from the sides of the bridge. She got her gloves and a bag full of crime scene gear and headed back.

A foot patrol showed up. She had Frank get them to clear the area. Handed one of the officers a roll of yellow tape to put around the scene. Handed the other a log book.

"Right down all our names," she told the man. "Time we got here, what we did, where we walked, that kind of stuff."

That cop looked around. He was young, his face was freshly shaved. "Isn't it a bit late for that, detective?"

"Do it," she said again, holding out the book.

The cop shrugged and took it.

She grabbed the rope and swung over the rail, feeling the tight nylon tug through her hands as she put her feet on the large knots. It was only a few feet to the platform, but as she descended, the salty air of the channel became something more rotten and fetid. It smelled like a red tide had come in, when dead fish by the score would lay belly up near the shoreline, the scales shimmering crimson.

The smell of death.

The temperature grew colder, on the platform, close to the channel's surface. Sitting under the shadows of the bridge, the water was gray and dark. Styrofoam cups and pieces of plastic bobbed there, gathered around the corpse. The water seemed cleaner out in the middle of the channel. The crescent arcs topping each wave glittered out there in the open, like curved knives flashing under the sun.

Baber stopped breathing through her nose. Down here the smell was much worse, it was all rotten. Baber put on her gloves and wished she had grabbed a handkerchief, something to wrap around her face. Wesleyan had been a trooper, hanging out here this long.

She shook her head, staring at the body. Corpses that had been in water a while were always horrifying to look at. The bodies were ugly things, many times no longer resembling the person who had once walked around, maybe staring at the same ocean.

This one was one of the worst. It had been beaten, just like the girl in the tattoo shop. Charley. Charley. There were hematomas all over her body, purple and black bubbles protruding from exposed skin. Some of those bubbles had burst, the skin open in ragged flaps, the edges of the wounds pale and wrinkled from the cold water.

Baber wondered if the body had just been dumped. If someone had stopped on the bridge, pulled the girl out of the trunk, and tossed her over the rail. Waited to hear the splash of the body in the water, then left. Maybe tied to a cinder block, a rope that had loosened at some point, to help her sink. Though there was no rope tied to the girl, that she could see.

Fish had nibbled on the corpse. Maybe other creatures as well. Not a lot, so the girl hadn't been in too long. Not for days or weeks, at least. But long enough bile rose up in Baber's throat, a warm and acidic taste that she couldn't swallow back down.

"Rough one," Wesleyan commented, shifting a moment, as if his legs were tired of squatting. When he did, the body shifted, the neck turned, revealing the girl's face.

Baber closed her eyes a moment. Not wanting to, but having to.

God, the poor girl's face. She was young, with skin that might have been tan, in life. Her face had been beaten, just like her body. The skin over her cheek had burst open, and the flesh pudgy and swollen around that eye. The other eye was open and unfocused. Soggy, wet, and glazed over.

"That's not all," Wesleyan said. The girl's hair was thick with wetness, and dark. It lay across her face, and the cop reached out a gloved hand to move some of the strands aside.

"Jesus," Baber said.

Someone had cut off the girl's ear. The skin was puckered there, around the ear canal, with little nibble marks around it. A whiteness of bone there, where the skin had pulled back from the skull, and the cut cartilage.

Baber looked up. Forcing the bile down in her stomach.

"Frank," she called.

"Beebs." The big man was above her, leaning over the rail. Taking everything in.

"We're going to need forensics on this," she said. "Soon."

"Is it her?"

She shook her head. She didn't know, there was no way to tell. Her skin was dark enough, and she was the right size, but that was all she could tell, from the state of the body. "It could be."

"You know forensics is going to take a bit," he said.

"What about Travis?" she asked. "He owes us."

"He's on nights," Frank said.

"What's the backlog like?" she asked, knowing Frank had already called.

He shook his head. "The normal," he said. Which meant a large line at the morgue. "Plus there were some shootings in South Boston that have been given priority."

He paused a moment. "From up top."

Baber swore. Not wanting to think what she was thinking. What Frank was thinking. And she needed this body IDed. She needed to know if this was Angela Martinez.

"Call Travis anyway," Baber said. "See if he can find a way to get on it. Tell him it's important."

Frank grunted, which she knew meant *not effing likely*.

She focused again on the body. Feeling the way the girl was beaten. The pattern was similar to the girl from the tattoo place. Too similar. Not many people delight in that kind of punishment.

Her gut told her it was the same person. Likely a guy, with the physical violence. It couldn't be coincidence, two girls beaten in the same way, found on the same day.

She really, really wanted to know who killed both. Needed to, now. Things were escalating, and Baber felt like she would be too late, if she waited on anything.

"Baber," Wesleyan said. His voice low, like he had already guessed the answer. "Anyone coming to relieve me?"

She shook her head, coming to a decision. "Likely no one soon," she said. "Pull her up on the boards and tie her down."

Wesleyan looked up. "You know that'll fuck up forensics."

"You get that from a book, Wesleyan?" Baber said. She knew it would fuck up the scene. But by the time they got information, it would be too late to do anything about it.

"Fuck you," he said, though the words didn't carry any real force in them.

"Stay here if you want," she said. "Or pull her onto the planks. Maybe tie her there. It's not going to matter much."

The sad thing was, it wasn't going to matter. Even if this was a normal case, and someone wasn't trying to stop Baber from finding the truth. This was just another corpse in a city that could produce many more, if it had a mind to.

Baber climbed back up the rope. The nylon dug into her hands on the way up, roughly cutting into her palms as she hauled herself back up. Not that she noticed, her thoughts were elsewhere.

None of this was going to matter. Not to the girl. The time for mattering for her was long gone.

Angela had pictures, of friends, and what looked like a younger version of herself. A sister. Baber thought, if the morgue was going to be slow, maybe she could find the answer there.

CHAPTER
THIRTY-EIGHT

Whelan knew where Angela was.

It was hard for me to sit still and hear the old man out, after he told me that. Part of me was worried, anxious. The part that felt the urgency rising around me, like a charge that kept building and building and building. It felt like years since I had met her at the bookstore.

It had only been a few days.

Whelan wanted to help. I needed to keep swinging, and was willing to take it. We agreed, there would be no conditions between us. My goal was to rescue the girl. Not carry out vengeance. He smiled when I told him that, as if he knew that anything I did would be more than what he had. As if he was gambling that I would do more.

I gave the guns back to the bodyguards. They took them, unhappy. The south guard gave me an *I'll-see-you-again* look, which was fine with me. If he wanted to, he could find me, and we could settle whatever thing he had then.

Whelan talked to the professional.

While he did, I walked over to the railing, leaning against the chilly metal bar, looking out over the harbor.

The cargo ship was a small dot now, heading out to sea. The large wake behind the vessel was gone. The big swells of water that had once bobbed craft in front of me had collapsed back into the harbor's dark surface, leaving nothing behind but the tiny lapping of shrunken waves against the pier.

The energy which had once roiled over the surface, now hiding below.

There were different cages, I realized. There were cages of routine, holding back a dark betrayal-fueled anger. There were cages of regret, held gently by circling arms. And there was the large cage of the ocean, with all the power and anger and sorrow buried inside cold, dark waters.

I was a different person than a few days ago. And I was also the same. Anger. Sorrow. Betrayal. Vengeance, it could all be held in deep, dark depths. There would always be a placid face on the surface, but anything could break the water at any time. Like the flick of a tail of a sea monster, it would rise. Like the deadening wake, it would die away.

The professional came over. His eyes alert. "I'm going to take you somewhere."

"The girl?" I asked.

He shook his head. And he wasn't going to tell me anything else. I got the feeling Whelan already felt like he had spoken too much, out here in the open, where anyone could hear anything. Maybe the old man felt like the risk was worth the reward.

I followed him out. The restaurant was the same leaving as it had been coming in. Relaxed people enjoying their Friday lunches. Looking forward to the weekend. Conversations about plans and dreams over a good meal, bundled with a cocktail or a glass of wine. Nothing in their world had really changed for them, no matter what had happened on the patio.

It had just changed for me. Like the ship, I was pointed in a direction. I knew where Angela was. I was headed that way.

We got in the car. A dark black Lexus. As soon as the locks clicked shut, he reached his hand over. His jacket sleeve slid back, showing me the same athletic tape wrapped around his arm as the other day.

"James," he said.

"Hurt your arm?" I asked.

He looked at it, shrugged. "Got cut the other day."

It hit me. The mercenary, and the blood at Angela's place. "You were in her apartment," I said. Probably looking for the drive.

"Maybe," he said. "Until I got caught."

"Young guy?" I asked. Remembering how the mercenary had looked. "Crew cut? White T-shirt?"

"That's him," he said.

"You were looking for the drive?" I asked.

"A few days ago something got emailed to Whelan," James said. "Until then, he hadn't known about the drive, Angela, nothing."

"What was the email?" I asked.

"Apparently the drive had been encrypted," he said. "Someone had tried breaking it. There was a program on the drive, something Ben had put on it, and that program sent an email to Whelan."

Angela's courses had stood out to me, because I hadn't been able to figure out her major. She could sing. Had done a lot of acting. At Harvard, she had been something special. Kirschke had said she was bright.

And then I remembered the computer science class. Data Security.

Angela had been trying to break Ben's encryption. Not knowing who she could trust. Just knowing what had killed her boyfriend.

Ben had something on the drive to alert his father. Who was being watched by the governor. Who likely had seen the email too.

I wondered why they hadn't reached out and protected Angela.

James's face was sad, when I asked the question. "It all went down too fast. He got the email, the email told us what Ben had found, and where he was headed. Maybe an hour later I was at the girl's apartment, to find her."

Whelan had probably been excited. Having a chance to exact his revenge. James had probably been sent there as soon as they understood what had happened.

But Angela hadn't been there. Hadn't known any of that was going on. She was just headed to a bookstore, to finish up a project.

You have that look.

"She wasn't there," I said.

James nodded. "I let myself in, took a peek around. Thought I'd see what I could find."

He buckled his seatbelt, started up the car. The engine hummed, and lukewarm air flooded out of the vents.

"Turns out, all I found was they keep making them younger, and faster," he said.

He seemed like a nice guy. Who did the right thing, when he could. Cautious, too. Someone I wouldn't have minded working with, back in the day.

"You were there," I said. Realizing something. "It was you who sent her the text."

James looked at me out of the side of his eyes. He didn't look happy. "I did what I could. It just wasn't enough."

It bothered him, her kidnapping. He pulled the car into traffic. The radio was on, tuned to a news station. A voice, a young woman by the sound, read something off her notes about the upcoming election. Then she went right into traffic patterns. It was a small voice, running underneath our conversation.

The way James spoke told me something. Making them younger and faster. Talking about the pipeline of soldiers.

"You were in," I said. *In* meaning the military. Which usually meant, in our world, Afghanistan.

"I was," he said, pulling the car into traffic. The engine had a low, thrumming purr that spoke of power, well taken care of. He glanced at the mirrors out of the sides of his eyes, and when he did, they paused on me. "You too."

I doubted I'd be able to find anything on the man. Certainly not on my own. Maybe Aaron could. James was definitely a professional, and knew how to keep himself separate from Whelan. Still, I went fishing. "You're pretty cautious."

He held both hands on the wheel, at ten and two. "You know like I do, there are two ways to stay alive over there. Either you're really good at killing, or you're really cautious."

James slowed down as we approached a traffic light, and clicked on the blinker. The ticking sound was loud enough to be heard over the news.

"I know my strengths," he said.

I stayed quiet. James did too. The sky was the blustery bluish gray of a pending storm, something the clouds seemed to hold back from those of us below, as if everything and everyone waited on the first rumble of thunder.

The traffic wasn't light, but it was easy for James to navigate. Although I could feel the urgency in me, pushing me onward, faster and faster, the man drove at a steady pace. I took a breath, then another, trying to settle myself. I was the hare, James was the tortoise, and both of us would get to wherever when we got there.

North. Across Fort Point Channel, on Seaport Boulevard. South of us, the flashing lights of the police car I had seen at Summer Street Bridge were gone, though traffic had backed up from that area, causing us to stop along Seaport for a bit.

Then we were navigating Boston proper. Keeping on Seaport until we could get on the interstate, where we picked up speed taking I-93 northwest past Bunker Hill and Charleston. Always heading north, until we were out of Boston and into Medford.

"You going to tell me who we're meeting?" I asked.

James turned the radio down. "We've got a guy watching the governor."

Whelan had found a way to keep tabs on things, even if he had been threatened. Maybe thanks to James.

"No names," I said.

He nodded. "Everything verbal. Everything cash, through multiple parties. Nothing online, digital, or spoken out loud, if we can help it."

"And so far?" I said.

He shrugged. "You know like I do, there are no guarantees."

We took an exit off near Medford. Fellsway. Weaved our way through less-crowded streets. It was early afternoon now, before everyone headed home and then headed back out to celebrate the weekend.

For those celebrating.

There was a shopping center ahead. The red-dotted sign of a Target. Next to a coffee place, a small gym, and a pharmacy. We pulled through the parking lot until we got in front of the coffee place, parked and got out of the car.

My leg hurt a bit, getting out. An ache of staying in one place too long, combined with the sharp pains of the stab wounds as I got out. I flexed it a bit.

James hit the key fob. The Lexus beeped twice, though the lights didn't flash. We walked in and ordered a couple of coffees, and took a table in the back. A dark wood table, round, with four chairs spaced around it. Both of us sat facing the door.

The coffee was strong and bitter. Hot. I sipped it and waited, comfortably quiet. James too.

He had been in Angela's apartment. Had met the mercenary there. Had lost, but gotten away.

"You recognize the man?" I asked.

"Who?" James said.

"The guy in Angela's apartment," I said.

"Yeah," he said. "He's one of a hundred young guys that get out, every year. Guys that don't play by the rules."

"That's not what I meant," I said. "You know who he is?"

James shrugged. "Not his name. Or where he served. Just enough to know he's not the kind of guy I'd hire."

He sipped his coffee.

"Maybe when this is done, I'll look him up," he said.

"He may not be around," I said. At least, not if I saw him again.

A man walked in about halfway through my coffee. An everyday kind of man. Brown shaggy hair, not cut well. Not too long, but not too short. He wore a loose jacket, rumpled around him. Jeans and sneakers. Dark blues and grays and browns, in color. Nothing memorable about him.

I watched the man order a coffee. Standing at the register like he had ordered the same coffee every day, as if this was his spot. Everything the man did, he did it in a way he belonged.

He grabbed the coffee after it was made, left a tip in the little square plastic tip box, then headed our way. Taking a seat in the same manner that he walked in. Like this was something he did every day.

Close up I saw he was a day past needing a shave. He had brown eyes, unremarkable. If he was the guy that watched the governor, he was good.

The man nodded at James. James nodded back. Then the man pulled out a small manilla folder from his jacket, emptying the contents on the table.

Photos slid across the surface. Black and whites, likely to save on the cost of developing them. My guess was the man did all his own work, and that guess was confirmed when he pulled another small envelope out and handed it to James.

James checked the envelope. It looked like negatives were in this one.

I looked at the photos. Picked the first one up that caught my eye. A black Escalade, pulling through iron gates, the truck on its way up a driveway.

"That was Wednesday," the man said. His voice light.

The photo had been taken from somewhere above ground, but not too high. Just enough to see three-quarters of the truck, the roof, and the back. There were at least five figures in the truck, that I could see. Three in the middle seat, and although I couldn't see if the middle person was Angela, I was pretty sure.

More pictures on the table. I picked them up. One of an official-looking limo, black with tinted windows leaving. The car looked thick and heavy, in the way that armored vehicles looked. Like it carried more weight than a normal car would.

"Same day," the nondescript man said. Commenting on what I was looking at.

There was a house, not far up the driveway past the iron gates. Well, a mansion, up on a hill. Big trees around it, leaves brown in the fall. The house made of red brick, multiple levels, with a black roof and a chimney on the right, tall against the blue sky. A little turret on the other side of the home. Large windows on each level, with drapes pulled aside.

Another photo showed a close-up of some of the windows on the turret. The drapes there pulled aside, and someone standing behind the glass. Someone whose face was hidden by the window, but who had long, dark hair.

"Yesterday," the man said.

"Where is this?" I asked.

"It's a vacation place," James said. Leaving out the words *of the governor*, though I believe I understood him. "He goes there sometimes, like a home the man always circles back to. Like a base."

I flipped through a few more pictures. Saw another, and felt my heart beat a little harder. I picked up the picture.

A sports car at the gates. One of the newer Mustangs. Red, with the pony package. I saw the sports stripe down the middle, the tiny chrome emblem of a running horse on the door panel, glinting in the black and white light.

The driver's window was down. The driver was talking to one of the guards. The iron gate was half-open, and the driver faced the camera.

The mercenary.

I took a long breath and let it out. This was the place.

The man had a passenger, but with the heavy tint and the small rear window, I couldn't tell who that was. And I didn't need to know. The merc was enough.

"Where is this?" I asked.

"South Gloucester," James said. "Along the coast."

Not even an hour away, unless traffic was bad. Not too far. Not too far at all. The sky outside was still dark and gray. Before long I would head to Gloucester. I would get there at night. And I would hit them hard, and finish what I had set out to do, just a few days ago.

Maybe then I could get back to the life I had been living.

"I'm going to need a few things," I said, looking at the professional. Guns. A tactical vest. Things I had once worn like a second skin, but had shed, for this new person I had become.

The man smiled, as if he had already known. "I got a kit in the back of the car."

CHAPTER
THIRTY-NINE

Baber had dropped Frank off back at the department. He was better at lurking, and at being patient. His presence was a physical weight, wherever he stood. People felt him, even when he said nothing. If anyone could get someone to look at her body, it would be Frank.

The sun set ahead of her, the glaring rays flashing across her windshield. The sky still a blustery blue-gray above. Clouds floating west, above her.

She felt rushed, and drove that way. She didn't put her siren on, but she did bleep it whenever she got behind someone driving too slow in front of her. Then she would have to wait, maybe bleep the siren again, until the person realized they needed to get over. Then she had to wait until they actually got over, drifting slightly to the right, barely making it across the dotted lines before jerking the car back in front of Baber. They always did it over and over, sometimes glancing in their rearview, until the person driving felt safe enough to actually complete the move.

Baber hated drivers today. Cars weaved in front of her, meandered back and forth, drivers never using their turn signals, but following some sixth sense of when exactly they needed to pull right in front of her. Still, Baber made the best time she could. And she was able to get to Angela Martinez's apartment before rush hour truly set in.

Baber climbed the stairs and ducked under the yellow crime scene tape over the doorway. She and Frank had noticed the door jamb had been broken inward, when they had first arrived. They had found the apartment clean, neat and tidy, but a feeling of violence remained, maybe of some dark, angry act.

She had known something had happened, could always feel it, but hadn't known what until Hamilton had told her. The whole place had been tossed, he had said. But whatever had happened then, if she could trust Hamilton, it had been cleaned since. Sterilized. Leaving just a smell, something like eucalyptus mint, and maybe a hint of bleach.

Baber felt much like she did when she walked into the morgue. In that place the smell of Lysol always hung thick in the air. The metal tables always clean, the tile floor always spotless, yet somehow the scent of decay and death still lurked underneath all of the shiny metal tables and clean, white tile.

The apartment had that same sense of cleanliness. As if something dead had been here once, but it had been scrubbed away. Cleaned to leave something else behind, something sterile, just a pungent minty smell. Like a place no one had really lived in.

Baber walked through it, again. Trying to get a sense of the apartment now, with what she knew before. The bedroom had just one bed, but too many pillows. The towels in the closet seemed new, and were a bright blue, when everything in the bathroom was yellow. The shower curtain looked new, and the liner. She flipped the clear plastic back and forth. No mold or mildew on the bottom. No tiny white spots, where drops of water had dried, leaving a limey residue.

Baber went back to the kitchen. Looked at the wall by the dining room, at the photos. Angela in different places, on a stage, acting, singing. One of her in front of a boat, in the harbor, with a girl that looked a lot like Angela, just younger.

She grabbed that photo off the wall and called Frank.

"Beebs," he answered, his voice a low rumble.

"How's the morgue coming?" she asked.

"Travis is headed in now," he said.

Baber smiled. She knew the Frank trick would work. She used it sparingly, when she felt like time was critical. No one liked a mountain overhanging them, the feeling of a landslide rumbling above them, ready to be released with one misstep, or wrong word. The coroner there would feel that pressure, subconsciously, even with Frank just standing there and saying nothing. They would call in help, and the help would come.

"Good," she said. "Can you find me an address on a younger sister of Angela's?"

"You think she has a sister?" Frank said.

"Unless she has a friend that looks just like her," Baber said.

She could track the sister down, get her to come in, maybe help identify the body. Hopefully before the day was out.

"Hmm," Frank said. "One sec."

Baber stayed still, staring at the photo, trying to place the corpse she had just seen overtop of Angela. No matter how hard she tried, she couldn't reconcile the dead body with the smiling, beautiful girl in the picture. Or her sister.

"Got it," Frank said. "Luisa Martinez." He rattled off an address. It was further away, south of Dorchester, but east of where she was now.

She swore, but got back in the car and headed that way. It was a decent drive, and she didn't have to fight as much traffic, with it being early afternoon and everyone heading home. Just the normal amount. Which was still a bit frustrating.

Luisa lived along a run-down block. The place Baber pulled into was a tiny building, two floors high, old brick. There was a tiny strip of weeds along the sidewalk, maybe a foot wide, between the concrete and the building. Baber walked up a few stone stairs and entered the hallway.

The building had eight apartments, four on the first floor, four on the second. Two doors sat on either side of Baber. A pale yellow tile sat underneath her feet. She walked down to Luisa's door and knocked, hoping she was home.

Baber waited a moment, then knocked again.

Silence on the other side. A quiet, person never home kind of silence. Baber walked out front again, looking for a sign for a property agent. Then walked back inside and knocked on other doors.

The first one answered. "One moment," called out a young female. Baber heard the person walk to the door, heavy creaks of an old, wooden floor. Then she watched the peephole darken a moment.

Baber held her badge to the side of her face and waited.

There was a long pause, then the door opened.

A heavyset woman stood there. Young, and pasty white, with large flaps of skin layered under her chin. Thin stringy hair was tied up behind her head, which she had tilted oddly, as if wondering what Baber was doing here. And her eyes were open, maybe scared.

"Officer?" she said.

"Detective," Baber said. "Wondering if you have the landlord's number here. Or the rental agency."

"Are we in trouble?" the girl asked. She didn't seem like she had it all together. Her head made little motions, left and right, that made the skin under her neck twist, like someone wringing a towel.

"No ma'am," Baber said. "It's about your neighbors."

The girl's eyes widened. "You mean Luisa?"

"Yes," Baber said.

"I called the other day, she didn't answer," the girl said. "She was making a lot of noise though."

Noise. Like maybe getting beaten. Baber started to get a really bad feeling. "She didn't answer?"

"No," the girl said. "And the walls are thin. It was like she was moving stuff. Grunting and yelling, too."

A really bad feeling.

"Can you get me your landlord's number?" Baber said, moving down the hallway to Luisa's door.

"Are we in trouble?" The girl asked again, focusing on the wrong thing. "I mean, she was disturbing *us*."

Baber shook her head. "Get me the number, please."

She put her hand on her holster, looking at Luisa's door again. She tried the knob, and it was locked.

Fuck it, Baber thought, and kicked the door. Once. Twice.

"Jesus," the heavy girl said.

Baber didn't think she was going to get the number for her. The heavyset girl followed Baber down the hall, the floor creaking underneath her steps. If she had worried about others, instead of just herself, maybe Luisa would be here today. But apparently the girl was only concerned about how she might be in trouble. That and maybe the next meal.

The third kick opened the door up.

Inside the apartment was a mess. Shelves fallen to the floor. The couch flipped over. A kitchen table, on its side. A large potted plant, the red clay pot upended, with rich black dirt scattered across the floor. A trail through the dirt, as if someone had been dragged through it.

"Jesus," the girl said again.

"Miss," Baber said, staring at the girl. "Please get back in your apartment."

Maybe it was something in Baber's eyes, but the girl finally listened to her. The floor creaking quickly this time as she scooted back to her apartment.

Baber looked quickly around. Signs of a struggle everywhere. There would be no way to tell, but her intuition was telling her the same person that was here, had been at Charley's Angels.

There was a bathroom here too. With hairbrushes and combs, holding little strands of hair. She went back to the car, got an evidence bag, and put a hairbrush into it before zipping the seal tight.

She wasn't going to label it. She had a feeling this would all get lost, somehow. Especially if Baber called it in.

Instead, she closed the door behind her, leaving Luisa's apartment almost like she found it. Minus the brush.

Then she called Frank.

"Beebs," he said again. Like she hadn't just called.

"Got something," she said. "Travis there?"

"Just arrived," Frank said.

"I'm headed in," she said. "Tell him I got something for him to match up to the girl."

"See you then," he said, then hung up. He was a man of few words.

She started up her car and sat there, thinking. One hand on the steering wheel of her car. Two girls missing now. One body found.

If one of the sisters was dead now, she wondered how soon the other would follow. And, like always, she tried to puzzle out the why of it.

Hamilton knew the why. She was willing to bet on it.

Baber would drop the brush off and then go see the man. No matter what the lawyer had told her about staying away. Or the weird-ass shit about the stool and the four legs, or four branches. Whatever.

JAMES DROPPED ME OFF AT MY PLACE. I STOOD OUTSIDE A moment, holding the heavy gym bag he had pulled out from his trunk, feeling the press of people walking back and forth around me. The darkening sky above. The cool wind of fall, funneled down the street and stirring the leaves of the plants hanging from the windowsill of one of my neighbors.

It was late enough in the year that the plants had turned brown. I wasn't sure if they were alive anymore. Or why they remained on the sill. Maybe the person forgot, or life got too busy for them. Maybe the plant was one of those kinds that can survive a cold Boston winter. Or maybe whoever it was inside was just going through the motions.

I thought the last the most likely.

James had let me know he couldn't help. That anything he might do, would lead back to Whelan, and it was his job to keep his principal from being killed. His eyes revealed a little regret, as he had pulled the kit out of his trunk, and I had thought he was a good man. More like I had used to be, than the person I was, now.

You have that look...

The urgency had grown during the drive back to my apartment. It had swelled, like a tidal wave. A deep need, buried inside me, pushing me to rush out and rescue the girl. Once, that feeling had been the way I had been wired. Once, that had been how I had defined myself.

Now I just wanted this over. I had made many mistakes, chasing Angela down. Those mistakes had cost Charley her life. Had cost Angela, too. It was hard for me to believe that someone like the governor would employ someone like the mercenary, but after thinking about it, I guess I shouldn't be surprised. It was the way of the world now. And after all, the governor had proved he wasn't shy about killing someone.

So the urgency swelled. Became a tsunami. A desperate rushing of force, rolling over the waters, heading to shore. Flooding harbors and capsizing boats along the way, tearing everything apart in a mad need, leaving just me in its wake.

The waves whispered to me, a throaty, gurgly voice. It reminded me that I had caused all of this. Charley, beaten, killed. Angela, maybe the same by now.

I had started the mercenary on his path of beating women. Of carving earlobes from their heads. Of tying me up, and stabbing me, just to even the score between us.

Who was I, to think I could go back in time and be the person I had been? What path could I possibly follow that would take me back to that man? That trail was long overgrown, the path hidden in brush and bramble. I had tried to walk it, and it had led me to a dark ravine, full of loose rock and shale, the slightest stumble of which would cause an avalanche that would bury me.

Actions had consequences. At the beginning of this I had chased the truck, not thinking, just *doing*. A pretty girl had sat and talked to me at a table, I had felt some connection to her, and somehow that had led to me chasing after Angela.

That had been the step to lead me here. The routine had been broken, and the quiet rage inside of me had found an outlet. It was what had led me to the here and now. It was what had first stabbed the mercenary. It was what was driving me, now.

Not the guy I had been. Not the guy who wanted nothing more than to protect his friends. Not the guy who had grabbed a lifeline, a pretty girl's interest, in order to try to save himself from the dark world he had built.

I wasn't who I had been. I would never be. I was the guy that got Charley killed. That had some other guy carving pieces off of women.

That was the guy I was now, and that guy wasn't going anywhere.

Sadly, I understood all of this too late. Too late for Charley. Maybe even too late for Angela.

But I would try.

A man pushed past me. His shoulder bumped my chest, and I took a step back to catch my balance. My leg twinged a bit, where the bones had been broken. The tape there stretched tight around my thigh. The man kept walking, hunched over, staring at the phone in his hand. Dark jacket puffed out a bit, as if he had been thinner, once.

I had called myself Crosse. I thought I had *that look*. I hadn't realized the red cross on the shield wasn't colored paint, it wasn't even my blood, it was the blood of innocents, and all that could leave behind was rust, a crimson stain that ate and ate into the metal plate.

I swallowed. A bitter taste remained in my throat. The ache in my leg kept aching. The tape kept digging into my thigh.

I wasn't the man I had once wanted to be.

I wasn't going to be that man, ever again.

I would do this thing. I would rescue Angela. I could do that, at least. Even the man I was now. Then I would go back to my routine. Beat out whatever it was in me that wanted to help others. Build the dark world my consciousness craved and pull it over me, let the blackness surround me, and drown.

I wasn't strong enough to carry the weight I used to carry. Not anymore.

I got to my apartment. The ammonia smell was worse, so I cracked open the windows, not worried about the rain. If a storm was coming, so be it. Then I dialed the thermostat down, and flipped the fan switch from auto to on. I hoped circulating air would mellow the scent of urine out.

I'd probably come back to a water-soaked apartment that still smelled like piss, but that was tomorrow's problem. I needed to finish this, now. Today.

I changed out my jeans to something darker. Checking the wounds in my leg, the bandages, and thinking it all was good enough. Then I grabbed a black T-shirt and slid that over my head, tugging the cotton over my shoulders and arms.

All my tennis shoes had white soles, so I picked a gray pair and colored the sides with a black Sharpie. The black marker left wet streaks, and no matter how much I let the ink dry, some white remained. I smeared what I could, and smudged the rest, hoping altogether it would be dark enough.

I opened the gym bag. James had struck me as cautious, and nothing inside indicated otherwise. I pulled out a black tactical vest, like the old Interceptor Body Armor I used to wear in the service. Not the full kit, but enough to cover me. The vest was heavy, with a ceramic plate already inserted in both the front and back.

James was definitely cautious.

The armor was a little snug, but after putting it on I could still move around. I put on a black leather jacket and zipped it up and down, flexed my arms, then took the jacket off. It would work, it wouldn't restrict anything I wanted to do.

James had a few grenades in the bag, tucked into a side. An MP5 as well. I left it there. If I needed something that used that much ammo that fast, then I was in more trouble than a submachine gun could get me out of. I planned on going in quick, and getting out the same way.

There were two Glocks in there, as well. The ones law enforcement used, with nineteen rounds to each mag. James had plenty of extra mags in the bag, and a nice suppressor. Plenty of spare mags. I took everything out and set it all on the table. Then I worked the slides, handled the guns, getting a feel for them. So they both would become a part of me.

I would have no questions, no doubts, when I needed them.

It got darker outside, becoming the black of night. The window reflected the light over the dining room table, and out of the corner of my eye I saw my reflection, a dark man in a light room, wearing a vest of ceramic plates. The table became the break room table from my nightmare, except there was no case in the middle of the table. No vials of a virus, no Aaron with a smoking gun off to the side, no missing Sam and definitely no suit of armor.

Not on me.

I snapped the magazines in and dropped them out, and became the black of night. I stayed sitting at the table and dry-fired both Glocks, listening to the clicks and clinks as I handled each. The routine wanted the television on, but the mercenary had put a nice foot-sized hole in the middle of that, so I just paid attention to the sounds of traffic outside instead. The rushing of cars, the heavy rustling of the wind, the sounds of doors opening and closing, the occasional horn, loud in the night.

A combination shoulder rig was in the bag. Something that would allow me to carry both guns and cross-draw each. I put it on and snapped both guns in. I was left-handed, and part of me wondered if I could still shoot as well with my right as my left, and a larger part of me stayed unconcerned about it.

I screwed the suppressor on the gun I like better. I put that Glock in the rig under my right arm. Put the other gun under my left. If I needed that one, I wouldn't be worried much about being silent.

After that, I put on my jacket. Tested the fit again. At that second, I went back to the bag. Grabbed a couple of the frag grenades there. One for each pocket in the jacket. Then, I felt like I was ready.

I still sat on the table though. Then I reached back behind me, to the kitchen counter. Picked up *The Faerie Queene*, and flipped to where I had stopped, in what had seemed like another life.

Maybe that was the point I had really known.

In the story, the knight had gotten trapped. Had faced a giant and had been betrayed. Had swung until he could swing no longer.

He had lost. Been beaten. He could blame the betrayal maybe, but the truth was, he just wasn't good enough.

The lady had found a real champion. Someone with glittering, shiny armor. A bright shield. A ray-like lance. Outfitted in gold, and diamonds, jewels that hadn't been gifted to the knight, but instead had been something the man had earned.

The lady for some reason still searched for the beaten knight, bringing the new knight with her. The new guy easily beat the giant. Had rescued the beaten man. Then the lady had taken the old knight to a place where he could recover and heal.

Not a place that smelled like urine. Not an old uniform soaked in piss. I looked around at the mess that was my apartment. The dark reflection in the bright glass of the cracked window.

My hand found my phone. I called Kirschke's office. I didn't believe he would be there, this late on a Friday night, but by chance, or whatever, he answered

"Professor," I said.

"Well look who it is," the professor said. "How's the story?"

"I don't think it's what I thought it was," I said.

"You should really come in sometime," Kirschke said. "Wednesday nights, we're all up here."

A small part was interested. But the larger part demanded the routine. When I was done with this, I would go back to that routine. That person.

"The other knight," I asked. "Is that King Arthur?"

"The one in the first book?"

There was more than one? I flipped through *The Faerie Queene*, some of the pages were wrinkled and folded, from getting thrown. I got to the end and saw there were six books, in total.

The small part of me wanted to finish it. I think that part believed in something in the story. But I hadn't even made it through the first book before giving up.

"Yeah," I said.

"It is," Kirschke said.

"I don't understand," I said.

"What?" he asked.

"How's the first knight the hero?" I said. The first monster the knight had faced had left its spawn behind. The knight had challenged other knights in the field, and had beaten them, but those knights hadn't seemed especially tough. Just something to make the knight feel good about himself.

The giant had easily taken the knight down.

"I mean, how easy is it for another person to come in, at the end, and kill the giant?" I said. "It's like the first knight failed at everything he did. Everything he tried, things just got worse."

"Have you finished it?" Kirschke said.

I snorted. All six books that I hadn't known about? "Not even the first book."

"Maybe you should," he said. "Maybe it's not the story you think it is. Maybe it's not just about slaying a dragon."

"What is it, then?" I asked.

"Read it," Kirschke urged. "Then come in and talk about it. Next Wednesday,"

The small part of me wanted to agree, but I forced it down. Told that voice to shut the fuck up. I didn't want to be that guy anymore. It was the whole reason I was here, now.

Kirschke sensed the conflict in me. Sensed that there was a part of my life wrapped up in what I had read. Angela, telling me I had *that look*. Telling me to not be faint, and to show what I was.

The story had snuck up on me. I had been interested, at first. I think that small part of me had hoped it would lead me back to who I had been, but I was just as lost as the knight. Then the kidnapping had become killing, a killing I had been responsible for, and I just wasn't capable of shouldering that burden, anymore.

"Maybe," I said.

Kirschke knew I wouldn't.

"The offer stands," he said.

"Sure," I said. "Thanks."

I didn't give him a chance to say anything else.

Whatever the story was, it wasn't me. It wasn't going to lead me back to who I had been, any more than any other fairy tale. It was a book, a bunch of words, and in the end those words didn't matter compared to the actions.

I called Sara next, to keep her updated. I didn't tell her anything Whelan had told me, believing the man would want that kept quiet, but I let her know I had found Angela, and I was going to get her.

"And she's up where?" Sara asked. "Gloucester?"

"Yeah," I said.

"You driving your car there?" Sara said.

It was the quickest way for me to get there. I told her I was.

"You're not worried?" Sara asked. "With all the people having *accidents* lately?"

I knew what she meant by stressing the word. But I wasn't worried. However they were causing the accidents, those people needed to know the exact car I was driving.

They couldn't just Google that information. The name I had bought the car under was an old name, something I had worn when I had gotten out of rehab. Later, after leaving the Branch, my name had been changed to Hamilton.

Hamilton didn't own a car. If someone wanted to find out what I was driving, they'd have to tie the car I was driving to my old name.

That link only existed in a database that no one was even aware existed.

I told Sara I'd call tomorrow. Tomorrow this would all be done. Then I hung up. Put on my jacket again. Zipped it over the vest and the guns, the leather of the coat stretching a little around the rigs. Went and used the bathroom. Looked at the counter there, where rolls of bandages and tape sat around the sink. Washed my hands, and ran them through my hair, down my face. Took a deep breath and stared in the mirror.

It was the face of a man at his end. A man clothed in darkness, armored in a vest and some plates, aching and wounded inside. A man who might be ending something, soon. One way or the other.

Like the knight, I had failed slaying the giant in front of me. The monster was too big for me to come to grips with. Too large in scope. And here in the real world, there was no King Arthur coming to my rescue. No lady to take me somewhere and heal the wounds I carried.

I stepped outside the bathroom.

Aaron stood there, in the door. One hand on the knob. Staring into the kitchen.

His gaze turned to me. His nose was wrinkled. I guessed the smell in the apartment was worse than I thought.

We stared at each other. I wondered what he was doing here. Not in Boston, but *here*.

Neither of us spoke, but his face was sad. Like he was with me in the hospital, sitting by the bed, watching me get the news that whatever cancer ate at me, that the sickness was incurable.

He opened his mouth.

I looked away.

And the black phone rang, from its hole in the wall, the dull echo ringing over and over and over, like the tolling of a bell.

CHAPTER
FORTY-ONE

Aaron stepped inside the apartment.

I held a hand up and walked to the kitchen. Stood in front of the wall and laid a hand on the casing of the phone. Felt the vibrations tremble through the plastic, as the handset rang. I knew those vibrations had traveled along a physical line, buried deep under the earth, from wherever Sam called from, to here.

To me.

I picked up on the fifth ring.

"Sam," I said. My voice tight, controlled.

"J," she said back.

"I'm busy," I said. Not wanting to deal with Sam, with the anger that came up from her betrayal. But also not able to let it go. I wondered if I ever would. I had put in the phone line, knowing she could find the number, believing there would be a day of reckoning then between us.

Then I could move on with my life.

Leave the routines and the nightmares to others.

But some monsters are too hard to slay. Some monsters live on, they just change their shape and form. They evolve and grow and spawn other creatures, who spawn others, always twisting their way into your life, living on no matter how many times you faced them.

It was something I couldn't defeat. The rage at what had happened to me. And Charley had paid the price, for the monster I couldn't beat.

Hard to see a world where the knight could succeed, with that.

Sam's voice was soft, concerned. "I think I know why," she said. "You being you."

My fist tightened around the handset. Sam felt so much like the Sam of *before*, but the two of us were in the *after*.

"You don't know me anymore, Sam," I said.

I turned a bit. Faced the dining room. The mess there. The picture of her and I in a boat in Venice, just our hands holding a pair of oars, the frame face down on the floor.

My throat tightened. "I didn't know you, either."

Aaron and I had been together a bit when Sam had come to our group. She was confident in her work. Great at what she did, one of those people who could pick up a laptop and do anything. A must have, in today's world of cyber technology, hackers, and the dark web.

The hum of the phone line still tied us together, Sam and I. A current underneath. And then there was a catch, like a half-sob, from her side. Or maybe the sound was one of the million switches between us, transferring the line from one connection to another.

"This is harder than I would have ever thought," she said. Her voice, normally light, maybe a little rough.

I couldn't say when I started to feel something for Sam. Or her for me. As confident as she was at her work, she had been shy around me. Nervous. Always looking away after our eyes met, tucking her blonde hair behind her ears.

Aaron had joked about it once. Sam had blushed. I looked at her then, and that time she didn't look away. Our eyes caught, the flush grew across her cheeks, her eyes open and inviting and deep.

Hard was an understatement.

"I'm busy now Sam. Call back tomorrow. That way things can be settled, between you and I."

"I didn't know, J," she said, almost crying out. "How can I *know*?"

Her voice *was* hoarse. But didn't, wouldn't, can or can't, none of those were important now.

"Whatever you knew or didn't know," I said, my voice low. Cold. "None of that matters now."

It didn't. Not really. Not now. Now was for saving the girl. Something I had once been good at. Something I hoped I was still good enough at.

Once I did that, I could get back to the routine. Get rid of all this emotion. This complicated mix of hate and rage, the pain at losing her, the fury at what had been done to me. The sense of loss, of who I had been, of who I wanted to be, of who I was now. A broken shell of a man who found a way to hurt others, instead of help.

I would finish this with Sam tomorrow, this thing that broke me, this thing two years in my past. I would find her, I had put it off long enough. Whatever she had been paid to steal the virus, whatever country she had switched allegiances to, none of that would protect her.

It had been too long.

Two years.

I realized then what had happened to me, and what had happened to Ben, both had begun two years ago. Things otherwise not connected in this world, had wound up tied together, in Boston.

And these events didn't just affect me, either. It was more of an *us*. The three of us. Sam. Me. Aaron.

The connection *hummmed* at me. Aaron's stare dug into my back, I felt it like heat, like a laser probing my conversation. He was just hearing one side, but he would be filing what he heard away, putting it together, like Aaron did. Like Sam did, as well.

The two of them were always better at the *knowing* of a thing. Not me. I was the guy good in a fight.

The expendable one, it had turned out.

"Maybe it does matter," Sam finally said. "You need to know what's going on, over there."

"Not interested," I said.

"You need to be," she said.

"Stop," I told her.

The word was almost a scream, and loud enough that Sam did. How could she think I would trust something she told me?

One lie always led to another. The lies would grow and fork into more and more, all covering up the truth. The monster always birthed a thousand more.

Actions mattered to me. Not words. Because in the end, it's the only thing that was pure. The *doing* of a thing.

Never the saying.

The realization of that was powerful in me.

I couldn't trust anything she told me. Anything Aaron told me. I couldn't *trust*.

I could only *do*.

Maybe the silence had gone on too long, between us. Sam started to speak again. So I slammed the handset of the phone onto the receiver.

The phone jingled. The drywall collapsed inward, the hole opened more, and the case of the phone fell inside the wall. The handset hung there, outside the hole, dangling from its new, flat gray cord.

I clenched both hands tight and held back a real scream, something from deep inside. My eyes shut tight, just breathing deep breath after deep breath, letting my chest swell against the vest, then relax. The smell of piss and asparagus was strong, I could taste it in the back of my throat. But I just breathed deeper.

Then I opened my eyes. Jerked the gray cord from the phone. The phone jangled from deep inside the wall. I yanked the other end from where the cord plugged into the white plastic cover on the wall. Tossed the cord aside.

Sam's last words were telling me not to trust. Fitting enough. She wouldn't have to worry about that, with me. I had that part down.

I faced Aaron. His face was still sad, hell maybe it was always sad now. Sometime during the call he had closed the door to the hallway. Maybe to give me some privacy. Probably to keep the smell in the apartment from spreading.

He held the book in his hand, as if he had picked it up off the table, while I had been talking. *The Faerie Queene.* "Brother," he said, simply.

We had been that, once.

"What do you want?" I asked him.

"You reading this?" he asked back. His voice slow and hesitant, as if something ate him from the inside.

I just stared at him. Feeling goosebumps ripple up and down my arms, feeling my heart thud harder in my chest.

I wanted to fight someone. Anyone.

Aaron finally answered. "Man, I just stopped by," he said. "I didn't like how we left things."

"You didn't?" I said. "Me neither. Not yesterday. Not two years ago."

Aaron's eyes opened slightly. He looked hurt, and his head made a little shaking motion. Once. Twice.

"Brother," he said.

"Stop," I told him, like I had Sam. "Don't *brother* me this or that. Don't stop by and see how I'm doing. Just go."

I had something to do now. Something I would do or die trying. One last chance to help someone. Then tomorrow I would get back to old things.

Aaron looked at my jacket. He would recognize the bulges under my arms. He would see the vest.

"You found her," he said.

I didn't think he knew how close I was to swinging. To pushing him out of my apartment. Out of my life.

"You're going to get her?" he asked. "Now?"

"Go," I told him. My voice thick.

I needed to do this one thing, and I would return to pick this all up. Sam. Aaron. The routine.

"You want backup?" he asked.

Aaron should have known better than to ask.

"You want me to trust you," I said. "Backing *me* up?"

"You know, I'm getting a little tired of this," Aaron said. "This *woe is me* bullshit. I'm your friend, man. I'm your *brother*."

"Sure," I said. We had been brothers once.

"Man I've never forgotten you saving me back then," he said, then stepped closer, so that he was chest to chest with me. He still held *The Faerie Queene*, and the book ended up between us. "*Never*."

I stared at him. The moment came on. I could feel it. My fingers curled up in my left hand.

Aaron felt it too. We stood eye to eye. He smiled, darkly, one side of his lips curving up.

"Fuck you J," he said. Then thumped the book against my chest. "Fuck you, *Crosse*. Easier now for you to run, isn't it?"

"You saying I quit, Aaron?" I asked. My voice low. I struggled against the feeling of fighting, of *wanting* to fight.

"I'm saying you used to be better," Aaron said. He looked at the apartment, the kitchen floor, the uniform stained with piss. "Now look at you."

"What's it fucking matter?" I said. "Let me do this. Get out of my life. Let me go. Take care of whatever the Branch needs here and *go*."

"It matters because the Branch is breaking, man," Aaron said. "It's fucking breaking, and here I am trying to help my brother, when I really need him to *help me*."

Aaron's voice was full of hurt. And pain. It was tired. As if he had been fighting a losing battle for a long time.

That was a battle I understood. Deeply. Irrevocably.

"You were the best of us once, man," Aaron said.

He was wrong, there. He still remembered the old me. He thought that person still existed.

Maybe that was the only thing that kept me from swinging.

I looked away.

"Let me go, Aaron," I said.

I went to move past him. He held the book against my chest, it rested between us, a solid square wedge. I felt him, looking at me, though I didn't look back. I stared at the door behind him, the door to the outside, the door to rescuing the girl.

"Let me go," I said again, quietly.

Aaron let his hand fall away, and stepped aside.

I went to the door, opened it, and paused.

Aaron and I had done some good together. And he was still trying to do it.

Maybe he was right. Maybe quitting was easier. Some monsters though, they were too hard to face.

"Don't be here when I get back," I told him. A person who had once been a good friend. A brother.

Then left.

Traffic was neither better nor worse on Baber's way back to the station, but it felt slow. She knew it was the feeling of urgency driving her, that whatever was happening was happening *now*. So the cars on the road felt like logs on a river, always piling up in front of her, slowing down, stopping at the slightest curve.

The night sky was black above her. Headlights flashed from the other side of the road, people with their high beams on, no matter they were in the middle of a city. The bright halogens that kept getting brighter, with every new car or truck. At some point all the lights would have a sun-like intensity, would all blend together so that the night would dissolve into some kind of pseudo-day.

And the car companies would still keep making the lights brighter.

She got to the station and parked. There were at least plenty of spaces, with the dayshift headed home. There was just a single smoker in the smoker's box where she and Hamilton's lawyer had talked. Baber pushed down the sudden need for a cigarette, grabbed the evidence bag and got out, slamming the car door shut and heading inside.

The station was a little more empty at night, but carried a darker sense inside. Cops walked with a focused purpose, there was none of the hustle and bustle of daytime, of people rushing down the halls with sheets of paper fluttering to the ground behind them.

She headed to the morgue, taking the stairs to the basement before opening the door there to a cold, brightly lit hallway. Baber turned right and headed to where Travis would be, the heels of her pumps striking the tiled floor in little click-clacky sounds, her nose wrinkling at the sharp disinfectant smell.

Frank appeared from far off, all the way down the hallway, leaning against the wall. He was large in the distance, and grew larger as she neared. One eyebrow raised at the bag she held in her hands.

She handed him the bag. It seemed small in his hand.

"Angela had a sister," she said.

"Had?" Frank asked.

Baber nodded. "Her place was a wreck. Someone tossed it, likely when they killed her."

"You think it was her we found in the channel?" Frank said.

She nodded.

"That doesn't make sense," he said.

Baber knew what he was talking about. It didn't make sense, none of this did. Not the kidnapping, not the murder at the tattoo shop, not the murder of Luisa, if the body they found was Angela's sister, and not Angela herself.

"One thing Hamilton is right on," she said, "Is that this is something big. Something way above our paygrade."

Frank pursed his lips. "Always comes down to it, something like this. People in power."

It was basic, but it applied. People with or without. Baber had seen it a thousand times. People didn't have something, so they took it. It happened in muggings, robberies, people would up the ante and the same robberies would become homicides.

It wasn't necessarily always about money, emotions ran hot, people wanted to love or wanted to be loved, maybe they just wanted sex, whatever. It always came down to that, who had what, and who else wanted it, and how much power did they have, to get it.

Didn't matter what the power was. It could be a knife. A gun. Or a pen.

"You nailed it," Baber said.

"What?" Frank asked.

"It doesn't make sense," she said. "The warrant was one thing. Someone has some power, and they are using it to cover things up. Distract us. But that's just one thing."

"The beatings," Frank said.

"There's some emotion in play, with the power," Baber agreed. "Because beating someone to death takes anger, and rage, and hate."

"Hamilton has that," Frank said.

Hamilton did. Had it in spades. Baber had felt the emotions, deep within him. But she had looked at his hands, as they were fingerprinting him. His knuckles hadn't been swollen. So she shook her head. "He didn't do it."

"Could've ordered it," he said.

"Hamilton?" Baber said. "Not that guy. He's someone that does things personally."

"Maybe," Frank said, then corrected himself. "Probably."

Baber wondered about the Fourth Branch. The further she was away from the lawyer, the easier that story was to dismiss as a fairy tale. But the man had been convincing. Emotionally so.

His knuckles had been clean, too. She still remembered the way he had held the cigarette, the back of his hand to her. His thumb moving across the screen, as he showed her the pictures of Hamilton, the soldier.

She blinked, bringing herself back to being with Frank.

He was frowning at the brush.

"Have Travis compare the hair," she said.

"He's in there now," Frank said. "Middle of the autopsy."

"Get him on it," she said.

"He's not going to like it," Frank said.

"He doesn't have to like it," Baber said. "He owes us, so he's going to do it."

"Want DNA?" Frank said.

"I don't care," Baber said. "Whatever he can get done the fastest. Just have him tell me if that's the sister or not."

"Where will you be?" Frank asked.

"Going to Hamilton's," she said.

"Wait up," he said. "I'll tell him and come too."

"Stay here," she told Frank. Travis could be obstinate. He might finish the autopsy before beginning the hair analysis. And Baber knew, she could *feel*, that time was tight. "Get Travis on the hair."

"Beebs," Frank warned. He understood how Baber felt, the need to save someone. He got into a case just like she did, but he had been around longer, and had learned how to be patient.

She knew there was too much in the air to wait, though. The emotional component told her that. People were getting killed. And Hamilton knew the why, she was sure of it.

So Frank gave her the stare. The one that said Baber was being foolish. That Hamilton was a risky go for her alone.

She had seen a different side though. Hamilton hadn't had to warn her back when they had brought him in, but he had. And she still saw a part of him in the picture, the one where Hamilton was sleeping next to a medical tent, duct-taped and everything.

"We don't need it for a court," Baber said to Frank. "Just tell me if Travis gives you the thumbs up or down."

He shook his head.

"I don't like it," Frank said. "You should wait."

"We don't have time," Baber said. "You know that, right?"

Frank looked at her, with his patient stare. The one that had seen many more cases than she had. He had been a detective for ten years, before Baber had started. Maybe he knew that another case was around the corner, another murder to be solved, but Baber wanted *this* one.

"Call me when you get there," he finally said.

"I will," Baber said. "Call me as soon as you know."

Frank nodded.

"And don't let word get out about this," Baber said, rolling her eyes to the floors of the department above the morgue.

She wanted to make sure she was free to chase the case, until she found its end. She didn't need more interference from above, or redirects. Not from her captain, the lieutenant, or whoever was giving them the orders to fuck with her case.

She slapped Frank on the shoulder and headed back to the car. If the body was the sister, then Angela was still in trouble. And with two girls now beaten to death, Baber felt like Angela's life couldn't be measured in days. Not anymore. Not if someone was killing her family.

FORTY-THREE

It hadn't taken long for me to reach Gloucester. There had been some cars on the road, some traffic, people heading out of town for the weekend, but not much. The road was curvy and hilly, wrapping around where the sea ate into the rocky beaches, then heading up into the cliffs. The drive became somewhat hypnotic with me being one of the few cars on the road.

I was okay with what I had to do. I didn't know the governor, but had no problems killing him, if he was there. Same for his guards. Angela was there. The mercenary was there. Everyone at the mansion would know what was going on. They all had made their beds.

I passed the home almost without realizing it. The brick mansion rested on a hill, back to the water, perched above the cliffs. A rolling stone fence blocked off the public from the acreage, the lawn green for this late in the year, the grass surrounding the home. A garage sat to the left, a big building for eight or ten cars, maybe. A pool and pool house to the right. Trees poked out behind both of the smaller buildings, to the north and south, amidst decorative brush.

I drove by once more. The stone wall lay between the road and the home. The driveway began at a guard shack and a set of wide iron gates.

From there the white pavement rolled around the house and circled back to the front, in a big O shape.

I chose the south end, for no reason other than it was closer to Boston. There I drove the sedan off the road over the shoulder and into the woods, weaving it slowly between a few trees, backing it into brush a good distance, so that oncoming traffic lights wouldn't flash across the car.

I shut off the car. Then I made the call. I pulled out my cell phone and dialed the number the mercenary had left.

"Talk to me Goose," the mercenary's voice was light, as if he was having fun.

"I got your drive," I said.

"Interesting timing," he said. "Took you long enough."

"Yeah," I said. "You want it or not?"

"Oh, I want it," he said. He gave me a location and a time. Where the walkway lead into the Boston Commons. An hour from now.

Long enough for him to get there.

"You bringing the girl?" I said.

"Of course," he said. "It's why I picked the Freedom Trail."

He thought it was funny. Neither of us laughed. We both knew it was a lie for a lie.

"You got a name?" I asked.

"Does it matter?" he said.

I did want to know the name of the man I was going to kill. Maybe in the end, names didn't matter. Maybe what we were wasn't in a name, but in the deed.

Maybe that's why I pushed myself to rescue Angela. To balance the scales for Charley. And if I killed this guy too, that would tilt them my way a little more.

"I guess it doesn't," I said.

"Do I have to go through the whole speech?" the man asked. "The *kill-the-girl* one, if you try anything?"

"Nah," I said. "I understand that part."

I knew he was going to kill her anyway. It was just a matter of time, with no USB drive to be found anywhere. They would get rid of her, me, anyone linked to this. Then the governor could plot his path to the presidency, if not with a clear conscience, then at least with a clear record.

"See you in an hour then," he said.

He seemed really cavalier about things. Maybe that was his personality. He was young, with a lot of growing to do. Not that he would get a chance to do those things, after I found him.

That would be later, though. After I rescued Angela.

And it was time for that, now. Finally.

I got out. Shut the door with a quiet click. The night around me was dark. The trees were a low overhang above me. Crickets began to chirp up, silenced only for a moment by me parking the car. Behind the crickets was the sound of the surf, waves battering stone beaches, far below me.

The storm promised throughout the day had never come, a bank of fog had rolled in though, as if the gray clouds had sank during the evening and hovered around everything. Somewhere, far out to sea, a fog horn blew, a long and lonesome sound that echoed over the crashing of the surf.

I headed north, picking my way through the trees and the brush. Taking a little care with where I placed my right leg. It didn't take but a few minutes for me to get to the fence surrounding the property. It wasn't a proper wall, just seven or eight feet high. High enough that it kept people inside from seeing anyone approaching.

According to the guy watching the place, there weren't any cameras, either, at least around the wall. Maybe it was hard to host parties and events, if you looked like you were hunkering in for World War III. Maybe the mansion wasn't meant to be a long-term hideaway for anyone, or a place where the governor expected to run a group of mercenaries.

Either way, it was easy enough for me to jump up and grab the flat stone top of the fence and pull myself up and over. No iron spears at the top. No barbed wire, or broken glass. Just cold rock, a smooth surface.

I went up and over. Dropped down behind the stand of trees on the southern side of the house. My leg twinged a bit at the landing, but the grass was springy and thick. They must irrigate the hell out of it. I crab-walked across the ground to a stand of brush, looking to see if anyone had noticed me.

The stand of trees rested to my right. The pool house was near on my left, the pool nestled between the mansion and the little building. The clear blue water shimmered a bit under the illumination around the home.

The front of the mansion rested between the pool house and mansion. A couple of trucks were being pulled to the front there, from the garage. Two black SUVs, like the one that had kidnapped Angela. Tinted windows, a mirror-like black, brightly reflected the lights on the front of the house.

I waited and watched. Two large groups of guys left out the front door. They were dressed in tactical gear, like S.W.A.T. teams. Each man held an assault rifle, some of them had breaching shotguns slung around their backs. They had done this sort of thing before, all of them walked with a purpose.

I could hear mutters and small talk among the men, but I was far enough away that I couldn't make out any words. Just the snicks of doors opening and the thumps of the doors shutting, after each truck filled up.

I didn't see Angela. Which I had figured on. It was the obvious play, keeping her here. A safety net, in case I didn't have the USB drive.

Whether I did, or didn't, the tactical teams told me the mercenary didn't want me making it to the next day. Tonight was the night. Whatever was happening, whatever was going to be done, it was going down now. Just like I had felt.

The governor was going to cut his losses. He had waited long enough. He knew the longer this played out, the greater chance he would get caught.

The trucks headed out along the driveway. The gates there were open, and the vehicles didn't stop. They smoothly pulled onto the road, the rear ends of each bouncing briefly where the driveway connected to the highway.

Then they pressed the gas and headed down the road. Into the night. The gates closing behind them.

Then the gates closed.

The crests of the surf collapsed against the rocky beach below, in rhythmic motions, over and over. In and out, in and out. Little *wishes* and *washes* of sounds echoed up the cliffs to where I stood.

I had a couple of hours, now. Especially if I could do this quietly. I looked around at the house, the bright lights over the lawn surrounding the mansion, the tall tower-like structure perched above the roof, little fancy crenellations surrounding what looked to be a walkway around the tower.

I realized the tower was built almost like a lighthouse. Looking out far over the ocean. Over the bank of fog hiding the surf and the beach, the crashing of the waves.

The lighthouse was lit, though all the curtains were drawn shut. Heavy drapes that left only a faded circle of illumination to surround the roof around which the turret was perched. Maybe I imagined it, but I thought a shadow moved behind the drapes.

The fog horn blew again, further away. Deeper in the mist. The ship, hidden, but heading out to sea. The cloud bank was thick and dark over the water, stretching below the mansion, stretching further and further away. It seemed to go on forever, and I wondered what other monsters hid there, deep inside the pall-like murkiness below, and if, at the end, I was about to join them.

FORTY-FOUR

Baber raced up the stairs to Hamilton's place, taking them two at a time. Thumps echoed from the stairs as her pumps pounded the floor. She pulled herself up along the banister, turning at the top of each staircase with a quick spin, and was almost out of breath by the time she got to his floor.

She had called Frank before running into the building. The large man hadn't got word back from Travis, but swore the tech was on it. Frank had told her he still waited outside.

Who the dead girl had been was going to be important.

She got to Hamilton's floor, stopping to take a few large breaths. Feeling her heart race with the exertion. Then she gathered herself and walked to the man's door.

Which was slightly open. A sliver of a crack of light coming from the inside of the apartment. And then someone swore.

She put one hand under her jacket, wrapping her fingers around the handle of her Springfield XD. A 9mm her father had bought her a long time ago, and that other cops made fun of her for carrying. It was a nice gun, well-made, just not the standard Beretta or Glock that a lot of the officers today preferred.

She leaned to the side of the trim and toed the door open. It swung inward on quiet hinges. Baber peered through the crack, as the opening widened, revealing the apartment behind it like a panoramic shot in a movie.

The lawyer stood there. Aaron. A white apron was tied around his stomach, and the man held both of his hands up. Each hand had a plastic glove on it, the blue rubber latex kind. He held a green sponge in one hand, and a bottle of some kind of foaming cleaning spray in the other.

Aaron stood there, quiet. Both of his eyebrows raised. A square bucket of cleaning supplies next to him. The man grinned.

"I surrender," he said.

"Burr," she said, pulling her hand out of her jacket, stepping inside. "What are you doing here?"

"Pretty evident, isn't it," he said, still holding his cleaning supplies up.

There was a lemon-lime smell in the kitchen, from the counter. Something else too, something dark. Pungent. Something maybe cooked into the floor there.

Baber looked around. The apartment had been tossed. It looked a little like what had happened at Luisa's. The couch was at an angle in the living room, all the pillows missing, large rips in the front and back.

"You do this?" she asked. Then thought maybe it had been Hamilton. Maybe he had finally snapped.

Which didn't explain why Aaron was cleaning up the place, though. The television was sitting on its stand, but it had been smashed. There was a hole in the wall behind the kitchen, and black trash bags were everywhere. All of them were plump and full and tied together tight at the top.

Except for the one next to Aaron. It was open, some pale yellow blocks of foam cushion poked out. The foam blocks were mixed with crumpled white paper towels and a green sponge.

"Close the door, will you?" Aaron said.

Baber tried, but it wouldn't stay closed. The jamb had been busted on this side, but she was able to push the door hard enough that the latch of the doorknob clicked and held the door shut.

"Where is Hamilton?" she asked.

"Off doing Hamilton things," he said.

"What's that mean?" she asked.

Aaron smiled. He tossed the sponge into the bag of trash, set the bottle of cleaner on the counter. Everything was clean in the apartment, as if Hamilton was moving out.

"You know I'm not going to tell you that," he said.

Baber wondered if Hamilton had found the girl. If the man was going to save her now. And then she wondered if maybe he had found out about the dead body. If he knew if that body was Angela's or her sister's.

She remembered the anger hidden inside the man. The dark fury.

"You need to tell me where he is," she said.

"Actually, I don't," Aaron said.

Baber set her jaw. If she brought Aaron in, he'd just get right out. There was nothing she could arrest him on.

And she knew he knew that as well.

"He can't be the law," she said.

"Oh he's not the law," Aaron said. "He's never been that."

She thought about the picture of Hamilton Aaron had shown her. The pictures. The one of the soldier by the tent.

The other man, tied up to a chair. Rage blazing in his eyes. Veins popped up on his forehead, as he strained against the bonds that held him in place.

If the first man was the friend, the protector, what would the other man be?

Judge. Jury. Executioner.

"Something to drink?" Aaron opened the fridge. It was empty, except for a six-pack of beers. Something amber in color. He pulled out two, popping both tops and making sure each of the tops made it into the trash.

He held a bottle towards her.

"He can't do this," Baber said.

"I think you'll find he can," Aaron said, finally setting her bottle on the counter. Taking a swig of his.

She didn't have a choice, she was going to have to bring Burr in. Hamilton too.

"Bring me in if you have to," he said. "You know where that'll go."

"Fuck," Baber said.

Aaron just smiled. Drank more of his beer. Then waited, leaning against the counter. As if he had plenty of time.

She could feel it racing though.

"Just tell me," she said.

Aaron frowned. "Tell you what?"

"Whatever it is you want to tell me," she said.

"Where's the fun in that?" he asked. Glancing at her beer.

She sighed, grabbed the bottle. Sipped it. Leaned against the counter, so that she was face-to-face with the man.

Up close she could smell his aftershave. Something tobaccoey. His eyes flashed, as if something electric twisted between her and him.

Dangerous.

She took a larger sip. The beer was bitter but hinted at something fruity. Raspberry or blackberry.

Maybe she could get Aaron on her side.

"Let me show you something," she said. She pulled out her phone, opening the photos. Putting a picture of the dead girl on it.

Aaron looked at it. Then he took another drink and stayed silent.

She thumbed through the pictures. She had gotten a few. And one of the missing ear, the skin puckered and white around the edges, the bone and the cartilage.

Aaron took a deep breath. She thought she saw a hint of recognition in his eyes.

"You see it, don't you?" she said.

"What?"

"It's the girl," she said. Leaving out the sister.

"It's not the girl," Aaron said. Confident.

Gotcha, you bastard.

"So who is it?" she said.

Aaron frowned, as if really seeing that last picture. "Is her ear cut off?"

"It is," Baber said. "Think it was a message?"

"I don't know," Aaron said, but his voice was less confident.

"And if it was, who was it to?" Baber asked.

"I don't know," Aaron said, but his eyes went to the door. Then they widened, the green irises sparkling, as if he had just had a realization. Something from out of the blue.

"I can guess," she said.

The man stood there, the beer forgotten in his hand. His gaze went from the door to Baber, a few times.

So she pressured him a little more.

"You know, she was beat just like the girl in the tattoo shop," Baber said.

Alarm flashed in his eyes then. Whatever realization he'd had, it seemed to lead to another. He whitened to an almost pale.

Her phone rang then. It was Frank. She set her beer down on the counter and held up a finger to Aaron, answering the call.

"Frank," she said. "Tell me."

"It's the sister," Frank said.

So Hamilton was on his way to save the girl. They had found the kidnappers, and he was going to rescue her.

Which didn't speak to why Angela Martinez had been kidnapped to begin with. And why would the sister be part of this at all? Unless there was an element here out of control, which the beatings spoke to.

While she was talking to Frank, Aaron finished his beer. Tossed the empty bottle into the trash, almost listlessly. Then he picked up some more cleaning supplies out of the bucket next to him, as if he was going to clean some more.

"You on your way?" she asked Frank.

"In the parking lot now," he said.

"Still at Hamilton's," Baber said.

"Be twenty or so," Frank said. "Depending on traffic."

Aaron walked around, wiping down surfaces already cleaned. Every now and then he stopped and sprayed air freshener into the air, something clean and eucalyptus smelling, with maybe a hint of mint.

"I'll be here," she said. "Got company."

"Hamilton?" he asked.

"No," she said. "His friend."

Frank chuckled. From the large man it was more of a rumble. "That man have friends?" Frank said. "See you soon."

Aaron was in the living room, still spraying the air freshener. He placed his hand on the television, for a moment. Then straightened the picture frame on the coffee table, his fingers lingering on it for a moment.

"It was her sister," Baber said. Taking a deep breath of the better-smelling air. Happy to have something cover the dark smell in the apartment.

"I see," Aaron said. His voice a little troubled. The man sprayed a little more of the air freshener, the can of smell-good making little *shushing* sounds each time he pressed the top down, releasing a misty fragrance that clouded the room.

The man stepped closer. A few feet from Baber. His face was still pale, but composed. As if he had figured out something.

She felt she was missing something too. She took a breath. Then another. Something about the scent tickled her brain. Or maybe she just liked it. "What is that smell?" she said.

"What?" Aaron looked at the can. "Teagarden." Then he smiled, his face almost back to its regular tanned color. "I guess maybe it's Boston Teagarden."

"I've smelled it somewhere before," she said, searching her memory. Then realizing exactly where she had gotten the same eucalyptus mint scent.

Angela's apartment.

It had felt clean. Sterile. Baber had gone through and felt violence there. Something in the back of her mind had been convinced. Everything in the apartment was too clean, too organized.

As if someone had cleaned up something horrible there. Someone who wore gloves, even an apron. Someone who liked things a certain way.

Maybe even someone who had a bucket of cleaning supplies in his car.

Her gaze went to his hand. Then the bucket. Then back to Aaron.

Aaron watched her. His grin turned inward, as he followed her train of thought. It was like he could sense exactly what she was thinking.

So the man knew—at the exact moment she knew—Aaron had been part of kidnapping Angela.

"Well," Aaron said, dropping the can of air freshener. "This is unfortunate."

She went for her Springfield.

Aaron was faster.

CHAPTER
FORTY-FIVE

THE SOUND OF THE TRUCKS ECHOED BACK FROM THE ROAD, the rumble of the pair of engines getting softer and softer as they headed down the hill. The gate shut behind him, letting out one large creak as the heavy iron swung closed.

Then it was just me, the crickets, and the washing of the surf below.

I stayed at the edge of the pool. Looked at the big brick home of the governor over the glimmering blueness of the water. The pool was slightly L-shaped, sitting close to the side of the mansion before wrapping around the back of the home.

I could always feel the moment, when it was time. When no one was watching. When it was just me and the night and whoever was inside the home. It came in the quieting of the crickets, a silencing of the wind, a brief pause in the washing of the surf.

The time was now.

I moved around the back of the mansion, silently, quickly. Skirting the edge of the pool. The back of the house towered above me, thick bricks leading up to the roof. Up close the mansion was much bigger, it felt like a fortress, or stronghold.

I found a patio in the backyard. It led to a large set of double doors to the house. The patio was old, made of cobblestone, and it was easy to sneak across it to the back of the mansion, right by the set of doors there.

They were glass, and were the kind of doors that slid into the wall on either side. Each of them was tall, made of thick glass with black frames, with pale blinds down the glass on each. The blinds on each were tilted open, giving me easy vision into a large chef's kitchen behind the doors.

I stayed there a moment and peeked in. The chef's kitchen was enormous, black marbled countertops, stainless steel appliances. Multiple ovens, a big two-door refrigerator. A pale beige tiled floor, and the same color backsplash.

No one was there. Which was good, because no one expected me. I hoped the team that left had been most of the force here, and that they had just left a few guards here. It's what most people would do. If there were just a few, I could sneak in, grab the girl and leave.

By the time the team came back, I'd be long gone. With no one the wiser.

Of course, if enough guards were here… Well, I would have to take care of them. I didn't see a maid, cook or butler. With luck they were gone for the weekend. I wasn't optimistic about it, but it was late on a weekend night, and anything could happen.

Any way about it, I wasn't shy about shooting anyone. Not tonight. Whoever was here had been here with lots of guys with lots of guns. I'd take that into account, if I came up on someone. But it my mind, everyone inside the house was fair game.

I tested the door. It was unlocked. I opened it and slipped inside. It was warm, the heat was on in the house. The kitchen smelled of chowder, though there was nothing on the stove, just the faint whirring of the microwave.

Which I found hanging on the wall, a stainless steel box, lit inside, with something round rotating under the lights. The microwave was right by the refrigerator. The fridge was next to a thin door, something that swung both ways, for people to carry food out and in.

Another door led out, at the far end of the kitchen. Not a lot of places in here for me to hide. I moved that way.

The microwave dinged. The sound was loud in the kitchen.

I froze.

The sound of footsteps came from beyond the service door. A person walking without any concern. Heavy feet on a wood floor, *thump thump thump.*

I drew the pistol with the silencer. Then flowed over to hide behind the door. It swung open. The door had a glass port in the center, like you see at restaurants, and a flash of dark hair and pale skin appeared in it. Dark clothes, like the tactical gear the groups wore in the trucks.

The door shut.

It was tactical gear. The man turned away from me, towards the microwave. A pistol hung in a holster off his right hip.

Whatever was going to happen, was going to happen now.

I reversed my grip on the pistol so I could hit the man with the butt of my gun.

At the same moment he stopped, like he had forgotten something, and turned back. The motion was quick, and he saw me out of the corner of his eye.

I swung anyway. The blow glanced off the top of his head. He shouted and went down, then grabbed at my legs. I swung again, connecting with the back of the head. A spatter of blood arced over the kitchen floor, and the man went limp.

"Larry?" a voice called from down the hallway. Questioning.

I kept my swear silent. Knelt on the floor. The man's arms fell off me. Quieter steps came down from the hallway to the kitchen door. As soon as the round window darkened, I fired a few times, the suppressor quiet.

Someone thumped to the floor behind the door.

I opened it and dragged another man in. Another one from the team, dressed in dark clothes that smeared the floor with red.

The house had felt quiet, coming in. Now it thrummed with energy. A high-voltage current charged with life or death.

I made my way down the hallway. It opened into a large room, like a living room, only much bigger. Mansion-sized, with the ceiling thirty feet above me. Couches and cabinets lay everywhere, elegant pieces of dark gray on a darker floor, with beige end tables and one large coffee table with some kind of rock, maybe a piece of granite, on the center of it.

Black duffel bags lay everywhere. On the arms of chairs and couches. On the floor. But none on the coffee table. Handles of shotguns poked out of most of them, breaching weapons. A vest lay here and there, other smaller pistols and magazines. So this was the staging area. Where the team had gotten ready, before they left.

The front door of the place was in front of me, out of the hallway, across the room. Stairs led past me to my left. They ran up the wall and then angled at ninety degrees to the second floor.

The sound of a guitar broke out, a lone chord playing, the theme from *Top Gun*. It came from a television, and I found it to my right, across the large room. It was mounted on a wall, at least a hundred inches in size, movie credits rolling down the television. Then the screen flicked from channel to channel, pausing a moment on an old black and white movie where Frankenstein held his arms out and walked towards me, out of the screen.

Another guy stood by the television. He faced away from me, a remote in hand, pointed at the screen. He flipped it from Frankenstein and went through the channels, pausing here and there.

"You guys got the soup?" he called out, absentmindedly.

I just shot him once. Blood sprayed the wall and television. The man fell to the ground. The remote fell with him. It must have hit a button, because all of a sudden the sound from the television rocketed up. The channel surfing had ended on a sports channel—motocross—and the sound of the race blared through the house.

Well, I thought. *That was that.*

Things were going to happen faster now. I headed up the stairs. The sound would bring people. I had no idea who was left, and I didn't want to get pinned down in this big room, and I didn't know who was where.

I did know Angela was at the top of the house. I felt safer on the move. And I could get there as fast as I could get to the remote.

At the top of the stairs there was a balcony, spreading left and right, each side leading into a big hotel-sized hallway with plenty of rooms. I needed to find another set of stairs here, that led up to the third floor, and the tower room.

On a whim I chose right. I walked to the side, like I belonged. Opening doors to bedroom after bedroom. A large marble bathroom between each, one of those with dual vanities and a large stand-up shower. Veined rock everywhere.

A door opened behind me. From the left hallway.

"You guys going to turn that down?" A voice called out.

Then, "Hey."

I turned and saw the man. He was reaching for his gun. I had mine in hand.

He went down.

I headed that way. Chances were, people were going to be between the bottom floor and the tower room. I checked doors that way, wondering how many people were left. If there was anyone out front that was coming in.

I finally hit jackpot. A library, or den. The door I had opened revealed a tiny entryway, a blank wall right ahead of the opening. I turned right and saw I had found the right room. A large, plush red rug, tall floor-to-ceiling bookshelves surrounding the walls. A big oak desk in the far side of the room, right underneath some windows looking over the cliffs.

A fireplace, with a suit of armor standing guard next to it. It took me a moment to see a tiny set of stairs in the corner of the room, across from the knight. One of those smaller spiral staircases, that wound around itself, going up to a small door above. The tower.

I smiled to myself. The long journey over the past few days was about to end. I could finish this, then get back to my life.

I stood in the doorway too long. The door jamb exploded next to my ear, at the same time as a gunshot rang out. Splinters of wood stung my cheek.

I dove into the library, more cracks splitting the air behind me. I worked my way to lay against the wall that had rested at ninety degrees to the doorway. Well, not against the wall there, but the bookshelf that was the wall.

More gunshots. Single reports, firing repeatedly. Sidearm fire, no assault rifles yet. Still, the wall across from the doorway developed a sudden case of holes. Bullets dug into the wall there, thudding into the frame of the house.

The place was well-built, brick on the outside and thick wood on the inside. Thunks of bullets hit the wall above me, but nothing broke through. Yet.

My mind went to the shotguns and rifles below. I didn't have a lot of time. The staircase was behind me, but if I ran up now the gunmen in the hallway would just follow me. We'd be trapped in the tower with no exit.

The shots stopped. Voices sounded from down the hallway, it was hard to make out the words with the ringing in my ears, but I thought two people. Then a shout from someone below, maybe a third.

I worked my way around, so that the wall, bookshelf, and doorway all formed a T, with the bookshelf being the middle. I took a peek and got a glimpse of someone working their way down the hallway. I took a shot and was rewarded with the man dropping down. I rolled back before I could see anything else, as return shots kept drilling the wall to the side, the floor, all around.

Time was wasting. And it wasn't like I was sneaking in, anymore. I glanced at the stairs. Looked back at the doorway. Then grabbed one of the grenades out of my jacket and pulled the pin. Let it cook for a few moments, then tossed it down the hallway with a tuck of my hand.

There was a warning shout, then a big explosion shook the floor, the walls, everything around me. I was up and through the door even as books fell off the shelves inside the room, as the knight tipped over and rang against the brick fireplace.

The grenade had caught the guy I shot. If he had been alive before, he wasn't now. There were just a few pieces of him littered in the hall-way. A leg here. A head there. Blood splattered what was left, the floor, the walls, the framing inside the walls, the detonation opening up the walls and revealing wooden bones.

I felt alive in a way I hadn't in a long time. My heart beat steady, not racing, as if my body knew exactly how much blood I needed and when. Like a car built for racing, I was built for the fight.

Smoke and flames danced down the hallway in front of me. I strode through the gray fog, the soot drifting through the air, the charred wooden edges of the blast. A large, gaping hole in the floor now lay between me and another guy, wide enough there was no way across. I shot him before he realized I was there.

Another guy was on the stairs, heading up. He held an M4 against his shoulder. He got a bullet as well, and dropped with his rifle clat-tering against the banister. Shouts now echoed from the bottom floor, more people likely flooding into the great room, trying to figure out who was here, how many, and where we were all at.

It was just me. And I loved it. Goosebumps rippled over my fore-arms, the gun felt great in my hand. I had no idea how many people were below, but I thought there couldn't be many more, unless the tactical teams had come back already.

It didn't matter. I wanted to take them all on. It was a fight to turn back around. The grenade had done its job. Anyone coming after me would have to find another way up.

I had a moment. And Angela waited.

I flowed back into the room, a ghost in gray haze. Up the stairs, not feeling my leg. Opened the door, and saw her, standing across from me.

Angela.

The octagonal room was brightly lit. It was large, with a big circular light hanging from the top of a pointed ceiling. Each of the eight walls was more window than wall, though I only saw the drapes hanging across each section. Thick red curtains, pulled tightly shut, all around me.

Angela was there, across from me. She had a hand inside the drapes, hung up there. Her face was battered and bruised, swollen, under hair that lay flat over puffy cheeks. She was very different from the girl in the bookstore. The girl with the motorcycle, who had been so alive then, in a way I had lost. That I had lacked. Still lacked.

Now she was more like me. More dead inside, than alive out. Her face and emotions just a shell, wrapping the blankness within. A bandage on the side of her face, dark and mottled with old blood.

Her eyes widened, as much as they could. Her irises, that had once shone with a golden glint of interest, poked out from her swollen face. Her look more of a wince than anything else.

I remembered our moment in the bookstore. The laugh inside the eyes, hiding a secret pain. A pain she had overcome in some way. Me, wondering if that was possible.

Now I knew the answer. The evidence lay before me. Pain could be masked. Hidden. It may even retreat for a while, like when the tide occasionally pulled the sea away from the shore.

But the pain always came back. It was consistent that way. Pain wore away on you like surf against the sand, the frothy foam of the sea hiding the current eating the coast underneath, until all that was left of the shoreline was a pitted, twisted version of what it used to be.

We were all eaten by the waves that crashed against us. Eaten by the tide of life. Eaten by the icy currents twisting around us. Eaten by the waves spawned by some monstrous torment, the creature splitting the surface of the ocean we all swam in, the sheer size of its titanic bulk hidden deep below dark, watery depths.

Those of us suffering the monster were marked only by what we had left. What remained of us, of our fight. The only sign of the creature's existence was the erosion of the shore. The constant nibbling of our souls. We all walked around less than we had been, consumed by the waves crashing against us, watery echoes of the leviathan's passage, dark swells that rolled on long after the monster had passed.

The deadening wake.

My hand had tightened on the gun.

Angela recognized me. Almost stepped back in that moment, her head tilting. I could almost see her wondering why I was there. Trying to link up what had happened in the bookstore to the *now*.

But she couldn't. I couldn't. I was lost maybe, but I was here. And that was enough for me. For now.

Her mouth opened then. Almost in warning. At the same time something told me to *move*.

I was in the fight. And when I was in the fight I felt things around me that others had sworn was a sixth sense. There was no one better. Not even now, not even after the past two years.

I ducked to the side. Felt the butt of a gun slide across my back, the hard metal falling harmlessly off of my shoulder.

I swung around, grabbing that arm, yanking it across my body so that I was belly-to-belly with whoever stood behind me. I placed my gun directly into the center mass of that person and pulled the trigger a couple of times.

It was the mercenary. His lips were curved in a sardonic smile. As if he had known I would be here, and not in Boston.

Which was a good thing for me. It would save me the trip back to kill him.

The bullets thumped into his chest. He wore a vest, but the shots carried a lot of force, pieces of metal traveling at thousands of feet per second, and all that force pounded into his vest and spread into the flesh and bone underneath.

A big exhale came from the man. He folded over, slightly. But he was good, and he grabbed my gun hand and twisted it away, even while losing his breath. Even while we struggled against each other.

We stood toe-to-toe. Each of us held the other's gun hand. I held his arm up, but his finger twitched a few times, firing his gun into the top of the tower. The lights there shattered, burst, and sparks showered around us.

The room darkened. The two of us fought. Quick. Trying to maneuver our leg inside the other's leg, trying to get a knee in a crotch and end the fight right there. Each of us trying to pull our gun back towards the other.

He was shorter than me, now that we were before each other. But we were of a similar size. Shape. And intentions.

Both of our arms were locked, straining to move. Our legs pressed against each other. Our fight felt like it went on for an hour, but it was just a few seconds. Time was funny that way.

His expression was a mix of a grin and a grimace. Like he couldn't help it. Maybe, like me, he was good in the fight too. And liked that he was good. Liked it too much. I had seen that in Angela's face. In the pictures of Charley.

I screamed and head-butted his face. Once. Twice. His nose burst and warm blood splashed across my face. The mercenary went limp.

I was still screaming. I swung his body around and tossed him down the stairs. He fell against the tiny railing, it broke, and then the mercenary tumbled over it and hit the floor. Hard.

He looked up. I pulled the second grenade out. Pulled the pin and dropped the grenade. The last thing I saw before I shut the door was him trying to scramble away.

I ran over to Angela. I felt the ticking of the clock inside me, my body counting the seconds left until the explosion. Something I knew intuitively, from a million other times.

Angela flinched when I brought up the gun, but I was shooting the window behind her. Heard the tinkling and cracking of the glass as I gathered her in my arms and dove through the same window.

The drapes protected us from the glass. We landed on the outside of the turret, me on the bottom. The outside walkway was hard concrete, and I rolled with Angela in the drapes and the broken window until she was against the lower outer wall of the walkway, and my body was between her and the tower room.

The boom shook the turret room. The walkway underneath us. The entire roof, around the tower. I felt the concussive force like a giant fist below the two of us, punching up through the mansion.

Luckily, the mansion was well built.

Unluckily, there was no way down now.

Well, maybe there was one.

I grabbed Angela and pulled her up. She looked okay, more alive than she had been in the turret room. Her eyes narrowed on me though, and she resisted my tug, even after I climbed over the wall around the walkway.

"Who are you?" she asked. "What are you doing here?"

"Later," I said. "When we're free."

She laughed, something bitter and dark. "We jumping off?"

The mansion was three stories high. So jumping wasn't something I wanted to do. But there was a side of the house where we could.

Angela stood a little above me. It was a short drop from the walkway to the roof. I pulled her hand again.

"Yes," I said.

She shook her head and swore. When she did the bandage fell off the side of her face. Maybe the dive through the window had dislodged it.

I grabbed her chin, tilted her head forcefully left and right. Angela resisted for a second, at least until I had seen both sides of her face and let her go, swearing softly. The bandage had covered a gash in her cheek, where a bruise had swollen enough to burst, probably after getting beaten. But Angela had both ears.

So the mercenary had lied to me. Another girl had gotten scarred just so he could do his thing in my kitchen. Stage his scene. Part of me wondered why he hadn't just cut Angela, but the larger part of me smiled, hoping he had enjoyed the grenade. Karma is always a bitch.

"You mad because they beat me?" she asked.

I shook my head. I was always mad. Telling her why, about Charley and the mercenary, would take too long here. "Later."

"You keep saying that," she said, and some of her old self came back, the evocative woman I had met in the bookstore. Someone full of confidence, and a self-knowledge about overcoming pain to emerge triumphant in life. "I don't think it means what you think it means."

I barked out a laugh at that. Shook my head. Felt a little better about our odds. If Angela could joke about it, I felt like I should, too.

I took her across the roof. To the opposite side of the mansion, where the pool waited, nestled against the house.

I had to convince her. But it wasn't that long of a jump. Just the highest of a high dive. I made sure she knew not to go headfirst, that this was more of a cannonball situation.

I would have gone first, but I wanted to make sure Angela would actually jump. I asked her if she trusted me. She said she didn't even know me. But she said it with a smile, and jumped right after.

I followed her in, after watching her paddle her way to the pool's edge. It was a short jump. For a moment I hung weightless in the air, the wind rushing around me, clean and pure. As if I was stationary, and the pool was actually rushing *up* to meet me.

Then a splash. The water was cold and clear. My ass bounced off the bottom of the pool, but not hard, and I swam up easily. Angela was already pulling herself up on the far side.

There was just a hop over the wall and a quick run to the car, after that.

Only then, when the two of us were in my sedan and I had fired it up, when Angela was strapped into her seat and asking me questions, did I allow myself to believe it was done. And that I had done it.

CHAPTER
FORTY-SIX

Baber came awake in a running car.

She kept her eyes closed. Her hands were bound together. Strapped together by what felt like a wire tie, and resting in her lap. Her head throbbing a bit, from a spot on the back of her skull.

A seat belt was pulled tight across her chest. Baber sat in a nice leather seat of a car. The engine was large and powerful, it hummed underneath her. The vehicle was something luxurious and big, she could smell the new car smell. The radio was on and tuned low, a pop song was on, something about being there and rare and remembering things, all too well.

The engine shifted down. The car took off. Went a few feet, then stopped. She gently fell forward until the seat belt caught her. Baber kept her eyes closed.

"Awake, I see," Aaron said, his voice coming from her left, from the driver's seat.

She stayed silent. Baber hadn't trusted him, not really, not with his crazy story about four branches of the government, the example of the four-legged stool. But she had felt connected to him, she had been attracted to him, even though she knew he was dangerous.

That attraction had blinded her a bit. Baber hadn't trusted him, she told herself again. But she had missed something, with the attraction and the story about Hamilton and the photos. Something that led to her kidnapped in this car.

Aaron seemed to be okay with waiting for her to talk. The song played out and went to something else. An older pop song about a wrecking ball. The car stopped-and-go*ed* a little further, the vehicle smoothly pulling out, smoothly stopping, over and over like waves hitting the beach.

Aaron finally swore, but it was a swear without any real meaning behind it. If anything, it was exasperated.

"The traffic here," he said, maybe to her, maybe just saying it out loud.

Baber wondered if she still had her phone. If Frank could track her that way, once he came to Hamilton's place and didn't find her there. It would seem odd for Aaron to make that kind of mistake.

Her arms weren't tied to anything. Just each other. Baber could move them around, if she wanted to. She could look for her phone. Or maybe launch one good swing at Aaron, and take that moment to unlatch her seat belt, pull the handle of her door, and jump away from wherever he was driving her.

Maybe not the best of plans, but it was what she had.

"I love pizza," Aaron said, out of the blue. Then, with a bastardized Italian accent, "Nothing-a more American than a good pizza pie."

His tone had her finally open her eyes. It was the sound of a grin, mixed with a faint sense of sadness.

The car was nice, something luxurious and large. Five rings linked together were nestled in the middle of the dash, the logo of some company too expensive for a detective. Everything was dark and gray inside, the dash, the seats, the floor.

They were stopped at a traffic light, the lead car in a parking lot of an intersection. Somewhere in north Boston, if she recognized the streets right. Rows and rows of brake lights stared at them from the road ahead. Red eyes, glaring at Baber in the night, as if mocking her for being exactly where she was.

Baber shifted in the passenger seat. The seat belt was the only thing holding her there. Aaron was looking to the left. Now was the time, if she was going to try anything.

She happened to glance past Aaron. A pizza shop sat there at the corner. A little mom-and-pop place, without a lot of ornamentation.

It was nothing special. Just a family place that served pizza by the slice. Tall glass windows with a neon sign across the top. A deli counter inside, with pizzas on the rack under the glass there. White cardboard boxes stacked on one side. An older person at the register, and someone ordering a pizza in front of them.

Something about the tone of Aaron's voice had stopped her. Regret? Sadness? Memory?

Whatever it was, it held a bit of truth.

A horn blared from behind them. It jolted both Baber and Aaron. The light was green. The red eyes ahead of them blinking, as the cars moved and stopped, moved and stopped. Aaron grinned a little self-deprecating grin and moved their car through the intersection, giving a little wave to the rearview.

The horn blared again.

"Some people," Aaron said, glancing at Baber. Putting his hands back at the ten and two positions.

"Where are you taking me?" she said. Her voice surly.

His smile spread wider. "With me."

"Why?" she said. Frank would be hunting for her, even now. "You've got to know that's going to bring the hammer down on you. On Hamilton. Can't be good for your Fourth Branch."

He snorted a bit. His head bounced up and down once, as if acknowledging what she had said. "It definitely isn't good, you're right about that," he said. "But I'm not kidnapping you."

Baber lifted her eyebrows. Held her arms up, showing him the wire tie. "Oh?"

"I admit that's what it looks like," Aaron said. He looked smooth and powerful at the wheel. "I had to make a snap decision. I didn't want to bring you along. But I also didn't need a bunch of cops stopping me."

"Stopping you," Baber said. "From what? From a second kidnapping?"

He looked over. "It's not a kidnapping."

She held her arms up, higher.

Aaron sighed. Pulled a knife out. A quick fear burst up from her belly, lodging firmly in her chest. The man was smooth about everything, and she wondered if he would cut her open just as elegantly as he might slice open a pear.

But all Aaron did was quickly snap open the knife, one-handed, and reached around the wire tie binding her wrists with the edge of his blade and his thumb. With a quick slice, she was free.

That knife was sharp. Those ties were thick. Most of them had strands of metal running through them.

Aaron put the knife away.

Her arms were free. The fear in her chest slipped away, almost as fast as it had come, leaving just the thudding of her heart in her chest. A thudding that subsided, with every breath. Until the tense moment had almost never existed.

Now was the time for her to jump out of the car. One hand on the seat belt, one on the handle of the door. But, *dammit*, she was curious now.

Aaron waited, as if he already knew what she was going to do. Or say.

Baber took a breath, let it out. "Stop you from what?"

His grin told her she had been right. "Saving my boy," he said.

His boy could only mean one thing.

"Hamilton?" she asked.

"The one and only," he said.

"You said he found Angela," she said. "And was going to rescue her."

"I did," he said.

"So that means you know where she is," Baber said.

"It does," he agreed.

She searched her mind, wondering what had changed back at the apartment. Aaron had been happy to let Hamilton go out on his own. Then she had showed him pictures of Angela's sister. And something had almost immediately changed in the man.

He had realized something. And that something had changed how he had felt about what was going on. He had seen the pictures of the sister, and had *recognized* the sister, even beat up and bloated. Had recognized her, because he knew what Angela looked like.

"You had her all along," she said. One hand itched for her gun. Or a set of handcuffs.

"It's a long story," he said.

But if Aaron had Angela, if he had been behind the kidnapping, then why would he let Hamilton go rescue her? Something didn't make sense there.

"The pictures I showed you," Baber said. "What about them?"

"What about them... what?" he said, a little mockingly.

"What about them changed your mind?" she said.

The small smile at the corner of his lips told her the man was eating himself up inside. He had realized something, something that had changed his view of the world. Of his own actions. His eyes burned quickly with an intensity Baber hadn't seen in him before, a deep, dark fire. It scared her a little, reminding her of Hamilton. How that man felt, danger, violence, coiled up so tight inside it was ready to spring.

"Two years," Aaron said, his voice low, a whisper. Something he might be unaware he was saying. "Two damn years."

Two years. What was he talking about? Back when Hamilton had been injured? Or something else?

"You going to tell me?" she finally said.

Aaron changed the subject. "You like pizza?" he asked.

"Sure," she said, realizing he wanted to change the subject. Wondering where he was going. Everyone liked pizza. There wasn't anything about it to not like. Melted cheese, tomato sauce, a thin crust not quite crispy, just hard enough to hold.

But it wasn't what she wanted to know. So she repeated her question. "How did you fuck up?"

"Nothing-a more American than pizza pie," he said again. His voice still carried that note in it, the sad one, and a hint of the fake accent, as if it had been something he had said many a time. A fond memory? Something happy? Sad? "The best slices I ever had were in a little place in New Mexico."

Something in his tone told her he was reliving a memory. The softness of his voice, the slight tinge of remembered sadness, the hope of happiness.

"We were kids," he explained. "My sister and I. My mother was an immigrant, in the country illegally, working two jobs to pay the rent on a place the landlord kept charging her more for. Extorting immigrants."

"Money was tight," Aaron continued. "There were times I saved up a few dollars. Hustling. Working odd jobs, running errands. So when I saved up enough, every few weeks, I took my sister to the pizza place across the street from where we lived.

"My sister had jacked-up teeth," he said. His face twisted in a snarl, as if angry at the world for something he and his sister had no control over. "She would never grow up to be pretty. She knew it. Not like me," he finished bitterly.

Baber wondered what Aaron's sister looked like. Aaron was straight off a magazine cover. She sensed he knew his looks, used them even.

Speaking about them now, in the way he compared himself to his sister, it gave him a depth she was unaware he had.

She felt it now, in how Aaron talked about his sister. As if she were an angel. Someone worth anything. Everything. Baber had felt something similar before, when Aaron had been talking about Hamilton, saving his life. The first photo.

She felt that same emotion from the man now, something he kept in tight check. Revealed only when he was so deep in it that he couldn't hide it anymore.

Love. She realized the word she was looking for. A tightly coiled emotion, inside the man. Deep and wrapped up tight. Passionately hidden. Violently protected.

She forgot where they were.

She thought Aaron had as well.

"It was just the two of us, against the world," he said. "My mother, always out working. Two, three, four jobs at a time. So it was me and my younger sis, together. No television. No electric, sometimes. Books, when we could find them. Comics, mostly. They were cheap, and I'd read to her, pretending to be one of the heroes there. But pizza night, that was the thing she loved most. And that was the thing I loved to do most for her."

He let out a breath, something long and deep and winding. "The smell of that place, the cheese and pepperoni, the hot bread, it meant the world to me, when I could take her there and get us a slice."

Baber could almost taste the pizza. Feel the shop around her. A small place, heavy on Italian seasoning. Maybe garlic in every inhaled breath. The warmth of the pizza oven, heating the small restaurant.

Aaron shrugged. Maybe trying to let the memory go. "Tiny things, right?" he said. He looked left, as if expecting to see the shop there again. But it was something else now. Another coffee place. The mom-and-pop place was blocks behind the two of them now. The pizza place he was speaking of, even further.

Baber wondered where this was going. She should be getting out of the car. Running for it. Calling Frank. But there was a rawness to Aaron, a realness, that hypnotized her. There was something in the man that pulled her in, made the inside of the car feel like it was part of the tale, as if Baber was outside of normal time and space, watching something unfold in front of her.

Her curiosity got her in bad places sometimes. Luckily, it was only matched by her drive. The two had made her a good detective. And they had solved a lot of cases for her. So she decided to ride this out.

"One day the old man there asked me who we were," Aaron said. "He was the owner, his wife had been dead a long time, he was sixty years old. We got to talking, him and me, an old man and a young boy. We got to be friends. At some point he met my mama. Maybe I bought her a slice. And then he did us a favor. He married her. Adopted us. Paid all the red tape to make us legal. Then took care of us. Put us through school."

Aaron looked over at Baber.

She sat there, waiting.

"He's the reason I believe in America. People like him. He's the reason I do what I do."

"Do what you do?" Baber asked. She realized he was talking about the Fourth Branch. That whatever she felt about how crazy that story had been, Aaron still believed it. She wondered if she was crazy for even wanting to believe it, too.

His glance told her he knew what she was thinking.

"I remember when the man came home one day," Aaron said. "He had taken my sister to the dentist, and got her these god-awful braces. Shiny steel all in her mouth—but her smile..." The man choked up, took a breath, then another. And another, letting each breath come out in a shaky exhale, a warbling whistle.

He couldn't finish the sentence. A hand left the steering wheel, wiped his cheek, then retook the two positions on the wheel. He shook his head, finally tried a grin, and it stuck. His next words were a whisper, as if he was still reliving that memory. "Her smile…"

Baber looked away. She was viewing something too personal, something the man hadn't shared with anyone before, maybe. For a moment she just let him drive, and she watched the dark storefronts slide by on the right, darker pedestrians mingling together and separating again, as they walked down the sidewalks.

The stop-and-go traffic became a little more go than stop. They were out of north Boston, heading north-northeast. Too late for her to get out of the car now. If she had ever really wanted to. The car picked up pace. The song on the radio was one of those weird ones, where the singer used some kind of voice modulation, as if something electronic and fabricated could ever add something real to their music.

"People like him," Aaron said, his voice thick, "are why I joined."

Baber knew he wasn't talking about whatever service he had served in. Whatever military, or government agency. He was talking about his wild story. The Fourth Branch.

She looked at him. He was focused now. Serious. The dash lights lit up his face just enough for her to see his eyes, glistening in the shadows of the cab of the car. "People like him?" she asked.

"Yeah," he said. "People who *are* the American dream. Who believe deeply in it, who live their lives by it. People like you. Like Hamilton."

She was someone who lived by facts. It was what she had to use, to solve the case. To prove.

But she had a gut, too. And a lot of times she used that gut, those instincts, to get to the facts. To get to things she could prove. And while she couldn't believe in this branch Aaron talked about, the deep emotion in him had her believing him *enough*. Trusting her gut, to get her to a place she could find the facts. To a place where she could prove.

She had seen the pictures of Hamilton. The first one, she could believe that man loved the American dream. Had lived it. The second picture though, that man was mad. Not just angry mad, but maybe insane mad.

She would see this through, though. See if she could rescue the Martinez girl. And if possible, figure out which of those pictures that man really was.

"So we're going to save him," she said. It might have sounded like a question, she wasn't sure.

Aaron's head nodded up and down, once or twice. His hands were locked on the wheel. His body tight, as if preparing for a fight. But a small smile crept over his face, even as he stared far down the blackness of the road ahead of them. Maybe because Baber had used the word we. Or maybe he was just ready.

CHAPTER
FORTY-SEVEN

THE CAR SEEMED COLDER. PROBABLY BECAUSE THE TWO OF us were wet. The water from the pool had dripped everywhere, and soaked from my pants into the seat. I wrestled the jacket off, tossing it into the backseat, before firing the car up. It responded with the low humming purr that all four-cylinder vehicles had. I clicked the ventilation over to heat, and the fan to high.

The vents responded with cold air, blasting from the dashboard. Angela shifted hers so they didn't blow directly on her. She was shivering, arms wrapped around herself, but all I had was the wet jacket. I made a motion to it, but she just shook her head.

I pulled the car slowly through the woods. It bounced over roots and rocks, over the edge of the shoulder, and smoothed out as we got onto the road. I punched the gas then, wanting to get as far away from the mansion as fast as possible. The car responded by taking off in the slow lurching speed-shifts only an under-powered sedan had. As slow as those lurches were, Angela seemed uncomfortable with them, bracing herself in the seat.

"I don't know if we're safe yet," I said, checking my rearview, seeing only darkness behind me.

We were out of the mansion, but safety was still a nebulous thing, something hazy, indistinct. I wasn't sure when it would be concrete, but I was sure it would start when I got back to my place and called Baber.

I could hand Angela over to the detective, then. I trusted her. And I could come back to the governor's mansion and clean up what I had left. Make sure that I hadn't left the mercenary alive. Make sure the teams he had sent back to Boston were discouraged from ever coming back to Massachusetts.

The sedan lugged its way up a steep incline. We were still in the hilly part of the coast. The earlier fog had made its way inland, and I kept clicking the headlights from low beams to high, back to low. Low barely illuminated enough of the road, high threw back too much of the light into my eyes, reflected by the thick gray mist.

The warm air finally kicked in. Angela took a breath and held her hands out over them. I turned the center vent, the one closer to me, her way.

She laughed. Dark, but also happy. Almost a surprised kind of burst.

"What?" I asked.

"Show what you be," she said, shaking her head. Her voice carried that timbre all people who worked stages had. "Be not faint."

The line she had quoted to me at the bookstore. The one about the knight, the one that had me reading the book. I shrugged it off.

"Spenser," she reminded me.

"I know," I said. I had read the book. Well, some of the book. And I wasn't anything like him, not that knight. Not his fight, his struggles. There was no woman wanting to rescue me, no Arthur Pendragon coming to save me, to help me become a better person.

What I was, the world didn't need to see. And I was okay with that, I told myself again. The routine would be all.

After this night.

Angela kept shaking her head, as if in disbelief. "Of all the people for me to sit next to..."

The same thought had occurred to me, more than once, these past few days. If it had been a coincidence, it had been one of those lightning strike kind of chances. The billion to one kind of odds.

Life wasn't a story. I had told Kirschke that. It was something earned. It was scars, and fights, and coming out just an inch ahead of whatever you faced. There were no knights rescuing princesses from dragons, no happily ever after.

Part of me wanted to help Angela, still. I thought she might still be in shock, though she was handling things well. It might be hard going from being locked up and beaten, tortured for something she knew, that if she gave it up, would mean her death. Maybe she had known it was her death anyway. Me showing up, it would have been like pulling a winning lottery ticket. It would have been something hard for her to believe.

The joke was on my lips. *It wasn't anything different from my usual Wednesday,* I was going to say, as if the two of us were back in that bookstore and I was mocking my own routine. But the words felt corny to me, so I pushed the comment away.

I was closing up, I realized. Returning to who I was, when I had met Angela. Getting ready to button my life back up.

I took a breath and let it out. Tested it. Felt the anger inside, hiding, but also being pushed down. As if the dark emotion realized the routine could beat it, *had beat* it before, and was about to subdue it again. Like the bitter fury was okay with waiting, until the next time it was needed. Until the next time I had someone tied up and helpless in the kitchen.

Beating myself up wouldn't fix what happened to Charley. Rescuing Angela wouldn't, either. Nothing would even that scale for me, would fix what I had done.

But my life was broken, anyway. What was one more jagged piece to the puzzle that was what I lived? What I was now was nothing like what I used to be, and if I had done something good, and something bad, and those scales weren't even… Well, I would have to be okay with that.

Whether I was, or wasn't.

"How'd you do it?" she asked, finally. Realizing I wasn't going to say anything. It did feel like we were back at the bookstore, with her prompting me to say anything about myself. With me reluctant to do so, as if who I was and what I had done weren't worthy enough to speak of.

But I told her some of it. Not about Charley, or the cops. About talking to Kirschke, the mention of which brought a small smile to her lips. I told her about Sara, and our discussion. How Sara had covered Ben's wreck. About the reasons she thought Angela had been there, too. About the back and forth, between Sara and I, when we realized what might have happened in Ben's wreck, and the governor's car accident.

I didn't tell her about the mercenary, about reading the book, about my first thoughts on Whelan selling a device to the black market. I didn't tell her about Aaron or Sam or anything else. So shortening it all up like that made it seem so easy, basically I had just found Whelan and talked with him, and then came to get Angela.

Her eyes had gotten sad, inside the cab of the car, after I had mentioned the wreck and Whelan. I wondered aloud about why they had come to find her, now. About the possible pieces. The drive. Her computer courses. Her trying to get into the drive to see what was there, and the chain of events that had led to.

She smiled, a sad twist of her lips. "I had to know," she said. As if explaining. As if carrying the drive and not knowing had been eating her alive.

"Know?" I repeated. Actually being the one doing the prompting. I focused on the road, it was hard to see through the fog, but I kept thinking headlights navigated the same soup behind us, so I tried going a little faster. The engine responded with a whine. The car responded with a burst of speed through the haze.

She nodded, took a breath. Her hand placed hard against the dashboard. "It almost went down exactly like you said. Ben was so frantic. He was trying to explain everything to me, in the car. He had come up to get me. We were driving to Canada. He had handed me the drive and told me this crazy thing, how he had found out the governor had been killed. That he had all the evidence.

"He was driving so fast, and he wasn't making any sense. I was telling him to slow down, even when he was telling me how it had all been done. That we might be in danger." She closed her eyes, a soft sad closing of the lids, that at the end became a tight painful wince. "I'm still not sure what happened. All of a sudden that car was tumbling over and over, flying through the air. Ben was screaming something like *oh my god they found us*, I think his hand was wrapped in mine, but the car tumbled over and over and I was just thrown clear."

The cabin of the car was quiet, with her story. Her voice, the timbre, a low purr that echoed with her words. I could see it happen. The car hit the guardrail, flip over. Everything frozen in that one moment in her memory. Ben reaching out, every word crystal clear. Both of them screaming. The crumpling of metal. The shattering of glass. Then a burst of pain as Angela was thrown clear.

"I woke up down the side of the hill," she said. "Somehow, the USB drive still in my hand. I crawled up and looked, and saw the cop looking at the Porsche." Angela took a moment here, as if trying to not remember that part. "I knew Ben was still there, still inside, could see the windshield, could see…"

Little wonder she had stayed hidden then. Hearing some crazy story about how her boyfriend had found out the governor had been killed. Hearing him tell her about how the accident had been done. Telling her he had proof of it, on the drive.

And then the same thing happening to them.

She had thought quickly. Angela had guessed, likely correctly, that no one had known she was with him. And that guess had led to another, that if anyone had learned she knew the same thing Ben had, then she would be just as dead as he was.

I gave her a moment, adjusted the rearview. Flipped the high beams to low again. We were going sixty-five on a curvy road in the fog. The headlights behind us drifting further back in the murk.

Her voice was soft now. "I still remember his fingers getting yanked from mine. I wake up sometimes, at night, and can *feel* them, you know?"

The timbre in her voice echoed in the cab of the car. It paired perfectly with the whispering rush of the air from the vents, the high-pitched whine of the engine as we headed up another hill. Her voice was magical, it pulled me into the picture she painted, it tugged at memories of my own and let them unfold.

Sam and I, in a gondola in Venice. The feel of her hand in mine, on the oar, steering the boat. The feel of her laugh, as she pushed back against me.

The feel of the mattress, soaked in sweat, as I awoke in fear, every night. The ghostly fear of a chisel tapping against my leg, the ghost-like hammering into my bone. The burned in memories of Aaron on the floor, and Sam gone.

The feel of the understanding of a thing, once it had been done.

I knew. I knew all about memories that would never leave. Those things shaped you, long after they were actually gone.

"I know," I said, my voice rough.

Angela looked at me, and nodded. As if she understood me. As if we understood each other.

"It's why I just ride now," she finally said. Trying to explain her hand on the dash, maybe. "If they could do that to us then, I knew they would come after me, if they knew I was there too, with Ben."

"Hey," I finally said. "You're safe now."

She smiled, the sad smile. Her eyes, holding that hidden pain. What had first attracted me to her, in the bookstore. A common soul. "I want to believe that."

If there was one thing I could do, it was protect someone. I didn't think that part of me was gone. Not yet. Sometimes, in my darkest moments, I thought the routine was something put in place by that part, by me, trying to protect what was left of... me.

So this time I tried a joke, though I felt like it fell flat. Like the parts inside me that conveyed tone and feel, things like a grin, a twinkle in the eyes, those things didn't know how or when to appear. It all came out gruff. "I've been told I have that look."

She laughed, and the laugh was real. It made the cabin of the car less stuffy, more open. It even got me smiling. "So you actually read *The Faerie Queene*?"

"Yeah," I said. Then corrected myself. "Not all of it." Hell, I wasn't through the first canto. Whatever the hell the canto was.

Her hand snaked into mine. Her fingers slender, thin, long. Warm. The touch of an artist.

My hand wanted to ball up. I forced it to stay open. Forced my fingers not to tremble, or shake.

"What'd you think?" she said, softly. And then it was just her and me in the car.

"I don't know," I said. A moment later. "I don't think I am who you think I am."

"Hey," she said. "You're here, aren't you?"

That was the thing. I was here. But what it had cost others... that was too high a price.

I wanted to be vengeance. I wanted to do the right thing. I wanted to be the consequence for other people's actions. The vengeful, *just* consequence when people decided to do whatever the hell they wanted. When people made the kind of choices they felt like they could make, because there was no one to stop them. No one to correct their assumption.

What I learned though was that, if I wasn't careful, those same kinds of consequences came back to visit me. I had learned that the world didn't view me as some kind of hero, some knight rescuing some girl. I had learned, deeply, that the world was an unfair place, it didn't care about things like reasons or well-meaning goals or *the desire to do good*. All actions had consequences, no matter the intention of the person performing the act.

I never felt like the ends justified the means. But the means never justified the end, either. There were no heroes and villains, the world was just a soupy gray, some people more gray than others, maybe. Some people darker, a blackish stain, and some people lighter, like a pair of foggy headlights, bobbing behind me, in the rearview mirror.

Angela caught my gaze. She felt the sudden shift of tension. Her fingers tightened on mine. "What?"

I shook my head. I had let off the gas listening to Angela, with us going up and down hills, and now we were headed back up an incline and only going fifty-something in the fog.

I pressed the accelerator. Felt the car lurch up the hill, straining to add power, but getting faster. Then I glanced in the rearview.

The headlights picked up speed. Stayed behind me. Large, powerful beams from an expensive car, the bright LED lights cars had nowadays.

I swore, under my breath.

"What?" Angela asked again.

"We'll be okay," I said, as if automatic. But I didn't know if that was true. I could just push the gas pedal down and hope we could get away. Get free. Then come back to punish these people. The mercenary, if it was him.

Angela's face had paled. Her hand braced against the dashboard. Her fingers clutched in mine. The seat belt, tight against her chest.

I wanted to let go of her hand, but she wouldn't let me. I had to steer one-handed, pushing the automatic of the four-cylinder through its change into high gear, trying to get it to climb the hill faster and faster, the fog rushing over us in streams of thick gray tendrils that slipped over the windshield. Like some old smoke-stack train chugged along the hill in front of us, and we drove through the clouds of smoke it left behind.

We flew up the hill, leaving the headlights behind us dropping further and further back. Then we crested the top, breaking free of the fog, the night clear above us, the fog waiting below us, on the other side of the hill.

The road descended sharply. I couldn't tell if it curved or not. The fog was too thick.

I hesitated, then hit the gas. And found I didn't need to. The car was still accelerating.

We descended into the soup. I had no idea where we were at. The car was at eighty, ninety, going faster each second. The whine of the engine, climbing higher and higher. No matter that my foot was off the gas pedal. With no knowledge of whether the road ahead was straight or curved.

A cold realization washed over me. This was how it happened. How the previous governor had been killed. How Ben had been murdered, too.

Then a second, deeper understanding washed behind it. A bigger wave. A broad, far-reaching crest. Something I knew intuitively, all at once, and yet the knowledge was so large it was also something I couldn't fathom.

Aaron and the Branch weren't here to stop the sale of the technology behind those deaths. They weren't here to stop the acting governor, or his band of tactical teams and thug-like mercenaries. Or to take this GPS tool of murder off the board from the world.

They were here, behind it all.

There was only one way to track this car to me. It couldn't be linked from the license plate, or the name I used now. It could only be done from the VIN of the car, the vehicle identification number, and that number was only linked to my real name in one database. Something that had both the car and the name in the same place.

The Fourth Branch was behind all these killings.

The knowledge paralyzed me.

"Oh god," Angela whispered. Her fingers so tight in mine that pain radiated from the knuckles. The car weaving back and forth on the road, faster and faster.

The words, the action, got me moving.

There was nothing I could do.

Her words got me moving though. I pumped the brakes, and the engine instantly redlined, the car swerved on the road. I let my foot off the brake, trusting the road to be straight for long enough for me to figure out something.

The steering wheel remained in my grip, and the car felt like I could still control it, but if the engine blew I would lose it. Pulling the emergency brake, switching the sedan off, both of those would leave me at the mercy of whatever the car wanted to do.

All I had left was something crazy.

The car sped down the hill, the tachometer climbing, the engine whining, almost like even the car worried about what was about to happen.

I yanked my hand from Angela's. It felt difficult for our fingers to pull apart. I pumped the brakes once, twice, with hard jabs of the pedal. Then I swung the steering wheel at the same time as the last pump of the brakes, a hard turn. Like I was trying to take a ninety-degree turn into a parking lot.

We were lucky. I had slowed the car enough that it didn't flip over. Squeals screamed through the night, as the tires drug along the road, as the car swiveled so that the trunk of the sedan now pointed down the road. Angela and I were traveling fast, backward, staring through the windshield and back up the hill. The tires squealed and slid as the momentum of the car drove us farther and faster downwards.

I pulled the emergency brake and looked out of the back of the car, in the direction we were sliding, not sure how fast we were going, just knowing it was way too much. Too fast. The engine redlined and then gave out. There was a boom from under the hood. I didn't care much, most of what I was doing was just trying things.

We went off the road. The squeal of tires became the low scratching rumble of something heavy dragging through rocks and dirt. I tried to steer the car, tried to keep the trunk of the car between us and whatever we were about to hit, though there was no steering the sedan now, it was just a three-thousand pound sled on rubber rails, tearing through the ground at an unknown rate of speed. Something heavy and monstrous blasting through the thick gray fog.

The heavy mist whipped by, over the rear windshield, over the hood of the car. Like we traveled back in time. Like everything I had ever done was being reversed.

Angela leaned forward in her seat, hands pressed tightly against the dash, whispering over and over. Her hair covered her face. Her words indistinct, in the rumbling of the sedan over the earth, though I understood the message.

The car dropped down the hill like a train off its tracks, like a roller-coaster off its rails, everything too fast. There was nothing I could do to stop it. My stomach lurched at every bounce and drop. Then we were weightless, like we were flying through the fog, the rumble of the car dragging through the dirt became an eerie silence.

I looked at Angela. Her face was turned to mine. The lights of the dash illuminated just her cheeks, her temples, her forehead. Her eyes, pressed tight together.

I half-turned in my seat. Looked out the rear window. Saw nothing but gray, stained red with the taillights of the car.

Wherever we were going, this was going to be it.

We landed. Stopped. Immediately. The car slammed against something it couldn't move aside. Briefly, for an instant, the trunk of a tree revealed itself in the taillights of the sedan, the tree outlined in the crimson glow.

I'd say there was a lot of pain, but that would have been an understatement.

Fortunately, it all went black.

"I had forgot about the people," Aaron said.

"People?" Baber asked.

Aaron nodded. "Yeah. People like the man who took care of my sister. Like Hamilton. Like you."

"I'm not following," she said.

"The Fourth Branch, it doesn't exist to enforce rules," Aaron explained. "Keep a government in place. It was created to protect the people."

He shook his head.

"Somehow I forgot that," he said. "Or placed it second, or third. Somehow I thought I was doing good, for a group of people. For America. I put them all together, under one thing."

Aaron wasn't really making sense. They were one thing, one country, one group.

"But they are," she said.

But Aaron kept shaking his head. "They aren't, not really. And there are hints everywhere, what we should stay on guard for. Reminders. *Protect against all enemies, foreign and domestic.*"

Baber looked at Aaron. Really looked at him. His fingers were tight on the steering wheel, locked in the ten and two positions. Whatever truth he had stumbled on, whatever he feared he had missed, the realization had really hit him, hard.

This Fourth Branch really exists, she thought. *At least, for him it does.* Baber couldn't stop there, though, her curiosity was engaged, and her detective mind had to figure it out now. *So if it's breaking, if this Branch really exists, did Aaron realize he's too late? That whatever it was he started preparing for has already happened, and that he's too late to save it. That this Fourth Branch is already broken?*

Baber didn't have to believe this Fourth Branch existed, to search for reasons, motives, to extrapolate forward what someone might do, when faced with that information. Choices, decisions, that was all human nature, and she was good there. That was something she could figure out.

Aaron and Hamilton worked for some government agency.

Something had happened two years ago, changing Hamilton.

Aaron was part of that, in some way.

"You think you might have caused it," Baber said aloud. "Whatever happened to Hamilton."

Aaron looked at her quickly. Then back to the road. They were heading more east than north now, at a good pace. They traveled along the coast, the night was dark, the ocean was dark, and between the two a fog hung, thick and heavy. Baber could tell they'd be in that bank soon, it crept inward, off the water, pushed in by some slow-moving wind.

"Maybe," Aaron said. "I'm starting to think Sam saw the cracks long before I did. She might have not known who to trust."

He was speaking too fast now. Coming to realizations. Baber didn't know who this Sam was. What Aaron was talking about.

And if this Sam didn't know who to trust then, would Aaron be having the same problem now?

"You have to understand," Aaron said. "I *believed* in what we were doing. To my core. Everything I did, I did for a man in a pizza shop. For a sister, with braces. For a mom, stick-thin and worn out from work, just trying to take care of her kids. For an America where things like the pizza shop and my sister could become the norm, for *everyone*."

He was talking to her, but Aaron's voice also carried this wondering tone. Like someone talking themselves through a memory of the past. As if part of him was rooted in the feelings he was talking about, the feelings of the past. And another part of him was trying to drag that part into the *now*.

Baber didn't think he was trying to convince her of anything. It was more likely Aaron was trying to come to grips with the new knowledge he had. He was trying to convince himself. Or maybe Hamilton, or whoever this Sam was.

"She couldn't have trusted me," Aaron said, finally. "I believed too much."

The memory he was working through had played out. He had taken what he had learned, looked back at whatever had happened, and come to his conclusion. His voice was sad, low, and almost broke as he said the words.

Baber wondered what had happened then. Two years ago. Whatever it was, between this Sam and Aaron and Hamilton, it sounded like it had changed everything. Maybe for all of them.

Her detective mind kept working. When had Aaron changed? When had the realization hit him? What moment or thing had finally convinced Aaron?

It had been when Baber had shown him the pictures of Angela's sister.

It had been like Aaron had been struck by lightning. His tanned skin had turned almost white. He had wandered into the living room, coming to grips with it. Then Frank had called Baber. Stealing precious moments from her, where she might have seen the transformation in Aaron, where the realization had become the new action.

"The sister," she said.

Aaron nodded. "The sister."

So he knew the sister existed. And, she guessed, Aaron knew who had killed her. Who had likely beat up Charley. And who likely had Angela, now.

"I need it all," Baber said. "If you want me on board."

He barked a laugh. Something bitter and self-recriminating. "If I knew it all, I wouldn't be here, now." He looked at her, serious. "*You* wouldn't be here, now, either."

Meaning he wouldn't have needed to bring her along. Which told her, he would have stopped whatever was going on. At least, Baber got the feel Aaron felt like he could have done something about it.

"Still," she said. "I can't be in the dark."

"Yeah," he said. His voice short, clipped, still bitter. "It'd be nice if I wasn't, either."

He went through it. What had happened to Ben Whelan. The previous governor. Why he was here now.

It almost sounded like a movie. It was so far out Baber had trouble believing it. A piece of technology, that could kill someone at a whim. At a distance. Anywhere in the world.

Aaron had been sent ostensibly to protect the governor from it. He had been told Angela had the information on a drive, and that he needed to find the drive. That the life of the acting governor had been at risk.

Aaron hadn't questioned those orders. He thought they were inviolate. Golden. But, after the past few days, he had begun to question. Maybe it was seeing Hamilton again, seeing what had happened to his friend, what he was like now. Maybe it was all the memories of back then, with Sam. Whatever it was, he started to wonder.

It had all locked in at Hamilton's apartment. When Baber had shown him the picture. Everything crystallized, became clear, in one giant lightning strike of thought.

Aaron talked about what had happened two years ago. What had happened between him and this Sam. What had happened to Hamilton. Who Sam was. Why the black phone was in Hamilton's apartment. And half of a mysterious virus, gone.

"The thing was," Aaron said. "The virus wasn't active, in itself. It was unique. It needed to be present in a host's body, and then it could be triggered, in the presence of another agent."

"Like the Batman movie?" Baber said. And when Aaron looked confused, she explained. "There was one where, when two different things were bought and mixed, like lipstick and orange juice, the two different chemical agents would react, and that reaction killed whatever person wore the lipstick and drank the juice."

"Maybe kind of like that," Aaron said. "This wasn't chemical, though. It was viral. There was a base virus that would be spread all over the world, like a cold. Leaving a special antibody in place, something that had reacted to that specific strain."

"That would be like the juice, maybe," he said. "The second virus wasn't contagious. Maybe you could say it was like the lipstick. It had to be applied in a certain area, more of a surgical strike. Put it in the air, food, a drink, and whoever had encountered the first virus would fall over dead."

"That sounds crazy," Baber said.

"It *is* crazy," Aaron said. "But it's the kind of thing we were designed to do. At least, that's what I always believed. Protect the United States from things like that. From all the things people in power could use to enforce their will, their wants, on others."

The way he said that made Baber think. Enforce their will. If someone had spread the first virus through the world, and they had this second virus, then that person could blackmail anyone. Demand anything.

"All they would have to do is threaten to release the second virus," she said.

And they wouldn't have to blow up a city, to show the effectiveness of the virus. They could easily target small, highly visible groups of people. Actors on a set. News anchors on a feed. Politicians at a campaign dinner.

"Exactly," Aaron said. "In my mind, what the Branch did, we protected America from things like that."

A moment later. "I mean, if I could tell you all the things we've done. Things we did, to protect the people…"

Baber had the feeling, again, that this Branch was real to him. As incredulous as it sounded. She wondered why it was invisible. Why it wasn't a real part of the government. Like everything else, especially if it did the good Aaron believed it did.

And then she started to get it. *Protect against all enemies, foreign and domestic.* The Fourth Branch was in place not just to protect America from the outside world, but to protect America from itself. And what Aaron was telling her was that part was breaking. That this branch couldn't, or wasn't, doing that, anymore.

"Sam saw something in the pattern," Aaron said. "Something I missed, until now. The things we were protecting the world from, maybe we were gathering them instead." He shook his head again, like what he had missed had been so obvious. "The person we were taking our orders from, he was gathering these weapons. I can see it now."

"Why?" Baber asked. That was the question, if this agency really existed. "If this Branch was here to protect us?"

Aaron took a long moment to answer. While he thought, the car passed into the bank of fog. Immediately the glare of the high beams reflected back at them, and Aaron flicked them to low.

"I think it just maybe got to be that time," he finally answered. "Look at the world today. The internet spreads things like wildfire. People look at their phone for the news, in little two hundred word chunks. They go from Hollywood to third world countries, to starving kids to what one politician says about another, all in the same stream."

Baber didn't see how that made sense.

"I guess I'm telling you I don't know for sure," Aaron said. "This is just a feel thing. Maybe the realization is too new, for me. But the Branch serves the people. And we serve the people by—mainly—keeping politicians in check. Watching for those that abuse their power, and when they do, putting the scandal out there for the people to see. It makes it easy, right?"

"Are you saying things like Watergate?" Baber said.

"That's how we would do things," Aaron said. "But look at what's happened lately. People get blowjobs in their offices. Others are accused of working with the Russians. Some ride the private jet of a pedophile."

Aaron sighed. "It used to be that people could read the news, digest it, talk about it, and come to a conclusion. Use that conclusion to drive an action," he said. "Now, people flick to the next two hundred word block of text. Catch whatever their favorite athlete or celebrity or influencer is doing. The important stuff never gets thought about. Never gets acted on, other than maybe a retweet with an angry emoji."

Aaron was still working through the realization. Baber thought it must be part of the realization that had hit him back in Hamilton's. These thoughts had been brewing inside of him, but the shape of them was new to him, and she thought he was still trying to figure out how it all went wrong. How and when it all had changed.

Though she understood some of what he was saying. The perception of what people were reading, seeing, what news had been, and what it was today, it *was* wildly different. Baber felt it too, in her job. It was funny, how many cell phone cameras today caught the police doing something wrong.

Not that she was defending those cops. The law was the law. But all these cameras in the world now, and all these videos of cops doing something outside the law. Never a video of a guy snorting coke before beating his girlfriend. Never a video of the beating, either.

Funny how that worked. It made her job harder. Baber didn't quite accept it, but she worked with it. There were people out there needing help, and she had to do what she could for them.

"Like having a hand tied behind your back," she said.

"Yeah," Aaron agreed, appearing to be lost in his realization. "Yeah."

The bank of fog was thick. It hid the road in front of them, and they had to slow down. The car had fog lights, but Baber didn't see where they did anything to help. Just a faint illumination of black pavement, a white line on one side, double-yellow on the other.

Baber worked on some realizations of her own. What happened in a world where people got their information from social media? Where the perception of what people thought could be shifted quickly, almost violently, away from whatever a politician didn't want their attention focused on?

Those politicians could get away with things. And they had started to feel untouchable, maybe. And they likely had lost whatever fear that they'd had, that someone, somewhere, would hold them accountable.

So, the GPS device. This Fourth Branch of Aaron's could use it to maybe scare a politician straying into that kind of god-mode. Maybe the virus as well, if it was what Aaron had mentioned. If the first part of the virus was basically inert, until it mixed with the second part.

There was a problem with all of that though, no matter how good the intention. It was a dangerous path, a slippery slope. Once you have something like the virus, or the GPS device, it wouldn't be long before you had to use it. The politicians would make you. *People* would make you. It was human nature, to press the limits of authority.

So you would have to talk yourself into it. After repeated warnings, after making threats. The person at the very top of this branch, or agency, would talk themselves into it. Just to show them. *At some point, her dad used to say, you have to quit talking, and start doing.*

At some point, maybe the person in charge of the Fourth Branch had seen where all his talking was going. Where it would end up. And he had decided to start doing.

His intention, probably good. But a line still had been crossed.

"You realized it all when I showed you the picture," Baber said. "Why?"

Aaron smiled. "I didn't like the guy. Someone the governor had hired. So I looked into him, as much as I could. The guy had a dishonorable discharge."

"Military?" Baber said.

"Yeah, kicked out," Aaron said. "And it took a bit, but I finally found someone who told me. Someone in his old unit. Apparently he liked counting kills over in Afghanistan. Trimming ears off. Had a violent streak, too, that grew over time. The soldier I had talked to had stood up to the guy once, and took a beating from him."

The picture of the girl. Missing an ear. Beat to death.

"That's when you knew," Baber said.

"That's when I knew," Aaron echoed. "But at that point, who could I trust? Who could I tell?"

He had tried to tell someone, Baber realized. He had tried to talk to her, out at the smoke pad. Maybe Aaron had been at Hamilton's for the same reason. There was something happening in a world he believed in, utterly, something he couldn't figure out, and he didn't know who he could tell.

"I understood Sam, then," Aaron said. "Understood everything that had happened to her. Why she had fled when she did. She must have waited until the last second, hoping to see something happen, hoping to see that she could trust me. Hating herself for not. Wanting to see some sign, and knowing she couldn't take the chance. Knowing she couldn't let that weapon get back."

Had Aaron told Hamilton? Was Hamilton someone Aaron felt like he could trust? Baber wondered what had happened between the two there, and why Aaron had let Hamilton go rescue the girl.

Aaron felt a little broken to Baber. Not like Hamilton. Not that far. But enough. Aaron couldn't follow the orders he had been given, but he also couldn't do anything about it. Because if he alerted the people above him, that he knew what was going on, they would likely take him out.

Maybe even right now. Using this car. And the GPS Device.

Baber shivered, and wrapped her hand around the seat belt.

Maybe that's why Aaron had let Hamilton go. It was what he could do, with what Aaron had around him. If Hamilton was who Aaron said he was, then the girl would be safe, and the weapon would be out of the hands of this Fourth Branch. Aaron would probably be clean of any suspicion.

Then Aaron could sit back and watch and see what happens. Figure out who he could trust, by the orders he was given next.

It was what Baber would do, in Aaron's place. She felt for him, if what he was telling her was true. He had been stuck between a rock and a hard place, with no way out, and a hard memory of two years ago that would forever stick with him. When he could have done the right thing, had this Sam person trusted him.

Baber shook her head. *People*, she thought, *always being human*.

That word stuck with her. People. Something Aaron had talked about, at the very beginning.

"You said it was about the people," Baber half-said, half-asked.

"It's what it should always be about," Aaron said. "Something I had forgot. Or at least, I let other things become more important."

He blew out a big breath. "It always should be about the person next to you. The old man who owns a pizza shop. The soldier who always puts his life in front of others. The detective who works long hours for little pay." He smiled his sad smile. "Once you start grouping those people together, making them all some nebulous thing like *America*, or *the voters*, or *this political party*, it becomes so easy to justify things. You know the saying, the needs of the many..."

"Outweigh the needs of the few," Baber finished. Aware of the line.

Used in plenty of movies, by the bad guys at the end, justifying the action they were about to commit.

"The thing is, if you focus on the few, help those people out, that's all it takes to make the world a better place. Instead, people always want to group themselves together," Aaron sounded frustrated. "Just help your neighbor. Get a girl a piece of pizza. Who knows, maybe it turns into a pair of braces."

Maybe it would, Baber thought, but most people weren't that way. Easier for them to pick a group of people and blame them for their problems, like cops, or rich people, or *The Russians*, then do something about the neighbor who might need someone to mow their lawn once in a while. The parent needing someone to take them to the doctor.

It was the sad side of being human. Easier to blame, than accept. And once you were blaming, it became easier to justify things to yourself. Easier to steal a few dollars, drink a little more, justify this drug or that one. Way easier to head that way, than meagerly save up change until you could buy a sister a slice of pizza.

"The world will never be like that," Baber said. "People just don't think that way."

He shook his head. "That's why it's so easy to fuck up. Once you start down that path, once you start thinking of people as *this* group, or *that* one, it's easy to blame them for whatever problem you're facing," he said.

Aaron closed his eyes, tightly, for a second, and Baber glanced at the road ahead, the blank fog they drove through, the refraction of the lights against the little glistening bits of mist, and she feared they would plunge suddenly off the road and into some unknown world.

But then he opened them again, and the drive went on.

"Once you start blaming those groups for your problems," Aaron said. "You forget all about the old man in the pizza shop."

FORTY-NINE

THE PHONE WAS RINGING. THE BLACK PHONE, THE BELLS shrill, insistent, but also, oddly muted. I thought I had ripped the cords from it, I thought it had been ripped from its place in the wall, in my life.

I went to answer it, but my feet wouldn't move. They were oddly light. It was my arms, my head that was heavy. The phone kept ringing though, louder and louder. I pressed my eyes tight and opened them, found myself... *back in the dream. Standing in the office. Or the cave. It seemed to be both now. The phone, ringing on the table in the center, like a cartoon phone, ringing so hard it vibrated on the table. The rings came over the casing waves, like the ocean, swelling as the phone bounced on the table harder and harder, then waxing as the trembling of the handset relaxed...*

The rings kept pulsing, in that rhythm.

I blinked, shook my head again. I knew I wasn't asleep, but I couldn't remember where I'd been. Where I was at. All I knew was that I was back in the nightmare, my feet frozen again on the floor. The boots a rusty metal, not clean, like the suit of armor back in the library room at the mansion, but so rusted the joints couldn't move. So rusted the metal was almost black with it.

And oddly, my feet felt so light. Though I couldn't move them.

The office walls ran with the same word, over and over. Error, scrawling in its crimson trails. The cave of the monster itself. Like I lived here. Like I was the monster.

Warm wetness ran down my face. I wiped at it, and dark blood came away, almost black, like the boots. When I looked at my hand the word Error was being written on it, over and over, just like the walls. I wiped my face again, looked at my palm again, and now more of the word scrawled across the skin, as if multiple invisible hands penned the script, in the same rhythm, one above the other.

Everything was about rhythm. Everything moved at the same pace. The pulsing of the blood, the ringing of the phone, the looping of the letters, as Error was written all around me. Even the smell of Turkish coffee, always strong and present in the dream, thickened in the air until I could barely breathe, for the scent of it. Thickened in waves.

I pressed my eyes tight. Opened them.

Still in the dream. The table remained in front of me. The phone morphed back into a closed case. Into a motorcycle helmet. Into a case again, now open. One vial missing. One broken.

The ringing muted, softened a bit, until I could pick up gunshots down the hallway. The shots letting me know the soldiers were coming. These sounded different. In a moment I would turn to face them, but for now I remained, staring at it all in front of me. At the nightmare that had tormented me, every night, for two years. At the puzzle of my life, at all the jigsaw pieces, pieces seemingly from different puzzles, crying out for me to put them together.

The morphing case/helmet/phone.

The smell of Turkish coffee.

The scrawling of the word Error.

Sam, gone.

Aaron, laying on the floor, still. This time wearing the same rusty suit of armor I had on. A rusty red so dark it too was black, so that I almost couldn't see Aaron, he blended so well with the dark floor of the cave.

The gunshots grew louder, and became a slow rhythm of their own.

I frowned. Focused on the case. Stepped forward with the intention of grabbing the second vial.

The dream let me, this time. I picked up the vial and the glass morphed in my hand, becoming the motorcycle helmet, the receiver of the phone, the vial, rinse and repeat, over and over again. It flickered so fast it became a blur.

The bullets got louder behind me. They were strange this time. Not the fast repetition of assault rifles, but single shots, fired in a pattern. Like someone was squeezing a trigger, to some slow beat of a drum.

A pressure built heavier and heavier in my head, as if a knowledge built there, something that gathered and grew until it was too big for the container that held it. The words scrawled in the office/cave sped up, became sloppy, the even lines began crisscrossing each other. The morphing of the case/helmet/phone flickered faster, becoming one big blur.

Until I screamed and squeezed it in my hand, hard. Until I felt something crunch, in my hand, inside me, I didn't know.

It became the phone. The phone shaking so hard it was hard to grasp. And then shrilly ringing in my hand. The ringing loud in my head, so loud it overwhelmed my scream and became everything I could hear...

———

I CAME TO, UPSIDE DOWN. STILL IN THE SEAT OF THE SEDAN, it was the car that was upside down, resting on its roof. I hung in my seat belt. Everything hurt, as if I had run through a gauntlet of people swinging clubs at me. As if a giant had held me in his hand and shook me for all he was worth.

The ringing from my dream remained. Became the muted ring, like what they showed in the movies, when a grenade goes off too close to someone. I felt that way, like I was swimming in a shaky world around me.

I pawed at the strap of the seat belt. My muscles had trouble moving when and where I wanted them to move. They responded long after the thought. My hands were slow, sluggish, and moved way after I told them to.

Blood ran down my face. Warm. I wiped at it with my hand, the best I could. I had a headache, not just from the wreck, but from the pressure of all the fluid in my body pushing its way to my skull. I had no idea how long I had hung here.

I groaned, turned to look at Angela.

The roof of the sedan caved in between us, punching an angle of metal into the cabin that divided us a little. But Angela hung from her seat belt as well. No engine block pressed into her lap. No tree trunk had broken through the windshield and slammed into her.

She was there, upside down as well, and unmoving. Both of her arms hung limply. Her hair fell loose around her face, and I couldn't see her eyes. I couldn't see if her chest moved, if her eyes fluttered, if she was dead or if she was smiling, waiting for me to wake up so she could laugh and say something like *can you believe we survived that?*

I had a bad feeling though. I needed to get out, and get her out. Get us to safety. For all of this to end like this, here, now...

It was just a few days ago. She had smiled at me at a bookstore. The smile had pulled me out of the life I had been living. I didn't want to admit that I had needed that smile. That I knew the life, the routine I had crafted had only one ending for me.

Maybe I thought it had been meant to be. Maybe I thought Angela was the once-in-a-lifetime chance for me to change. To find a way back to who I had been. Who I thought I was meant to be.

I might have gotten her killed, instead.

I screamed, it came out more like a long, bubbling groan. I tried to move, flexing my fingers. A tingling ran into them, and my hands became less like lumpy, thick pillows. My fingers curled up, twitched, I felt the tips of them dig into my palms.

I focused on finding the clasp of my seat belt, pushing one hand up next to me, inside of the chair, around where the seat belt clicked into its receptacle. The console was pressed tight against me, I stretched myself some to give my hand more room, bracing my other hand on the roof of the car and turning to the driver's side window.

The mercenary sat there. In the open driver's door. Squatting on the ground. He was upside down in my sight. His nose broken and swollen. Blood staining the front of his shirt. But the man smiled a wide smile, as if he had been watching me.

He had his gun in his hand. Pointed up into the air. As if he had been shooting it. Maybe in a slow, pounding rhythm.

"Hey," he said. "Remember me?"

I screamed again, or tried to. It was just a gasp, now. A moan. My body wouldn't respond right. I wrestled in my seat belt, I reached out for his hand, for his gun. The reach was too slow. Far too slow. He popped me on the temple with the top of the pistol, the metal stabbing into the side of the bone there.

A tiny explosion of stars washed over me. More blood leaked down my face. I wiped my face again. Found the mercenary now held a knife in the hand opposite his gun hand. With that, he sliced the webbing of the seat belt holding me up.

I fell to the roof of the sedan. My arm barely supported me, slowed the fall enough that it was more of a collapse. Everything hurt. My head, my legs, my arms, everything battered by the wreck. Broken ribs screamed at me, I struggled to breathe. I curled up on myself, on the roof of the car. There was a lot of blood here. Maybe more than one person's. I looked over at Angela and thought I saw her eyes were open, still. The irises rolled up into the top of her head.

I screamed again. This time it was loud, and lung-emptying. All I could see in front of me was her smiling across the table from me.

Show what you be.

Who was that? Other than a man who killed everything he touched?

"I thought you might," I heard the mercenary say. He grabbed me by the back of my vest. Dragged me out of the car. I reached out for Angela, a slow grasp of my hands.

I dug for something, anything. Anything to get me moving. The anger I had carried for two years seemed to be gone. Like I had nothing left. Nothing in reserve.

I pawed feebly at the mercenary's grip.

He dragged me along. The ground was wet and heavy around me, like thick loam with hard fingers of roots that clawed along my skin. It smelled like dung, like a heavily fertilized field, as if the forest we were in was ancient. The wet earth came away as I was drug across it, my pants smeared with a black mud.

The mercenary dragged me around to the back of the car. I was dead weight, but he did it easily. Like I had wheels on me, like I was one of those wagons he toted behind him.

"Well, lookie there," he said, almost to himself.

He dropped me, back by the trunk of the car. After the sedan had collided with the tree it must have rolled a bit more down the hill, sideways, until it had stopped wherever it was we were now. The car was all broken up, punched up and dented metal, shattered glass, splintered plastic. The trunk gaped open behind me, like a big mouth, and all of it swelled up out of the fog around us, as if the broken car was some dead creature, surfacing from the depths of the gray mist.

I struggled to move, to put my knees underneath me. My feet were light, almost like they were feet belonging to someone else, but they began to tingle a bit. Like the nerve-endings there had begun to fire. Hundreds of pinpricks needled the soles of my feet.

The mercenary had walked forward, into some brush behind the car. He picked something up there, pulled it up out of the low-lying fog, and held it high in front of him.

The motorcycle helmet. It had been in my trunk. I had left it there, in what seemed like another life.

The mercenary turned to face me, the helmet in his hands. It seemed important to him. His smile had gotten larger, and more twisted. "I love getting two birds with one stone," he said.

He was satisfied. He smiled that kind of smile. He talked to himself, but he was aware of me, aware he had an audience.

To me it was a clown's smile. The grin of a performer. The broken nose, the black eyes, gave him that impression. Of a man hiding behind a face he put on for the rest of the world.

Maybe that was me though. Maybe between the two of us, he was the real one. Maybe I was just someone who was pretending.

I didn't understand where I was. Who I was, other than I was lost. I had stuck to this routine, I had carefully crafted a life to keep me away from things like this. Out of places and times that would only remind me I wasn't the man I used to be.

I had been someone capable of keeping people safe. Of keeping them alive. Who wouldn't be this shell of a man, stained in mud, collapsed and broken on the earth.

I had only wanted to save the girl.

Something ignited then, in my chest. A flame. Small, but furious.

I was so tired. Tired of this life. Tired of the nightmare. Of the routine. Of the paralyzing feeling inside my chest, that I was frozen in this place in time, doomed to the same fate, over and over.

What was I holding myself back for? Why was I constantly on guard against the anger inside me? I had tried to stay out of this world. Maybe harder than anyone had ever tried. I had kept to myself, kept to my routine, stayed out of everything and away from everyone.

I thought, if I just carefully swept along the surface of the water, I wouldn't disturb any of the monsters below. Instead, a monster had watched me. Trailed me, from hidden depths. Had bided its time. And, when it was so inclined, that creature had come up and eaten me.

The monster, the creature, its spawn, whatever it was, it had always known I was there. Always. I couldn't have hidden from it, no matter how I had tried to hide myself. No matter how insignificant I had tried to make my life.

No matter how small we make ourselves. No matter how quietly we paddle across the surface of the ocean, we always left some trace of ourselves. It was just life. The only way to not leave a wake behind you was to be dead.

The flicker of anger bloomed. White-hot heat burned in the back of my skull. Somehow, I had gotten to one knee. The fury I had locked up inside me, the fury of a wasted life, pushed out of my chest, radiated down my spine, pushed air into my lungs until they swelled, until I felt bigger, stronger... *greater*.

Anger was a power all its own. Uncontrollable, maybe. Not without its own consequences. But power.

Despite everything I had done to hide, despite just wanting to help someone else, despite just wanting to save a girl, the world had taken another chunk from me. A monster trailed me, from its depths, swimming after me, taking little bites when it could. Sam. Charley. Aaron. And now, Angela.

The white-hot flame seared those words in my brain.

The mercenary was fumbling with the helmet. He tucked his gun into the back of his pants and used both hands to pop the modular part up. He had it facing me, so that the front of the helmet opened, the wings on each side open and flowing down each side, as if a hidden wind still lifted them.

He peered inside the helmet. If it could, his grin grew wider. He reached a hand into the helmet, on the side, where most bikers now had a Bluetooth earpiece, and he pulled out a small USB drive.

"I'm not good at math," he said, holding the drive out. "But I think that's three for three."

It was then he realized I was standing.

His eyes opened wide. He started to drop the helmet. I was already charging him.

He got his gun up just as I collided with him. There was a pop, muted with the pulsing anger in my ears, and something thudded into the vest. Then I hit him and we flew into the brush behind him.

Branches broke around us. He pulled his gun down and fired a few more times. I thought the vest caught those, but to be honest, I was past feeling anything. All that burned in me, anything I felt, was consumed in the anger. In the heat.

Not a righteous anger. Not justice. Not even vengeance. Just the anger of a man who felt like he had been wronged. That life had been unfair. That, no matter the good he had done, life had still fucked him, and when he had withdrawn from the world, life had followed and fucked him some more.

It was time to fuck that life back.

We rolled through the brush. I grabbed his hand with the gun. Ripped some of his fingers back and broke them. He screamed, the gun dangled from his index finger, still stuck in the trigger. I twisted the gun, snapped his finger, twisted and ripped the digit off.

His scream ran out of air. He was trying to knee me, to punch me with his other hand. I felt none of it.

Something came out of my mouth too. Not a scream, but a roar.

I snapped my elbow into the side of his face, once. Twice. His nose broke again and threw blood to the side. Then I was standing, picking the mercenary up, and I swung him against the trunk of a tree.

His back bent around the tree. There was a cracking sound. Then he dropped to the ground.

My chest heaved. I drew in air, deep pulsing breaths of the fog around us. The air was wet and humid, cool, but that coolness didn't matter to me. It wouldn't quench the fiery anger.

I stepped out of the brush. Stood next to the mercenary, flipped him over onto his back. He screamed again and tried to swipe at me with his hands, but he was the one that was slow this time. His legs just lay there, twisted around each other, like they couldn't move.

His eyes blinked at me, a couple of times. His mouth opened and closed, like the mercenary wanted to say something, but couldn't come up with the words.

So I spoke for us both.

"You could have survived," I said. "I just hurt your knee. And your pride. But you took it out on an innocent girl, instead."

I wasn't looking at his face, though I was aware of his eyes looking at me, searching me for something. I was looking at the ground around us. Searching for something else. I noticed the drive. Picked it up and put it in my pocket. And kept looking.

"Maybe it was a pattern. Maybe you just like beating people. Or just girls," I said. "Whatever it was, it made you think you were a match for me. It made you think that you were this badass."

I found what I was looking for. The mercenary's gun lay off to the side. I picked it up, took his index finger out from where it still lay in the trigger guard.

"You thought no one could touch you," I said, holding the barrel of his gun against the middle of his forehead. "How about now?"

His mouth opened and closed. No words came out. His eyes shimmered, glistened with an awareness we all have, when we are this close to death. When the monster takes its last bite.

"Exactly," I said. And pulled the trigger.

Headlights lay ahead of them, stationary. On the other side of the road, the illumination muted in the fog, but pointed to the left. Off the side of the road.

Aaron slowed down, pulled their car off to the same side, making a huge U-turn to park behind the stationary car. He flicked on his hazards, like he was just some Good Samaritan, checking on a fellow traveler.

"What are you doing?" Baber said.

"This'll be it," he said, engaging the emergency brake, but leaving the car running. "Stay here."

She still didn't know what to think, but staying in the car wasn't going to be an option.

He got out quickly, one hand on the top of the window of the door. His jacket open right below the hand, where he could access his gun, quickly.

"Hey friends, you guys okay?" he called out.

The car ahead of them was parked at an angle. It was on the shoulder, but pointed off, just a little. The mist thickened and swirled ahead of their headlights, so that little tiny points of crystals flickered in and out of existence.

No one answered from the car ahead. Its driver's side door was ajar, a tiny beeping sound reporting that the door was ajar, an obnoxious *binging* sound repeating over and over.

Baber looked out her window. The blacktop of the shoulder ended in the edge of the road, thick grass took over from there, but within a few feet that grass descended out of view, sloping downward, and then it too disappeared.

She popped her door open. Unclicked her seat belt and got out. Squatted next to the road. Parts of the grass were torn up there, recently. Two parts, trails the size of a tire. As if a car had flown over the side.

As if someone had lost control of their car...

"Someone went over the side here," Baber said. She couldn't see too far into the fog, but she guessed they were on a good-sized hill. She took a couple of steps into the mist, the ground didn't just drop off, but she could feel it slant underneath her feet.

Aaron walked forward, took a peek inside the door. "Some blood here," he said. "Side of the door, drops on the seat."

He left the lights in the car on, but shut the door. The binging of the door stopped, leaving an emptiness in its place. The night around them was quiet for a moment, one of those quiets so deep that Baber thought she kept hearing the door ajar alarm.

"Hear that?" Aaron asked.

Baber listened. It was so quiet around them, as if the two of them were in their own world. Then maybe, *maybe*, she heard a pop. Far below them. "Gunshot?"

"I think so," Aaron said. He left the other car and headed to the trunk of their car, his pace quick and fast. Stalking.

She turned and followed, meeting him at the back. The taillights glowed red on the pavement, but even so, she could pick out a thick rubber trail of fresh tire tracks, headed off the side of the road. Twin, thick, dark streaks of blood across a darker surface.

Aaron noticed it too. And just shook his head. Popped the trunk open. In the back was a bulletproof vest, one of the nice military models, tossed over a bag. Aaron picked the vest up, looked at it, then looked at her.

"You're not going to stay here, are you?" he asked.

She arched an eyebrow at him. "What do you think?"

He grinned at her. "Then you get the vest. Might be a little big, but it should work."

"Then I get a gun too?" she said.

"Your Springfield's in the bag," he said, pulling something large from the bag. An assault rifle, something with a green polymer frame, a slick, futuristic sight and a shorter than usual barrel. Baber thought it was one of the Steyr AUGs, a bullpup assault rifle.

He waggled his eyebrows at her.

Baber rolled her eyes and put the vest on, tugging it over her jacket. It was large, almost too large, but she could cinch the straps tight enough to keep it snug over her. Then she reached in and found her Springfield.

"Magazines?" she asked.

Aaron shook his head. "Really wasn't planning for you to be in the gunfight," he said.

"You were planning for something," she said.

"Not really," he said, checking his gun. "Just prepared."

She looked in the bag. Some grenades, C4, magazines for the Steyr. Everything a budding terrorist needed. "Some preparation."

He held out a hand to her. Baber paused. Then she heard it too.

Twin engines. Two vehicles with big eight-cylinder engines, climbing the hill below them. As if they had been right behind Aaron and Baber, on the road. Roaring through the fog, as if the drivers were racing back.

Then she saw headlights, below them, on the road.

Aaron waved her down, and she took a knee behind their car. Aaron did the same, closing the trunk with a light, snapping click.

Two trucks drove into view, one following the other. Big sports utility vehicles, all black in the gray fog. They paused at the edge of the light, so that they appeared as shadowy blocks at the edge of all the illumination from the headlights.

Their engines rumbled, low. Like a purr.

Aaron knelt next to Baber. His back pressed to the car. Both of them risking tiny peeks over the trunk. Waiting.

The lion-like trucks waited too. One engine picked up a bit, as if the driver had goosed the gas, slightly. The wind shifted around the hill, a brisk breeze blew across the road, and the fog lightened into a mist between them all.

Then everything was clear.

A bright flash came from the window behind the driver of the first truck. A high-pitched whine split the night. Something hard and with a lot of velocity behind it *thunked* into the trunk of the car. Just a foot ahead of where Baber had been risking her peeks.

She ducked, just as the one gunshot became many. Multiple whines split the night. Automatic rifles, spraying the air. Tracers of bullets ran past the two of them, stabbing into the road behind Baber, more *thunking* into the car.

"See," Aaron winked at her. "Always Be Prepared."

He rolled to the side of the car and, in a smooth motion, sighted in his Steyr and returned fire. Controlled, pulling the trigger in little three-round bursts.

Then Aaron rolled back, pushing Baber to the side of the road and following her. Even as they moved, more gunfire lit up the car. Glass shattered behind them.

"You got to get down there," Aaron said. "Help Hamilton."

"What are you going to do?" she asked. "Hold off the army up here?"

Bullets skipped along the surface of the road. The tires of their car blew in large, booming explosions. Above all that, Baber heard voices coming from the trucks.

"For as long as I can," he said. "So be quick."

She looked down. The fog had cleared over the road, but the thick bank remained below. Here and there treetops crested the bank, thick clutching hands of dark scarecrows, as if they were warning her away.

"You know," she said. "I'm still not sure about him."

Aaron's grin remained, but his eyes turned inward. "You would have been, one day," he said.

The gunfire started eating up the car in front of them. Whoever was firing at them kept up a steady, torrential pace.

Aaron winked, and she saw he held a grenade in his hand. Baber wasn't sure when she had even seen him grab one.

"Go," he said. "Save Hamilton, if you can. For me."

"You know..." She hesitated one last second. "I don't know you that well, either."

"Yeah," he said. "But I know you."

Aaron pushed her a bit, down the hill. Just a nudge. He winked at her, and pulled the pin on his grenade, counted a few moments and then tossed it down the hill.

An explosion followed, a bright flash of light with a booming sound, something that dwarfed the gunfire around them. Screams and shouts came from the area of the trucks.

"Go," Aaron said. With one last nudge.

Baber took a breath and started descending down the hill. Into the deeper, darker fog. It swallowed her whole, and even then she couldn't help but feel a tingling in the middle of her back, right in the center of her spine, as if a sniper had her locked in their sights, with one finger lightly pressing the trigger.

FIFTY-ONE

Baber kept making her way through the fog. The gunfire stayed constant above her, loud, but dwindling as the slope of the hill got steeper and steeper. It wasn't long before she pulled off her pumps, snapping the heel off of each with a shake of her head.

The ground was wet, cold, under her feet. The grass, scratchy. She shook her head and put her pumps back on, kept working her way down the hill. The thick grass became brush, she waded further and further into that, until somehow she stumbled upon the trail of the car that had gone over the edge.

She followed the trail, it was as if someone had drug a wide shovel ahead of her. Bits of brush yanked out of the ground, thick chunks of earth missing in spots, small saplings cracked and broken.

If Hamilton had gone over the edge here, she wasn't sure he was alive.

Then she heard another shot, and she was sure it came from below, though she wouldn't have put money on it. There was just too much gunfire around.

The smaller saplings made way for larger trees. The vest was too big on her, and caught on the clutching arms of dead branches. For a moment she wondered if she would get out of this alive. She shook her head, thinking of Frank, and knowing that if she did get out of this alive, what the mountain of a man would say to her.

Beebs, his voice would rumble, *I told you*.

She grunted a laugh. That's what he would say. But that's all he needed to say. He had told her, but she had followed her gut, and those instincts had led her here.

She yanked herself out of more branches, tearing the sleeve of her jacket. Then kept following the car's trail. Ahead and down the slope from her, she finally saw lights in the fog. Red taillights, glaring crimson eyes in thick fog.

For a moment she looked up, far above. She could no longer see any of the lights from the road, the fog was too thick, none of the tracers or the flashes of gunfire from barrels, none of the headlights. There was still shooting above, but it was quieter down the slope. Baber had no idea how far she had descended. Once she had started going down, the smaller steps had become larger, gravity-assisted leaps and bounds.

However far, whoever was in the car had to be hurt. Or dead. She couldn't imagine, after traveling the distance, that anyone had survived.

She came to a tree, a thick trunk, cracked almost in half at the base. As if some giant had struck it with a huge, dull axe. The bark at the impact site was smashed in a V-shape, almost crushed, and the sap of the tree pushed out from under the rough skin of the tree as if it were bleeding.

Baber found bits of plastic, metal, and glass in the bark. Evidence of a great collision. More of it rested around the grass and brush, which flattened out below her. The car had struck this, then kept going down the slope. Maybe rolling.

She worked her way downhill, following the trail of the car. Finding bits and pieces of it, torn off as the vehicle had kept rolling. A side mirror. More glass. A clear covering of a headlight, jagged where it had broken off.

She entered a small area, almost a clearing of sorts. The grass was high and thick around her, except where the car had rolled through, so the trail remained easy to follow. The glow of the crimson eyes grew brighter, even if the bank of fog seemed to grow thicker around her.

Shapes resolved in front of her. A car, maybe a sedan, though it was so battered it was hard to tell. Definitely something with four doors. The car rested upside down, the trunk open and facing her, though the back of the car pointed slightly away from her. The passenger side of the car was opposite Baber. Closer to the downhill edge of the clearing.

She stopped for a moment by a motorcycle helmet, laying in the ground in front of her, like it had been dropped. The face shield was up. Baber picked it up, it was a white helmet, though there were spots of mud on it, and maybe darker drops of blood. Wings spread out to either side, angelic wings, so that they wrapped around the helmet and met at the back.

Angela's helmet, Baber realized. And a very wrong feeling came over her. She dropped the helmet, and gripped her Springfield with both hands. Circled around the back of the car, wary. There was some brush to work through, the small brittle branches cracking and crunching as she drug her legs through them.

A few trees spotted the landscape at the corner of the sedan. They marked the beginning of the forest below. A body lay there, against one of the trunks, and a thrill of fear ran through Baber.

She knelt by the corpse. It was a man she didn't recognize. He lay on the ground, his back to the trunk, a bullet-hole in the center of his forehead. His eyes open.

Somehow, the man still looked scared. As if, dying, he had looked into the face of a monster. And had carried that image into the afterlife.

She wondered who he was.

"That's your guy," a voice said. Tired. Lost. Haunted.

Hamilton.

Baber turned to the voice. The passenger side of the car. Hamilton sat there, his back against the sedan, both legs straight before him. Arms to his sides, as if he had collapsed there. A body lay next to him, on the ground.

Her muscles tensed. His voice had that effect on her, the voice of a reaper, come calling. The emotionless tone of death. Baber's fingers tightened around the grip of the Springfield. Hamilton didn't move though, and she couldn't see if he held a weapon.

He didn't seem surprised to see her.

"The guy?" she asked, carefully.

"The guy who beat Charley to death," he said. His reaper's voice closed, empty.

She frowned and searched her memory. "The tattoo shop girl?" she said.

"The tattoo shop girl," Hamilton echoed, with a sigh. Then, again, as if the name was important to him. "Charley."

If Hamilton was telling the truth, the dead man here was the guy who had killed Angela's sister, too. She wondered if Hamilton knew that, and decided not to tell him. Not right then. She wasn't sure he was in the right frame of mind to take it.

"Who's on the ground next to you?" she said. The fog seemed thicker near the ground, and made it hard to see. And as harmless as Hamilton looked, she was afraid to take a step closer.

His head moved in the darkness, as if he went to speak, and then couldn't. It bobbed up and down once, then again. A long, drawn out breath escaped him, catching in the middle, like a sob.

Hamilton held both hands up. Maybe, realizing why Baber wasn't stepping closer. Each arm moved slowly, as if he lacked the energy to do even that. Both hands were empty, and one motioned her closer.

She took careful steps towards the car. Towards Hamilton and the body. The ground was wet and soft around her, sinking slightly under her feet.

The body was Angela. Baber swore, and knelt next to the girl. Blood had caked on her face, and she could see the girl had been beaten in the past. She lay on her back, her arms to her side, her eyes staring sightlessly up into the air.

"I tried," Hamilton said, his voice breaking. "Maybe I shouldn't have."

Baber looked over at him. And knew, doing so, she would have this third picture in her mind of Hamilton forever stamped into her brain.

The first one Aaron had showed her, the one of Hamilton sitting next to a medical tent, duct tape around his shoulder, rifle nestled in his lap, sleeping, patiently waiting to see if his friend survived the surgery.

The second one, of a furious Hamilton. Strapped to a chair. Eyes mad, angry, veins popping. Sweat over his skin, a bright fluorescent light baking him. His mouth open in a silent scream.

And this third one now. Hands now down at his side, as if he had no energy to lift them anymore. Face covered in blood. Wet trails under his eyes, where the blood had dried and caked, and tears had streamed. Eyes open, lost, haunted.

A man lost. Whatever had happened here, Hamilton would never forgive himself. He would blame this on his actions.

She had been right, not telling him about Angela's sister. This was a man on the edge, who could teeter either way, and she had no idea what he would do, whichever way he fell.

"Hamilton," she said. "I'm going to need to see if you're armed."

She didn't have her cuffs. And for a moment didn't know what to do, if Hamilton was armed. If he resisted. And, what was worse, Baber realized she had lost track of what was happening above her.

The gunfire had gotten closer. Louder. Began to echo along the surrounding hills. It was hard to make out, but it sounded as if Aaron was making his way down here. A second explosion rattled down the slopes. Maybe another grenade.

Then silence. She wondered if Aaron was dead. If he hadn't made the descent through the dark fog, into whatever hell this was.

Then he appeared next to the car. At the back, on the other side of Hamilton from Baber. The Steyr gone. Covered in mud and dirt, as if he had stumbled a few times in the wet earth on his way down. As if Aaron had worked his way down so fast, he couldn't have stopped an occasional fall, as the slope steepened underneath him.

"We got to go," Aaron said, out of breath. He looked back the way he came.

"I'm not sure we're going anywhere," Baber said, nodding to the side of the car.

Hamilton's head swiveled to Aaron.

It was right then Baber understood she wasn't going to stop anything from happening with Hamilton. Whatever hung in the balance, whatever knife's edge Hamilton balanced on, whichever of the three different pictures of the man she held in her mind, the scale had fallen, he had slipped off that edge, and the three Hamiltons were about to become one.

"You lied," Hamilton said. The words short, each one a bite of controlled fury.

"Brother," Aaron waved, almost absentmindedly, glancing back from up the hill. As if unaware of what was going on in the man sitting on the ground. "We got to go."

"You lied," Hamilton said again. The words even angrier. His reaper's voice carrying some new emotion, dark and brittle and breaking from the strain.

"Hamilton," Baber said, holding her gun on the man. "I need you to calm down."

Hamilton dragged one leg up, then the next, and pushed himself up the side of the sedan. His back slid up the side, the car rocked just a little, under the movement. The gunfire picked up from above them, whines zipping through the forest, bullets smacking into trees.

"Brother," Aaron said, finally pulling his attention from up slope. "Whatever it is, let's talk about this later. You know, after the people stop shooting at us."

Aaron looked at Hamilton. Maybe then, he saw the same thing Baber had. His eyes flicked around quickly, picking up glance the girl's body. Realizing who that was. Picking up the dead guy, the merc, against the tree trunk, a few feet away.

Then it looked like Aaron realized what was happening.

"Shit," Aaron said, softly.

"*You lied*," Hamilton screamed, his words echoing out of the fog, up the hill, and into the dark skies above. His face twisted in anger and rage and fury, veins popping out of his head.

"*Hamilton*," Baber yelled, her gun suddenly up, ready to pull the trigger.

The man was fast. Hamilton grabbed Aaron, wrestled with him against the side of the car. The sedan rocked a few times, the roof crunching with the motion. The two circled each other, limbs moving in a blur, Hamilton beating on Aaron, Aaron trying to defend himself. The fight went on for just a few seconds, until Aaron's back was against the sedan, Hamilton holding him, one arm tucked under Aaron's chin.

Aaron held both arms out, to his sides. Hands open. "Brother," he said. He sounded tired. His voice sounded... thick.

"You lied," Hamilton said again. Baber couldn't see his face. "You're a liar."

"It's not that simple," Aaron said.

"It's always that simple," Hamilton said.

Aaron's eyes closed. "I know that now," he said. His voice quiet. "I know, man."

They stayed that way for a long moment. Baber circled them, got to the side, where she could see their faces. Aaron was pale, composed, quiet. Almost... sad.

Hamilton's was the face from the chair. Veins ran thick by his temples. His jaw taught. Teeth gritted. Blood, caked and dried on his face.

Eyes burning.

"Hamilton," Baber said. "Let go. Or I'm going to have to shoot you."

"I know," Aaron said again, softly. "I'm so sorry brother, for everything. I understand, again. It's about the person."

Hamilton hesitated. Looked at Angela. Looked at Baber. Looked back at Aaron.

"Let's go," Aaron said. "Let's get out of here, and I promise you can take it out on me there. Sam was right, John, you were right, everyone was right but me..."

Gunshots rang out. Whines and whizzes through the trees. Aaron pitched forward, against Hamilton. Something hit Baber's shoulder, picked her up and tossed her to the ground.

She lost her gun. Baber lay on her back, the ground cold underneath her. She went to look for it, and realized her arm wasn't really responding where she wanted it to go. Then a hot pain flashed through her body, from her shoulder. A hot wetness spread from that area.

She had been shot. She winced and dragged herself back, until she hit a tree. Pulled herself into a seated position, looked at her shoulder.

The bullet had hit the edge of the vest, come out the other side. That arm wouldn't move at all, but a lot of blood was coming out. She felt hot, but a shuddering coolness flashed over her as well, and a cold sweat broke out over her forehead.

The gunfire was heavier now. Bullets fired thunked into the car, thwacked into trees. Hamilton still stood in front of her, motionless, his gaze down, bullets somehow missing him.

He was looking at Aaron. Who was seated, back against the car. As if he had slid down the side of the sedan. There was a smear of something dark behind Aaron, on the car. He had one leg splayed to the side, as if Aaron had just collapsed.

Aaron looked at her, and winked.

Then he died.

For a long second Baber didn't register anything. The moment was surreal. She wondered what in the hell she was doing here. Sitting in what felt like a war zone. She was a detective. She was just a detective. And here she was, going to die at the bottom of a hill, in some bank of fog, still not really quite believing all of it.

"Hamilton," Baber said. Her voice a whisper.

Hamilton stood there a few moments. Bullets hitting all around him. He stared at the man underneath him for a long time, uncaring. Then the man looked at Angela. And finally, his gaze turned to Baber.

"Hamilton," Baber said, not sure what she was going to say.

His eyes flashed to her shoulder. She felt like the man saw everything. His eyes, so angry and furious a moment ago, cycled through thousands of emotions. Fury, haunted, angry, sad, bitterness, despair, his eyes flashed through them all, and settled on some dark pool of something she couldn't identify. Maybe the closest she could come was... acceptance.

Hamilton nodded at her. He found her gun, off to the side. Picked up another one, next to the body of the first man, the guy who had beaten Charley.

Baber couldn't tell if she was getting delirious from blood loss, but she could swear he headed up into the thick fog. Heading up the hill, into the storm of bullets. His stride focused and sharp. As if Hamilton already knew that nothing would touch him.

Maybe he was right. The reaper never feared his own death.

A few moments later there was an occasional sharp, single pop. Followed by another. Baber thought she recognized the sound of her

Springfield, but maybe that was just her imagination, making details more real to her.

Whichever, soon there were shouts and cries from above. Questioning. Then screams, and panicked fire, as if the people shooting at them realized there was a monster loose, among them. Single pops. Automatic fire. Muzzle flashes, muted in the fog.

Soon after that, there was silence.

Baber awoke sometime later. Hamilton was kneeling next to her, he had one hand behind her back, and was tugging on a roll of duct tape, wrapping it over her shoulder and underneath her arm. She wasn't sure if it was the sound of the tape ripping, or the tugging, that had caused her to wake.

He tugged a final time, causing Baber to almost scream, then tore the tape. His face was calm, composed, his eyes revealed nothing of what had happened. Knelt next to her. Her eyes flashed past Hamilton, up slope.

"No one is left," he said.

"Hamilton," she said.

"No one," he said. As if that was important to him.

She found Aaron. He remained where she had seen him last, facing her, back against the car. His eyes closed now.

"I don't think you're going to lose the shoulder," Hamilton told her. "But you're going to have to rehab like a son of a bitch."

Baber had no idea what to say. What to do. The world she was in felt crazy, surreal. As if the fog surrounding them had transported her to a different place, a different time. A place where people could kill each other, with viruses and GPS devices, where people could have shootouts on the side of the road.

A place where a guy like Hamilton existed.

Some voices spoke, out of the blue. Muted, and next to her. She couldn't make out what they were saying. She wondered if she was imagining things, imagining someone talking to her, narrating this new world Baber found herself in.

Hamilton picked something up that was next to her leg.

A phone. The screen had a call open, she watched the time tick upwards under the number 9-1-1. The voice grew louder, it sounded like a young man, almost panicked. "Sir, you need to tell me your name."

"That's not important," Hamilton said. "You have units on the way?"

"Police are on their way," the young man said. "But I need your number and name, sir. It's important in case we get cut off."

Hamilton hit the red button on the phone. Dropped it in Baber's lap.

I guess they got cut off, she thought. A little dizzily. *Likely the blood loss.*

She snorted. The screen went to a background, and Baber saw the photo of Hamilton on it. The one by the tent. It must be Aaron's phone. She wondered if Hamilton had seen the photo, and then thought he must have.

Hamilton looked at her funny. "You should be good," he said.

Good. Like any of this could be good.

"This is crazy," Baber said.

"Yeah," Hamilton said, and then sighed. He seemed smaller afterwards, like the action had deflated him. "Yeah."

"Things like this don't happen," Baber said.

"They do," Hamilton said. "You just weren't aware of them."

She wondered what she would tell people, when they found her. What she would tell Frank. She wanted to tell people the truth, but what was that? What would people believe? What did she believe?

All she had was bits and pieces, crazy stories, unbelievable tales. Her eyes went to Aaron. The Fourth Branch. Who would believe that?

She wondered who Aaron would show up as, when they tried to identify him. What kind of life would be in that database? And would it be anything like who he had been.

Baber hadn't known the man long, but she doubted it.

"He said you were the best of them," Baber said, looking at Hamilton.

Hamilton glanced back at the man, his friend, and nodded. When Hamilton turned back his eyes shimmered a bit, as if they were wet. His jaw was set. "Maybe that was true once," he said. "Not anymore."

He fell silent, but stayed next to Baber, on one knee. As if, once he had done what he had done, once he had killed everyone, closed Aaron's eyes, taped Baber up, Hamilton had returned to being a statue. An empty shell, where before the container had been nothing but fury and anger and torment.

Baber wondered what would fill that shell now. What he would do now. What would fuel the man in front of her.

Neither of them moved. The pain in her shoulder was a throbbing ache, hot and wet. Every so often, when Baber breathed, a shooting pain would radiate from the joint and she would wince.

But that was it. She was silent. Hamilton was silent. The forest was silent around them. She could hear herself breathe. She couldn't hear Hamilton, at all. He was still, a statue. His eyes looking past Baber, past the trees, as far as she could tell, past everything.

Around them the forest began to speak. The wind rustled the branches above. Crickets began to chirp, low at first, then gaining in strength, like a wave. An owl, somewhere, hooting its call.

Then sirens. Faint. But coming.

Hamilton got up. She knew he was going to leave. She knew she likely would never see him again.

What was she going to tell Frank? What was her partner going to tell her? He wouldn't leave it at *I told you so*, but what in the world could she really say? It wasn't like she believed Aaron, believed in the Fourth Branch, any of that.

Still...

"What am I going to say?" she asked him.

"You'll figure out something, Baber," Hamilton said. He paused. "I'm sorry about all this. I'm sorry it all happened. I wish in some way I could have avoided it, but I'm starting to think I won't ever get away, not from any of this."

"You can't leave," Baber said. "You killed all these people."

"Did I?" he asked. And glanced over his shoulder, at Aaron. Baber hadn't noticed, but the man was holding her Springfield. And another gun, in his second hand.

"You can't stop me," he said, a ghost of a smile flickering into place, a sad smile. It wavered for a long breath, then disappeared. "I don't know what to tell you, Baber. But be careful what you say. Who you tell. This isn't over, yet."

Hamilton was warning her. He didn't know how far things went up. But he knew, like she did, that some of those people were still in place. That what they were dealing with now was likely the lowest branch of the ladder.

This Fourth Branch seemed real enough to him.

Baber looked over at Aaron. Wondered about the old man in the pizza shop, if that guy was even alive. Or his sister. And if they were, if they would ever know about Aaron. How he had lived his life. How he had chosen to die.

"This is crazy," Baber said again.

"Life is," Hamilton said. "I used to think it was different, once."

The sirens grew louder. The warbling echoed down the hill, loud through the fog.

"See you detective," Hamilton said. "I've got something I have to finish."

And then he was gone.

The first thing Baber heard was the beeping. Her eyes stayed closed, after she had passed out, after Hamilton had left. She was lying down, that she knew. Her left arm was cold, but the rest of her was warm, with a heaviness, like a thick blanket, on top of her. There was a smell of new sheets and cleanliness, but those things didn't comfort her like the beeping.

The beeping of a monitor, in a hospital.

Slowly things came into focus. Not in her sight, but her hearing. The murmuring of people talking outside. The thumping of a wheel-chair or a hospital bed being pushed and maybe hitting a wall. The beeping of the monitor. And the heavy, deep breaths of someone in a chair next to her.

Baber opened her eyes. Everything was fuzzy, like her eyes were too dry. She blinked them a few times, until her sight cleared up. Focused on the whiteboard across from her, with a nurse's name on it, the meds they were giving Baber, and the last time she had been checked on.

Midnight.

Frank was next to her. Too large for the small chair he was in. One of his legs laying in another chair, that was turned to face him. He still had on his thick trench coat, and his arms were folded across his belly. The window behind him was black, where Baber could see through the slits of the blinds.

He grinned when he saw her wake. The gap-tooth grin of an old boxer.

"'Bout time," Frank rumbled.

Baber took a few breaths. Tried to speak. Her throat was dry and raw. Her left shoulder hurt, where they had bandaged it. There was an IV running into the back of her wrist, likely why her arm felt cold.

Frank wiggled a tiny plastic cup. The motion looked silly in his large hands. But there was a straw in the cup, and he held it close to Baber's face so she could sip it. One pull, then two, of cool, iced water.

"Thanks," she croaked.

Frank nodded.

"How long?"

"A few days," he said.

She frowned. Frank had family. "You been here the whole time?"

He nodded. Pulled a phone out of his pocket. "Got your cell."

Not her cell. The phone Hamilton had given Baber, after he had called the cops. That was all she needed to know.

"You know?"

"I'm piecing some of it together," he said. "Maybe later, you tell me the rest."

He nodded outside. Past the door. Out into the hospital. "Good chance the lieutenant will be here in the morning. Captain too. They've been here both days. You stirred up a shitstorm."

She grimaced. Tilted her head forward. Frank automatically gave her the straw, and Baber gulped down more water.

"It was bad, Frank," she said.

"I figured," he said. "Best I can think, maybe you forget it all."

"They'll never buy that."

"Hard for them not to," he said. "You been out two days... All the blood loss. The trauma." He shrugged. "Easy enough explanation."

Maybe it would work. Maybe that could be enough. Because if she said anything about Aaron, or Hamilton, she would be on someone's list. She might already be on that list.

She couldn't afford to be higher.

"I don't know Frank," she said. "I don't know."

"Give it time," he said. "Maybe tomorrow you say you can't remember. Take it day by day."

It might be the only thing she could do. At least, until they knew more. Until they found the person at the top.

"Another thing," Frank said. "I stopped by his place."

There was no need to say who. They both knew he meant Hamilton.

"It looks like he's split," Frank said. "His place is all cleaned out."

Baber thought he meant *up*, not out. She shook her head. "Aaron was cleaning it. Something happened there." She remembered a dark and pungent smell, underneath everything. And she smiled a bit, a wistful smile, at the image of Aaron spraying his Teagarden spray over the living room. "Something bad."

"Nah," Frank said. "He's gone. There was a picture that used to be there, gone. A few other things. The uniform."

He paused.

"The phone was still there though," he said. "It started to ring when I was leaving."

There was a long moment then, as if he was remembering, and thinking, and even drugged and tired Baber wanted him to finish. "What, Frank?"

"I answered it," he said. "A little voice said something on the other side. A woman."

"What did she say?"

"The voice said, 'Is he dead?'" Frank said. Then he tilted his head. "Then she said, 'No, wait. Don't say anything.'"

Baber waited some more. She wasn't feeling great, her shoulder was in pain, and she was worried about the captain. "And?"

Frank grunted. His eyebrows lifted. Both of them. He held both hands out, like he didn't know. One of his large maws holding the tiny plastic cup of water. "That was it. She hung up."

Then the big man shifted in his chair. As if there had been something more. Some sound, or word, or *something* the woman had said or wanted to say.

Well, Baber could figure that part out. And maybe she could do more, maybe she could find out where that person was. She thought she owed Hamilton that, but maybe this woman owed him more.

But for now she had bigger concerns now to worry about. Her captain, her lieutenant, one of them had been a part of this. Which meant they were on the take. Which disgusted her, and was something she resolved to take care of.

As soon as she could.

Baber let out a breath. "We're in a big mess, Frank."

Her friend's grin was sympathetic, but also comforting. "We always are. Best I can tell, we just keep doing what we do."

She was falling asleep again. She could feel the tiredness come in quick, as if this brief expenditure of worry and fear and energy was more than her body had. Still, she wanted to know. "What's that?"

"Take it one case at a time," her partner said, staying in the chair. A comfortable mountain of a rock. "And let the chips fall where they may."

She may have heard the last. She may not have. But she knew what he was saying. Take each case and work it. Climb their way to the top. Figure out who had done what. The right way.

Not Hamilton's way.

Though her last thought was about the man, before falling asleep. Baber couldn't help but be comforted that Frank had the cell phone Hamilton had given her. It was nice to have that option.

Just in case.

CHAPTER
FIFTY-FOUR

I sat in darkness.

The room was comfortable, the temperature was neither too hot nor too cold. It was just right. Every now and then the fan would kick on, there would be a stir of air across my face, a scent of lavender, but other than that, nothing else moved.

Maybe that was the nature of hotel rooms. A slight sense of movement, followed by the emptiness of something always in transition. Of never really being a home to something.

It was dark in the room, empty except for me, pieces of a suit discarded on the floor and the bed. A spare set of shoes, a striped blue tie.

At least the chair I sat in was comfortable. It was tough to not fall asleep. I had been waiting a while, and the chair had cushioned my body as soon as I had sat into it. It had hugged me, and pulled me back so that I slouched a bit, a book on my lap, as if I was getting ready for a late night reading session.

The truth was, I was just waiting. And I was still sore. Still bruised. It had been a few weeks since the mansion, since Angela and Charley, since Aaron. Time had passed, but a few scars remained. Some scars probably would always remain.

My index finger kept running over the cover of the book. My fingertip caught the edge of the paperback, as if the cover had been folded, or curled, and wouldn't lay straight. The edge made a little flicking sound, every time my finger brushed over it. The book was warm on my leg, I had been sitting here a while now, and the tome seemed to soak up whatever heat my body had radiated.

The past few weeks I had come to some realizations. I thought of them as guideposts, in my new journey. They hadn't all come at once, and I was sure there would be more, because the destination I had in mind was far away, and I wasn't sure I knew how to get there. Not, at least, from where I was at, right at this moment.

I had talked to Sara, given her what I could of what happened. More than I should have, probably. Sara had published some of it, had tried to get all of it, had harassed the officers at the accident, the governor, the investigation of the shooters, but in the end her editor had shut most of the story down. Sara had just lacked real proof.

And we both knew what happened, without proof.

I had seen Whelan one last time as well. Given him what had happened. We had met at the same restaurant, on a similar Friday, with vessels cutting wakes across the harbor, both real, and imaginary. He had seemed less happy than he should be, but then, it wasn't quite over for him. Maybe tomorrow, he'd be happier.

He had offered me money. I had declined. The things I felt like I needed to do in life, now, well, taking money for those acts would twist them. Make them less pure. There was right and there was wrong, and somehow, taking money for either of those things brought them both into some gray world, where intentions became nebulous, and acts more vague. It's why we lived in a world of rules and regulations, where lawyers could stall death sentences for murderers for decades, where others adhered so closely to what the law said, because to make one little misstep on a warrant was to let a criminal go free. Where what people said was so different from what they did.

I wanted to be clear about my purpose. Clear about my next few steps, pure in my actions. Most of all, I wanted to feel like I was doing something right. Something *just*.

The fan kicked on again. A low humming through the room. A puff of breeze across my face, light. The scent of lavender.

It was a nice room, situated high up in the hotel. The very top floor. Outside, and below, there were sounds of people celebrating. The calls of young men, with one too many cold beers in them, drifted up to me. The high-pitched echoes of young women followed.

It was a night for celebrating.

Angela would always be dead. No matter what I had done that day, or who she had met. Whether she had met me at the bookstore, or hadn't. I understood that, in my brain. It was the other part of me that wouldn't accept it.

She had plugged in the drive, tried to find out what Ben had known, and had started a sequence of events that would have ended with her being kidnapped and killed, whether or not I had ever been involved.

But I *had* been involved. And getting involved, I had gotten Charley killed. Angela had a sister, and likely what I had done to the mercenary had marked her for death as well.

And Aaron. He had died too. Trying to save me, at the end.

He still had the picture of me, on his phone. The person I had been once. And maybe, the person I was trying to be again.

I wasn't sure I was worth any of them. Actually, I was sure that I wasn't. As certain as Aaron had been, something in me fought what he believed.

But, maybe all journeys start that way. With a few faltering steps, to an unknown destination, just a hint of a direction, of where you want to be.

So, I had circled back to something I had known once. About being there for that person who needed me. Or someone like me. About not thinking about some evil, some third world country, some crime happening the next state over. About helping the person in front of you. And then the next.

There were a lot of evils in the world. A lot of bad people doing bad things. It would be impossible for me to fix all of them.

But I also couldn't hide from them, anymore. Especially when they happened to me. I could no longer hide in a routine. Live my life like a turtle, plodding along, ducking in my shell whenever something jumped out at me.

I had thought, after Sam and Aaron, and the lost virus, after my torture and getting my leg broken, over and over, that I wasn't fit for the Branch anymore. Not because I had been broken, but because something in my brain, the part of me that wanted to believe I was always doing the right thing, the good thing, the *just* thing, had been broken.

The anger had overwhelmed me. The betrayal had killed the part of me that believed, if I did good things, that those acts would protect me. Keep me safe. That because I was doing something pure, and right, that some force would keep me alive. Keep me on the frontline.

But bad things could happen to me, too. I wasn't special. I knew that now. I knew I had been wrong about Sam, about what had happened back then, about the Branch, because my brain had been trying to tell me for two years. Nightmare after nightmare.

Only now, could I come to that realization, though.

There was a sound at the door. The beeping of a keycard, I thought. Then someone trying to turn the handle of the door, but it remained shut. The beeping again, the handle again. The person shook the handle, as if it were the door's fault.

I agreed with the person outside. I didn't like the new hotel cards either. The ones they keyed to the room. The cards never seemed to work right. The old keys seemed more trustworthy, in some way. More real.

Though most of the time the keycards worked. People used them regularly, and when the door didn't unlock, it was usually the operator.

Like now.

Finally, the beeping and the handle were operated in the correct sequence. The door opened. A man walked in, stumbling a bit. Maybe a bit inebriated, after his celebration. I watched him wave a goodnight to someone outside, then shut the door.

He stumbled around. There was a nice desk, sitting in front of some floor-to-ceiling windows, looking out over the city. He walked over to it, placed the keycard on the desk, watched it fall to the floor, then bent down and tried it again.

This time the card stayed.

He blew out a breath, steadied himself against the desk, finally turned on a light.

He was young, older than me, but still young. Late thirties, maybe. Dark hair with a hint of gray that women would find attractive, and that media outlets loved. A person who radiated authority. Who would look good behind a podium, addressing the nation.

He was also tall. Wore a nice coat, something gray and pinstriped. A darker gray suit on, almost a charcoal-like color, underneath. A blue tie with a Windsor knot, no stripes, still tied around his throat.

There was a little kitchen to the side of the desk area. He walked in, came out with a cold beer in his hand. Something dark in the bottle. He took a big drink of it, pumped his fist, as if still celebrating, and then stumbled again. Against the desk.

The card fell to the floor again. As the man bent over to grab the card, the beer poured all over the floor. It sounded like someone pissing.

"Well," the man said aloud, "Fuck."

He bent back up, straight from the waist, like a drunk would. Sat the beer on the desk with a careful thunk. Then the man walked into the bathroom to get a towel. Came back with something white and big and fluffy and sat down to scrub the floor with it. He sat on his ass, with each leg on either side of the spill, and leaned forward with the towel. All with the careful, exaggerated motions of someone who maybe had one too many. Or five too many.

But, it was a night for celebrating.

He never saw me. The whole time he went back and forth. Granted, just the desk light was on, and the illumination didn't quite reach the chair I sat in. And he was focused on his task. But still, you would think he'd notice a stranger in his room...

I had to finally introduce myself.

He sat on his knees, blinking, towel held loosely in his hand. Looking around as if wondered what it was he had heard. Or maybe, who he had heard. And where he had heard it from. His eyes went to a large television, next to the chair I was in.

So I introduced myself again. Gave him a wave with one hand.

Finally, he saw me.

"Who the fuck are you?" the man asked. Blinking.

He had drank quite a few too many. So this wouldn't feel as good as it should. But I believed it would still feel good. Feel right. Maybe even just.

It was a night to celebrate, after all.

I stood up, the book in one hand. Walked across the room to him. The carpet was thick and plush, my feet sunk into it, with each step. It was a very nice hotel, suitable for a man who had recently claimed the Office of the Governor.

The man watched me walk. His eyes narrowed, as if he had seen me before. As if he was trying to place me.

I kept the book in one hand. My fingers ran over the edge of the cover, all the edges of the pages, bound tightly together. I flicked the edge, occasionally, but otherwise remained quiet. All the way until I squatted in front of him. Putting my face right in front of his.

I smiled, but it wasn't a happy smile..

He finally recognized me. "*You.*"

"Me," I said.

His face showed real fear, then. Like I was some monster, crawling out from under his bed. Some leviathan from the deep. As if he had been swimming, out in the harbor, and something cold and slick, with maybe a rough bite to it, had just brushed his leg.

The fear sobered him up, and he scooted back, until he hit the desk. He looked to the door.

"I'll scream," he said.

I shrugged. "People everywhere are screaming tonight," I said. "It's a night for celebrating."

I reached my hand out, slowly, and fingered the knot on his tie. "Congratulations on your victory."

He swallowed, the muscles of his neck forcing the motion so hard, I could hear it. The loud sound of the gulp.

"They'll never believe I killed myself," he said.

"Good," I said, keeping the smile on my face. The fake one. "Good."

"I can pay you," he said. "Whatever you want."

I had already turned down money for this. "I'm not sure there's an amount, friend."

"Just tell me," he said. "Whatever you want, I'll give it to you."

I was sure he thought he could. He had a lot of pull, as the governor of one of the original states. He would have a lot more, in his mind, as the future president. He probably dreamed of everything he could have then. Everything he could do.

"I'm sure you think you can," I said. My finger still brushing the cover of the book.

"So tell me," the man said. His gaze went to my hand, and he repeated himself. "Whatever you want."

"Whatever I want," I said. Like I was musing. "That's something that's been tough for me to figure out."

"It's easy enough," the man said. "Money? I can get you whatever. Power?"

I thought about both.

"I have a jet, too," he said. "You want to go anywhere, we can make that happen. Whatever you want, we can make it happen."

Make it happen. Like he was a genie, and he could do anything, for anyone.

The real thing he was saying was, he felt like he could do anything, *to anyone*, for a price.

He was about to discover the consequences of those types of thoughts. Of the actions, for where those thoughts led.

"I think you can help me," I said.

"Whatever you want," he said. "I can get it."

"What about... justice?"

He was on his way to saying more, but stopped then. Confused. Perhaps wondering how he could acquire something like that. How he could pay for it.

"You know, I used to believe every action deserved a consequence," I explained. "So, when a person is kidnapped, I kind of assumed I was going to be the consequence to whoever committed that action. It was a natural feeling for me."

I held up the book. *The Faerie Queene.* "Maybe I even believed I was a hero. Or that I could figure out how to be one again. That this was going to be some kind of movie, or story, where I saved the girl, and we all lived happily ever after."

His eyes tightened, and he peered closer at the cover, like he might be seeing double. Reading the author's name aloud, as if trying to get it. "Spencer?" he asked.

I corrected him. "Nope, it's not about him. It's not even about justice, I don't think. It's more about... a journey."

He looked at the cover again. Leaned closer.

"I don't get it," he said.

"I don't know that I do, either," I confessed. "I think I know the destination, and I think I know the way there, but once you start walking, well, the path changes some. It gets rocky. It meanders through a forest a bit. I mean, I know where I want to go, but getting there..."

I let out a big breath. "Getting there's the issue."

His eyes lit up then, as if he could help. "You need a private jet? I told you, you can borrow mine. Go anywhere in the world you want."

He winked at me, like he was sharing a joke. "No getting lost, with that."

"That's not what I'm saying," I said. And I shook my head. I didn't think he'd get it, but then, how could I expect him to, when this was me still figuring this out. "I guess I'm saying I think I know where I want to go. And I think I'm taking the right steps to get there. But there's no way to really tell. I'm going to have to learn this, as I go."

I waited a moment. "I've got to know who I want to be, and just take the best step in that direction I can."

This guy was shaking his head. Lost. The old acting governor, the future governor, whoever he was acting as, he was also frustrated. And angry at his frustration. As if he was looking at something he thought he could puzzle together, but just lacked the capacity.

I guess I understood.

"Yeah," I said. "Like I said, it's something I'm figuring out."

I set the book down on his desk. Placed correctly to the corner, so that a person walking into the room would see it first.

"I'm a bit lost," I said. Still trying to explain it to him, maybe. More likely, just thinking aloud. For myself. "But I'm finding my way."

He tilted his head. As if things would make sense, if he just looked at them from a different angle. As if it was only the alcohol confusing him. As if maybe he was having a bad dream, something he could wake up from, if he only could see the end of it.

There were a lot of people like the governor in the world. Giants in their fields, politics, money, military. Giants in their towns, their cities. People who did what they wanted, whenever they wanted, no matter who they stepped on while they did it.

Those people thought that the bill wouldn't come due, for them. Virtue wasn't a thing anymore, and a lot of people thought no one would hold them accountable, for their actions. *Could* hold them accountable. And maybe, in the past, that might be the case.

But I was around now. I was taking steps through their forest. Their hills. Sooner or later, I would find them. In their caves. In their castles. By their fountains. I would find the monsters, the giants, the dragons, the people who hurt others, and they would regret the day that I did.

"I'm not getting it," the governor finally said. Angry, as if it was my fault he didn't understand.

So I got a little closer. Made sure he saw my smile. It felt real to me then, and I guess, maybe it was.

"Let me put this clearly for you," I said. "There's a lot of people in this world who think the rules don't apply to them. I believe I'm here to correct that assumption."

He was scared, but also angry. Like he believed he was above these things, *this*, me in front of him. Consequences.

"You kill me, and people will come looking for you," he said. "Powerful people."

I kept my smile on.

"Sure," I said. Understanding that rule very well. "Let them come."

I stood. Picked the current and future governor up by his arms. As tall as he was, he was lighter than I thought he'd be. He offered no resistance, and his legs drug across the carpet.

"Please," he said, his voice a whimper. "I'll be better."

"No," I told him. "You won't."

I carried him around the desk. He didn't fight. His whole body had gone limp. Dead weight. As if he, now, understood.

He couldn't stop begging. Though his words were quiet little whispers. Prayers to himself, maybe. "Please," he said again, over and over. "Please."

"There are a lot of people in this world," I told him, placing his back hard against the window. The glass cold against my fingers. "People you never see, who suffer the consequences of things you decided. People who died, people you *know* you've killed, people you've stepped on to get to wherever the hell it is you want to go.

"And doing all this, you just always assumed no one would ever hold you accountable for your actions."

Like people who tried to live life the right way. Who tried to help others. But maybe who didn't have the power, the skillset, or the commitment to see their desires through.

My smile turned real then, for the first time.

"You were wrong," I said.

Then I swung him against the window. Once. Twice. Hard thumps. The hotel was old, the windows weren't the newer storm windows, they were made of rustic old glass from back in the 1950s.

The windows cracked. Then shattered in a tinkling of glass, the shards flying out into the night. The governor screamed, following the glass. The scream went on long, and dwindled as the man fell. Until the cry bounced off the street, echoing faintly back up to me, along with a solid thump. A splattering sound, when he hit the pavement.

Then a moment of perfect silence. A pause, as the world registered what had happened. Then the screams began. Horns blared. Shouts from below. And, after a bit, sirens.

It was a night for celebrating.

A breeze blew in from the air outside, I took a breath of it. It was clean, and fresh, and new. Cold, crisp air, of late fall. Or maybe early winter. The kind of air that came after everything had died, after everything was dead and buried under layers of ice and snow, and those that needed it waited for rebirth.

———

Enjoy *The Deadening Wake?*

There will be more of Crosse. A story is in the works, actually *stories* are in the works. I love the idea of the Fourth Branch, of a hidden organization built to help our country weather future storms, and what might happen as the centuries pass.

So while you're waiting, help get the word out about the Crosse Series by leaving a review for *The Deadening Wake* at your bookseller of choice. Even a few words would be greatly appreciated.

After that, come visit chrisjcranford.com and be a part of the Crosse Universe, as well as other series I've written. Discover all the other worlds I'm building. Or just reach out and say hello.

I look forward to meeting you.

ABOUT THE AUTHOR

When Chris isn't trying to figure out how to write a bio, he spends time contemplating the fate of the universe. Probably while walking into a door jamb. He's accepted that the two go hand-in-hand.

He currently resides in Florida, though he has some Magellan in him, and loves to wander.

It is his dream to write stories that – through their telling – influence others to live a little better. Stand a little taller. Smile a little wider. Hold someone a little longer. Fiction should be the dream real life aspires to be.

Dogs are his buddies. Football is his hobby. Books are his passion. Find out more about Chris here:

www.chrisjcranford.com

facebook.com/chrisjcranford

x.com/chrisjcranford

instagram.com/chrisjcranford